A Winter's Wish

Tracy Corbett started writing in her late twenties. As well as writing novels, she's written several short stories, pantomime sketches and magazine articles. Tracy describes her writing style as modern tales of romance, with engaging quirky characters, who overcome adversity, grow as people and conclude in satisfying optimistic endings. When she's not writing, she enjoys amateur dramatics, gardening and music. She works part-time for a local charity.

Someone Like You
A Winter's Wish

Tracy Corbett

A Winter's Wish

1☉ CANELO

First published in the United Kingdom in 2021 by

Canelo
31 Helen Road
Oxford OX2 0DF
United Kingdom

A CIP catalogue record for this book is available from the British Library.

Print ISBN 978 1 80032 333 9
Ebook ISBN 978 1 80032 332 2

Look for more great books at www.canelo.co

Printed and bound in Great Britain by Clays Ltd, Elcograf S.p.A.

1

For all my amazing colleagues at Citizens Advice,

you're stars – each and every one of you x

Chapter One

Samantha Tipping emerged from the toilet cubicle wearing her new 'dress-to-impress' business outfit and checked the results of her makeover in the wide mirror. It wasn't a conventional look. The tan-coloured linen trousers were tailored for a man, as were the navy waistcoat and polka dot tie. But the recycled white dress-shirt was freshly ironed, and teamed with the smart navy trilby hat she'd found in a retro store in Clapham, she felt appropriately dressed. More importantly, she was ready to face the hordes of guests that would soon be arriving. Including the press, local dignitaries and potential funders. Not to mention her parents.

Her enthusiasm took a dip.

Shaking off her trepidation, she checked her reflection in the mirror. Happy with the outcome, she twisted her thick wavy hair into a knot and tucked it under her hat. Aside from her flushed cheeks – reddened from hours of cleaning ahead of today's launch – she felt confident, if somewhat nervous. There was a lot riding on today.

Shoving her dirty cleaning clothes into a carrier bag, she exited the toilet block and glanced at her watch. There was just enough time to carry out one last check before The Crash Pad officially opened to the public.

Her pulse rate kicked up a notch, reminding her of what was at stake. Today was the culmination of years of dreaming and months of hard work. When she'd purchased the rundown care home just over a year ago, her dream of opening a night shelter for homeless teenagers had been a few scribbled ideas in a notebook. The reality of what lay ahead only came to light when she'd set about obtaining the appropriate planning approvals. Not only had she had to work with contractors to ensure she adhered to the strict building regulations, she'd also had to convince Lambeth Council she was up to the task of safeguarding minors.

In the end, she'd compromised on her desired ideals, and settled on providing a service for sixteen to twenty-one-year-olds, which eradicated the need for Social Services' involvement. It still meant liaising with the Adult Social Care Team, but the rules weren't quite so restricting, so it enabled her to get the project off the ground.

And now the end was in sight. After months of hard graft and overseeing building renovations, her dream was about to become a reality.

She couldn't be more excited. Or petrified.

She made her way through the large open-plan communal area to the cafe. Norah and Emily had done an amazing job getting the space ready. The design matched the rest of the shelter, with its bright industrial lighting and exposed scaffolding, accented with colourful modern furniture. The small wooden tables were handmade, with recycled napkins, and decorated with potted herbs grown in the shelter's rooftop garden.

The chalkboards were colourful and enticing, decorated with Emily's loopy handwriting and listing all the food on offer, from hearty meat stews to vegan not-sausage rolls. The countertop was lined with pre-baked goods, freshly made sandwiches and wholesome salads, a nutritional balance to the chips and pasties warming in the oven.

The scent of homemade mushroom soup permeated the air, reminding her she'd skipped breakfast. She'd been too nervous to eat.

Norah opened her arms as Sam approached and pulled her into a hug. 'Well, don't you look adorable,' she said, rocking her from side-to-side.

When Sam had advertised for help to run the shelter, she hadn't known what to expect in terms of applicants. But she was quickly discovering that managing volunteers was an entirely different dynamic to working in a paid environment. Not that she was complaining. She'd never experienced this much warmth from her family, let alone from her work colleagues.

Sam stepped back and tipped her hat, allowing a wave of dark curls to escape. So much for taming the mane. 'Do you approve?' She straightened the trilby, deciding it would be easier to keep her hair loose.

Norah smiled.

'It's perfect.' Her Dublin lilt was as infectious as the glint in her blue eyes. 'You'll knock 'em dead.'

That was the idea. 'Is everything ready?'

Norah nodded. 'All's grand. We'll not let you down.'

'Oh, I know you won't.' She touched the older woman's arm. 'You've both been absolute stars. I couldn't have done it without you.'

Which was entirely true. It was one thing to make plans to open a night shelter, but running it was another matter altogether. As she was already discovering. And they hadn't officially opened yet.

Dealing with young homeless people would require patience, understanding and a lot of resilience. Norah's experience came from a long career as a paediatric nurse, followed by a stint running her own catering company, and all while raising four children singlehandedly. Whereas Emily had lived on the streets for four years before finally being housed by the local authority a few months ago. Between them, they had enough understanding and empathy to cope with whatever difficulties occurred. And there were bound to be problems. She wasn't naive enough to think otherwise.

Emily appeared from behind the counter, her hands smeared in pink chalk. 'Hey, Sam. Nice hat.'

'Thanks. I got it from the retro shop.' She admired Emily's leaf-patterned green dress, a match for her parsley-coloured eyes. 'Pretty dress. New?'

Emily blushed. 'Charity shop.'

'What a great advert we are for recycling.' She checked her watch. 'Oh, God. It's almost time.' Panic was starting to kick in.

'It'll be fine.' Norah gestured to the vast open space filled with colour. 'Who couldn't fail to be impressed by this?'

Sam looked around. Norah was right. The walls of the old care home had been knocked through to make one large open-plan space. Around the edges, individual beach huts had been constructed, each one painted in stripes of bright colours and containing a single bed. There were fifteen huts in total.

In the centre of the space was a communal area, filled with potted palm trees, comfortable sofas, a pool table, and giant squishy beanbags. Skylights in the high ceiling flooded the space with daylight, enhanced by the strip lights hanging down from the scaffolding. A huge mural painted on the end wall depicted a beach scene, complete with palm trees, golden sands, wispy clouds and an enticing blue sky. It was a place to dream, to escape, and to hope for more.

The shelter was basic in its construction, rustic in its design, but carefully thought through in terms of providing a welcoming, calming, and secure place for homeless young people to spend the night.

'Let's hope potential funders agree with you,' Sam said, the butterflies in her tummy playing havoc with her attempts to remain composed. 'I'm going to check the roof one last time.' She blew them a kiss. 'Good luck.'

Emily crossed her fingers. 'You too!'

Norah gave her a thumbs-up. 'Go get 'em, girl.'

Satisfied the catering was in safe hands, Sam headed upstairs to the rooftop garden. Outdoor space in Streatham was in short supply. The care home hadn't been blessed with huge grounds, so she'd had to come up with an inventive way of creating a garden.

Having somewhere to grow produce was imperative. Not only because it was good for the environment and improved poor mental health, but if they could grow their own vegetables then it would keep costs down and make them more sustainable long-term.

Setting up the project had almost wiped her out. They had enough funds to run for a year, but after that they'd need to generate further income streams if they wanted to keep the project going. Something that was playing on her mind.

She headed for the 'Staff Only' area and used the long pole to unhook the catch on the loft ladder. The sound of grating metal made her teeth itch as the ladder rattled down. With extra funding, they'd be able to construct a more robust method of accessing the roof, which would mean they could set up a gardening project and encourage those staying with them to grow their own food. But for now, using the makeshift ladder would have to suffice.

Sam climbed up and opened the hatch at the top.

Bright sunshine made her blink. It was a lovely autumn day, the last of the summer sun clinging on, as if reluctant to depart for another year.

She stepped onto the roof and was immediately hit by the smell of African basil. The rooftop was still awash with growth, despite the shortening days. Rows of carrots, beetroot and pumpkins filled the raised beds. The herb garden attracted a few lazy bees, and the last of the tomatoes provided a splash of colour.

Only the sound of busy London traffic threatened to spoil the tranquillity. The skyline was dominated by grey buildings and the chimney stacks on the disused industrial warehouse on Streatham High Road blotted the view. But if you didn't look upwards, you could believe yourself to be in a pretty country garden somewhere in rural England, rather than a rundown area of South London.

A gust of wind dislodged her hat.

Laughing, she caught hold of it before it disappeared over the side. As much as she loved her new purchase, she wasn't about to launch herself off the side of a building to retrieve it.

A bang made her jump – the hatch door had caught in the wind and slammed shut.

She went over and tried to lift it up, but it wouldn't shift. She tugged harder. No joy. Kneeling down, she tried again, easing her fingers under the latch, but it wouldn't budge.

After another few attempts, she was starting to get agitated. The guests would be here any minute. She needed to be downstairs ready to greet them. She tugged at the door again, but it was firmly stuck.

Damn.

She ran over to the edge and looked over. The car park was filling up, the guests were arriving.

Shielding her eyes, she looked for Fraser, who was manning the door, hoping to attract his attention. He was her latest volunteer recruit, an ex-Royal Engineer who'd been medically discharged from the British Army following an altercation with an IED. Even minus a leg, his large frame and 'don't-mess-with-me' attitude made him a formidable person to have overseeing security. But she couldn't see him.

She called out anyway, hoping he'd hear. 'Fraser!' Her voice disappeared in the wind. She tried again. 'Fraser? Are you there?'

No response. And she didn't even have her phone on her.

Sighing, she looked around, hoping for inspiration. Maybe she could use a shovel to bust open the latch? But then she'd have to pay for repairs.

Her only option was the fire escape.

Sam didn't mind heights. She'd spent her early years on the slopes of Lech am Arlberg and Klosters being forced to socialise with other well-to-do families, but her aptitude for downhill slaloming hadn't prepared her for imitating Spider-man. At least he had webbing to secure him to the wall. She was going to have to descend the building via an unstable and creaking metal ladder that immediately parted company from the brickwork when she lowered herself onto it.

Gripping hold, she descended slowly, praying the ladder would hold up and that no one would witness her humiliation.

But the fates were not on her side.

Voices could be heard below. People milling about. A crowd was gathering.

Oh, hell.

The ladder creaked louder, drawing attention. There was a drop of about six feet from the bottom of the ladder to the ground. How the hell was she going to negotiate that?

Then her mother's voice cut through the air, 'Samantha? Is that you?' Her tone indicated that she really hoped it wasn't, even though she feared it was.

The sound of talking faded. Everyone stopped their conversations to focus on the woman dangling from the fire escape.

As if the situation wasn't bad enough, her mother appeared directly below, her tan Chanel fitted-suit a far cry from Sam's hand-me-down charity shop bargain. 'What on earth are you doing?' she said, as though her daughter was 'acting out' and not genuinely stuck. 'Get down from there.'

Whether it was the disapproving note in her mother's voice, or the ladder shifting beneath her, she wasn't sure. But before she could ensure a safe landing, her grip loosened on the handrail and she tumbled inelegantly to the ground.

A collective gasp filled the air – which thankfully masked the numerous expletives tumbling from her mouth as she hit the ground with a thud, knocking the wind from her lungs.

Fortunately, she didn't land on her mother – who was glaring at her like she'd just murdered a kitten. Or worse, sprayed gravel over her Valentino Garavani courts.

Although pain rendered Sam momentarily speechless, she didn't appear to be badly injured. A bloody scrape on her hand was the worst of it, along with a grubby left knee.

So much for making a good first impression.

And then a flash startled her. Brilliant. The press had arrived. Her day was getting better by the minute.

'And what are you wearing?' her mother hissed, gesturing for her to get up and 'stop messing about'.

It was typical of her mother to focus on what people would think, rather than whether her daughter was okay. It was the story of Sam's life, how she never failed to embarrass the Tipping family, this time by launching herself from a building and wearing charity-shop clothes. Oh, the shame of it.

She heard laughter.

Her brother.

A hand reached down and pulled her to her feet. 'Christ, Sammy, you sure know how to make an entrance.' He brushed dirt from her once-white sleeve.

Max Tipping looked like something from a style magazine. His pinstriped three-piece suit was custom-made, no doubt by a top Savile Row tailor, and his haircut and trimmed-beard probably cost more than Sam spent in a month on food.

Behind him stood her father, his tweed suit teamed with a lightweight grey sweater, open-neck shirt and shiny brown brogues, a match for his year-round tan.

All three of them stared at her. But at least her brother's expression conveyed amusement rather than disappointment.

Sam's preference for second-hand clothing had never been approved of, even as a teenager. The idea that photos would be appearing in the newspapers of her looking 'like that' was clearly of abhorrence. Well, tough.

She wasn't about to be shamed. Not today. Showing up to a charity event for homeless youths dressed like they were attending a royal garden party was hugely insensitive. Her parents would never understand that, so it was pointless to mention it.

Plus, she didn't have the time.

'Thank you for coming,' she said, forcing a smile and ignoring the sting in her hand. 'I'm so glad you could make it. It means a lot to me.'

'We're eager to see what our money has paid for,' her father said, frowning.

Sam bit her lip. It would be too easy to retaliate. 'The flat was my twenty-first birthday present, Dad. So really, it was my money to use.'

Her mother tutted. 'No one in their right mind would sell a highly sought-after property in Dulwich to fund a…' Her perfectly powdered nose wrinkled as she searched for the right word, 'charity.'

'If we'd known what you had planned, we might not have bought it for you,' her father chastised.

Sam's smile became a little more forced. At the time, she'd wished they hadn't. The flat had felt like a bribe, a way of trying to keep her in line. Still, it had come in useful now. Without it, she couldn't have financed her dream.

'I hope you don't expect us to bail you out when you run out of money,' her father said, glancing up at the 'Welcome to The Crash Pad' sign.

'Not going to happen, Dad.' Even though running out of money was a distinct possibility.

The cavalry arrived in the shape of Fraser, who tapped his watch and beckoned her over. It was show time.

'Excuse me, I'm needed elsewhere. Make your way inside. Have a look around. Refreshments are being served in the cafe.'

She loved her family, but they were never going to see eye-to-eye.

As she limped towards the door, she spotted the Mayor – instantly recognisable by the distinctive civic chain of office around his neck.

Sam went over, introduced herself and thanked him for coming. His aide indicated they could only stay a short while; time was of the essence. But she was grateful he'd at least put in an appearance.

As she ushered everyone inside, she spotted several people making a beeline for her family. She was used to it. Some people were seduced by money, others notoriety. The Tippings of Holland Park provided both.

Her brother mingled with ease, smiling and shaking hands with dignitaries and common folk alike. Max Tipping was a born seducer, equally successful at making financial trades as he was flirting with women. He'd tripled his inheritance within the first five years of working in the City, and already owned several properties. He'd ticked every box on their parents 'wish list' for a how a Tipping offspring should live. And good luck to him. He deserved his success. Just as her sister did.

Tara was a high-flying plastic surgeon, currently residing in LA, where she reaped the rewards of pandering to the insecurities of the Hollywood elite.

Was it what Sam wanted? God, no. Her idea of success didn't centre around money. She wanted to make a difference in the world, help others, and be of some use to society. Not work sixty hours a week betting on share prices or reducing someone's double chin.

But her siblings seemed happy, and that was all that mattered.

Thankfully, everyone gathered looked suitably impressed with the building. There were lots of approving nods and photo taking, which was good. But she decided it would be best to get her speech out of the way before anyone lost interest. People's attention spans were notoriously short.

Still shaken from her fall, Sam climbed onto the low wooden table by the sofas and cleared her throat.

Switching on the microphone, she tapped the end. 'Hello? Can everyone hear me?'

The chatter in the room quietened and everyone turned to face her.

She wasn't a born public speaker, but she was hoping that her passion for the project would override her nerves. 'Thank you all so much for coming today. Your support is very much appreciated.'

Deep breath. Remember to smile.

'Today is a very special day for us. It's been long-time dream of mine to open a night shelter for the young people of South London.'

A sea of faces stared at her. Some interested, some less so.

That was the thing about tackling a difficult subject. It didn't always evoke compassion. If she'd started a charity to support sick children or orphaned animals, everyone would be on board and singing her praises. But mention the growing issue of young people being forced to sleep rough and it was a truth society didn't want to face.

But it wasn't enough to discourage her. People needed to know the reality of what life could be like without a supportive family, money, or privilege.

'When you think of someone being homeless, your mind probably turns to people sleeping rough on the streets and begging for money. They must've done something to deserve it, you probably say. Why don't they get a job? Why are they relying on the charity of others? They'll only blow the money on drugs or booze. Right?'

She took a deep breath and made eye-contact with the Mayor, who nodded – unlike his aide who was glued to her phone.

'But homelessness is often the result of having no other option. No one would choose to live on the streets if they didn't have to. Circumstances sometimes leave people with no other choice. Last year alone, over a hundred thousand young people across the UK asked for help with homelessness. But this is just the tip of a very big iceberg, and it's feared that many more are affected who simply don't come forward.'

A few people looked uncomfortable, shuffling their feet and looking anywhere but at her. Including her parents. Sam supressed a sigh. Airing political or contentious views had never been encouraged in the Tipping household.

'Homeless people often end up sofa-surfing, squatting, or living rough on the streets,' she continued. 'If they're lucky, they might get offered temporary accommodation by their local council, or find a place in a hostel. But none of these living situations are easy, and those sleeping rough will frequently get abused, robbed, or get moved on by the police.'

Her mother's mouth straightened into a line. This was not a topic for 'polite society'.

But Sam wasn't to be deterred. People had to understand how unacceptable the situation was.

'So how does a young person find themselves homeless? There are many reasons. Sometimes their family life is so awful that leaving is safer than staying. Can you imagine that? Being too afraid to go home?'

She looked around the audience, willing them to understand. A few people shook their heads. Was she winning them over?

'Those who leave the care system often find themselves homeless. As do children who are excluded from school, or who get caught up in gang culture. We all hear stories on the news about knife crime, but can you imagine living in an area where nightly stabbings occur? Or of being too afraid to leave your house in case you get attacked?'

Her father's expression indicated she was being too dramatic. It was a look she'd experienced many times as a teenager when she'd wanted to attend rallies, or protest for social change. He clearly felt she should have grown out of it. Aged twenty-nine, she was hardly likely to now.

Steadying the shake in her hands, she continued, 'The impact of being homeless can be devastating. It can contribute to poor mental health, exacerbate physical disabilities, and cause severe illness. Not to mention the risk of drug and alcohol addiction.' She'd seen the effects first-hand. Seven years as a social worker had exposed her to all kinds of horrors. 'This charity has been set up to try and mitigate some of those risks. We're not offering a miracle cure. We're not naive enough to believe the problem will go away. But we're hoping that by providing a bed for young people who have no other place to stay, it might enable them to deal with some of their other issues.'

A few tilted heads indicated people were listening. That was something.

'If you're fighting to survive on the streets, or sofa-surfing, it's impossible to get a job, find a permanent home, or invest time in education or personal development. And these things are essential in order to live independently and contribute to society. They're not luxuries. They're basic human rights.'

Her mother flinched on the words 'human rights'.

But Sam had more to say. 'If nothing else, we aim to provide these young people with a hot meal, washing facilities, and a bed for the night. Because no one deserves to be homeless. And certainly not someone who's still a teenager.'

Lecture over.

She smiled and scanned everyone's faces, wondering if she'd won them over. 'Thank you for listening. The Crash Pad will officially open its doors to the public tomorrow night. We've already had referrals from several local agencies asking if we have beds available, so that tells me the problem is very real and this project is desperately needed.'

The Mayor's aide made a motion to leave.

Sam had to get in quick. 'If you'd like to support us, then we'd love to hear from you. Whether it's donating funds or volunteering with us, this is a community project and it'll only be successful with everyone's continuing support.'

She gestured to the cafe. It was time to woo them with refreshments.

'I'm sure you're all eager for a drink. Please feel free to look around. Try the delicious home-cooked food from our cafe and chat to our volunteers, some of whom have been affected by homelessness at some point in their lives.'

'But not you,' a man called out, causing heads to turn. 'You've never wanted for anything, have you?'

Oh, hell. One of the reporters. She might have known one of them would put the boot in.

Sam glanced at her parents, who looked annoyed rather than uncomfortable. Bad press wouldn't be welcomed.

Her cheeks burned. 'You're right. I haven't. I was fortunate enough to have been brought up in a secure environment by loving parents who've never let me go without.'

She smiled at her parents, trying to show them that she wasn't an ungrateful child, she just didn't share their political beliefs. 'Not everyone's as lucky as I am. I'm extremely proud of my family, who've turned up today to support me and support this charity.' She gave her parents a thumbs-up. 'I only wish the teens accessing this shelter had the privileges I've had.'

The Mayor nodded.

Her brother shouted, 'Hear, hear!' and started clapping. God, she loved Max.

Her confidence returned. 'Any other questions?'

Several hands shot up.

Oh, boy. It seemed she wasn't getting away with simply making a speech.

It was interrogation time.

Chapter Two

In the five years Jamie Lawson had worked at the *South London Herald*, he'd covered all manner of bizarre stories. From the petty theft of a German military helmet, to a mass brawl that had broken out at a Morris dancing competition. But he'd never witnessed a ninety-year-old wheelchair-bound woman being arrested before.

Far from looking perturbed as the officer secured the handcuffs around her wrists, Ida Newton grinned from ear-to-ear and flirted shamelessly with the young officer apprehending her. She waved at the other care home residents, revelling at being in the spotlight.

'Can you look this way, Ida?' Jamie snapped a shot of Ida kissing the officer's cheek.

She was a co-operative subject, he'd give her that.

'Lovely. Now lift your hands so we can see the handcuffs.' Words he'd never imagined saying to a ninety-year-old woman.

'When do we get to ride in the squad car?' Ida's eyes shone with mischief.

The officer stood up. 'I have to read you your rights first, Ida.'

Ida squealed with delight.

The officer cleared his throat. 'Ida Newton, I'm arresting you for breach of the peace. You've been having way too much fun on your birthday and the neighbours have been complaining about the noise.'

'Tell them they can join in,' Ida said, making the care home staff laugh.

Jamie took another photo. He'd timed it just right.

'You do not have to say anything,' the officer continued. 'But it may harm your defence if you do not mention when questioned, something which you later rely on in court. Anything you do say may be given in evidence.'

'The music isn't loud enough and I need more wine,' yelled Ida, waving her handcuffed-hands about.

The police officer grinned and pretended to note down her words. 'I'm sorry, Ida, but you'll have to come with me to the station. The chief inspector may want to give you an official caution.'

'Is he handsome?'

'*I* think so, yes,' replied the officer, making everyone laugh.

Jamie scribbled down a few notes on his iPad, ready to draft his story later. He followed the staff outside and positioned himself by the police car so he could photograph Ida being wheeled out by the officer.

It certainly made for a more interesting story than his usual assignments, or writing his regular column, Pet of the Week. Hearing about Fluffy's toilet habits, or Bruiser's appetite for eating shoes, wasn't exactly a barrel of laughs and often resulted in him being bitten. The sooner he could hand the feature over to the next unlucky sod, the better.

Over the past few weeks he'd been asked to cover parking issues at the new gym and the story of a motorist who'd been injured by a falling tree. Not exactly the dizzy heights of journalism he'd hoped for. The paper wasn't a national, but it covered all of South London, so there were meatier stories to be reported on, he just hadn't been assigned any of them yet.

He glanced at Ida, who was now seated in the back of the squad car and wearing the officer's hat. 'Lock me in the cells and throw away the key,' she cried, playing to the crowd.

Good old Ida. He snapped another shot.

'You're a very compliant prisoner, Ida.' The officer got in the car. 'I normally get a lot more grief than this.'

Ida waved to the gathering crowd. 'Don't forget the siren. And the blue flashing lights. I want all the neighbours to see.'

Jamie took a few last shots as the squad car drove off, sirens blazing, blue lights flashing. It certainly drew intriguing looks from the residents of Wimbledon.

Happy that he'd captured the story of Ida's birthday surprise in full, he left them to enjoy the rest of the party.

He was still smiling as he walked up South Park Road and onto The Broadway where the newspaper offices were situated.

When his phone rang, he assumed it would be Frances from the office, asking him to pick up a sandwich for her on his return. She had the appetite of a horse. But he was surprised to see his former foster carer's name flash up on the screen.

'Hey, there, Peggy? Everything okay?'

'You tell me.' She sounded cranky.

He stopped walking. What had he done? 'You've lost me.'

'I haven't heard from you in weeks.'

Ah, so that was his crime. He mentally kicked himself. He'd been meaning to phone Peggy for a couple of weeks, but somehow work kept getting in the way. 'Sorry, I've been busy.'

'Too busy to visit the woman who practically raised you?' Peggy wasn't above using emotional blackmail to make her point. 'I've been worried about you.'

He rubbed his forehead. 'I'm sorry, Peggy. My bad. How are you?'

'Old age isn't for the weak.'

He rolled his eyes. Sixty-seven was hardly old; look at Ida, still flirting with police officers at ninety. 'Are you ill?'

'Not ill, just wearing out.' She sighed. 'What about you? Tell me how you're doing?'

He resumed walking, relieved she wasn't calling with bad news. 'I'm good, thanks. Working hard, agonising over West Ham, eating too many takeaways. The usual.'

'You need to eat better. Why aren't you cooking for yourself? I taught you how to cook, didn't I?'

'You did, Peggy. But every time I make your Jamaican curry the neighbours complain.'

'Complain? Why would they complain?'

'Because I haven't invited them round.'

Her laugh was big and throaty. 'You don't fool me, boy. I won't be tricked by your compliments. When are you coming to visit?'

'Soon, I promise.'

'When?'

He'd almost forgotten how stubborn she could be. 'Let me check my diary. I'll text you some dates.'

'No texting. I can't use that blasted phone you gave me. Call and speak to me, like God intended.'

Jamie smiled. 'Okay, I'll call you. Like a good Christian boy.'

She tutted. 'That'll be the day.'

'Excuse me? You dragged me to church every Sunday for seven years.'

'And have you been since?'

'No, but that's because you scarred me for life. I'm too afraid someone will make me stand up and sing "Raise Up". It still haunts me.'

'You have a beautiful voice. And going to church changed you, you became a better boy.'

'That wasn't church, Peggy. That was you. God can't take any credit for turning my life around.'

'Ah, you're a good boy.' He had to hold the phone away from his ear when she blew her nose. 'But you'd be a better boy if you visited more often.' And there she was again, the Peggy he knew.

'I'll visit soon, Peggy, I promise. I'll call tonight and fix a date. Okay?'

'You'd better.'

He wouldn't dare not. Peggy was a big-hearted woman, but she wasn't someone you wanted to cross. He'd made that mistake enough times as a teenager to know that behaving was the much safer option. 'I've got to go, Peggy. Chat later.' He hung up.

He'd reached the newspaper offices on The Broadway. The *South London Herald* was situated on the fourth floor of a generic office block. It was open-plan with ugly green partitions erected to create individual work areas. Frosted windows ran the length of the room, obscuring the views of London. The ceiling tiles were stained and yellowing, highlighted by stark strip-lighting.

They weren't a big team. Only four reporters, the technical editor, the boss, and one secretary, but it wasn't a bad place to work. It just wasn't where he wanted to be in another five years' time. He had bigger ambitions, with dreams of becoming a hard-hitting documentary filmmaker. But for now, he had to make do with Pet of the Week.

No sooner had he sat down when Gurdip Singh's face appeared over the top of the partition. 'Boss wants to see you.'

'Right now?'

'No idea. He was looking for you earlier.' Gurdip rested his chin on the partition. 'You been covering a story?'

'Ninety-year-old woman arrested for breach of the peace.' He picked up his notebook. 'She was carted off in her wheelchair. Lights flashing, sirens blaring. The lot.'

'For real?'

Jamie rolled his eyes. 'Of course not. It was a birthday surprise laid on by the care home.'

Gurdip looked disappointed. 'Shame.'

Jamie shook his head. His colleague wasn't really hard-hearted; it was just the journalist in him. No one would want to see an elderly woman arrested. At least, he hoped not. 'Better luck next time, right?'

'We live in hope.' Gurdip sighed and sat back down at his desk.

Like him, Gurdip was looking for his big break. The story that would propel them from local reporters into big-time journalists. But until that elusive break came along, they had to make do with mundane issues that were fun to cover, but would never set the newspaper world alight.

Jamie walked towards Gareth's office, which took up the entire back section of the room. It was a glass monstrosity filled with manly leather furniture, including a huge armchair with matching footrest. The desk was double the size of everyone else's, and the side wall was filled with flat-screen televisions, each one tuned into a different news channel. His boss liked to be abreast of developing stories, although it probably had more to do with demonstrating his status as 'top-dog'.

Gareth Gascoigne was a forty-something ex-footballer whose brief stint on the bench at Stoke City had been ended by a knee injury. He'd switched to sports journalism before progressing to the tabloids. His claim of being a relative of Paul Gascoigne had aided his progress and gained him access to numerous events, but years of drinking, followed by a messy divorce, had seen his fortunes tumble from the heights of the *Daily Mirror* to running a regional paper.

When Jamie tapped on the glass, his boss looked up from his laptop and beckoned him in.

'Jamie, mate. How's it going?' The sleeves of his pink shirt were rolled up and his tie was at half-mast. Deep circles rimmed his bloodshot-eyes.

As Jamie entered the office he was hit by a waft of stale cigarette smoke. Gareth had never been one for adhering to health and safety regulations.

'You wanted to see me?'

'Take a seat.' Gareth took a swig of black coffee and wiped his mouth with the back of his hand. 'How was our jailbird?'

'Entertaining.' Jamie sat down on the 'interrogation chair' as the staff called it, an uncomfortable plastic contraption that numbed your bum if you sat still for too long. 'I've got some great shots. Ida wasn't shy in front of the camera. And the police officer was up for a laugh, so it'll make for a good human interest story.'

Gareth nodded. 'Any fit nurses?'

Jamie raised an eyebrow. 'Excuse me?'

'At the care home? I hope you got some shots of a few hotties.'

'Err… no, I was focused on covering the story about Ida.'

Gareth looked disappointed.

Jamie should probably be used to his boss's inappropriateness after five years of working for him, but it still made him cringe. Sexual harassment laws were another regulation Gareth ignored – as his poor colleague Frances knew only too well. As the only female reporter, she was forever having to avoid Gareth's roaming eyes. He'd yet to pinch her bottom – at least, as far as Jamie knew – but he never held back with the smutty innuendos or leering suggestions that she should wear shorter skirts to work.

Thankfully, Frances was adept at dealing with Gareth's flirting and would put him back in his box by mentioning his thinning hairline or growing beer belly, which was usually enough to shut him up.

Gareth sat back in his chair. 'You've done some good stories of late. I was impressed by the piece you did on the reduced bus service and how it impacts pensioners.'

'Thanks.' High praise indeed. Gareth didn't hand out compliments easily.

'It was a fucking boring story, but you managed to make it interesting.'

Jamie hid a smile. His boss was the master of giving with one hand and taking away with the other. And besides, he doubted anyone could make a story about a bus exciting... except maybe Keanu Reeves.

'You're good at finding an angle.' Gareth pointed at him. 'You make it about people. You get the reader to *care*.' He used air quotation marks on the word 'care', as though no one really cared about these things, but that wasn't the point. 'Sentiment Sells Papers' was a phrase Gareth used in staff meetings when he was trying to boost the team's productivity.

'I appreciate that, Gareth.' It was a half-hearted compliment, but he was grateful nonetheless.

'So you should.'

His boss was a modest soul.

'How long have you worked here now, two years?'

'Five.'

Gareth frowned. 'What?'

'I've worked here for five years.'

'Fuck me, where does the time go.' Gareth rubbed his unshaven chin. 'Then it's about time you covered a bigger story. Before some wanker from the big-boy papers nabs you.'

Jamie tried to contain his excitement. A big story? He'd been praying for a big story for the entire five years he'd worked here. Something he could get his teeth into. Something that would make a name for himself. He sat up straighter, eager to hear his assignment. 'I'd really appreciate that, Gareth. I'm ready for a big story.'

Gareth opened a folder and handed Jamie a photo. 'Ever heard of Max Tipping?'

Jamie looked at the photo of a forty-something man dressed in a flash suit. He was on the phone, standing outside a posh office block. 'No, should I have?'

'He's the finance director at Quinton International. One of the private banks in London. Share prices for the company have risen dramatically over recent months.'

'And you think something dodgy's going on?'

Gareth handed him another photo, a grainy shot taken from a distance of two men.

Jamie squinted at the picture. 'Is that the same bloke?'

'Yep.'

'Who's the other man?'

'No idea. Some other loaded posh-knob.'

In the picture, Max Tipping was handing the other man a thick envelope.

'Drugs?'

'More likely money. Something that might account for the bank's share prices suddenly rising.'

'Where did you get the photo?'

'My girlfriend. She attended some fancy charity dinner at The Dorchester last night. Max Tipping was there as a representative for Quinton International. He presented Great Ormond Street with a big fat cheque. She remembered him because he was a bit of a charmer.' Gareth rolled his eyes.

'So?'

Gareth pointed to the photo. 'The other guy in the photo was sat next to him at dinner. At the end of the night, my girlfriend was getting in her car, when she saw them talking. It caught her attention because they were acting shifty, glancing around, checking no one was watching them and keeping to the shadows.'

Jamie looked at the photo again. 'Doesn't necessarily mean anything dodgy was going on.'

'Then why not hand over the envelope during dinner? They spent the whole evening sat next to each other, laughing and boozing. If they had nothing to hide, why wait until they were in the privacy of the car park before handing over the envelope?'

He had a point. 'And you think it's worth investigating?'

Gareth shrugged. 'If it was any other city-boy trader it wouldn't be worth the effort, but Max Tipping is the son of Christina and Richard Tipping.'

'I haven't heard of them either.'

'They're big-wigs in London society. They hobnob with royalty and other loaded toffs with more dosh than they know what to do with. Their photos regularly appear in the media, usually linked with one worthy cause or another. Totally superficial, of course. It's all about appearances.'

'So they wouldn't want their son exposed for financial irregularities?'

'Fuck, no.' He handed Jamie a set of mock-up prints. 'We're running this story tomorrow.'

Jamie read the headline. 'Help for Homeless Youngsters.' Below was a photo of the Mayor cutting through a large pink ribbon. Jamie scanned the article. A new night shelter was opening in Streatham for under twenty-ones. Good. More beds were desperately needed.

'What's this got to do with Max Tipping?'

Gareth handed him a group photo taken outside the shelter. He pointed to a dark-haired woman standing next to Max Tipping. 'That's Max's sister, Samantha. The shelter is her project.'

Jamie looked closer. She looked a lot younger than her brother, and she was wearing what looked like men's clothes, complete with polka dot tie, waistcoat, and trilby hat. It was a far cry from Max Tipping's tailored city-boy look. 'You think she's involved?'

'That's for you to find out.'

Jamie studied the woman, her long wavy hair and open smile. She didn't look like an obvious suspect for financial fraud. But it wouldn't be the first charity to front a money laundering scandal.

'Whether she's involved or not, she's our way in.'

Jamie glanced up. 'How so?'

'Max Tipping isn't an easy man to get to. There's heavy security at the bank and he lives in a fancy, gated pad manned by a security guard. His parents' place is like fucking Fort Knox.' He leant forward. 'But the sister is advertising for volunteers to help at the shelter.'

'You want me to volunteer there?'

'It's the perfect cover. You can observe without suspicion.'

Jamie couldn't believe what he was hearing. 'You mean, like a proper undercover operation?'

'You up for it?'

Was he ever! 'Christ, yes.'

Gareth wiped his nose with the back of his hand. 'Better than Pet of the Week, right?'

Just a bit.

'Thanks for this opportunity, Gareth. I won't let you down.'

'You'd better not. If this bastard is up to no good, then I want him exposed. You hear me? Take the fucker down.'

Jamie stood up. 'My pleasure, boss.'

Exposing the devious dealings of a privileged family who'd probably never suffered a day in their posh self-centred lives was his kind of story.

Chapter Three

Sam was quickly realising that she'd been lulled into a false sense of security. The opening night of The Crash Pad had gone surprisingly smoothly. Only seven teens had turned up, so they'd easily coped with demand and provided a hot meal, shower facilities and beds for all who'd queued. There'd been no dramas, no problems, and the night had run like clockwork, just as she'd hoped it might.

The second night had proved slightly more challenging. Ten young people had required beds, and although there'd been no major issues to deal with during the night, this morning she'd discovered a torn pillowcase, a missing pool cue, and a pile of sick in the male toilets. Still, it was nothing she couldn't deal with and it was only to be expected. A project like this was never going to be totally plain sailing.

Tonight, however, was proving to be another level of test entirely, and it was only seven p.m. A few lunchtime stragglers had yet to leave the cafe and were ignoring Emily and Norah's polite requests for them to depart. Plus, there were already seventeen people lined up outside, which meant at least two were going to be turned away.

The urge to hide in the loos until the unlucky ones had been rejected was tempting, but Sam knew that wasn't fair on her volunteers. This project was about trying to make a difference, not cure the world of homelessness entirely. Even if they opened shelters all around the UK, they still wouldn't meet demand. But if they could help a few people turn their lives around, then it was a job well done. She had to keep reminding herself of that.

Her phoned pinged. Fraser needed her by the entrance.

Bracing herself for another tough situation, she made her way through the colourful communal area to reception. A trestle-table was set up by the front entrance, ready for the night receptionist. But as they'd had no luck recruiting anyone for the position, they were having to make do without for the time being. It wasn't the most glamorous or desirable of positions, but it was disappointing not to be able to fill it.

It was pitch dark outside. Nonetheless, Sam could still make out the line of bodies queueing at the door, their hunched shoulders and resigned expressions visible under the security lighting.

Although the autumnal days were still relatively warm, the temperature at night was rapidly dropping. The thermometer on the wall hovered at six degrees. Not freezing, but not camping out weather either.

Fraser was waiting by the glass doors. Some of the kids were shivering, moving from foot to foot in a bid to keep warm while they waited for the shelter to open.

Sam didn't envy them. 'Is everything okay, Fraser? Why haven't you opened up?'

He nodded behind her. 'Slight problem.'

She turned to see an elderly gentleman leaning on a walking frame.

She went over. 'Can we help you with something?'

He smiled. 'Cuppa wouldn't go amiss, love.'

'I'm sorry, sir. But the shelter is for under twenty-ones only.'

'That's what he said.' He nodded towards Fraser. 'But he said to ask you.'

Sam glanced at Fraser, who was wearing his big army coat, the collar turned up. 'I wondered whether we could make an exception.' His eyes lowered to the old man's feet.

Sam glanced down and saw a pair of heavily worn slippers. The soles had come loose from the tops and they were tied onto the man's feet with string. Her heart contracted as her eyes travelled over his faded grey trousers and thin jumper. 'What's your name, sir?'

'Harold Jones.'

'Nice to meet you, Harold.' She extended her hand for him to shake. 'I'm Sam. Do you have anywhere to stay tonight?'

'I have a place in Ambleside Avenue.'

That was something. At least he wasn't homeless. 'Do you live alone?'

'I do now.' He blinked away tears.

As much as she'd tried to imagine all the scenarios she might encounter when opening a night shelter, this wasn't one of them. 'Well, Harold, we can't offer you a bed, but I'm sure we can stretch to a cup of tea.'

He squeezed her arm. 'Bless you, dear.'

She turned to find Fraser grinning at her. He gave her a thumbs-up. 'Nice one.'

Except she'd just broken one of her own rules. She was going to have to develop a thicker skin if the project was going to succeed. 'Are you okay to deal with the queue if I take Harold through to the cafe?'

'No problem.' Fraser unlocked the doors and stood back to allow the queue to move inside.

They filed through the doorway like obedient puppies. A diverse mixture of shapes, sizes and ethnic backgrounds, bound by the commonality of homelessness. Most of their clothes were dirty and the scent of stale sweat accompanied them as they entered. They looked painfully young, scared, and distrusting.

'Please make your way through to the communal area.' Sam smiled in the hope it might ease their trepidation. 'Hot food is being served in the cafe, and you'll find towels and toiletries in the shower blocks.'

A lad glanced up and half-smiled. The others kept their gazes fixed to the floor and shuffled passed.

Emily appeared in reception, her knitted red hat the exact same shade as her deep auburn hair. She watched the guests troop past, her expression a mixture of compassion and relief.

Only a few months ago she'd been sleeping rough herself. She knew better than anyone what these kids suffered. But Emily's story was a reminder of why The Crash Pad was needed. A place to help those who through no fault of their own had ended up on the streets.

'We need you in the cafe, Sam. One of the lunch-time stragglers has been on the booze,' Emily whispered, checking no one could hear her.

Sam frowned. 'Seriously?'

'The girl with the camouflage jacket. She's refusing to hand over the bottle.'

The shelter had a strict 'no drink or drugs' policy. There were signs attached to the walls stating that any infringement would result in immediate eviction. Sam had hoped it wouldn't be an issue, but clearly, she'd thought wrong.

But before she could respond, Fraser's arm blocked the doorway as the fifteenth kid stepped inside. 'Sorry, we're up to capacity. No more tonight.'

The girl who'd missed out looked stricken. 'But I've being queueing for hours.'

The lad who'd been number fifteen in the queue turned when he heard her speak. He walked over. 'She can have my place,' he said, hoisting his rucksack onto his shoulder.

Sam intervened. 'You don't have to give up your place. That's why we have a queue system. You're entitled to a bed.'

The lad shrugged. 'She needs it more than I do. I'm less likely to get hassled on the streets than she is. I can look after myself.'

It was a chivalrous act and one that tugged at Sam's heart strings. The girl waiting at the door was scarily young, but the boy didn't look much older himself. 'Do you have somewhere else to go?'

'Sure. There's a nice doorway in Streatham High Road I've got my eye on.' He half-grinned. 'I'll be all right. Maybe see you tomorrow night.' He headed out the door.

Emily rushed after him. 'Wait a moment.' When she was sure he wouldn't go anywhere, she ran back to the main area, letting the doors swing shut behind her.

Fraser let the girl queueing at the door inside.

'Thanks,' she mumbled to the nice lad who'd given up his place, scuttling past, as if fearful he might change his mind.

'No worries. Sleep well,' the lad said, with a wry smile.

Emily reappeared in reception and handed the lad a takeaway carton and paper bag. 'I hope you like tomato soup.'

He smiled at her. 'Who doesn't?'

'There's a hot pasty in there too.'

His smile widened. 'My lucky night.'

'I'm Emily,' she blurted, her cheeks colouring.

He raised the cup of soup, as if toasting her. 'Thanks, Emily. I'm Alfie.'

Emily's blush deepened. 'It was nice of you to give up your place for that girl.'

He shrugged. 'Anyone would've done the same.'

She watched him leave. 'No, they wouldn't.'

But he didn't hear. He'd already disappeared into the night, searching out his doorway on Streatham High Road.

Sam sighed, saddened by the exchange. But she was impressed too. Emily had shown such kindness towards the lad. The girl had a big heart.

Sam gestured for Fraser to shut the doors. 'You can lock up now.'

Another shelter rule was that once everyone was inside, they weren't allowed to leave until morning. If they did, they couldn't come back. It was the only way to ensure everyone's safety.

Fraser bolted the doors. 'All done.'

'Thanks, Fraser. I might need your help with something in the cafe.'

'Sure. I'll check the windows are shut and be right with you.'

Sam reverted her attention to Harold, who'd been patiently waiting by her side. 'Sorry about that. The cafe's this way. Do you need a hand?'

'I can manage, thank you, dear. Speedy Gonzales, they call me.' He shuffled along on his walking frame.

Sam held his arm, afraid he might fall. He didn't look very steady on his feet. But walking at a snail's-pace meant she had time to observe what was happening in the main area. A few guests had collapsed onto the sofas. Most were queueing at the cafe counter, being served by Norah.

Sam spotted the drunk girl immediately. She was slumped over one of the cafe tables, her hand gripping the vodka bottle, swinging it from side-to-side. Not good.

Sam led Harold to a table away from the girl and held the chair for him as he sat down. 'How do you take your tea, Harold?'

'Any way it comes,' he said, landing heavily on the chair.

She patted his arm. 'Coming right up.' There was something she had to do first. She went over to Emily. 'Can you get Harold a cup of tea? I'll deal with vodka-girl.'

Emily frowned. 'Be careful. She looks unstable.'

'Don't worry, I will be.'

She waited for Fraser to reappear before approaching the girl, who was mumbling to herself. 'I'm sorry, but we have a no alcohol policy at the shelter,' she said, keeping her voice low. 'I'm going to have to ask you to leave.'

'Fuck off.' The girl swung her arm, nearly hitting Sam with the bottle.

A few kids looked over, no doubt intrigued by the situation. Sam had hoped to extricate the girl without causing a scene, but maybe that was wishful thinking. A battle awaited, and she wasn't exactly built for combat or practised in martial arts.

Thankfully, Fraser was.

With lightning speed, he removed the bottle from the girl before Sam could even blink. Despite the girl protesting, swearing, and trying to wrench herself from his grip, he eased her out of the room with minimal fuss.

Once again, Sam was grateful for Fraser's army training.

And then a loud crash startled her.

She turned to see two lads entangled in a brawl.

It took her brain a few seconds to absorb what was happening. Time seemed to slow. Or maybe it was just her reaction time that had slowed. Her feet were rooted to the spot as the two lads scuffled with each other. They fell against a table, knocking it over, sending plates smashing to the floor. Food went everywhere.

The two girls seated at the table ran for cover.

A crowd gathered, fascinated by the fight.

And then a flash of steel caught her eye.

Holy crap. One of them had a knife.

She jerked forwards, her mind and body in turmoil. She needed to call the police… Stop the fight… Protect the others… All of which couldn't be done simultaneously.

Fraser came to her aid again. He ran towards the boys, his false limb affecting his gait, and barged into the boy with the knife, sending him tumbling backwards. He disarmed the boy and pinned him to the ground, all before Sam had even moved a step.

Fat lot of help she'd been.

Her stress levels lowered enough that she could move, and knowing she needed to take control of the situation, she climbed onto a chair and clapped her hands. 'Show's over. Can everyone relocate to the communal area or go to their allocated room while we clear up.'

The onlookers reluctantly began to move.

She jumped off the chair. But when the second lad involved in the fight tried to follow the others, she ran after him. 'Not you,' she said, catching his arm. 'You need to leave.'

'Why? I ain't done nothing.'

'I'm sorry, but fighting isn't tolerated here.'

'I was defending myself,' he objected, as Sam led him to the exit. 'He started it. Fucking unfair.'

Sam had no idea whether she was being unfair or not. She hadn't seen who'd started the fight, and had no idea what it was about. But she knew she had to set a precedent. If she put up with any kind of bad behaviour, the place would descend into chaos and her idea of a supposed safe haven would be no safer than the streets.

'Am I barred?' the lad asked, as she unbolted the door.

'Only for tonight. You can try again tomorrow.' She opened the door for him. 'But if there's any repeat of tonight's behaviour, then you're out again. Understand?'

He ambled off, still mumbling about the unfairness of it all.

Who said life was fair? Certainly not her. Alfie had been turned away tonight so someone needier could have his place. And now they had two places spare. If life was fair, then Alfie wouldn't be sleeping in a doorway on Streatham High Road while two undeserving lads abused the kindness of volunteers.

Blue flashing lights were approaching. The police. Great.

Sighing, Sam held the door open as two officers exited the squad car.

'We've had reports of an incident?' the older officer said, approaching the building. 'Lad with a knife?'

'Through here. My colleague has him apprehended.'

'You didn't search the kid before he came in?'

Sam shot him a look of annoyance. 'This is a night shelter, not a prison.'

The officer raised an eyebrow. 'Then you're asking for trouble.'

She tried not to feel aggrieved as she followed him into the main area and led him over to where Fraser had the kid pinned to the floor.

The officers took control and searched the lad. They confiscated the kitchen knife, a knuckleduster and a small bag of what looked like cocaine. Oh, great.

Sam inwardly cringed. Things were rapidly spiralling out of control.

The lad was handcuffed and led out to the waiting squad car. Fraser went with them.

Sam joined Emily and Norah and helped clean up the mess. The table leg was broken and all three dinner plates were smashed. Yet more expense. And she'd only just forked out for the loft hatch repair.

Worse was to come.

The older officer returned and asked to speak to her in private. She showed him into the storage-cum-laundry room, where he spent the next ten minutes tearing into her for not having better security protocols in place and letting the second lad involved in the knife fight leave before they could question him.

As a former social worker, he told her she should know better. And he was right. It wasn't like she hadn't dealt with her fair share of incidents over the years, but she'd hoped that by trusting these kids and treating them with kindness, it might deter any serious bad behaviour. Evidently not.

The policeman also criticised her refusal to adopt a belongings search before allowing the guests access to the shelter, for not recording details about who was staying at the shelter, and for not having more staff on duty to cope with incidents such as a kid pulling a knife.

Throughout the reprimand, she stood still, eyes downcast feeling like a scolded child.

He used words like 'irresponsible' and 'naive', which were accusations regularly thrown at her by her parents.

It was only as he was leaving that his tone softened. 'I know you're trying to help these kids. You want to make a difference, I get that. But unless you run a tighter ship, this won't be the last incident we get called out to. If word gets out this is a soft place, you'll be inundated with lowlifes using it to peddle drugs and initiate knife crime.'

Shame burned in her cheeks. 'I don't want that, but I don't want to distrust them either. They deserve to be treated with dignity and respect. I don't want to treat them like they're criminals, especially when most of them haven't done anything wrong.'

The officer looked at her like she was the biggest schmuck on the planet. 'You're dealing with troubled teenagers. These are streetwise kids, and like all kids, they need boundaries. If you want this project to work, you're going to have to toughen up. If you don't, the place will be closed within a month.'

'I can handle it.'

'You might not have a choice. We have the power to shut this place down if we think it's proving to be a hazard.'

'It's not—'

'And I won't hesitate to recommend its closure if incidents like tonight become a regular thing. The council won't be happy either. They'll revoke your licence if this place causes unrest in the community.'

Tears pricked her eyes. 'It won't come to that.'

'Then get your act together before someone gets seriously hurt.' His tone had returned to reprimanding. 'If you don't, then you won't be helping anyone. Least of all these kids.'

She closed the door behind him, needing a moment to compose herself before re-joining the others. She was still shaking from witnessing the knife fight, and now she'd been chastised for being naive, clueless, and irresponsible. It was like being a wayward teenager all over again.

All she'd wanted to do was help. To make a difference. But it was proving harder than she'd anticipated. It wasn't like she'd expected it to be a breeze; she just hadn't anticipated quite so many hurdles in the first week. Maybe she was naive after all.

She slumped against the pile of spare bedding and let her head drop, unable to prevent the tears from falling.

Had her parents been right?

Had she bitten off more than she could chew?

God, she hoped not.

Chapter Four

Emily started when the boy next to her shouted. It was an instinctive reaction, an inbuilt defence mechanism to sudden sounds. It was the same when people touched her unexpectedly – she'd strike out involuntarily. Not meaning any harm, just self-preservation kicking in.

But there was nothing to be alarmed about. The boy hadn't even seen her, he was yelling at his mates across the corridor, running to join them ahead of class. As the boy reached his mates, he slapped one of them on the back and laughed, oblivious to the unnerved state of the girl he'd left cowering by the doorway. Why would he notice? He probably had no idea what it was like to live in constant fear, or wonder where your next meal would come from. She was glad he was clueless. She wouldn't wish that experience on anyone.

Pushing herself away from the wall, she checked her surroundings and headed down the corridor. A group of girls were clustered together checking their phones. One of them glanced over, assessing Emily's second-hand camel coat and worn Doc Marten boots with the rainbow laces. Unimpressed, the girl reverted her attention to whatever exciting thing was happening in the world of social media.

Emily pulled her knitted hat lower and scuttled away, wishing the college wasn't so big. She wasn't comfortable in crowds. People made her nervous. Open spaces made her nervous, as did enclosed ones. In fact, most things made her nervous – something few people understood.

People assumed she was fearless, that living on the streets had toughened her up and desensitised her to everyday dramas. It was the opposite. Living rough was surprisingly simple. Brutal, but simple. It was re-joining society that was proving hard.

She checked her map. The location for her induction session was in the main auditorium. Sucking in a deep breath, she pushed open the door.

The noise was overwhelming. Her state of nervousness increased as she scanned the room. There were people everywhere. Kids talking, laughing, scrolling through their phones or listening to music, all without a care in the world. They looked untroubled, some bored, others excited by the start of a new chapter in their lives. Albeit a delayed one.

A fire at the college over the summer had prevented the term starting in September as scheduled, but there was no evidence of any fire damage now. The place was pristine.

Emily looked around. A few of the other kids looked nervous, sitting alone on the raised seating, heads down, trying to appear invisible. She could relate; even before she'd left home she'd never been one of the cool kids in school. Coupled with being an only child, was it any wonder she lacked extensive social skills?

Aiming for a seat at the back, she stepped around a group of kids blocking the gangway. She clutched her patchwork bag to her chest, her hands clammy and shaking. It took all her willpower not to bolt.

When the local authority had eventually housed her, she'd hoped it would be the start of her new life. An opportunity to begin afresh and shed her anxieties. But even after several months of living in her cosy bedsit, her self-preservation instincts were quick to kick in. She felt like a lioness in the wild, alert and skittish, torn between hunting for food and hiding from predators. Would she ever feel safe? She hoped so. But it would take more than a few months to repair the damage caused by four years living rough.

A man appeared on the stage at the front of the room. He introduced himself as the principal and welcomed them to the Bromley campus. It took a while for the room to quieten, and he had to wait a good few minutes before being able to address the group.

He spoke with enthusiasm about the college's new and improved facilities, and how they'd turned the tragedy of the fire into a positive and used the opportunity to modernise the college. The campus now offered several cafes and a common room, where students could play table tennis, use the snack machines and make new friends. He spoke about the multi-faith prayer rooms and the fitness centre, complete with weight-room and gymnasium.

It was mind-blowing. A gift. A privilege.

And yet none of the other kids seemed that impressed.

Most of them were glued to their devices, their boredom thresholds already exceeded.

They had no idea how lucky they were. And why should they? They'd probably come from loving homes, with doting parents and wanted for nothing. Emily didn't envy them. She just wished her circumstances had been different.

She'd enjoyed school and had always got good grades, despite the difficulties at home, and she'd hoped to do well in her exams and attend university, but that wasn't to be.

She was now nineteen years old and didn't have a single qualification to her name. Her status as care leaver meant she was given special dispensation and offered a college place despite her lack of formal education. The fact that she'd only been in care a short time didn't matter to the powers that be. They liked their labels, and 'care leaver' meant she had access to support services. 'Homeless teen' didn't.

She glanced down, unaware she'd been biting her nails. There was blood smeared around the cuticles. Self-conscious, she sat on her hands, preventing herself from chewing again.

The principal continued talking excitedly about the college's facilities, and it was another forty-five minutes before he finished the induction session. After this, they were invited to use the canteen for refreshments before heading to their first class.

Emily waited until the room had emptied before leaving. She couldn't face a busy canteen. She went to the loo and then searched out the classroom circled on her map.

It was a big room with large windows that magnified the sunshine hitting the glass. Heading for the back, she chose a seat by the far window. She'd feel less claustrophobic if she could see outside.

The classroom overlooked the sports field. It was filled with kids wearing athletic attire. Some were running around the track. Others were standing around socialising – a skill she'd yet to acquire.

Volunteering at the shelter had helped. She could relate to the homeless kids and the other volunteers were sensitive to her situation. They didn't crowd her, or ask too many personal questions, and they didn't judge her. Something she suspected wasn't going to be the case with her fellow college students.

She unearthed her phone and checked the screen. No new messages. Not that she'd been expecting any. But it occupied her hands and stopped her biting her nails.

The room began to fill with other students.

A blonde girl stopped by her chair. 'OMG! What's that?'

Emily didn't immediately register the girl was talking to her.

'Is it from the Jurassic period?' The girl let out a snort of laughter.

Emily looked up, realising the girl was referring to her old-style pay-as-you-go phone.

'Has it even got a camera?'

Emily shook her head.

The girl exchanged a look with her mates. 'Any games?'

Emily felt her cheeks grow warm.

'Tell me it has access to Wi-Fi?'

Emily shoved the phone in her pocket, hoping the girl would go away.

She didn't.

'My nan's phone is more current than that. Why don't you upgrade?' It was said in such a matter-of-fact way, as though the girl couldn't fathom why any sane person wouldn't have the latest device.

Emily wanted to tell the girl to mind her own business, but she knew it would only inflame the situation. Instead, she shrugged, and said, 'Maybe I will.'

The girl flicked through her sparkly gold device, her long nails manicured to the same perfection as her micro-bladed eyebrows. 'I've got the latest iPhone. Unlimited monthly data.'

Emily nodded. 'Nice.'

What else could she say?

Clearly bored with Emily's lack of response, the girl gave her a critical look and re-joined her friends.

Emily sensed they were talking about her. She heard comments about her 'Poundshop notebook' and lack of make-up. They concluded she must be 'poor' and decided she wasn't someone they wanted to 'hang out with'.

Far from feeling hurt, Emily felt relieved. Surrounding herself with kids who judged others by what phone they had wasn't her idea of true friendship.

Not that she knew much about having friends. There were a few girls on the streets she'd hung out with. More from a safety perspective than through any shared interests, but they'd had each other's backs, at least.

It wasn't until she'd applied to work at the shelter that she felt she'd met kindred spirits. The owner, Sam, was lovely, and so supportive and kind. She always wanted to help others and never made anyone feel unworthy, including Emily.

Fraser was like the big brother she'd never had, and Norah was like a surrogate mother. It was the closest thing she'd ever had to being part of a family.

A loud bang made her flinch.

A woman in chef whites appeared in the doorway. She was a burly woman with a big voice and no nonsense attitude. Slamming the door, she marched into the room and introduced herself as their course leader. She briefly explained the course programme and asked them all to introduce themselves.

'We'll start with you,' she bellowed, pointing to a kid at the front. 'Up you get. What's your name? Where are you from? And speak up so everyone can hear.'

Emily felt the blood drain from her head. No way was she about to stand up and tell a room full of strangers about her life. It was no one's business but hers.

Her agitation increased as one by one the kids stood up and spoke. Some were confident, some shy, but none of them had run away and lived on the streets, or been abused by a mentally ill mother.

If she'd known this was a requirement of the course, she'd never have signed up.

By the time the woman got to her side of the room, Emily was in full panic mode. Her heart racing, her hands clammy, breathing shallow and erratic.

The woman towered over her. 'Come on, girl. Don't be shy. What's your name?'

Emily tried to stand, but her legs felt like lead. She glanced around at her classmates, who were all staring at her like she had an octopus attached to her head.

She heard the words 'freak' and 'weird' being sniggered.

It was no good, she couldn't do it.

Grabbing her bag, she ran from the room, knocking into desks as she tried to escape. She ignored the woman calling after her and continued running.

Why had she thought she was up to this? She was a fool for even thinking she could cope with college. It was too much. Too suffocating. Too traumatic.

She pushed passed people in the corridors, ignoring shouts of 'Hey, watch where you're going!'

Tears ran down her face as she ran.

She gulped in air, trying to escape, hampered by a tightening throat.

Finally, daylight. She'd made it outside. She was free.

And then she saw a familiar face.

Norah was sitting on the low wall outside the front entrance of the college.

She stood when Emily neared and opened her arms. 'Oh, love. Come here.'

Emily collapsed into her arms.

She had no idea how long they stayed like that, hugging. Emily crying, while Norah rubbed her back and made soothing noises. Eventually, the tears subsided and she allowed Norah to lower her onto the wall.

'How... how did you know?' Emily wiped her nose with her sleeve.

Norah dug out a tissue. 'I was afraid something like this might happen. Here, love. Blow your nose.' She waited until Emily was calmer. 'Today was a big deal. I figured it might be a bit overwhelming for you. I'd hoped you'd be okay, but I thought I'd best be here in case you weren't.'

Norah's kindness evoked more tears. 'I shouldn't have enrolled. I can't do it. Why did I think I could do this?'

Norah waited until the tears subsided. 'Of course you can do it. And you know more than most that nothing in life worth having is ever easy.'

Emily sniffed. 'But I didn't even make it through the first morning. I'm useless.'

'You're far from useless, love.'

'But I fell at the first hurdle.'

'Then get back up and try again.' Norah hugged her tighter.

'It's too hard.'

'Now, listen to me.' Norah angled her body to face Emily. 'Nothing will ever be as hard as what you went through on the streets. College is a piece of cake compared to that.'

Emily shook her head. 'But I don't know how to behave, how to interact with people.'

'Sure, you do. You're the most mature and sensible young woman I've ever met. You constantly amaze me. After everything that's happened, you've still managed to turn your life around. Not many youngsters could do that. You dug deep, kept believing and look at you now? Living in your own place, training to be a chef, and helping other youngsters to make the same transition. You're an extraordinary young woman, and don't ever forget it.'

'I can't go back in there.'

'Yes, you can. But not yet.' Norah gave her a squeeze. 'Sit here for a while, and then we'll go back in together, okay?' Norah opened her bag. 'I brought you a packed lunch. You'll feel better after you've had something to eat.'

Emily unwrapped the sandwich Norah offered her. 'Tuna mayo? That's my favourite.'

Norah rolled her eyes. 'That's why I made it, you daft thing. Eat up.'

Emily obeyed and took a bite. It was delicious. Her relationship with food was still complex. Too many years spent flipping between starving and scrabbling for scraps.

'So what happened to upset you?'

Emily swallowed awkwardly. 'The lecturer wanted me to introduce myself and say a bit about my life. I freaked out. No way was I going to tell a bunch of strangers what happened to me.'

Norah looked thoughtful. 'Yes, that is a tricky one.'

'I didn't know what to do, so I ran.'

'You could've just told the truth.'

'What, that I'm an abused runaway? No way.'

'But that's not all you are, is it? You could've said... Hello, my name's Emily. I have my own place, and I currently volunteer as a cook at a night shelter for young people. I'm here because I want to train to be a chef, and one day I want to run my own restaurant.'

Emily paused, her sandwich halfway to her mouth. Could she have said that?

Norah nudged her. 'Who couldn't fail to be impressed by that? I know I would, and I'm sixty-nine.'

Emily lowered the sandwich. 'Seriously?'

'And you wouldn't have been lying. It's the absolute truth. We all have bits of our lives that we'd rather not share with others. The trick is to find the positives and focus on them, rather than dwelling on the painful parts.' She stroked Emily's hair. 'You're doing so well, love. I know it isn't easy, but don't let a fear of what others think prevent you from achieving your dream. Half these kids are only here because they've no idea what they want to do with their lives. You do. And you should be really proud of that.'

Emily accepted the offer of a drink. 'How do you remain so positive all the time?'

Norah gave her a wry smile. 'I go by the old adage, fake it till you make it.'

'Don't you ever get sad?'

Norah shrugged. 'Of course I do. No one goes through life completely unscathed. We all have our burdens to carry. It's how we deal with them that counts. Life is rarely all good or all bad, it's a mixture of both. But you mustn't let the sadness you feel about your past prevent you from feeling positive about your future.'

Emily pondered her friend's words. Sadness was the only real emotion she was comfortable dealing with. It was like an old friend. A comfortable feeling she recognised and wasn't afraid of. It was the idea of happiness that unnerved her.

But maybe it was time to face her demons. What was the saying…? Feel the fear and do it anyway. Could she find the courage to be happy? It was a scary thought.

She finished her sandwich and stood up. 'Thanks for lunch, Norah. And for coming here today.' She kissed her cheek. 'I wish my mum had been as lovely as you are.'

Norah raised a hand. 'Stop that, you'll make me come over all unnecessary.'

Emily picked up her bag. 'I'd better go inside. I don't want to miss any more classes.'

Norah's smile filled her entire face. 'Good on you, girl. Knock 'em dead.'

'I will.'

Emily's smile faded as she turned away from Norah, her trepidation returning. But there was no way she could let Norah down.

However awful it might be, she was determined to complete this bloody course.

How else was she going to achieve her dream of becoming a chef?

Chapter Five

Sam tore away the protective cover on the newly acquired flipchart and removed the marker pen lid. It reminded her of her days as a social worker when she'd attended countless planning meetings to discuss a child's welfare. It was a part of the job she'd never enjoyed; making the decision to remove a child from their family home was never easy. The assessment meetings would often last for hours, with various agencies discussing the best way to deal with safeguarding concerns. Evidence would be produced, analysed and dissected, in the hope they wouldn't make a rash decision. No one wanted to break up a family unit if they didn't have to.

She'd much preferred the hands-on part of her job, visiting clients, engaging with children and their families, and assessing first-hand whether there was any real risk. Sometimes there was. Thankfully, often there wasn't and the family could be left to get on with their lives. But if she'd thought her days of chairing risk assessment meetings were behind her, she'd been wrong.

She wrote 'Action Plan' on the first page of the flipchart and turned to address her waiting audience.

Norah, Emily and Fraser looked at her expectantly. They were squashed inside the laundry room, currently acting as a makeshift office.

'I think everyone agrees it's been a challenging first week,' she said, trying to keep her tone light, despite her shredded nerves. 'No one expected it to be a breeze, but we've had to deal with a few unforeseen issues.'

The knife fight being one of them. The image of the blade slicing through the air was still imprinted on her brain, as was the police officer's bollocking she'd received afterwards. His scolding words continued to ring loudly in her ear, accusing her of being foolhardy. Annoyingly, he was right, which was why action was needed. Hence this morning's meeting.

'We've also received a complaint from the local authority,' she continued, noting the disappointed looks on her colleagues faces. 'Someone who lives in a neighbouring property has written to the council asking for us to be shut down.'

'Some people are so narrow-minded,' Norah said, looking disgruntled. 'Can't they see this place is needed?'

'It's disappointing, I agree. But we need to be seen taking the community's concerns seriously. I feel it's important to keep the neighbours onside.' Sam was doing her best to remain upbeat, but her positivity was waning, despite her best efforts.

'We've only been open a week,' Norah said, sounding unhappy the project was already under threat. 'You'd think they'd cut us some slack. Selfish lot.'

Emily chewed on her thumbnail. 'I don't think people mean to be selfish. They probably don't object to the shelter, they just don't want it on their doorstep. You know the saying, out of sight, out of mind.'

Sam couldn't agree more. For someone so young, Emily was incredibly insightful.

Fraser leant against the door, his arms folded, one booted foot crossed over the other. 'Was the complaint about something specific?'

Sam re-read the letter from the council. 'Noise levels during the evening when people are queuing up outside and an increase in litter. Particularly drug paraphernalia.'

The disgruntled resident had unhelpfully sent the council a photo of a disused needle with their complaint letter, supposedly found outside the building. Not exactly a good advert for the shelter.

'I feel as aggrieved as you do,' Sam said, trying to hide the true state of her anxiety.

It wouldn't be helpful for her colleagues to know she was questioning her ability to run the project. 'But it's made me realise we need to make some changes. When I met with the police a few months back to discuss security, I thought they were being too draconian in their recommendations and I didn't want to succumb to such a strict regime. But in hindsight, I realise I was wrong to ignore their advice. We need stricter rules.'

It wasn't that she'd been arrogant in ignoring them, it was just that she'd assumed seven years as a social worker had equipped her to cope with whatever incidents might arise. Despite her involvement with traumatic cases like the parents who'd put razor blades in their baby's nappy, most of the cases she'd dealt with as a social worker had come about through neglect. It wasn't the kids' behaviour that was questionable; it was the adults'. Which is why she'd decided to ignore police advice and introduce as few rules as possible when opening the shelter.

It was only now she was realising she should have listened to the experts and not assumed she knew better.

She looked at her volunteers. 'We've already introduced a no drink or drugs policy, and we don't allow anyone to come and go once they've been offered a bed, but it's clearly not enough. We need to make this place safer and less open to incidents like we had last week. So, I'm looking for ideas.'

Emily raised her hand. 'The cut off time could be earlier, to reduce the noise levels later in the evening.'

'Good idea.' Sam made a note on the flipchart. 'What else?'

'Much as I hate to suggest it, we probably need to carry out an assessment before offering the youngsters a place.' Norah twisted on her chair, so she was facing the others. 'A short questionnaire to find out more about them and ensure they're not minors. Some of them barely look sixteen.'

Sam frowned. 'Do you think that'll resolve the problem?'

'Not completely, but it should reduce the risk. We can't check ID, because most of the kids don't have any kind of formal identification, but it makes the service more personal. We stop being anonymous and become real people who're genuinely trying to help them. It might make a few of them think twice before doing anything destructive.' Norah looked around, gauging whether the others agreed with her.

Fraser nodded. 'If nothing else, it allows us an opportunity to suss them out before offering them a place. We'll be able to tell if they're high or pissed and can exclude them before anything happens.'

Emily raised her hand. 'What about asking them to sign a contract agreeing to the terms and conditions of the shelter. Like I had to do when I signed up for college. You know, to show I understood the rules and I'd be kicked out if I broke them.'

'And I know you're against the idea,' Fraser chipped in, looking apologetic. 'But we need to search them too. Nothing too invasive, but a quick pat down to ensure no knives or weapons get smuggled in.'

Much as she hated to admit it, Fraser was right. The police had recommended the same thing when she'd met with them. But she'd dismissed the idea, too afraid of infringing young people's human rights. Perhaps it was a necessary evil. 'It feels so extreme.'

Fraser shrugged. 'How else are we going to know if they're tooled-up?'

Sam looked at Emily. 'Would you have minded being frisked? If you'd stayed somewhere like this?'

Emily shook her head. 'I was used to it. It's not nice, but it's not uncommon. Most kids feel safer staying in a place that has checks in place, than places that don't.'

Well, that was something.

Feeling a little more heartened, Sam tapped her lip with the marker pen. 'It'll make processing the queue more time-consuming. And we still don't have a night receptionist, so that's going to make it harder. But I agree it's something we need to implement.' She wrote 'Body/Bag search' and 'Assessment Form' on her list.

Norah pointed to the racks of bedding stored in the laundry room. 'We should probably sign the youngsters out too and check they haven't helped themselves to anything they shouldn't have. We've already lost four pillows this week.'

Something Sam was painfully aware of, but accusing them of stealing felt like another insult. Guilty until proven innocent, rather than the other way around.

But they couldn't continue losing stuff and like it or not, things were being nicked. If it continued at this rate, her depleted finances would run out a lot sooner than anticipated.

She added 'Exit Check' to the list, her hand growing heavier with each entry. 'Anything else?'

The group looked at each other, before shaking their heads.

'And you're sure it won't feel too much like prison?' Sam asked, wishing there was another option.

'This is a world away from being banged up,' Fraser said, with such conviction she wondered if he was speaking from experience. 'All you're asking for is a little respect.'

Norah nodded. 'As Aretha Franklin would say.'

Fraser grinned.

Sam smiled.

But when Emily said, 'Who?' they all groaned.

Norah patted her knee. 'Oh, to be so young.'

Fraser pushed away from the door. 'Adhering to rules and accepting boundaries is part of life. If these kids are going to re-join society, they'll need to understand that. Asking them to enter into a contract is a good life lesson. Understanding there'll be consequences if they don't follow the rules is essential if they're ever going to live independently and hold down a job.'

He had a valid point.

Norah agreed. 'They get a meal, wash facilities, and a bed for the night, all free of charge. Asking them to behave, not stab anyone, and not nick anything isn't unreasonable.'

Sam sighed. 'I guess you're right.' She looked at the list. 'Okay, so we have an action plan. I'll make a sign for the door detailing our new policy. We'll start the new regime tomorrow. It'll give me time to draft the assessment forms.' She smiled at her team. 'Thanks for your help. I really appreciate your input.'

'Anytime.' Fraser opened the door. 'Whatever it takes to make this place work.'

Norah squeezed Sam's arm as she passed by. 'You're doing an amazing job. Don't let a shaky first week undermine that.'

'Thanks, Norah.' Sam needed all the reassurance she could get.

She followed the others out and locked the door behind her.

Locking everything away was a habit she was getting used to. She'd wanted to run the shelter based on trust, but that was another example of her naivety.

She followed Norah and Emily over to the cafe. It was approaching lunchtime, so they needed to be ready for business.

Fraser opened the front doors and allowed the people queuing to enter. Word had spread around Streatham about the quality food and reasonable prices, so they were attracting more than just a few homeless people during the day.

It was good to see the cafe busy and the extra income was welcome. If they could use more home-grown produce in the years to come, then profit and sustainability would be even better – assuming they stayed open that long.

At least they had a plan in place to improve things. Sam was determined to remain positive. However hard that might be.

She grabbed a roll of bin bags and a pair of rubber gloves from the kitchen and headed outside. Picking up rubbish wasn't her favourite job, but the sun was shining and it was dry, so that helped make it less grim.

The space outside was mainly concrete with a small car park at the rear and a driveway leading down to the main road. The hedges lining the border were overgrown and the brambles planted in the beds surrounding the building were prickly and devoid of foliage.

It could be so much more, even with the limited space. If the outside looked more maintained and attractive, it might dissuade people from using it as a rubbish dump.

Ideally, they could do with a covered porch area in case of rain, and a seating area so people could eat outside in summer. For now, though, her ideas would have to remain on paper. Her priority had been to develop the inside first and get the place up and running.

Shaking open a bin bag, she put on the yellow rubber gloves and knelt to clear away the rubbish shoved under the brambles by the front door.

Food wrappings, empty drink cans and random items of clothing she could cope with. Used condoms, cigarette butts and evidence of drug use was a lot more challenging.

Within five minutes she'd filled the first bag.

Tying the handles, she got up and carried it over to the industrial bin and removed the padlock. It spoke volumes about the desperation of someone living rough, that bedding down for the night in a dustbin was preferable to kipping on the streets. Hence the need for a padlock.

She returned to collecting rubbish, humming along to George Ezra's 'Paradise' as she tidied up. She needed something to distract her from the disgust of picking up a pair of soiled underpants. Gross.

As she reached under the brambles, her arm snagged on the thorns, leaving angry scratches along her forearm. '*Shit!*'

'Is this the night shelter?' a man asked, startling her.

She almost landed head-first in the brambles. 'Yes... but you'll have to come back later,' she replied, trying to regain her balance, embarrassed at having been overheard swearing. 'We don't open until seven. Although you'll need to get here early if you want to secure a bed.'

'Lucky for me, I have my own place.' He sounded amused.

She swivelled to face him, but nearly cricked her neck when she caught sight of him.

Holy hell. His smile made the most impact. It dominated his face, creasing his eyes and mouth, revealing perfectly even teeth. His hair was reddish-brown and wavy. His caramel eyes twinkled in the sunlight.

Jesus, there was no way this guy was homeless. His jeans looked new and his V-neck sweater definitely wasn't a charity-shop purchase.

Mortified by her blunder, she struggled to her feet and wiped her hands on her faded dungarees.

He held out his hand. 'Jamie Lawson. I'm looking for the manager.'

'You've found her,' she replied, automatically extending her hand... until she realised she was still wearing rubber gloves. 'Sorry. Excuse me.' She tried removing the gloves, but her hands were clammy and they wouldn't come off.

He watched her fumble, an amused expression on his face. 'Need a hand?'

'I'm good, thanks.' Finally, she managed to rip the gloves off.

He glanced at her badly scratched arms. 'Looks nasty.'

She wiped her arms on her dungarees, feeling self-conscious – although she had no idea why. 'Let's try that again,' she said, holding out her hand. 'Sam Tipping. Welcome to The Crash Pad. Is there something I can help you with?'

His hand was toast-warm, and coupled with his firm grip and disarming smile, she found herself slightly flustered.

'I'd like to volunteer,' he said, clearly unaware of the affect he was having on her.

'You would?'

He frowned. 'I thought you were advertising for help?'

'I am… I mean, we are.' She let go of his hand, checking she hadn't smeared him with blood. 'Come inside and I'll show you around.'

This attractive guy wanted to volunteer? Things really were looking up.

She headed inside, glad of a moment to compose herself and analyse her behaviour.

It had been a while since Sam had been attracted to anyone. She'd never considered herself particularly romantic, and she had zero ability to flirt, so relationships hadn't exactly been in abundance over the years. She'd chosen to focus on work, campaign for social change, and not waste her time searching for love, as so many of her friends had done. No man had ever mattered as much as trying to make a difference in the world.

Her brother often teased her and said she was like him – better suited to brief flings than indulging in anything more meaningful. Whereas her mother thought she'd never tried hard enough to find 'the one'. Christina Tipping firmly believed that her daughter needed to make more of an effort and would never settle down until she sorted out her wardrobe, introduced a better skin-care regime, and socialised with 'appropriate society'.

They were both wrong. Sam had no interest in flings or one-night stands, and the idea of slapping herself in make-up and pretending to be someone she wasn't made her shudder.

Love was about finding a connection. Sharing ideals and morals. Working together to make the world a better place. She refused to judge a person based on their salary, status, or family connections. Until she met a man who cared more about helping others than helping himself then she was perfectly content to stay single.

She glanced behind, unable to resist a quick look at the man following her.

Maybe this guy was different? He was certainly easy on the eye. Plus, he wanted to volunteer. If he happened to be kind, thoughtful, and cared about the environment, then he might be perfect.

But she was getting ahead of herself. Bloody hell, she'd only just met the man.

She led him through reception.

'This is the communal area,' she said, gesturing to the kids playing pool.

A few more were lazing about on beanbags, chatting.

'To the right, is our cafe. All the food is homemade and it's staffed by volunteers.'

'Impressive.' His gaze took in the colourful décor and furniture. 'You're not short of money then.'

For some reason this comment stung. She wasn't sure why.

He was smiling, so maybe she was reading too much into it.

'I wanted the place to look smart for the guests,' she said, feeling a tad defensive. 'A place where they could hang out and feel at home.'

'Home?' He raised an eyebrow. 'It's not like any home I've been in.'

She felt herself flush. 'Homely, then. A happy place. Somewhere they can feel looked after and safe.'

'Right. Before you toss them back out on the streets?'

She stared at him. What was his problem?

As if realising he'd offended her, he quickly back-tracked. 'It's a great place,' he said, trying to hold onto his smile, but it had lost its sincerity.

She wasn't sure what to make of him. One minute he was being charming, the next he was criticising her efforts.

Still, people often had their reasons. It wouldn't be fair to judge. Not without knowing a bit more about him. 'Do you live in London?'

A hand came up to rub the back of his neck. 'Yep. Leytonstone.'

'I don't know that area very well.'

'I don't imagine you do.'

Was that another slight? 'Are you working at the moment?'

'I work, yeah.'

When nothing more was forthcoming, she tried again. 'What do you do?'

He looked away. 'A bit of this, a bit of that. Admin mostly.'

Insightful. 'And you're looking to volunteer?'

He must have sensed the uncertainty in her voice, because his demeanour switched and a wide smile

64

appeared. 'I'm keen to make a difference and give back to society.'

Now why wasn't she convinced? His answer sounded false and rehearsed. Like he was reciting from a pamphlet. 'Do you have any experience of dealing with homelessness?'

His challenging gaze met hers. 'Do you?'

Who was interviewing who here?

'I was a social worker for seven years, so I hope I have some understanding of the difficulties young people face when a family unit breaks down.' Not that she needed to justify herself to him.

He didn't comment.

As much as she was desperate for volunteers, she owed it to everyone involved with The Crash Pad to vet anyone working here. And this guy definitely needed further investigation. When she'd interviewed Norah, Emily and Fraser, she'd had no doubt about their suitability. They came over as genuine, kind, and were ideal candidates. She couldn't say the same about this man, although she wasn't entirely sure why.

'I'll need to take a few more details from you, and I'll need two character references and a DBS check,' she said, aiming for an air of professionalism.

'Is that necessary? This is a volunteer position.'

She folded her arms, needing a barrier between her and the man who had seemed charming but was now annoying her. 'Regardless of employment status, the people who volunteer here need to be trustworthy and committed. We're providing a service for vulnerable kids. I have a duty of care to ensure their safeguarding. I would consider it a dereliction of my duty to put their safety in the hands of someone I haven't taken the time to properly vet.'

'Dereliction of duty?' His expression was a mixture of amusement and sarcasm.

Sam had the feeling she was being mocked, and she didn't like it.

If she wasn't so desperate for help, she'd be tempted to tell him to sling his hook.

'It's up to you,' she said, her attraction towards him long gone. 'I understand if you've decided against volunteering here. You could always try elsewhere. Another organisation may not be quite so scrupulous in their recruitment process.'

His smile faded. 'No, I'm happy to provide references. When can I start?'

'Once I have all the appropriate paperwork, we'll arrange a trial session and see how you get on.' She wasn't making any promises.

Only moments earlier, she'd been thinking he might be the perfect guy, and now she couldn't wait to be rid of him. Which only proved her point. People were hoodwinked by appearances. She'd looked into his seductive eyes and open smile and believed his inner character was a match for his outer beauty. More fool her.

She became aware of Harold queuing at the cafe counter. He was shuffling along on his walking frame, his slippers still tied on with string.

Eager to escape, she stepped away. 'It was good to meet you…?'

'Jamie.' He held out his hand. 'Jamie Lawson.'

She shook his hand, no longer affected by the warmth of his grip. 'Right. Well, thanks for the offer to volunteer.

Send me your references and I'll be in touch. You'll have to excuse me, I need to get on with running the shelter.'

'Thanks for your time,' he called after her, as she walked off.

She didn't look back, thinking it was highly unlikely she'd ever hear from him again. He hadn't exactly warmed to her. In fact, she'd go as far as to say he seemed to have a problem with her. Well, it was a feeling reciprocated.

Shaking away her disappointment, she went over to Harold, who was trying to unearth a five-pound note from his trouser pocket. 'Hey, there, Harold. Joining us for lunch today?'

His face broke into a smile. 'Shepherd's pie. My favourite. Would you like some?'

'No, thanks. I'm vegan.'

He frowned. 'Why?'

She laughed. 'Don't you start. I get enough grief from my family.'

'No wonder you're so skinny.'

Emily handed him his plate of shepherd's pie. 'Anything else, Harold?'

He glanced down at the five-pound note. 'Do I have enough for a custard tart?'

Emily looked conflicted. Technically, the answer was no, but when she saw Sam nod, she smiled. 'Of course, Harold. Custard tart coming right up.'

Harold handed Emily his crumpled note. 'You're an angel.'

'Enjoy your lunch, Harold.' Emily added a mug of tea to his tray.

Sam gestured to a free table. 'Take a seat, Harold. I'll bring your tray over.'

'Thanks, love. It's a bit tricky with this thing.' He tapped his walking frame and shuffled over to the table.

When he was out of earshot, Sam leant over the counter. 'I don't feel right taking his money.'

Emily handed her the five-pound note. 'Me neither.'

Sam joined Harold and helped him get seated. When he wasn't looking, she discreetly slipped the five-pound note back into his trouser pocket. 'Enjoy your lunch, Harold.'

'I will,' he said, tucking into his Shepherd's Pie.

Smiling, she went into the loos to wash her hands. Something she should have done before helping Harold with his food, but she'd been distracted by the appearance of Jamie Lawson. He'd momentarily befuddled her brain.

She ran the hot water and soaped-up her arms, wincing when the cuts stung. Then she glanced in the mirror. Oh, hell.

Not only did she have dirt on her face, she had a black marker pen smudge on her lip, her dungarees were smeared in blood and her ponytail was lopsided. Great.

It was just as well Jamie Lawson had turned out to be a disappointment. If he hadn't, she might have blown her chances.

She started laughing, causing a couple of girls to stare at her.

Pumping more soap into her hands, she began washing her face.

And to think her mother accused her of not having a suitable skincare regime.

Chapter Six

For the first time since venturing into a career in journalism, Jamie felt like a proper reporter. The morning had started with a six a.m. tube journey across London to the City, where he'd set up camp outside Quinton International bank and waited, camera at the ready, for Max Tipping to arrive for work.

It was now gone ten a.m. and there was no sign of the man. Jamie's enthusiasm was starting to wane.

At least the wait had allowed him time to survey the area. Quinton International was situated in the heart of Square Mile, the area of London frequented by the big global banks. When he'd first arrived, he'd tried to gain access to the ornate three-storey construction with its fancy glazed entranceway, but with no proof of being a client and no appointment booked, he'd been swiftly shown out by a smartly dressed security guard. It was certainly a far cry from the shabby *South London Herald* offices in Wimbledon.

Still, it was better than being stuck in an office all day. He checked his watch. 10:15 a.m. Still no show.

But this was all part of the role of an investigative journalist. Stakeouts were often laborious and time-consuming. Success hinged on patience, luck, and good fortune.

Maybe the man was off sick? Or on annual leave? Visiting clients? There was no guarantee Max Tipping would even be in work today.

It turned out to be none of these scenarios. It was simply that Max Tipping didn't do regular hours. At 10:30 a.m. he emerged from a black cab wearing dark shades and a navy pinstripe suit. Even then, he stopped off to buy a coffee and bagel before entering the plush city offices.

It was all right for some, Jamie thought. His boss would tear him a new one if he turned up so much as ten minutes late, let alone sauntered in at nearly eleven a.m. But that was just one of the many differences between them. Differences that had been determined by birth.

Whereas Max Tipping's early life had no doubt been filled with private tutoring, Norland-trained nannies and staff on hand to attend to his every whim, Jamie's early life had been filled with neglect and abandonment.

He'd never known his father and he'd watched his mother routinely abuse drugs before throwing up and passing out. There'd been no private jet, expensive sailboat, or personal chauffeur on hand to drive him to school. He'd had to walk the two miles unaccompanied, no matter the weather, and usually in ill-fitting worn-out shoes.

That was when he actually went to school. Often he'd had to stay home and care for his mother if she'd been on a particularly bad bender the night before.

He shook away the memory, unwilling to be dragged into the past. It was no longer relevant. He'd beaten the odds. He might be labelled a 'care leaver', but he hadn't allowed it to hold him back. He'd survived his difficult teenage years, scraped through his GSCEs, gained better A Level results and taken a gap year where he'd worked for a local newspaper. With his foster carer Peggy's help he'd obtained a degree in media studies and a postgrad diploma in journalism.

Could Max Tipping boast the same?

No. According to Jamie's research, he'd attended Harrow, then Oxford, barely passed his degree in Financial Economics and walked straight into a high-paid job in the City. Another example of how the privilege classes didn't have to work for their opportunities, but were handed them on a plate.

Jamie's sense of injustice built to such a crescendo he almost missed sight of Max Tipping re-emerging from the building only a few minutes later and hailing a black cab.

Reminiscing had caused him to lose focus.

Shoving his equipment into his rucksack, he jumped into a cab and followed Max Tipping to The Jugged Hare on Chiswell Street, where the man proceeded to enjoy a boozy lunch with four other suited-and-booted men, who laughed a lot, ate a shed-load of food and drank even more.

Jamie managed to charm the doorman into letting him use the facilities, where he snapped a couple of shots through a small window, but disappointingly he couldn't get close enough to hear any juicy snippets of conversation.

It was gone two p.m. by the time Max Tipping emerged from the restaurant and hailed another black cab, forcing Jamie to follow suit.

Instead of heading back to the bank, the black cab headed north, continuing for another half hour before reaching High Gate Golf Club.

With no clue as to their final destination, Jamie had watched in trepidation as the taximeter ticked over, leaving him with barely enough cash to settle the thirty-four-quid bill.

Following Max Tipping was proving to be a costly exercise. He was in danger of exceeding his expense account on the first day. His boss wouldn't be happy, especially if he arrived back at the office with nothing to show for his efforts.

If he'd known he'd be trying to gain access to a posh golf club later in the day, he'd have dressed more appropriately. Not that he owned any golfing clobber, but Levis and an army-green SuperDry bomber jacket weren't exactly helping him to blend in.

He hid behind a clump of trees and waited until Max Tipping emerged from the large glass clubhouse at the top of the hill. His posh pinstripe suit had been replaced with tan golfing trousers, a polo shirt and a baseball cap. The shades remained, despite it being an overcast day. The word 'poser' sprang to mind.

Max Tipping met with two other golfers, older men wearing similar sporting attire, who greeted each other with manly backslaps and more loud laughter.

Jamie used the zoom function on his camera to capture the meeting, hoping to identify the men when he got back to the office. He had no idea whether they were clients, colleagues, or shady business associates. But one thing was certain, they were loaded and his resentment for the privileged classes increased another notch.

No doubt the customers at Quinton International would be footing the bill for this little jaunt. Did they know? Or even care? They were probably so rich it didn't matter.

When the group finished teeing off, Jamie moved position, trying to get closer to the men without arousing suspicion. But the greens were so big there was no cover for him to avoid being seen. Today's reconnaissance mission was proving to be an expensive disaster, which meant he'd have to change approach. Something he wasn't thrilled about.

After visiting The Crash Pad on Monday, he'd hoped to avoid the need to volunteer there. Not because he had anything against helping homeless teens, but the idea of spending time with Sam Tipping wasn't something he was keen to repeat.

Seeing a photo of her ahead of their meeting had been one thing, encountering her in the flesh had been a different challenge entirely. He hadn't expected to find her so attractive. Or disarming. Or covered in dirt.

He'd expected a patronising superior attitude with an accent to rival the cast of Made in Chelsea. Instead, he'd discovered the woman on her knees cleaning up rubbish, dressed like an eco-warrior hippy and completely down to earth. For a few minutes, he'd forgotten why he was there and had instinctively responded to her wide petrol-blue eyes, slightly clumsy manner, and apparent lack of vanity.

Thankfully, sanity had kicked-in and he'd pulled himself together.

Unfortunately, his efforts to snap himself out of his trance had tipped him into rudeness, which had ended up making him sound like a judgmental tosser. Not helpful when he was trying to win her over so he could gain access to her brother.

Her warm smile had faded into a frown when he'd questioned her attributes for running the shelter. Her pleasure at having a potential new volunteer had been replaced by distain and distrust, and she'd made it abundantly clear she didn't think he was suitable volunteer material. He'd left, tail between his legs, embarrassed enough to hope he'd never have to see her again.

Unfortunately, Gareth had other ideas. His boss had managed to wangle two falsified character references and sent them to The Crash Pad, along with ID and a fast-tracked DBS certificate. Jamie's plan to adopt a false identity in case she Googled him and discovered he was a journalist had failed when he'd blurted out his real name. Meeting a beautiful woman was supposed to make a man forget his *own* name. In this case, it had made him forget his *false* name. But it was probably just as well. Falsifying references was one thing, there was no way he could have forged a DBS check.

This morning, he'd received a short email inviting him to a trial session at the shelter tonight.

It was time to concede defeat and call it a day. Lying on the cold ground carrying out surveillance wasn't helping to improve his mood. His neck was stiff and his bum was numb.

He packed up and headed home, where he showered, cooked pasta, and inspected the meagre contents of his wallet. He had ten quid left. He hoped Gareth would reimburse him. Although his boss was less likely to do so without a story in the bag.

At five p.m. he caught the bus to Streatham and headed for The Crash Pad night shelter, ready to volunteer and find out the truth surrounding Max Tipping. With any luck, his sister could be persuaded to spill the beans. If he could bag his story quickly, he'd be out of her life for good. Job done.

Jamie was aware he was being a tad naive. Getting the dirt on Sam's brother might not be as straightforward as he hoped. After all, he'd never done this before: his skills as an investigative journalist were untested.

He ignored the frisson of guilt nudging him in the chest. There was nothing to feel guilty about; he wasn't the one breaking the law. But maybe Sam wasn't either. Maybe she knew nothing about her brother's suspected shady dealings. Then again, she might be covering for him. Who knew?

Only one way to find out.

A queue had formed outside the shelter. A row of kids with their heads down, looking bored and resigned to their fate as they waited to be given a bed for the night.

He'd always assumed his own childhood had been the pits, filled with loneliness and emotional suffering. But perhaps he'd been one of the lucky ones. Being passed from one foster carer to another hadn't been fun, but he'd lucked out in the end and getting placed with Peggy Miller had been a blessing. And if Peggy hadn't been so stoic and determined to knock him into shape then maybe he'd have ended up like these kids, homeless and hungry.

It was a disturbing thought, so he made a mental note to phone Peggy tomorrow. A visit was long overdue.

He nodded at a couple of the kids as he walked past. Most refused to make eye-contact, but the lad at the back of the queue gave him a grin. 'All right, mate.'

Jamie nodded and headed for the door. He tapped on the glass.

A few moments later, Sam Tipping appeared.

The sight of her bunched his stomach into knots. Why, he wasn't sure. It was dread, probably.

Her long dark hair was pulled into a messy ponytail and she was wearing a man's shirt knotted at the waist. Her faded jeans had patches of miss-matched material sewn onto the knees, and her Converse trainers were old-fashioned and grubby… unlike her face, which was scrubbed clean and make-up free.

She looked like a young hipster about to head off to the WOMAD festival. She certainly didn't look like a woman nearing thirty whose family owned half of Holland Park.

'Good evening, Mr Lawson,' she said, opening the door. 'Welcome to The Crash Pad. How lovely that you're able to volunteer with us.' She didn't sound happy. Far from it. Her expression indicated it pained her to be civil to him.

He experienced another sinking feeling in his gut.

Jamie realised he was going to have to hide his true feelings if he stood any chance of getting a story on her brother. Allowing his dislike for all she stood for to show would only create a barrier, and he needed her to open up, relax, and not become defensive. Which meant he was going to have to fake enthusiasm for her ill-conceived charitable venture.

'Hi,' he said, trying for an open smile. 'It's good to be here. And please, call me Jamie.' His attempt to win her over was met with a sceptical raising of one eyebrow. He'd have to try harder. 'What would you like me to do?'

She nodded to the doorway. 'Help Fraser process the queue. You'll need to check the guests for contraband or weapons, and then send them over to the desk so they can complete the entry questionnaire.'

'Weapons?' Jesus, were they expecting gangland warfare? 'Is that really necessary?'

Her hands went to her hips. 'We wouldn't be doing it if it wasn't.'

'Sorry, course not.' Be conciliatory, he told himself. Don't antagonise her. He tried for another smile. 'I've got a lot to learn, clearly.'

'Clearly.' Her other eyebrow lifted to join the one already raised. 'Any questions?'

He figured it was too soon to ask about her brother. 'Nope.'

'Good.' She walked over to the desk and left him to make his own introductions.

Jamie headed over to the rugged man with dark stubble and distinctive limp waiting by the doorway. 'I'm guessing you're Fraser?' Despite the physical impairment, he didn't look like the kind of guy you wanted to pick a fight with. Not if you wanted to keep all your teeth. 'I'm Jamie.'

The man held out his hand. 'Good to meet you.' His grip was firm, his large hands calloused. 'Any experience of teenagers?'

'Only being one.'

Fraser grinned. 'That'll do. Don't take any crap. If you smell alcohol send them packing. And don't frisk the girls. Send them over to Norah.'

Jamie glanced over to where an older woman was waiting by the desk. She nodded a greeting and then looked away, seemingly unimpressed. Another tough nut to crack, he figured. More likely, Sam had filled her in on their meeting and the woman had a preconceived idea of him. And not a favourable one.

Fraser unlocked the doors and let the kids in. One by one they were assessed, frisked and sent over to the desk. It was a degrading process, like herding cattle ready for sale at market, but they all complied. He supposed the lure of hot food and a comfy bed was enough to dispel the humiliation of being manhandled.

A girl with matted dreadlocks pushed through the doorway, bypassing Fraser who was busy frisking one of the lads. She wore an expression Jamie recognised, pasty skin, dilated pupils, her gaze unfocused and vague. He'd seen his mother stoned enough times to know when someone was high.

Unsure of what to do, he let her walk by, not wanting to aggravate her by suddenly grabbing her arm. He knew from his experience with his mother that dealing with someone high on drugs was a precarious business.

The girl headed straight for the main area, but Sam spotted her and blocked her path.

The girl tried to barge past, but Sam wasn't giving in. She held the door closed, denying the girl access. But despite her determination she looked out of her depth as she tried to contain the girl, who was becoming increasingly more agitated.

Sad as it was to admit, Sam Tipping seemed ill-equipped to deal with the trials of homeless teenagers. She was one of life's apparent 'do-gooders', someone who was keen to rebel against her privileged background and help people, but without the necessary skillset or fortitude to do so.

Maybe he was being harsh, but he'd met too many people like Sam over the years. People with big ideas and opinions, who had no clue what it was really like to suffer. They liked the idea of 'helping the needy' and 'doing their bit', until they realised what was involved.

Very few had the stamina and determination to deal with the multitude of problems that arose from being taken into care. The attachment issues, the fear of abandonment, and the unhealthy relationship with food, family and friends, all resulting in the complex see-saw of wanting to be loved, but pushing away anyone who tried. Peggy had been the exception. She'd hung in there. And lucky for him she had.

The drugged-up girl became abusive, swearing and trying to force herself through the door to the main area.

Jamie wanted to intervene, but he wasn't sure what to do. He was no expert either.

Fraser glanced over and spotted the fracas. 'Take over, will you?' he said, limping towards the girl, leaving Jamie to deal with the queue.

Thrown into the deep-end, Jamie checked the number of tickets remaining and let in the last of the lads queueing, all of whom allowed him to frisk them and check they were sober without any fuss. Thank God.

Fraser escorted the stoned girl out of the front door, ignoring her insults and not even flinching when she spat at him. Jamie could only admire the man's restraint.

Jamie turned the sign on the door to FULL, much to the dismay of the young lad still waiting. His face fell when he saw the sign. 'You're kidding me?'

Jamie felt awful. 'Sorry, mate.'

'That's three nights in a row I've missed out on a place.' He ran his hand through his mess of dark hair.

'Perhaps you need to get here earlier.'

'I can't,' he said, slumping against the doorframe. 'I don't finish work until six.'

That was a surprise. 'You work?'

'Delivering pizzas, nothing permanent. But I'd rather work than be a lazy bugger.'

Jamie was impressed. 'Good for you.'

The lad shrugged. 'But it means I miss out on a bed for the night.' He swung his rucksack onto his back. 'That's life, I guess.' He hesitated before he walked off. 'Is Emily volunteering tonight?'

Jamie had no idea who Emily was. 'Sorry, I don't know.'

'Not to worry. If you see her, say Alfie said, hi.' A faint blush crept into his pale cheeks.

'Will do. See you tomorrow?'

'Maybe.' The kid ambled off.

Jamie felt bad watching him go. It seemed unbelievably cruel that a kid with enough determination to hold down a job was being punished for his efforts by having to sleep rough.

Then again, who said life was fair?

Certainly not him.

Chapter Seven

Wednesday, 14th November

When Sam heard one of the girls seated next to Harold burst out laughing, she glanced up from sweeping the floor, intrigued. It was barely lunchtime, but the cafe was almost full, the tables occupied by a mixture of homeless teens, a few business types examining the contents of a complex looking spreadsheet, and a mother and daughter chatting animatedly away, rocking a baby to sleep in its pram. A group of beauty practitioners from the local salon on Streatham High Road were seated nearby, enjoying an extended lunch, looking smart in their pristine white tunics.

It was a glorious sight. The colourful cafe bustling with activity and diversity. No dramas. No fights or issues, just a thriving community project. It was everything Sam had hoped it would be.

The success of the cafe was helping to counterbalance the issues they faced on a nightly basis when the shelter opened its doors to the homeless. And although things were slowly improving and they'd had fewer problems to deal with, it was still emotionally draining. Her nerves were on edge every night as she anticipated another fight, breakage, or alcohol infringement. But she wasn't about to give up. It was a work-in-progress. They were learning on the job and adapting to the challenges they faced. A real team effort.

Another burst of laughter caught her attention. The two young girls seated with Harold seemed fascinated by the old man.

Sam moved closer, hoping to hear a snippet of conversation.

The girl seated to his right was leaning on the table, her dyed pink hair tied into a messy knot, her chin resting on her hand. 'Is that why you learnt to dance, Harold? So you could pick up girls?'

'Got it in one,' he said with a wink. 'Twice a week me and my mates would go to the Locarno Dance Hall. The place would be packed full of youngsters. If you were a fella who could dance, you had your pick of the girls. I was the best dancer,' he said, proudly. 'The envy of my mates.'

'Who taught you to dance?' the second girl asked, fiddling with the sleeve of her black jumper.

'My brother, George. He was the oldest of us six kids, twelve years older than me. I idolised him. I wanted to do everything he did. He taught me to play cricket and football, as well as the foxtrot and jive. I even followed him into the army.'

'Did you fight in the war?' The girl's eyes grew wide in fascination.

Harold shook his head. 'That was before my time. George did, though. He was lucky to make it back. Took a bullet in the leg. Walked with a limp afterwards.'

'Couldn't he dance anymore?'

'Oh, it didn't stop him dancing. He was a bit lopsided, mind you.'

Both girls laughed.

'Is that how you met your wife?' Pink–haired girl asked. 'At the dance hall?'

A huge smile lit up Harold's face. 'I spotted her the moment she walked in. Dark wavy hair, big smile. She was wearing a blue dress that sparkled when she moved. I was smitten.'

The girl in the black jumper let out a sigh. 'So you went over and asked her to dance?'

He nodded. 'I pulled out all my best moves, trying to impress her.'

The girl smiled. 'Did it work?'

'We were married six months later. What do you think?'

They both giggled. As did Sam. She was enjoying their exchange.

Pink-haired girl shook her head in amusement. 'I think you must have been quite the charmer in your day, Harold. Do you miss dancing?'

Harold's smile faded. 'Not as much as I miss my Dorothy.'

The girl reached over and squeezed his hand. 'It sounds like Dorothy was a very lucky woman to have you in her life.'

Sam felt a lump in her throat. What a sweet girl, kind too. Like most of the kids here. It was what kept her going.

She only realised she'd been staring when a cough startled her. She looked up to see Jamie Lawson standing next to her.

For some inexplicable reason this annoyed her. He'd been volunteering at the shelter for three days now and seemed to be forever invading her space. Wherever she was, or whatever she was doing, he appeared... usually making her jump, as if he was trying to catch her out. Doing what, she had no idea.

It didn't help that he always looked immaculate. Not like her family in their expensive clobber and top-end accessories, but in a more natural relaxed way. Today he was wearing a teal-coloured top that accentuated the red in his hair. He was clean shaven, his wavy hair pushed away from his face in a casual style.

Maybe it wouldn't have irked so much if she hadn't been standing there wearing scruffy second-hand dungarees and a washed-out Radiohead T-shirt she'd inherited from her brother. Why did Jamie Lawson have to make her feel so... inadequate? She was normally fine with the way she looked. What was it about this man that got under her skin?

There was no real justification for disliking him, he was eager to help and he turned up on time. He carried out the duties he was asked to do and he never complained. But there was something about him that unsettled her.

Several times a day she'd catch him watching her, or suddenly appearing in her peripheral vision. It might be flattering if it weren't for the critical expression he wore. His face would crease into a frown as if he was trying to solve a riddle. The moment he'd realise she'd caught him staring, his expression would clear and he'd smile. But the smile never quite reached his eyes, and she had the distinct impression he was hiding something. What, she had no idea.

And now it was happening again. He was invading her space, snapping her out of eavesdropping on Harold's conversation with the two girls.

She resumed sweeping, ignoring the effect his after-shave was having on her senses. So what if he smelled good? It didn't count for much if underneath the polished exterior something darker lurked.

'Can I help you with something?' She tried not to sound prickly. After all, he was still a volunteer, whether she liked him or not.

'We're running low on potatoes and milk. Norah asked if you could pop to the wholesalers and pick some up?'

Sam's heart sank. They were getting through the stock at a rapid rate. 'I only stocked up last Thursday. I wasn't expecting to run out so soon.'

'The place is busy,' he said, nodding to the packed cafe. 'Isn't that a good thing? You must be turning a profit?'

Hardly. They'd deliberately priced the food to be affordable for the whole community, including those on benefits or low income. The plan was to cover costs, but not fleece the patrons. In hindsight, maybe that had been another example of her naivety. Far from being self-sustainable, she was regularly having to dip into her ever-depleting savings. The sooner the rooftop garden was contributing to their produce, the better.

She gave the floor one last sweep. 'I need to pop out anyway, so I'll stop off at the wholesalers.'

He continued to stare at her. 'Want me to come with you?'

God, no. She could think of little worse than being stuck alone with this man for any length of time. She'd ask one of the others. 'Thanks, but I'm fine.'

'Let me know if you change your mind.' He unleashed his smile, dimpling the creases either side of his mouth, which had once charmed her, but not anymore. Finally, he ambled off.

Good. She couldn't think straight with him always close by.

Unfortunately, everyone else was busy. Emily and Norah were still serving customers queuing at the cafe, and Fraser was mending the pool table, which had been damaged last night when two lads had decided to climb on it and start wrestling. Play-fighting or not, it had still resulted in a broken table leg.

Tempting as it was to carry out her chores single-handedly, it was easier and quicker to have two people loading up the car. So with some reluctance, she approached Jamie and took him up on his offer to assist her.

A decision she immediately regretted the moment they exited the building and she led him to the rear of the building where her car was parked.

He ground to a halt when he saw her vehicle partially hidden behind the wheelie bins. 'You're kidding me?'

She glanced up, unable to decipher his expression with the sun in her eyes. Why did he have to be so tall?

'Is something wrong?'

'That's your car?' He sounded incredulous.

Her hands went to her hips. 'Do you have a problem with that?'

His eyebrows lifted, accentuating the intensity of his eyes. 'Are you serious?'

She suppressed a sigh. She should have seen this coming. 'It's just a car.'

'That is not just a car. That is a Mercedes-Benz CLS Coupé.'

She felt her hackles rise. Trust him to know about cars. 'Your point?'

He turned to face her. 'You don't think it's a little insensitive to parade such a luxury item in front of home-less kids? Most of whom don't have enough money to buy food and whose possessions would fit into a single carrier bag?'

How dare he lecture her. He knew nothing about her. Or her principles.

'I don't parade it,' she said, failing to conceal her annoyance. 'Far from it, which is why I park it around the back and out of sight.'

'Because you know how it looks.'

'I'm well aware of how it looks, thank you.' God, she wanted to shove him in the chest. Sanctimonious prick. 'But I'm not about to change my mode of transportation just because you disapprove.' Even though at some point she fully expected to have to downgrade her mode of transportation to free up more funds. But having already sold her flat, she didn't want to further offend her parents by selling the car as well. Not until she absolutely had to.

But that was her decision to make, not bloody Jamie Lawson's. Who the hell was he to judge her?

She folded her arms in front of her chest. 'Now, are you going to quit with the snarky remarks and help me, or do I need to find someone else to come with me?'

He held his hands up in defence, no doubt sensing she was close to losing her temper.

Smart man. 'I apologise. I was surprised, that's all.' He followed her over to the car. 'Sorry.'

She should bloody-well think so.

Yanking open the driver's door, she climbed inside, still fuming.

A beat later, he climbed in next to her. His eyes widened as he sank into the cream leather seating. 'I'm guessing your parents bought the car for you?'

She gave him another glare. 'Not that it's any of your business.'

'You're right, it's not.' He gave her a sheepish smile. 'Nice interior.'

'But hardly practical for trips to the wholesalers.' She switched on the engine and shoved the car into drive.

'I never said a word.'

'Well, that'd be a first.' She revved the engine and swung the car out of the car park, her annoyance levels heightened. It wasn't exactly the best state to be in when driving a high-performance car. But at least the busy London traffic prevented her speeding. Thank heavens for small mercies.

She noticed Jamie had switched from looking disapproving, to admiring the lit-up dashboard. He let out a low whistle when she accelerated away from the traffic lights. Hypocrite.

He didn't need to tell her it wasn't a practical car. She was perfectly aware of that. If she had enough funds, she'd buy an old van for use at the shelter, but until they could source further funding, she was stuck using the Merc as a delivery vehicle.

Jamie didn't utter another word until they pulled up outside the Wash Inn launderette on Streatham High Road. 'Why are we stopping?' He strained to see out the tinted windows.

'Why do you think?' she said, exiting the car. 'We need potatoes and milk.'

'Are you being sarcastic?' he called after her.

'Who me?' She slammed the door, enjoying a smidgeon of satisfaction at cutting him off, and headed inside to collect the latest bag of laundry.

The amount of washing that was required had come as another shock. The duvet covers, pillowcases and sheets had to be changed daily, and the domestic washing machine she'd purchased couldn't cope with the bulk of the duvets – something she hadn't realised when she'd had it installed. Hence the need for regular trips to the laundry. It was costing a fortune in launderette bills, not to mention being time-consuming.

She returned to the car with the large bag of bedding and popped open the boot.

Jamie appeared from the car. 'Need a hand?'

'No, thank you. I can manage.' Which was a lie. The bag was huge and heavy and she struggled to lift it, but there was no way she was about to admit it.

He watched her try to ram the bag into the boot. 'Not exactly built for storage, is it?'

She stopped pushing. 'Will you quit with the snide remarks?'

'I didn't mean it like that. I was simply stating a fact.'

'Yeah, well, if I'd known my parents were going to surprise me with a car for my birthday I'd have asked for something more practical. Trust me, this isn't my choice.'

Now she sounded like a spoilt brat. Moaning about how Mummy and Daddy hadn't bought her the toy she wanted. She wasn't normally so prickly. What was it about this man that infuriated her so much?

She tried to slam the boot shut, but it ricocheted off the bulging laundry bag and flew back up, nearly clocking her on the chin. She jerked backwards to avoid being hit, tripped on the kerb and lost her balance. The next thing she knew, she'd landed between two bicycle railings and was now upended on the pavement, wedged between them. A situation which did nothing to improve her mood.

Jamie Lawson jogging over to check she was okay didn't help either. 'Are you hurt?'

Not physically, but her pride had taken a battering.

She tried to move, but couldn't. 'Are you going to help me up, or just stand there laughing?'

He grinned. 'Can I do both?'

When she glared at him, his smile faded.

Accepting his out-stretched hand, she allowed him to pull her to her feet. 'Thank you,' she said, trying not to sound ungrateful.

Unfortunately, her dungaree strap had caught on the railing and ripped. Great. Yet another repair.

He nodded at the damage. 'I think it's time they went in the bin.'

She inspected the torn strap. 'There's plenty of wear left in these yet.'

He raised an eyebrow. 'You're quite a conundrum.'

'How so?'

'On one hand, you drive a car that probably cost more than most people's annual salary and yet you won't throw away a pair of rotten dungarees that've seen better days.'

'I wouldn't expect you to understand.'

Not many people did. She came from money, so by default people assumed she lived a materialistic life-style. It never occurred to anyone that having spent her entire upbringing being exposed to endless wealth and witnessing excessive squandering, she might have more appreciation of the value of money than someone who'd been brought up with moderation.

He was watching her intently. 'Try me?'

'And subject myself to more of your delightful judg-ments? No, thank you.' She brushed loose gravel away from her backside and returned to the car, shutting the boot more carefully this time. 'If I'd wanted a lecture about my life principles I'd visit my mother.'

'She doesn't approve of your lifestyle?'

Sam rolled her eyes. 'You could say that.'

She often wondered what would make her mother proud. Partying every night with eligible beaus, probably. Squandering her inheritance on designer shoes and spending her days at the spa 'doing lunch'. But running a homeless shelter? Oh, the shame of it.

Sighing, she opened the driver's door and got inside.

Jamie joined her. 'Aren't you close?'

She gave a half-hearted shrug. 'Yes and no.'

He frowned. 'In what way?'

She turned to look at him. 'What are you, a journalist?'

He flinched. 'I was just making conversation.'

'Well, you'll excuse me if I'm not quick to share personal information. I've been duped too many times by people pretending to be genuinely interested, only to discover they have an ulterior motive and want dirt on my family.' She fastened her seatbelt.

'Are your family famous, or something?'

She studied his face. He looked innocent enough. Did he really not know who her family were? Or was he just feigning ignorance as so many people before him had done? 'Not famous, just notorious in certain circles.'

'Sounds intriguing.'

'Trust me, it's not.' She revved the engine. 'Buckle up. I need to make a detour and pick up some mending from my flat.'

If allowing Jamie Lawson inside her car was risky, letting him see where she lived was downright confrontational. She could tell by his body language he was confused even before they arrived at their destination.

Far from heading into the more affluent suburbs of London, she was zigzagging her way down the narrow side streets of Streatham, where rows of once high-end Victorian three-storey houses had been converted into multiple flats, housing an eclectic mixture of faiths, ethnicities and professions.

They reached Melrose Avenue and she slowed to a halt. She normally wouldn't leave her car parked in the road: it wasn't safe. She'd acquired one of the lock-up garages in the neighbouring street, but as they were only stopping off to collect her latest bag of mending she risked leaving it outside.

Letting Jamie know that she wouldn't be a minute, she jumped out of the car – only to discover he was following her up the pathway.

So much for protecting her privacy.

Tempted as she was to ask him to remain outside, she knew it would come over as rude, so she reluctantly invited him in. 'Mind the step,' she said, but only after he'd tripped up on the loose paving slabs. She pinned him with her sweetest smile and unlocked the front door. 'Oops.'

Rubbing his knee, he gave her a disgruntled look. 'Thanks for the warning.'

Served him right for laughing at her earlier for falling over.

When she reached the end of the narrow hallway, she stopped and looked around, trying to view it through a stranger's eyes.

The place wasn't big, sectioned into one quarter of the original building that had been converted into flats. She'd painted the hallway white, trying to bring some much-needed light into the place, and replaced the worktops and cupboard doors in the kitchen with cheap white Formica. It was simple, clean and clutter-free. Until you entered the living area.

She turned to find him frowning. 'Now what?'

He scratched his head. 'This is not what I expected.' His confusion was palpable.

Unlike the rest of the cramped flat, the lounge was the one room that had some character. It still had its original bay window and an ornate fireplace. She'd painted the walls a dark grey, a match for her sofa, and then brightened it with colourful accessories inspired by a holiday to Goa. The wooden floorboards were obscured by a huge Indian rug, woven in reds, oranges and golds. Matching cushions decorated the sofa. Panels of red voile framed the bay window and the fireplace was filled with assorted candles. Numerous plants filled the floor space and balanced on the mismatched wooden furniture.

It was her haven, the place she felt truly herself, but it wasn't exactly high-end.

He'd probably expected her to live in a fancy flash apartment with skyline views of London. Well, no more.

'This is great,' he said, absorbing his surroundings. 'Really homely.'

Well, that was a surprise.

'Thanks.' Not that she needed his approval.

He circled the room. 'No photos?'

'Not down here. Why?'

'Just curious.' And then he stilled. 'Do you have a cat?'

'Why would you think that?'

He pointed to the fireplace. 'Something moved. Over there.'

'Oh, that's probably Marvin.'

'Marvin?'

'Marvin the Mouse. I leave cheese out for him when I go to work.' She went over to the fireplace. 'Unlike his predecessor Elvis, he doesn't like eating with an audience.'

'Elvis?'

'Sadly, no more.' She paused for effect. 'He was caught in a trap.'

It took a beat before Jamie groaned. 'That's a terrible joke.'

'Then why are you laughing?' She searched the fireplace, but Marvin was nowhere to be seen. 'Anyway, I'd never use traps. It's inhumane. Elvis left the building of his own accord.'

Jamie shook his head. 'Is that another joke?'

She shrugged. 'What can I say? I have a gift.'

'You're a real stand-up comedian,' he said, moving closer to the door. 'I can't believe you have a pet mouse.'

'He's not a pet. He just visits from time to time. No idea where he comes from.'

'It doesn't bother you, having a mouse running about loose?'

She picked up the bag of mending from the floor. 'Why would it? He doesn't take up much room.' She nodded to the cramped space. 'Plus, it stops my mother from visiting. Every cloud, and all that.'

'You really don't like your mother, do you?'

'Sure, I do. In small doses. And before you say anything, trust me, she's a lot more disapproving of me than I am of her. I'm the square peg.'

Understatement of the century. No one in the Tipping family had ever even taken the bins out, let alone recycled second-hand clothing.

Jamie bent to inspect her wooden Indian elephant on the sideboard. 'You're lucky to have a family. Some people don't have anyone.'

And there it was, the judgemental remark she'd been waiting for. 'You think I don't know that? I love my family and they love me. But we don't always see eye-to-eye. It doesn't stop us caring or supporting each other. We just have very different ideas of how we want to live our lives.'

She slung the bag over her shoulder, and promptly knocked over one of the tall planters.

Oh, for crying out loud. What was wrong with her today?

Jamie gave her a questioning look. 'Are you always this clumsy?'

'Are you always this judgemental?'

'I don't mean to be.'

He could have fooled her.

She dropped the mending bag on the floor and repositioned the planter. 'Do you always get on with your family?'

He paused before answering. 'I can't say that I do.'

'Well then, perhaps you could stop giving me a hard time about mine. Okay?'

He picked up the mending bag from the floor. 'Fair enough.'

'Thank you.' She strode for the door. 'Bye, Marvin!'

Jamie twitched and glanced behind him, checking where he was stepping.

They left the flat and he put the bag of mending on the back seat of her car. The atmosphere had returned to being frosty and neither spoke as they headed off.

She glanced at him occasionally, puzzling to make him out.

She could sense he was doing the same.

Oh, well, it was no skin off her nose if he didn't like her. She had more important things to focus on.

After a few minutes battling with the traffic, she turned into Tandem Way. 'One last detour,' she said, grabbing a solitary space in the road. 'Stay in the car, I won't be long.'

She emerged from Clarks shoe shop ten minutes later. 'Hold this, will you,' she said, climbing in and handing him the shoebox.

'New shoes?' Once again he sounded incredulous.

'Slippers, not shoes. And not for me, for Harold.' Not that she had to justify herself, to him, or anyone else.

'Harold?'

'The old guy who comes into the shelter for lunch every day. His slippers are worn through and tied on with string. I'm worried he might trip over.'

Jamie lifted the lid and stared at the dark brown slippers, complete with Velcro fastenings and sturdy soles. 'That's really... kind of you.'

'Could you sound any more surprised?'

'Sorry, it's just—'

'What?' Why was it such a shock she'd do something nice for someone? Did he really have such a low opinion of her?

He held her gaze. 'Like I said, you're a bit of a conundrum.'

She gripped the steering wheel and pulled away, almost colliding with an oncoming vehicle, her annoyance bubbling to the surface once again.

Why she cared what this guy thought, she had no idea. She shouldn't care a jot if he approved of her, or not. It wasn't like she wasn't used to living with constant disapproval. Her parents criticised and challenged every decision she ever made. It didn't bother her.

Well, it did bother her, but she never let it deter her. She was determined enough to follow her own path in life and stick to her principles and not allow her family to belittle her ideas or dreams.

So why did this guy, whom she knew nothing about, have the ability to make her feel guilty for her choices? It made no sense.

She swung the car into the shelter car park and snatched at the handbrake. 'I would say thank you for your help, but next time I'll manage on my own. It might be less stressful.' She threw open the driver's door. 'What with me being such a conundrum, and all.'

'Err... Sam?'

'What now?' She jerked around to glare at him. 'What have I done now, eh? Driven too fast? Not been economical enough with my fuel? Used too much plastic? Polluted the environment with my big flashy car? *What!?*'

'You forgot to stop off at the wholesalers.'

Shit.

Chapter Eight

Friday, 16th November

Emily tasted the veggie chilli bubbling away on the stove. It had just the right amount of heat. A nice kick without blowing your head off. Hopefully, the kids at the shelter would like it.

Pleased with her latest creation, she gave the giant vat a stir and replaced the lid.

She had to admit that her college course was coming in handy, and she was only two weeks in. It was one thing to prepare a meal for one, but catering for large numbers required a different set of skills entirely. Her course was geared towards working in a busy restaurant, so all the workshops resulted in the production of large quantities of food.

Twice a week she was required to work in the college kitchens at lunchtime and help cook the food for the staff and students. It was quite a challenge. Mostly because it meant she had to work as part of a team, which wasn't her strength. She preferred to work alone. But if she wanted to achieve her dream of running her own restaurant one day then she'd need to learn how to manage people. It was a skill she was determined to develop.

She gave the tray of rice a stir and covered it with foil to keep it warm. The lasagnes weren't quite done, so she reset the timer for another five minutes.

Since introducing the shelter's new security regime, the cafe now opened at six p.m. rather than seven p.m, so it was a rush to get here on time each night, let alone have the food ready. But she was adapting to her new schedule and having a strict routine was good for her integration into society. According to her social worker, anyway.

Of course, volunteering at the shelter was also helping her personal development. Not only was she getting used to being around people, but Norah was teaching her to cook. She was a great mentor, patient and encouraging. It meant she was streets ahead of her fellow students in terms of culinary ability. Something which helped to ease the torment of feeling like a fish out of water in the frenetic college environment.

Norah appeared in the kitchen. 'Chilli smells good,' she said, opening the fridge to retrieve the prepared salads. 'Are you happy with the seasoning?'

'I've just checked it.' It was her first time in charge of the main dishes and she was nervous as hell. 'I hope people like it.'

'I'm sure they will.' Norah drizzled balsamic vinegar and olive oil over the salads. 'I'm looking forward to trying them.' She looked at the chalkboard attached to the wall. 'What have we got left to do?'

Norah had taught her to list all the tasks in order of priority on the board each day. That way nothing would be forgotten.

Norah read through the items. 'Soup, done. Bread, made. Chilli and rice, done. Salads dressed.' She turned to Emily, tucking her fair hair behind her eyes. 'How long for the lasagnes?'

Emily checked the timer. 'Two minutes.'

'Perfect. You've done a great job, Emily. Congratulations.'

'Don't congratulate me until people have tried it. It might be awful.' Her insecurities ran too deep for her to feel entirely confident. She liked the chilli, but would anyone else?

'You worry too much.' Norah came over and gave her a hug.

The sudden physical contact caught Emily off guard and she immediately shied away from the embrace. But then she was hit by a wave of guilt. 'Sorry.'

Norah stepped away. 'No need to apologise. It was my fault. I shouldn't be so touchy-feely.' She patted Emily's shoulder. 'What I should've said was, I'm so very proud of you. I want you to know that.'

Emily squeezed Norah's hand. 'Thank you.'

Norah cleared her throat. 'Enough with the sentiment. Let's get this show on the road.'

The timer pinged on the oven.

Grateful for an excuse to escape without offending her friend, whom she knew only meant well, Emily removed the lasagnes and carried the trays through to the cafe.

Norah followed with the vat of chilli, and soon the serving counter was filled with steaming hot food. All they needed now were some customers.

It took a while before the kids started filtering through from reception and appeared in the cafe. Fraser and Sam were manning the door tonight and carrying out the necessary checks. The atmosphere had certainly been less charged since they'd brought in the extra security measures. It wasn't only the volunteers who needed reassurance, it seemed the kids wanted a safe environment too. Who could blame them?

Emily tied the red Crash Pad apron around her middle and washed her hands ready to begin serving. As the kids patiently queued at the counter she spotted a few familiar faces. The shelter was building up a regular clientele. It was hardly surprising, when she'd been living rough she'd have longed for a place like this to stay at.

The first kid stepped up to be served. She looked like a frightened rabbit.

Emily gave her a warm smile. When you lived on the streets not many people smiled at you. They mostly avoided looking at you, or stepped over you, pretending you weren't there. 'Meat lasagne or veggie chilli?'

'Chilli, please.' The girl held out her plate, offering a faint smile as she was served a large helping of food.

As the queue grew and her chilli proved popular, Emily hoped she'd made enough to go around. Unlike during the day when they opened the cafe to the public, the evening session only catered for those staying at the shelter. But if all fifteen kids wanted chilli she might still be in trouble.

'Hey, there, Emily.'

She looked up to see the boy she'd met the other night smiling at her. 'Remember me? You gave me tomato soup.'

Of course she remembered him. How could she not? She'd been looking out for him ever since. Not that she'd admit as much. 'Yes, I remember. Alfie, isn't it? You gave your place up for that girl. It was nice of you.'

He shrugged. 'It was nice of you to give me soup. Which was very tasty, by the way.'

'Thanks.' She felt her cheeks flush.

He was wearing a dark blue checked shirt over a white T-shirt, and a green beanie hat. His boyish face had a smattering of light stubble over his chin. He was nice-looking, but in a subtle way. Not all chiselled and manly, but soft and kind. She liked his pale skin and light blue eyes. He looked gentle. Trustworthy. Like someone you'd want to... cuddle.

Embarrassed, she shoved the thought away.

He nodded to the serving trays laid out on the counter. 'Did you make all this? It looks amazing.'

Her blush deepened. 'Would you like some?'

'Christ, yes. Can I have both?'

He looked so hungry, she felt bad for denying him. 'I'm not really supposed to.'

'That's all right, I was being cheeky.' He held out his plate. 'Lasagne, please.'

She served him a large helping. 'When was the last time you ate?'

He frowned, as if thinking about it. 'Wednesday, I think.'

'You haven't eaten for two days?' Her shock made him laugh.

'It's no big deal.' He grinned, as though this was perfectly normal. 'I'll survive.'

But it was a big deal. No one should have to go without food. She knew how awful it was.

She placed two portions of garlic bread on his plate and added a side helping of salad. 'We have treacle sponge for dessert,' she said, wanting to ensure he had enough to eat.

His grin widened. 'Save me some, won't you?'

She nodded energetically. 'I promise.'

He moved away from the counter. 'Thanks, Emily.'

'You're welcome.'

Her eyes followed him as he wandered off. In fact, she was so busy watching him she nearly spooned chilli down the next person's front.

Scolding herself, she returned to focusing on serving the other kids, even if her eyes kept wandering over to Alfie.

He'd removed his green beanie hat and was seated at a table by himself, which wasn't surprising. Most of the kids were reluctant to socialise. They were like her, used to being alone, unaccustomed to having friends. As the cafe filled up, they were forced to share tables and soon the awkward silence was replaced by chatter as they relaxed and enjoyed the food.

Several of the kids returned to the counter and asked for seconds, something she was only allowed to do once all fifteen kids had been served. No one wanted to see any waste, so it was good to see the food eaten.

Alfie didn't reappear, so she saved him the last ladle of chilli and took it over. 'Room for a bit more?'

'Yes, please.' He accepted the plate from her. 'The lasagne was so good. Did you really make it yourself?'

She nodded, shyly. 'I'm training to be a chef at college.'

He looked impressed. 'Good for you.'

'I want to run my own restaurant,' she said without thinking, and then cringed. It was one thing to have a dream, it was another to voice it aloud. He probably thought she was a stupid naive fool. Kids like her didn't run their own business. 'One day, anyway.' Her cheeks grew hot. 'But it's a long way off.'

He frowned. 'How so?'

She fiddled with the tie on her apron. 'I don't have any qualifications, or money, or experience. So it's hardly likely, is it.' Now she felt stupid. She should stop talking.

'But you're at college, right? So you will have a qual-ification. And working here will give you experience, so you're two thirds of the way to achieving your dream.'

She blinked. 'I hadn't thought of it like that… Are you always this positive?'

'You won't get anywhere in life by being miserable.' He took a mouthful of chilli. 'Christ, this is good.' He ate some more.

Emily liked watching him enjoy her food.

'People are going to be queuing up outside your restaurant,' he said, shovelling in another mouthful. 'I'll be first in line. This is amazing.'

Her cheeks were burning hot now. She wasn't used to compliments.

'How come you're homeless?' she blurted suddenly curious, but then immediately cringed at her insensitivity. He just seemed so… together, so smart and mature for his age. He obviously hadn't always lived on the streets, he was too happy, for one thing. 'Sorry, none of my business.'

'That's okay, I don't mind you asking.' He wiped his mouth with the recycled napkin.

He had nice table manners, she noticed.

'Mum kicked me out when her boyfriend moved in. He didn't like me. Said it was him or me. She chose him.'

Emily sucked in a sharp breath. 'That's awful. Have you spoken to her since? Maybe she regrets her decision.'

'I doubt it. She's blocked my number.'

'I'm so sorry, Alfie.' Her heart broke for him.

At least her mum had the excuse of being mentally ill. But Alfie's mum had kicked him out in favour of a new lover. Talk about cruel.

'It is what it is.' But he failed to disguise the hurt in his eyes. 'It's not going to stop me living my life. I've got big plans,' he said, spooning in another mouthful of chilli.

'Oh, yeah?'

He drank some water before answering. 'I'm going to get a good job, own a big house, have loads of kids and love them unconditionally.'

For some reason her cheeks grew warm again. 'Is that right?'

He hummed. 'Just got to meet the right girl.'

Even if she wanted to look away, she couldn't. His blue eyes held hers with such conviction she felt like she was glued to the spot. 'Sounds like a plan,' she managed, her voice lacking any volume.

'I know, right?' His face broke into a huge grin. 'You promised me treacle sponge?' He finished off the chilli in one large mouthful.

'Coming right up.' She took his empty plate. 'Custard or ice-cream?'

'Can I have both?'

She laughed and went back to the counter to begin serving dessert, thinking about what an intriguing person Alfie was.

Far from letting what had happened to him dent his positivity or enthusiasm, he was determined to get a good job, buy a house, and make a success of his life. He just needed to find the right girl…

She dropped the serving spoon, making it clatter and causing a few heads to turn.

Alfie was watching her.

Why, she had no idea.

Chapter Nine

When Jamie left his flat, the sun was shining. It meant he wasn't about to get wet or freeze to death as he walked the fifteen-minute journey to Peggy's house. A visit was long overdue and he was looking forward to seeing her. She'd tried to persuade him to attend church with her this morning, but he'd used the excuse of playing football as reason not to go. She hadn't been happy, but she'd appreciated his commitment to the Leyton Harriers.

The knowledge that a roast dinner would be waiting for him when he arrived was helping to lift his spirits. A 5–0 thrashing and a dead leg for his efforts had been a depressing end to an already difficult week. He wasn't making as much progress in his case as he'd hoped, and his boss wasn't happy. Jamie working undercover was costing Gareth money. Something that always made him grumpy.

So far, Jamie hadn't discovered anything remotely useful about Max Tipping. Tailing the man hadn't unearthed any new information and neither had volunteering at the shelter. When he'd explained this to his boss, he'd been accused of not being devious enough in his efforts. Asking direct questions was never going to encourage someone to spill the beans, apparently. Trust was required. And if that failed, subterfuge was needed.

Jamie didn't like the idea of tricking Sam into revealing information, but getting her to trust him wasn't going to be an easy task either. Especially as so far he'd been a complete dick to her. He'd managed to offend her, annoy her, and press all her buttons. All the promises he'd made to be patient, non-confrontational and conciliatory, had proved impossible to adhere to. He was still trying to work out why.

He walked past New Spitalfields market, normally a hive of activity with stalls of fruit and veg selling fresh produce, along with an abundance of flowers. But it was Sunday, so the market was closed, which annoyed him further – he could have stopped off to buy Peggy a bouquet. Instead, he'd have to pop into the newsagents. He was a bad foster son.

His sombre mood was fuelled by an acute sense of disappointment. He'd had such high hopes of proving himself a decent investigative journalist, but he was floundering on his first assignment. He seemed unable to set aside his dislike of what the Tippings stood for in order to infiltrate the family. And that was never going to progress his career.

To top it all, Sam had confounded him by buying the old guy Harold replacement slippers. He'd been convinced she was simply playing at running a charity and that her commitment to the project was fleeting and shallow. But then she did something thoughtful and kind, like buying an old guy new slippers, and it skewered his opinion of her.

He reached the newsagents and emerged a few moments later with a box of Milk Tray. Not a great gift, but it was better than turning up empty handed.

Maybe he wouldn't have been in such a rotten mood this week if his research visit to Jonathan Campbell-Myer had gone better. Jamie had contacted the former city trader – who'd recently left prison having served an eighteen-month sentence for cooking the books – in the hope of gaining some useful insight into the world of insider trading. Interviewing someone found guilty of a similar crime might lead to a stronger and more insightful finished article on Max Tipping. But instead of finding a broken, remorseful man, filled with regret for scamming innocent people out of their pension funds, Jamie had discovered a cocky, arrogant arsehole.

Jamie had been polite, tentatively asking questions about why someone whose career was flying high had made the inexplicable decision to commit fraud, but the man was adamant he hadn't committed a crime at all. In fact, he was struggling to accept his guilt, despite over-whelming evidence to the contrary.

Jamie found it incredible that this supposedly intelligent and successful man had risked his personal wealth, reputation, and family to acquire more. Especially as the man was already loaded. It wasn't simply that he believed he wouldn't get caught, but a lack of recognition that he'd done anything wrong. The man felt absolutely no guilt for having ruined the lives of his victims. As far as he was concerned, *he* was the victim.

Jamie had left the man's lavish apartment reeling from the interview. So much so, when he'd arrived at the shelter later that day already agitated and had discovered Samantha Tipping owned a flipping Mercedes Benz CLS Coupé, he'd seen red.

Consequently, far from charming her so he could get to the truth, he'd argued with her, provoked her, and alienated her further. He was an idiot. A feeling further compounded when he'd visited her humble home.

He cringed at the thought. To say it wasn't what he'd been expecting would be an understatement. There were no lavish trappings on display, only an eclectic mixture of recycled furnishings. This insight into her meagre home life should have dispelled his anger. Instead, it had left him feeling ashamed and resentful.

Still, it was done now and there was nothing he could do about it. He just needed to work out how to make amends.

He arrived at Crownfield Road and stopped to clear his thoughts before heading in to see Peggy. It wouldn't be fair to turn up in a bad mood.

Taking a deep breath, he looked up at the redbrick house with its ornate porch and replacement double-glazed windows and felt his tension start to ease. The front had been turned into a paved area that could accommodate several cars. Something that was needed when you housed young adults. It was currently filled with various bicycles chained to the fencing, two mopeds and an ancient looking black Ford Ka.

Peggy had lived in Leytonstone all her life. Firstly, with her parents when they'd arrived in the UK as part of the Windrush generation, and then subsequently with her late husband, Ron. They'd both had successful careers in teaching, brought up three children and fostered dozens more. Peggy had retired from teaching now, but she was still on the board of governors and an active advocate for improving education within the Black community.

A sense of calm settled over him as he walked up to the front door. This place was the closest thing he'd had to a home growing up, the only constant in his life. He smiled as the noise from inside greeted him. It'd never been a quiet house.

He banged on the front door, hoping to be heard over the chaos the other side. Loud music blared out from the open windows above. Footsteps could be heard running up the stairs. After banging a second time the door swung open.

'Jamie, my boy!' Peggy's beaming smile was as bright as her patent shoes and jacket, under which she wore a loud floral dress. Her Sunday best – church attire. 'Why didn't you use your key?' she scolded, pulling him into a hug.

He didn't bother answering, mostly because he couldn't. Peggy had him in a bear hug, rocking him from side-to-side, expelling the air from his lungs.

'Come in, come in.' She dragged him inside. 'Turn that music off!' She bellowed up the stairs, nearly deafening him. 'I won't ask again! Sunday is the Lord's day... although heaven help him with this lot,' she mumbled, ushering Jamie inside.

The music cut off.

Peggy led him through to the kitchen. The décor hadn't changed since his teens. The walls were painted sunshine yellow, adorned with decorative plates. The space was filled with wooden furniture and a mismatch of crockery. Vases were filled with flowers from the garden. The room matched its owner: sunny and warm, and spilling over with love and chaos.

'Sit, sit!' she said, manhandling him onto a wooden bar stool. 'Tell me what you've been up to. It's been too long.'

'I know, I'm sorry. These are for you.' He handed her the chocolates.

She planted a big kiss on his lips. 'You're a good boy.' And then she gave him a sly smile. 'I was hoping you might bring someone with you today.'

'You were? Who?'

She tried for an innocent look. 'A girlfriend, perhaps.'

That old chestnut. He shook his head. 'Sorry, Peggy. No girlfriend.'

She looked disappointed. 'No one special at all?'

For some strange reason an image of Sam Tipping floated through his brain. He quickly shook it away. He didn't dispute she was attractive, but she was hardly girl-friend material. And it wasn't like she'd ever look at him twice. She was way out of his league, and he'd offended her at least half a dozen times. 'Afraid not, Peggy.'

'Shame.' She gave him a disapproving look and removed her jacket, hanging it behind the door. 'You're not getting any younger, my boy.'

'Thanks for reminding me.' He stretched across the table and pinched a handful of grapes from the fruit bowl.

Peggy washed her hands in the ceramic sink. 'By the time I was thirty, I'd been married for nine years and had three children.'

'But only because you'd met the person you wanted to spend your life with. I haven't. You want me to marry just anyone?' He popped a grape into his mouth.

She dried her hands. 'I suppose not.'

She didn't sound entirely sure, which made him laugh. 'Anyway, I'm concentrating on my career. Love can wait.'

'Don't wait too long,' she said, tying her yellow 'I've Got Flava' apron around her middle. 'I want to see you settled and happy.'

'I am happy.'

She pinned him with a glare. 'Lying is a sin.'

'I'm not lying.' He opened his arms in a 'look how happy I am' gesture. 'Life's good. I have my own place, I socialise with my mates, I have a good job. What's not to be happy about?'

She gave him a sceptical look and pulled on a pair of padded gloves. 'How's your job going?' She opened the oven door, wafting away a wave of steam.

'Good. I've been assigned my first undercover role.'

'Undercover?' She straightened, holding the tray of roasted chicken. 'Is it safe? Have you been forced to join a criminal gang?' She slid the tray onto the hob. 'I watch *Line of Duty*, I know how these things work.'

He laughed. 'I'm a journalist, not a cop.'

'Journalists get killed too.'

'Not when they're investigating a charity.'

'A charity?' She basted the chicken.

His stomach rumbled as the spicy jerk-chicken scent reached his nose. He'd missed Peggy's cooking. 'But the main focus of the case is the woman's brother. He's a financial trader.' Maybe he shouldn't be divulging this information, but it wasn't like Peggy would tell anyone.

She shoved the chicken back in the oven. 'And he's up to no good?'

'That's what I've got to find out.'

'How are you going to do that?' She dumped a bag of carrots in front of him. 'Make yourself useful.'

He reached over for the peeler. 'By volunteering at the charity and trying to get the information out of his sister.'

'Is she involved?'

Good question. He was still undecided. 'I think it's unlikely.'

Peggy handed him a saucepan. 'Then should you be using her to get to her brother?'

'That's how investigative journalism works, Peggy.'

She began chopping sweet potatoes. 'I'm not sure I approve.'

'How else am I going to progress my career?'

'I thought you wanted to be a documentary film-maker?'

'I do, but it's a tough area to break into.' He peeled the carrots. 'I'm hoping this case will be a stepping stone.'

They were interrupted by a lad of about fifteen appearing in the kitchen. He was tall and lanky and wore a Spurs shirt. 'When's dinner? I'm starving,' he said, removing a packet of crisps from the cupboard.

Peggy swiped at him with a tea towel. 'No snacking! Dinner will be ready when it's ready. Make yourself useful and set the table. We're eating in the conservatory.' She confiscated the crisps and shoved them back in the cupboard.

Jamie couldn't help smiling. It was a familiar scene. He remembered acting just as the lad had done. Pushing boundaries, testing Peggy to see if she was a 'keeper'. Luckily for him, she was.

'I'm Jamie,' he said to the boy. 'Former foster kid of Peggy's. Taskmaster, isn't she?'

The teen grinned. 'The worst.'

'*Oi!*' Peggy swiped at him again, but there was no force behind it. 'And you mind your manners too,' she said, turning on Jamie. 'You're not too old for a telling off.'

The lad collected cutlery from the drawer.

'This young man is called Ash.' Peggy's voice switched from scolding to caring. 'He's been with us for three weeks.'

Jamie nodded at Ash. 'All right, mate?'

The kid nodded back. 'Yeah, you?'

'Good, thanks. Are you here short term or long term?'

Ash shrugged. 'Who knows?'

'Well, you're in good hands.' Jamie winked at Peggy. 'Firm hands… but good hands.'

The kid grinned. 'I know.' He carried the cutlery over to the French doors. 'You staying for lunch?'

'Hell, yes. It's Jamaican jerk chicken.'

'Cool.' The kid disappeared into the conservatory.

Peggy watched him go. 'He reminds me of you,' she said, seasoning the sweet potato. 'Acts brave, but soft as snow under the surface. His mum has cancer. She can't look after him anymore.'

Poor kid. 'What's the prognosis?'

'Not good,' she said, with a sigh. 'I don't think she's long for this world.'

Jamie looked out of the French windows into the cluttered conservatory and watched Ash setting the table, his shoulders hunched, his skin pale and drawn. 'He's fortunate to have you in his corner.'

'The next few weeks will be a test for him. I'm praying for him.'

Jamie went over and kissed Peggy's cheek. 'You're a good woman,' he said, wondering if he'd ever properly thanked her for all she'd done for him.

He'd been a troublesome kid, forever causing problems, but she'd never given up on him. He wanted to express his gratitude, but somehow the words wouldn't come.

When tears threatened, he turned away before things became too emotional. 'Too early to cook the carrots?'

She patted his arm, seeming to sense his anguish. 'Put them on a low heat.' And then she pointed to an envelope on the kitchen table. 'Another letter arrived for you. You haven't told your mum your new address, then?'

He lit the hob, avoiding eye-contact. 'No point. I don't intend on replying.'

'You're not curious to hear what she has to say?'

'Nope.' He turned to face his foster-mum. 'What else needs doing? Red cabbage?'

'In the fridge. It'll need warming through.'

Spiced red cabbage was his favourite. He went over to the fridge.

Peggy followed him. 'She might have turned her life around, love. You never know.'

'Or she might still be a selfish drug addict.'

'If that were the case, social services would've taken your brothers into care.' She blocked his escape, determined to regain his attention. 'But they haven't, have they?'

'Half-brothers,' he amended. 'And they probably have by now. It's only a matter of time before she screws up.'

She passed him the envelope. 'Open the letter and find out.'

'No, thanks.' He emptied the red cabbage into a saucepan.

Peggy wasn't done. 'No one's saying you should play happy families, but you have three younger siblings who might benefit from having an older brother to support them.'

She didn't need to remind him he had family. He simply couldn't reconcile the fact that his mother had neglected him to the point where social services had taken him into care, but she'd gone on to have three more kids – all of whom had stayed with her.

Did his brothers even know about him? Were they curious? What did it matter, he had no interest in seeing his mother. She was a part of his past. She wasn't someone he wanted in his future.

Despite this, an ache filled his chest. He rubbed it away. It wasn't logical to feel loss. Peggy was the only mother he needed. He had no desire to reopen old wounds.

'It might give you closure,' his foster mother said, not giving up.

He stirred the red cabbage. 'What will?'

'Visiting your mother.'

'No way am I visiting her.'

Peggy confiscated the spoon and took hold of his hand so he couldn't escape. 'So instead you spend your days angry and resentful, punishing anyone who dares care about you?'

'I don't do that.' Even to his own ears he sounded defensive.

'Yes, you do.' She fixed him with her dark eyes. 'But you're a grown man now. No longer an angry and resentful teenager. You've beaten the odds and become a caring and thoughtful person who I'm proud to call my *son*.' She held firm when he tried to squirm away. 'You've nothing to fear from seeing your mother, but you've everything to gain.' She pulled him close. 'Even if it's just to gain closure. Because let's be honest, your fear of being abandoned again is the primary reason you're still alone.'

He flinched. 'I told you, I haven't met the right person.'

'And when you do meet them, are you going to be able to trust them with your heart?'

'It's not like I haven't had relationships.'

'Which you ended when things became too serious.'

'That's not—'

'Name me one girlfriend you didn't end things with?' She pointed the wooden spoon at him.

His brain flicked through the list of girls he'd dated. Laura, Kate, Andie. All of whom had been devastated when he'd broken things off. They'd been confused as to how things had gone from being great to him ending it for no apparent reason. That didn't make him a bad person, did it? He'd never cheated on them, messed them around, or been cruel. He'd enjoyed going out with them. He just hadn't seen himself spending the rest of his life with them. That wasn't a crime. Surely it was better to walk away than string a person along?

He shook his head. 'That's totally irrelevant.'

'I'm not blaming you, or accusing you of anything,' she said, still waving the spoon about. 'I'm just saying, you wouldn't be the first troubled kid I've fostered who finds it hard to trust. It's perfectly understandable. You've been hurt. It makes sense you'd protect yourself from further pain. And leaving someone before they have the chance to leave you guarantees you'll never get your heart broken.' She reached up and stroked his hair. 'But the price you pay is never truly allowing yourself to love someone, or being loved in return.'

'I've been in love,' he said, knowing it was a lie. He'd liked his girlfriends, cared for them, even felt genuine affection… but love? He couldn't truthfully say he'd loved them.

'You can lie to me all you want, my boy. You can even lie to yourself. But you can't lie to the Lord. He knows what's in here,' she placed her hand over his heart. 'And your heart is filled with fear.'

He wanted to object, to tell her she was wrong, but the words wouldn't come.

She offered him the letter again. 'At least read what she has to say.'

He hesitated, but took the letter from her. If nothing else to stop her badgering him.

She kissed his cheek, gave him a tight hug and returned to preparing the dinner as if nothing had happened. 'Time for gravy.'

He stared down at his mother's wonky handwriting. A rogue tear escaped and landed on the envelope, smearing his name.

Wiping his eyes, he shoved the envelope in his pocket. 'I'll go and help Ash set the table.'

He grabbed the cloth napkins and headed into the conservatory, eager to escape his foster mother's uncanny ability to undermine his carefully controlled pretence of being happy.

Chapter Ten

Tuesday, 20th November

It was an unseasonably warm day. The temperature had reached thirteen degrees and it was only eleven a.m. Sam had called a staff meeting, but instead of asking everyone to squash inside the cramped laundry room, she'd decided to hold the meeting in the rooftop garden.

Emily had baked mince pies for the occasion, and Sam had brewed a vat of fresh coffee and set up the wooden table and chairs next to the herb planters. She'd hoped, perhaps naively, that a fragrant backdrop might ease the ordeal of what they had to discuss. Trying to find a solution to the issue of turning away an increasing number of young people each night wasn't an enjoyable task, or an easy one. But ignoring the problem wasn't going to resolve it either.

After dealing with the more mundane items on the agenda, they paused the meeting so everyone could enjoy the mince pies and refill their coffee. Sam took the opportunity to visit the sensory section of the garden and run her hands through the decorative grasses. Breathing in the fragrances emanating from the wall planters, she instantly felt calmer. It gave her the respite she needed to gather her thoughts and try to find a solution to the problem they faced.

Word had spread around South London. The Crash Pad's reputation was growing and the shelter was inviting attention. Reports about how the young people were treated favourably had been a welcome boost. As had hearing glowing feedback about the quality of food on offer and the facilities provided at the shelter – which was great in terms of raising awareness and improving local opinion, but challenging when it meant more young people were trying to access their services.

Sipping her coffee, she smoothed down the front of her blue-striped top, noticing the grass stain on the sleeve. And to think she'd made an effort this morning. Glancing up, she caught sight of Jamie leaning against the water butt and instantly scowled. Something he'd said during his first visit to the shelter kept playing on her mind. He'd questioned whether they were really helping, or simply offering a short-term reprieve to a long-term problem.

His criticism had stung. She'd been so proud of The Crash Pad that she'd never stopped to consider the possibility that its bright welcoming décor, modern facilities and homely ambience might make someone feel worse about their situation, not better. She'd assumed their guests would welcome a cheerful respite from their otherwise challenging lives. But Jamie's comment about how she was dangling luxury in front of them, only to kick them out the next morning had hit a nerve. He'd implied that far from helping them, she was actually being cruel. Taunting them with what they could have had if only someone had loved, or cared enough about them not to throw them onto the streets.

It was a sobering thought. One that refused to budge.

What else could she do, though? She couldn't single-handedly solve the country's homelessness crisis. Wasn't it better to do something, than nothing?

Damn Jamie bloody Lawson and his judgemental remarks.

It didn't help that he'd shown up to the meeting looking relaxed and handsome in a white linen shirt and soft faded jeans. His caramel eyes crinkled in the late autumn sunlight, and his reddish-brown hair glowed like a flipping halo. A halo? An angel he most definitely was not.

He caught her looking over and smiled. To anyone watching, he appeared all charm and sincerity. But she didn't buy it. He was about as sincere as her brother Max when he was in full-on sales-mode and trying to persuade a hapless punter into buying whatever shares he was selling that month. Her brother's charismatic persona was merely a front for a ruthless game plan that usually involved someone handing over large quantities of cash.

What was Jamie Lawson's game plan, she wondered? Because whatever he said, there was more going on than him simply wanting to volunteer, she was sure of it.

When the team had finished their refreshments and reconvened around the table, she joined them and addressed the last item on the agenda. Demand exceeding resource and what, if anything, could be done about it.

'So... that's our dilemma,' she finished, keeping her tone light, despite the gravity of the situation. 'We don't have the funds to expand The Crash Pad right now or reconfigure the space.' She glared at Jamie. 'So, what do we do?'

He'd rather sarcastically pointed out that if she hadn't bothered with the pool tables, fancy lounge area or bespoke beach huts, she could have fitted in several more beds. Which might be true, but wasn't helpful to hear.

Besides, the guests needed something to occupy them in the evenings. It would be pretty soul destroying if there was nothing to do other than eat, shower and sleep.

'Turning people away was always going to be the reality of the situation,' Fraser said, wearing his heavy army overcoat, despite the warm weather. 'We can't help everyone.'

'I know, but it feels so cruel.' Sam placed her coffee mug on the table. 'I accept that we can't offer everyone beds, but I wish there was something we could offer them instead.'

'You mean like food parcels?' Emily raised her hand as if she were still in school. 'Like I did the other night for that lad, Alfie.' Her cheeks coloured. 'He seemed very grateful.'

Sam nodded at Emily. 'Exactly. It wouldn't cost too much to increase the quantities of food we produce. Although we'd need to buy takeaway containers of some kind. That might be costly.'

'I could speak to my mate who works in the army kitchens,' Fraser said, his camouflage coat almost lost against the evergreens. 'The military get through tons of containers, especially when they're catering on the move. They might be willing to donate the used ones, rather than chucking them away.'

Sam liked the idea of that. 'Brilliant, Fraser. Thank you.' She knew her team would have some ideas, they never let her down. 'But maybe we could offer more than just food in the parcel. You know, like a sleeping bag, or a blanket?'

'And a wash kit,' Fraser added. 'It's hard finding somewhere to wash on the streets.'

'Oh, I like that idea.' Then reality kicked in, and Sam's enthusiasm took a hit. 'But that will cost money. A lot of money. We're talking about five to ten parcels a night.'

'Have you thought about sponsorship?' Jamie leant forwards in his chair, resting his tanned arms on his legs. 'We could approach the big organisations in London. If you offer to brand the parcels with their company logos they might be interested in sponsoring them. It's free advertising.'

Sam thought about it. 'It's a possibility, but it sounds very time-consuming to organise.'

He shrugged. 'So we advertise for a volunteer fundraiser.'

Norah frowned. 'Do such people exist?'

Emily raised her hand again. 'I could ask at my college. I think they run marketing courses. There might be someone looking for work experience.'

Sam gave her a thumbs-up. 'That'd be great, Emily. Thank you. But even if we successfully recruit someone, it could take months. So, whereas I see this as a great long-term solution to the problem, we need to introduce something more urgently to tackle what's happening right now.'

'How about a donation drive?' Jamie's suggestion caused all heads to turn to him. 'Ask the public to drop off any bedding they don't need. Ask for the items to be in reasonable condition and prewashed so you keep the expense down, and then all we have to do is parcel them up.'

Norah looked impressed. 'That's a cracking idea. Like how the foodbanks run?'

He nodded. 'Low cost and easy to implement. Especially if we use social media to spread the word.'

Sam hated to admit it, but it was a genius idea.

Forcing a friendly expression, she gestured to Jamie… who was looking all smug, and handsome, and infuriatingly angelic. 'I think we have our winner.'

Emily started clapping. 'Go, Jamie!'

Fraser gave Jamie a manly slap on the shoulder. 'Nice one, mate.'

Sam had to agree, even if the effort of smiling was making her cheeks ache. 'I'll get onto it right away.'

'No need.' He relaxed back in his chair. 'I'll pick this up. You have enough to deal with.'

'That's kind of you, Jamie,' she managed to say, through gritted teeth. 'Thank you.'

'No problem.' He smiled, unleashing the full force of his charm. Damn him.

Out of the corner of her eye, she noticed Fraser and Norah exchange a glance. Their raised eyebrows indicated they weren't oblivious to the tension bubbling away between her and the shelter's latest recruit. In which case, she needed to make more effort to keep her feelings hidden. Jamie was a volunteer, after all. She should appear more grateful, less… agitated.

Norah stood up. 'We'd better get a move on. The cafe opens soon and we have sandwiches to make.'

Sam turned to the group. 'Thank you for your time and ideas,' she said, genuinely grateful she had such an amazing group of volunteers. 'I really appreciate it.'

Fraser gestured to the table. 'Need a hand clearing up?'

'No, I can manage. But thanks for offering. You head down, I'll join you in a minute.' She needed a moment to herself. Her feelings towards Jamie Lawson were getting more complicated by the hour. One minute he was criticising her, the next he was coming up with helpful ideas. It was hard to fathom.

As she cleared away the plates and switched her phone back on, it immediately rang. If the image of an angel appeared when Jamie was around, the devil incarnate flashed across her mind when she saw it was her mother calling. Oh, hell.

She braced herself. 'Hi, Mum. Everything okay?'

'Where are you?' Her mother sounded displeased. 'I've left three messages.'

'Sorry, my phone was off. I was in a meeting. Is something wrong?'

'Yes. Your father and I have been standing outside this godawful place for ten minutes knocking and no one has let us in.'

'You're here? At The Crash Pad?'

'That's what I said. Are you going to let us in?'

What on earth were her parents doing here?

She supposed she'd better find out. 'I'll be right down.'

Her mother tutted and ended the call.

With no time to clear up, Sam covered the remaining mince pies with a napkin and headed down from the rooftop garden, the metal ladder creaking beneath her as she hurried.

She ran across the communal area and into reception.

True enough, her parents were standing at the front door. Their disappointed expressions were visible through the glass, enhanced by the horror of being made to queue alongside a group of teens waiting for the cafe to open.

In contrast to the teens' casual sports attire, her mother looked like she'd stepped off the set of *The Devil Wears Prada*. Fitting, really, seeing as she'd just been comparing her mother to Beelzebub.

Christina Tipping wore a bronze-coloured embossed jacket over a fitted black dress. Four chunky gold necklaces hung around her neck, each one a different length, creating a strategically co-ordinated ensemble. Her dad looked far more casual, although she suspected his aviator sunglasses, blue suede jacket and light grey chinos weren't from M&S.

Unlocking the door, she let everyone inside. It was nearly midday, so it seemed churlish to make them wait outside for the sake of another ten minutes.

'Hello, Mother.' She leant in to kiss her mum's cheek.

Her mother recoiled. 'You're filthy,' she said, giving her daughter a disapproving look. 'Really, Samantha. Is it so hard to put on clean clothes?' She extracted a leaf from Sam's hair. 'Is that the top I bought you for Christmas?'

'I had an important meeting this morning. I wanted to look smart.' She hoped this might pacify her mother's desire for her to make an effort with her appearance.

'Is that a grass stain?' Her mother rubbed at the smudge on the sleeve. 'You really should be more careful. This item came from the Chanel winter collection.'

'Sorry.'

'Honestly, if I'd known you were going to be gardening in it, I would have opted for a high-street purchase.'

Sam blinked. 'You would've shopped on the high street?'

Her mother gave her a reprimanding look. 'Of course not. I would've sent Altamira.'

It figured. Her mother would never degrade herself by frequenting a chain store, she'd send her Brazilian housekeeper instead.

There was little point explaining to her mother she'd actually prefer high street brands to designer. Her lifestyle required practical clothing, they needed to be hard-wearing and washable, as opposed to dry-clean only.

'Hi, Daddy.' She hugged her father, who didn't seem much more approving than her mother. 'No golf today?'

'Your mother had errands for me.' He looked disgruntled.

'Shame. It's such a lovely day too.'

Her father gave her mother a look that said, 'See?' Which resulted in her mother glaring at Sam.

'Stop stirring.'

How was this her fault? She'd merely commented on the weather.

'Are you here for a specific reason? Or just interested to see how we're getting on?' She knew perfectly well it wasn't the latter, but it seemed impolite to assume they had an agenda.

'Do we need a reason to visit our daughter?' Her mother's insincere smile meant trouble was afoot. Oh, hell.

Suddenly struck by an idea, Sam decided to get in first, before they divulged their plan. 'Of course not. It's lovely to see you both.' See? She could do insincerity too. 'I didn't get a chance to show you the rooftop garden at the opening event. Let me show you now.'

She led them through the main area, determined to show off all they'd achieved.

Despite Jamie's criticism that the décor was overkill, it was still an uplifting space. The sunlight filtering in from the large windows hit the beach mural on the far wall, making it feel like they were on a topical island… and not in Streatham. Surely that had to be a good thing?

'As you can see, the cafe is proving popular.' She pointed to the potted herbs on the tables. 'All the food is homemade and we grow some of the produce ourselves.'

'Delightful.' Her mother was clearly doing her best to sound impressed.

Sam hooked her arm through her dad's. 'Do you still get involved with the charitable events at the airline?' Her father was the retired CEO of a worldwide airline.

'Occasionally, why?'

'I wondered if you could put in a good word for us? We're approaching various organisations to see if they'd like to sponsor our parcel scheme, and it occurred to me the airline might be interested. Especially as it's run by a member of your family.'

'Parcel scheme?' Her mother looked perplexed.

She nodded. 'We turn away several people most nights, which as you can imagine is heart-breaking.'

It took her parents a while to realise she was waiting for them to agree with her before continuing. Eventually, they both gave half-hearted nods and mumblings of agreement.

How touching.

'As we're not able to offer them a bed,' she continued. 'We want to offer them a takeaway parcel instead. Hot food, a wash kit, and bedding for the night. It's not the same as a roof over their heads, but hopefully it'll keep them warmer and it means they don't have to beg for food or money on the streets.'

Her mother's nose wrinkled. This was not 'polite' conversation.

'So, what do you think?' She looked at her dad, expectantly.

He frowned. 'What do I think about what?'

'Asking the airline to sponsor The Crash Pad?'

Her father glanced at her mother, who cleared her throat and said, 'Darling, a huge corporation like the airline has to consider its reputation.'

Sam frowned. 'Meaning?'

'They have shareholders and a board of trustees to appease.'

'But they regularly do stuff for charity,' she said, genuinely confused. 'We attended loads of fundraising functions when Dad was CEO. How is this any different?'

Her mother took her hand. 'Because the airline has to consider many factors before making the commitment to patronise a charity.'

'Such as?'

'Public opinion and goodwill.'

'Marketability,' her dad added.

'Marketability?' She looked between them. 'Oh, you mean the reality of kids living on our streets isn't very... what, palatable?'

Her mother lowered her voice. 'It's not exactly the sort of thing people like to talk about.'

'And that's the problem.' Her frustration bubbled to the surface. 'Nobody wants to face reality. Until society admits we have a problem nothing will get fixed. Wouldn't you like to be trailblazers? Stand up for social change and be at the forefront of tackling homelessness in this country?'

Her mother patted her perfectly coiffed hairdo. 'Frankly, darling, no. And neither does your father.' She turned her attention to the extended loft ladder. 'Are you expecting me to climb that?'

Sam clenched her fists. 'It's that, or fly.' The devil could fly, right?

Annoyed, she climbed the ladder. 'Coming?'

They could stay downstairs for all she cared.

As she reached the top, she was surprised to discover Jamie packing up the table and chairs they'd used for the meeting.

'I thought I'd make myself useful,' he said, shaking crumbs from the tablecloth. 'Everything okay?'

Before she could reply, her parents appeared at the top of the ladder.

She inwardly cringed. If Jamie thought she was a spoilt, rich, insensitive posh knob with no clue about living in the real world, what the hell was he going to make of her parents?

Therefore she couldn't have been more surprised when he came over and extended his hand. 'Mr Tipping, I assume? Delighted to meet you, sir.'

Sir? Sam felt her eyebrows almost touch her hairline.

'Jamie Lawson. I'm a volunteer at The Crash Pad.' He shook her dad's hand and then turned his charms on her mother. 'Mrs Tipping. It's an honour.'

An honour? Okay, what was going on?

'Can I offer you some refreshments? Tea, coffee?' Jamie's smile was on full-beam, dazzling her mother, who was never one to reject the attentions of a handsome man.

'No, thank you. Unfortunately, we can't stay long.' Her mother extended her hand. 'Jamie, you say?'

'That's right. Jamie Lawson.' He shook her mother's hand. 'Sam's told me so much about you.'

Sam nearly fell over. She'd told him diddlysquat. What was he playing at?

Her mother looked intrigued. 'Has she indeed?'

'It must be such a privilege to have two such accomplished and successful parents,' he said, really piling it on.

Sam baulked. When he'd used the word privilege to describe *her*, he'd almost spat the word. Yet here he was, sucking up to her parents, making out he was their biggest fan.

And besides, when she'd referred to her parents before, he'd claimed to know nothing about her family. What was he up to?

'Your charitable work is pretty impressive,' he said, still holding her mother's hand. 'I was reading about your support for the 100 Women in Finance organisation. Such a worthy cause.'

Christina Tipping beamed. 'I feel exactly the same way.' She covered his hand with hers. 'I think it's imperative that women are empowered and supported to succeed in business.'

But not charitable ventures, Sam added silently.

Jamie wasn't done laying on the charm. 'I imagine you're revered by many business women hoping to follow in your footsteps, Mrs Tipping.'

'Please, call me Christina.' Her mother gazed into Jamie's eyes. There was a long-drawn-out moment, before she suddenly seemed to check herself. 'Well, it's a pleasure to meet you. Isn't that right, Richard,' she said, as if suddenly remembering she was married.

'Oh, the pleasure is all mine,' Jamie said, ramping up the charm-offensive.

Jesus. Someone give me a bucket, thought Sam.

She glanced at her father, wondering if he found this as excruciating as she did, but he'd wandered off and was admiring her vegetable borders. Well, that was something. Either that, or he needed the distraction. She could empathise.

She was about to join her dad, when her mother said, 'It's funny you should mention the 100 Women in Finance organisation.' She turned away from Jamie's mesmerising gaze and searched out her daughter's.

Yes, I'm still here, thought Sam. Not that anyone would notice.

'We're having a little festive soiree at the house this weekend. Just a few close friends and associates. Nothing grand,' she said, which meant it would be a full-blown 'look at how rich we are' bash. 'It's part of our fundraising efforts for the organisation. We wanted to ensure you were able to come along, darling.'

Sam startled. 'Who, me?'

'Who else would I be referring to?'

Was she kidding? 'Sorry, I'm busy.'

'I haven't said when it is.' Her mother's polite tone faltered for a nanosecond, but she managed to hold onto her smile. 'It's Saturday evening, the twenty-fourth.'

'I'll be running the shelter.'

'Surely you can take one night off?'

Sam felt her blood heat. 'It's a homeless shelter, Mother. You expect me to close its doors so I can eat limp quiche and exchange small talk with a bunch of dignitaries?'

Her mother subjected her to a loaded look. No doubt because of the 'limp quiche' remark. Christina Tipping would never dream of serving quiche. It was the food of the lower classes. Only caviar and foie gras would suffice.

Sam and her mother simultaneously opened their mouths, primed to engage in one of their heated exchanges, when Jamie chipped in with, 'You know, it might be a good networking event.'

Sam glared at him. 'Excuse me?'

'It could be a chance to talk about The Crash Pad and invite sponsorship,' he said enthusiastically, turning his smile on her mother. 'There's no reason why Sam shouldn't talk about the shelter and drum up interest, is there? After all, it is a charitable event.' He opened his arms, all innocence and allure. 'And you must be so proud of all Sam has achieved. I mean, look at this place.' He gestured to the garden. 'It's amazing.'

Sam wasn't sure who was more stunned – her, or her mother.

Her mother swallowed awkwardly. 'Quite,' she said, avoiding eye contact.

Jamie turned to Sam. 'And I'm sure Fraser would swap shifts. You deserve a night off, you work so hard.' His eyes softened and for a moment she forgot where she was. 'It sounds like a very worthwhile cause, and you're all for helping those in need, aren't you?'

Sam snapped out of her reverie.

Was he challenging her?

'Supporting women in finance is hardly the same as offering homeless teens a bed,' she quipped.

'The Countess of Wessex is a Global Ambassador,' her mother added, straightening her shoulders. 'The organisation is supported by the entire royal family. Including the Queen. You could show a little more respect, Samantha.'

Sam's blood reached boiling point. *Respect?*

Jamie intervened. 'I'm sure Sam isn't being disrespectful, Mrs Tipping.' He then corrected himself. 'I mean… *Christina.*' His sultry emphasis on her name melted her mother's frown in an instant.

Sam groaned. Christ, she needed to take lessons from this guy.

'It's just that the shelter is as important to her as your charity ventures are to you,' he said, winning her mother over again with his charm. Or was it smarm?

Sam glared at him. Unlike her mother, she was no pushover, and she didn't need Jamie bloody Lawson fighting her battles for her.

Her mother softened. 'Indeed. And obviously, we want to support our daughter with her... project.'

Really? Sam folded her arms. 'Does that include asking Dad's airline to sponsor the shelter?'

Her mother struggled to hold onto her composure. 'Like I told you before, it's not a good fit. Now, do I have your assurance that you'll be at the soiree on Saturday? Your brother's going to be there, so I would like you there too. A united front.'

Sam closed her eyes. She tried to breathe in the scents around her, hoping it might ease her agitation, but she needed something stronger on this occasion. Neat gin, probably.

In truth, she'd rather pull out her own teeth with rusty pliers than attend one of her mother's soirees. But refusing wasn't worth the hassle.

Plus, as Jamie said, she could use it to network. 'Fine.'

Her mother's shoulders visibly relaxed. 'And please wear something suitable, Samantha. The dress code is black-tie.'

So much for the event not being anything grand. 'I'll have my jeans dry-cleaned especially, Mother.'

She was subjected to a look. 'That's not funny. I'll arrange for something suitable to be sent to you.'

Oh, joy. A ball gown, no doubt.

Her mother redirected her attentions to Jamie. 'Perhaps you'd like to accompany Samantha, as her plus-one?'

No way! 'He's busy,' Sam cut in. 'He can't make it.'

Without so much as a flinch, Jamie pinned her with a smile. 'Actually, I have nothing planned for Saturday.' He redirected his smile to her mother. 'I'd be delighted to attend. Thank you for the invitation, Christina. I'm honoured.'

Her mother blushed. Actually blushed. 'Well, aren't you a breath of fresh air,' she said, lowering her voice. 'Not like the types Samantha normally associates with.'

'I am standing here,' Sam said, feeling disgruntled.

Her mother offered Jamie her hand, which he dutifully took. 'I look forward to seeing you again on Saturday, Christina.'

'Likewise.' She patted his hand. 'Black-tie, don't forget.'

'I won't.'

After another long-drawn-out gaze, her mother extricated herself from Jamie's clutches and hooked her arm through Sam's. 'You can escort us back to the car, darling. The driver will be wondering where we are. Come along, Richard.'

Sam allowed her mother to lead her over to the ladder, but she glanced back at Jamie and gave him what she hoped was a suitably intimidating stare.

She'd be having words with Jamie bloody Lawson.

She was not happy. Not happy, at all.

Chapter Eleven

It was gone midday by the time Jamie arrived at The Crash Pad ready for his volunteer shift. He was in good spirits, buoyed by having made a breakthrough in the case. He'd managed to wangle an invite to Christina Tipping's fancy soiree tomorrow night. At the family home in Holland Park, no less. Even better, Max Tipping would be there. Which meant he'd have direct access to the family and their intimate circle of friends. He'd be able to get an insight into their behind-the-scenes-life. It was a gift. And he hadn't had to lie once.

Well, not much.

They'd invited him, hadn't they? And once the alcohol started to flow, tongues would loosen, and it would only be a matter of time before someone let something juicy slip. And then bingo, he'd have the lead he needed to crack open the case.

When he'd given Gareth the good news, his boss had almost combusted. But his jubilation hadn't lasted long. He'd gone on to warn Jamie not to 'blow this golden opportunity' or there'd be 'hell to pay' if he did.

Jamie wasn't going to let that happen. His story was about to make a major step forward. He just needed to focus.

However, his good mood was slightly dampened by the thought of encountering Sam today. He'd snuck away on Tuesday before she could confront him and he hadn't been at the shelter since. He didn't think for one moment this meant her temper had eased. She hadn't been happy about the way he'd schmoozed her parents. Her mum, in particular.

In fact, thinking about how he'd behaved around Christina Tipping made him cringe too. But he hadn't had time to formulate a better plan. He'd spotted the couple stepping onto the rooftop garden and recognised them from the press release photo. Seeing Sam's pained expression had confirmed his assumption that they were her parents, so he'd sprung into action.

His bluff had worked. Sam hadn't contradicted his bull-shit at the time, even if she had glowered at him like he was Lucifer himself. Her tortured expression indic-ated she suspected he was up to something, and she was right. Consequently, some fancy backtracking was required today to avoid a confrontation and eradicate any suspicion about his intentions.

He'd come up with a plan. Whether it worked or not would become clear in about… he checked his watch… half an hour. It was a gamble. A gamble that had cost him two hundred quid. He just hoped it paid off.

He reached the shelter's reception area and checked for signs of Sam. The coast was clear. Making his way into the communal area, he looked around to see the cafe tables were full. So much so, the patrons had spilled onto the sofas and beanbags in the recreation area to eat their lunch. It was good to see.

Despite his earlier scepticism about Sam's motivations for opening the shelter, even he could see this place was needed. And maybe Sam was more committed to the cause than he'd given her credit for. His opinions had been biased by her family connections, and that was unfair of him. He realised that now. A realisation that had added to his desire to make amends for his behaviour on Tuesday.

He spotted Emily and Norah serving behind the counter. Sam was nowhere to be seen. Phew.

He wandered over to the cafe and noticed the old guy Harold tucking into a large helping of beef stew. He glanced down and saw that he was wearing the new slippers Sam had bought for him. They looked comfy and snug, a perfect fit. No string in sight.

For some reason this brought a lump to his throat. He wasn't sure why. They were only slippers.

And then a voice said, 'All right, mate.'

He turned to see the homeless boy he'd met the first night he'd volunteered at the shelter sitting at a nearby table. The one who'd missed out on a bed because he'd been working. 'Alfie, isn't it?'

The lad grinned. 'That's me.'

Once again Jamie was struck by the kid's cheerfulness. He was cleanly shaven, his hair brushed, and he was wearing what looked like clean clothes. No mean feat when you lived on the streets. The lad was clearly resourceful. Which was just as well.

Jamie nodded to the plate of stew. 'Looks good. Tasty?'

'Christ, yes. It's like heaven.' The lad shovelled in another mouthful, his expression one of pure bliss. 'Emily can sure cook.' He glanced over to where the young girl was serving behind the counter.

Emily glanced over. When she caught his eye a faint blush crept into her cheeks.

Alfie smiled, a wistful look in his youthful eyes. It was a sweet moment.

Jamie gestured to the solitary spare chair. 'Mind if I join you?'

His voice ended the spell and Alfie broke eye contact with Emily. He felt bad for ruining their touching moment, but the kid didn't seem too distressed. 'Course not. Mind if I continue eating? I'm starving.'

'Be my guest.' Jamie sat down.

The other three kids sitting at the table were combining eating with tapping away on their phones. He had no idea whether they were homeless or not, but they were all pale and skinny, and he wouldn't bet against it. Strange that even homeless kids managed to own a device.

'Are you still delivering pizzas?' he asked Alfie.

The lad nodded. 'I don't know for how long.'

'I thought you liked having a job.'

'I do, but I don't want to deliver pizzas all my life. I've applied for loads of other things, but no one will take me on because I don't have a fixed address.' He ate more stew, washing it down with a mouthful of water. 'And I can't get a place to stay, because I haven't got a job.'

Jamie felt for him. 'Catch twenty-two, huh?'

'Plus, I don't have a deposit or anyone to give me a reference.'

Jamie remembered how challenging it had been when he'd first rented a place. The landlord had been reluctant to rent to a single lad only recently employed. He'd had to stump up six months' rent in advance and ask Peggy to be a guarantor. And that was despite him being in full-time employment with a regular income. How a kid like Alfie was supposed to meet those demands, he had no idea.

'What about Housing Benefit?' he asked, wishing he could find a solution. 'Or that new one they've brought in, Universal Credit. Couldn't you apply for that?'

Alfie gave him a wry smile. 'You try finding a landlord willing to take on a homeless person on benefits. They don't want the hassle.'

Sadly, Jamie could believe it. 'Have you been to the council? Can't they help?'

'I'm on the housing list, but I'm not a priority,' he said, with a good-natured shrug. 'I'm eighteen. I wasn't in care. I'm not sick or disabled. There's always someone who needs it more than me when anything comes up.' He continued eating. 'I get it, but it's hard.'

Jamie felt bad for the kid. It wasn't like he wasn't trying to make his own way in the world, he just needed a leg-up. 'Are you still sleeping rough?'

'Most nights, yeah. I've managed to get a bed here a few nights, but they've made the cut off earlier, so even if I'm working a day shift I miss out.' He shrugged. 'It is what it is.'

'You don't have any family?'

Alfie raised an eyebrow. 'Not any that give a crap.'

Jamie could relate to that. 'I wish I could help.'

'Nothing you can do, mate. But thanks, anyway. It helps coming here,' he said, glancing at Emily again.

Jamie looked around at the bright décor. 'You don't find it too… you know, fancy?'

Alfie laughed. 'Yeah, mate. I really hate having to eat tasty free food, shower using hot water and grab a few hours' kip on the comfy sofas before heading back to work. It's a real torture.'

Put like that, Jamie felt stupid for asking.

Alfie took another mouthful of water. 'What's your story?'

'Mine?'

The lad nodded. 'People who volunteer in these places usually have a story. Ever been homeless?'

Jamie shook his head. 'Not homeless, no.' Although technically he supposed he had been in a way. He'd certainly felt homeless at the time. 'I was taken into care aged seven.'

Alfie ate another mouthful of stew. 'Adopted?'

'Long-term foster care.'

Alfie shook his head. 'No one wants you unless you're a cute baby, eh?'

'Something like that.'

As a kid, Jamie had wondered why no one had wanted him. The carers he'd stayed with were kind and looked after him, but he'd never really believed they wanted him.

As an adult, he'd discovered it was virtually impossible for a child beyond the age of seven to form a meaningful attachment with a new family. Hence why it was so hard to find adoptive parents willing to take on older kids. Of course, at the time he'd just thought it was his fault no one wanted him.

Alfie sighed. 'Bummer.'

'That about sums it up.' But as painful as it had been, his sadness lifted when he thought about Peggy. 'Things turned out okay in the end. My last placement was a proper home with a foster mother who genuinely cared about me.' Even loved him. Definitely loved him. 'We're still close.'

Alfie raised his glass. 'Well, you can't ask better than that.'

The kid was right. He couldn't.

They were interrupted by a shadow appearing across the table. It was like a storm cloud gathering, shrouding them in darkness, and he experienced a sudden sense of foreboding. When she cleared her throat, he knew the tornado was about to strike.

'I want a word with you.' Her voice was low yet threatening. 'The laundry room, now.'

Resigned to a bollocking, he was about to obey, when his phone rang. He glanced at the screen. His delivery had arrived. Thank God for that. The cavalry was here.

He turned to her. 'Hold that thought,' he said, getting up. 'There's something I need to do first.'

'Convenient.' Her hands went to her hips.

It was hard not to react to the sight of her in a dark red tie-dye shirt, open at the neck, revealing a flash of illuminated skin. She looked… hot. As in, heat. Nothing else, of course. Who was he trying to kid?

Ignoring her outraged expression, he turned back to Alfie. 'Nice chatting to you. Good luck with everything.'

'Cheers, mate. You too. See you around.' The boy returned to devouring his lunch.

Jamie side-stepped Sam, who refused to move.

'You're welcome to come with me.' He headed for reception. 'Something's arrived you might like.'

'The only thing I'd *like* is to throttle you,' she said, marching after him. 'What the hell was that all about on Tuesday with my parents?'

Good question. 'I was trying to be charming.'

'I noticed.' Her voice dripped with sarcasm. 'Mind telling me why?'

'Just trying to be nice.' He pushed through the door leading into reception.

She followed him. 'Nice? At one point, I was about to suggest you and my mother booked a room.'

He winced. 'I wasn't that bad.'

'Excuse me?' She was right behind him, nipping at his heels like an infuriated terrier. 'I'm honoured to meet you, Mrs Tipping... I mean, *Christina*,' she said, imitating his voice. 'Your charitable work is so worthy, *Christina*. Let me lick your feet, *Christina*.'

He spun around to face her. 'I did not sound like that.'

'Yes, you bloody well did. I wanted to throw up.' They were trapped alone in the lobby. 'And what was all that crap about, *Sam's told me so much about you*? I've done no such thing.'

'Poetic licence.'

'Complete bullshit, more like!'

He backed away. 'I thought it might help.'

'Help?' She advanced on him. 'Help how, exactly?'

He held up his hands, trying to keep her at bay. 'You clearly have a difficult relationship with your parents. I could see you were thrown by their visit and I thought a friendly mediator might ease the tension.'

'Mediator?' Her eyes flashed with rage.

'You know, like an impartial go-between.'

She threw her hands in the air. 'There was nothing impartial about your behaviour. You sided with my mother. You were fawning all over her.'

'I was not.'

'Yes, you were.' She moved so quickly, he had to back away. 'You intruded on a private family moment and then shoved me under a bus.'

'How did I shove you under a bus?'

'By bullying me into going to my mother's blessed soiree tomorrow.'

'Don't you want to go?'

Oh, if looks could kill. 'What do you think?'

His back was against the front door. She was right in his face. She had him cornered.

'Anyway, I didn't side with your mother,' he said, struggling not to stare at her exposed neck. 'I defended you, didn't I? I told them what a great job you're doing with the shelter.'

She looked incredulous. 'Someone's changed their tune. The other day you were full of criticism. You said I didn't know what I was doing.' She pointed a finger at him. 'You accused me of being spoilt and privileged—'

'No, I didn't.' A twinge of guilt tugged inside his chest.

'Yes, you bloody-well did!' She jabbed him in the arm. 'You've done nothing but find fault ever since you got here. You shamed my car, told me I wasn't helping these kids, and implied I knew nothing about what homeless people needed.'

'I was wrong.'

She stilled, her face so close he could feel her breath on his cheek. 'What?'

He struggled to swallow. It was hard to focus when a beautiful woman was so up close and personal. Especially an irate one. 'I said… I was wrong. I misjudged you.'

There was a long-drawn-out moment where she stared at him. He was backed against the door with no means of escape. Her cheeks were red from yelling and her wide blue eyes pinned him with such force he couldn't move if he wanted to. And he didn't want to.

Then his phone rang.

'Sorry, but I really need to be outside.' Fumbling behind him for the door handle, he almost fell through the front door.

'I'm not done yelling,' she said, following him outside.

'Then you'll have to do it out here. Your new washing machine has arrived.'

'My what?'

The large delivery truck had backed up to the doors. A man was unloading the wrapped unit onto the rear platform. He pressed a button and the platform began to lower.

Sam stared in disbelief. 'What's going on?'

He took a deep breath. 'You're spending a fortune on laundry bills, right?'

Her frown didn't let up. 'So?'

'So... I thought this might help.' He gestured to the large package. 'It's an Electrolux semi-commercial washing machine.'

Sam didn't move. Or say anything. She just stood there, stunned.

Jamie wasn't sure whether this was a good sign or a bad omen. Maybe she needed convincing. 'It's suitable for washing bedding and duvets and has an extra-large drum. It has an excellent energy rating efficiency and is especially designed for small businesses.'

The colour drained from her face. 'I didn't order this.'

'I know you didn't. I did.'

Her head turned slowly to face him. 'Why?'

'To make amends.' He shrugged. 'I knew I'd stepped over the line the other day. I'm sorry. I've been a bit of a shit to you since I started here. Unfairly so. This is my feeble way of apologising.'

Her confusion didn't lift. 'By ordering me a washing machine? A washing machine I can't afford? It must've cost a packet.'

'I'm not expecting you to pay for it.' His words rushed out. 'It's a present.'

She recoiled. 'A present?'

'A gift. From me to you... I mean, the shelter. I got it off eBay. A bed and breakfast was closing down and they were selling it off. They bought it new six months ago for over a grand, but I got it for two hundred quid.'

Still no reaction.

'Bargain, huh?'

A few seconds passed.

A few seconds more.

And then she burst out crying.

Like, really crying – the dropping to her knees, letting out huge sobs, and wailing kind of crying.

Oh, shit. What had he done?

Buying her a washing machine was supposed to be a nice gesture. An apology. A way of showing her he was in the wrong and that he wanted to make amends. It wasn't supposed to make her cry.

He glanced at the delivery bloke, hoping he might spring into action and come to his aid, but he looked as alarmed as Jamie did.

What the hell should he do? ...Comfort her? Or steer well clear? He was torn.

But before he could make a decision, the delivery driver held out the clipboard. 'I need a signature.'

'Right. Sorry.' Jamie went over to sign the docket, watching in dismay as Sam dragged herself to her feet and stumbled towards the building, mumbling an apology.

He was desperate to go after her, but he needed to deal with the delivery driver.

The driver handed Jamie the clipboard and nodded towards Sam's retreating back. 'What's her problem?'

Jamie winced as the door slammed shut behind her. 'No idea.'

But whatever it was, he'd been the trigger.

And that wasn't a great feeling.

Chapter Twelve

Saturday, 24th November

Sam stared at her reflection in the mirror. She looked like a dismembered swan. What had her mother been thinking? She swivelled one way and then the other, hoping the sight of the ankle-length white feathered gown might improve on closer inspection. It didn't. She didn't have enough cleavage to keep the dress up, the feathers made her skin itch, and it was so wide she could barely fit through the doorway. There was no way she was wearing this dress to her mother's soiree.

She reached behind and eased down the zip, letting the heavy garment drop to the floor. Placing it back inside the box, she re-covered it with the tissue paper and shoved it under her bed ready to return to her mother, along with the sky-high white Manolo Blahnik stilettoes she couldn't stand up in, let alone walk in.

Her mother would be disappointed, but it wasn't like she hadn't tried. The dress just wasn't for her.

Sam wasn't like her mother. She didn't feel glamourous or confident wearing fancy clothing – she felt self-conscious and awkward. A white-feathered ball gown would invite attention. Comments. Stares. And that was the last thing she wanted when being forced to attend one of her mother's social events.

Hiding in the corner was more her style. The party wallflower. Happy to avoid scrutiny and let everyone else take centre-stage.

But she knew turning up wearing casual clothes wasn't an option either. She'd stand out even more than wearing a ball gown – like the only person at a fancy-dress party not in costume.

Therefore, it was just as well she had a back-up dress stored away in her wardrobe.

She'd bought the garment a couple of years ago from a charity shop in Kensington. It was amazing what you could pick up second-hand in the posh areas of town. The purchase itself had been a spur of the moment decision and one that was completely out of character. But she was glad she'd splashed out now as it meant she could wear something to her mother's event she actually liked.

Plus, it was designer, so her mother couldn't complain, right?

She unhooked the dress from its hanger and lifted away the protective covering. She held it up, hoping it was as special as she'd remembered.

It was.

The gown was a gorgeous dark teal colour and made from heavy silk that shimmered under the lighting. It was floor-length, with a fitted bodice and bias-cut skirt. Understated. Sophisticated. Not a feather in sight.

Unearthing her ancient black strappy sling-backs from the wardrobe, she slipped them on. They'd been worn so infrequently they still looked new. And besides, no one would see them under the long dress.

Stepping into the dress, she eased it up over her hips. The bodice was boned and off the shoulder, but it fitted perfectly and didn't dig in anywhere. Unlike the swan monstrosity, there was an extra sweep of material cut diagonally across the bodice to create a single shoulder-strap, so there was no danger of the dress slipping down and her flashing her mother's guests. Which was just as well. Her mother liked notoriety, not scandal.

Sam turned to face the mirror. Her up-do hairstyle still worked with the new dress, and her late grandmother's diamond-drop earrings provided a hint of glamour. She'd chosen a muted red lipstick and squirted on the Dolce & Gabbana Light Blue eau de toilette Max had bought her for her birthday. There was absolutely no way her mother could accuse her of 'not making an effort' with her appearance.

Right. Time to go.

She dropped her phone and twenty quid cash into her black clutch bag, and had just picked up her car keys, when someone knocked on the door.

Frowning, she went to answer it. She wasn't expecting anyone. It was probably the Deliveroo driver for next door. They were always getting the flat numbers mixed up.

But it was Jamie Lawson.

He was wearing a smart black tuxedo suit, with a white dress shirt and a hand-tied silk bow tie. His hair was fashionably styled and he was clean-shaven… and if she'd ever been in any doubt about the level of his attractiveness, she wasn't now.

He looked… gorgeous. And hot. So much so, words failed her. All she could do was stare – open-mouthed – which would normally have been excruciatingly embar-rassing and evoke a sarcastic retort from the man standing in front of her looking all… James Bond, but he appeared to be suffering from the same affliction as her.

'His eyes widened. His lips parted. And his gaze travelled slowly downwards and then back up, settling on her face. 'Wow,' he said, swallowing awkwardly. 'You look... beautiful.'

'Thanks.' Her hand came up self-consciously to touch her exposed neck. 'You don't scrub up so badly yourself.'

It wasn't the most sophisticated of compliments, but her vocabulary was seriously impeded by the sight of him all dressed up. Not to mention the humiliation of him witnessing her emotional breakdown yesterday.

'What are you doing here?' she finally managed.

'I'm your plus-one.' His eyes were fixated on her bare shoulders. 'I'm here to escort you to your mother's soiree.'

'Escort me? This isn't the eighteenth century.'

'It's still good manners for the man to pick up the lady.' Then he flinched. 'Sorry, woman. I wouldn't want you to accuse me of being sexist as well as old-fashioned.'

She rolled her eyes. 'Heaven forbid.'

'And after yesterday...' He paused, as if fearful of setting her off again. 'I wasn't sure if you were still angry with me. I didn't want to show up at your parents' house and risk another... you know...' he trailed off.

'Meltdown?'

He nodded. 'Also, I have no idea where your parents live.'

'Blast.' She snapped her fingers. 'Did I forget to tell you?'

He gave her a wry smile. 'I get it. You didn't want me to come, which I totally understand. But I promise to be on my best behaviour. No judgemental remarks. No sarcasm. Just someone who has your back.'

She viewed him sceptically. 'For real?'

'You have my word. Think of me as your wingman. Someone to help you get through the evening. Plus, I thought you might want to drink. It's a party after all, and I'm guessing you don't get to socialise much these days. Wouldn't you like to relax and enjoy yourself and not have to worry about driving?'

He was right.

Not that spending an evening at one of her mother's soirees was her idea of fun, but she could certainly do with a distraction. Her stress levels had reached boiling point. As evidenced yesterday when she'd burst into hysterical tears over a bleedin' washing machine.

'Fine.' She stepped out of the door. 'But one snarky comment and we're done, okay?'

'Okay.' He smiled – a big open smile that crinkled the corners of his eyes – the impact of which nearly knocked her off her feet.

Christ, and she hadn't even started drinking yet.

She closed the door behind her and accepted the offer of his arm as he led her down the pathway to the street.

'It's not a patch on your car,' he said, opening the passenger door of the black Vauxhall Corsa parked by the kerb. 'But I promise it's clean.'

'It's fine,' she said, climbing in. Contrary to what he might think, she wasn't someone who judged a person by their mode of transportation.

She rubbed her arms. The good weather of late had tailed off and she wondered whether she should have brought a coat. Not that she owned anything suitable. Her wardrobe was seriously devoid of evening wraps. Funny that.

Jamie climbed in the driver's side and started the engine. 'Are you cold?'

'A bit.'

He turned up the heater.

As he pulled away, she noticed he didn't have a satnav. But he seemed to be heading in the right direction, so she kept quiet.

They turned onto Tooting Bec Road and headed past Clapham Common, the expanse of greenery and trees masked by the darkness.

'So, about yesterday…' He glanced in her direction. 'You rushed off and I never got the chance to check you were okay. I searched for you, but Norah said you'd gone home. She said you weren't feeling too good.'

Understatement, if ever there was one. When Norah had found her in the toilets, Sam was curled up on the floor, spent from crying her eyes out. Talk about humiliating. But Norah had assured her it was just exhaustion and told her that she should go home and get some sleep. Which is what Sam had done. Mostly because she hadn't wanted to face Jamie.

'Sorry about that. I was feeling a little stressed.'

'Do you mind if I ask why?'

How much should she divulge?

She supposed there was no harm in admitting she was struggling. 'A combination of things, I guess. I haven't taken much time off over the last year, what with trying to get The Crash Pad up and running.' She'd been working twelve-hour days, seven days a week, for a long as she could remember. 'I don't get much sleep when I'm covering the night shift. And even when I'm not working nights, I lay awake at home worrying about the shelter. Worrying about what happens to the people we turn away. Worrying about not having enough money to keep the project running. And worrying about the safety of those who do stay at the shelter. It's exhausting.'

'It sounds it.'

She focused on the lights flickering on the Thames as they crossed Wandsworth Bridge. 'No matter how much we do, there always seems to be another challenge to overcome.'

His fingers tapped thoughtfully against the steering wheel. 'Not helped by dickheads like me making snarky comments.'

'It doesn't help, no.'

He grimaced. 'Sorry.'

'It's not just you. My stress levels have been building ever since we opened. And then yesterday… Well, I think my pressure valve finally erupted.'

'I'm sorry for making you cry.'

'It wasn't your fault. You were trying to do something nice. And it *was* nice. It was thoughtful and kind… it's just—'

'Just what?'

She paused. 'It made me feel inadequate.'

'Inadequate? How so?'

'Replacing the washing machine for an industrial unit was on my to-do list. Along with a load of other things I need, but haven't bought yet, because I've almost run out of money.' She fiddled with the fabric of her dress. 'And then you show up with a fancy-pants commercial washing machine, like it's no big deal, and… I…'

He glanced at her, but didn't say anything.

'Oh, I don't know. Part of me felt relieved. Part of me was grateful. And the other part of me wanted to punch your lights out.'

He frowned. 'Why?'

'For interfering. For resolving a problem that was mine and no one else's. It infuriated me.' She smoothed down her dress, realising she'd been creasing it. 'I know that sounds crazy.'

'A bit.'

She shot him a glare.

'I didn't mean it like that,' he backtracked, reaching out to touch her arm and then recoiling, as if realising it was a bad idea. 'But aren't you always saying that running the shelter is a team effort? Everyone pitches in. This was my way of helping. We haven't exactly got off to the best start. I needed to make amends. Especially after Tuesday.'

'Thanks for reminding me,' she said, groaning. 'And people wonder why I'm stressed?'

A beat passed. 'What's the deal with you and your parents?'

She didn't immediately answer.

They turned onto Holland Park Avenue and drove passed the rows of grand Georgian houses. Each one an advert for what life was like for the fortunate few.

Eventually, she said, 'We don't see eye-to-eye.'

'About what?'

'About everything.' Resting her hand on the door handle, she glanced down at her manicured blood-red nails. 'I've always been the odd one out. They've disagreed with every decision I've ever made. My choice of friends. The university I went to. My career as a social worker. It was never what they wanted.'

'What did they want?'

She sighed. 'For me to be a plastic surgeon, like my sister. Or a fat-cat city banker, like my brother. A respectable career, with a lucrative salary and an impressive standing in the community. Something they could boast about to their friends.' She'd scrunched up her dress again and had to prise her hands away from the fabric.

'But you never wanted that?'

Sam shook her head. 'I think they hoped with enough persuasion I'd eventually see the light and switch paths. But when I sold my apartment to start up The Crash Pad they finally realised it wasn't going to happen.'

'I sense your parents don't support the project?'

'God, no. For months they tried to talk me out of it. But I refused to cave-in. I was determined to do something useful with my life.'

For a long while he didn't speak and concentrated on driving. He seemed conflicted; his expression was one of puzzlement, as though he was struggling to understand her complex life. Join the club, she wanted to say.

The tip of the Italianate Pump House in Battersea Park came into view along with the stadium lights of Stamford Bridge as they entered the borough of Kensington.

After another long pause, he said, 'You have done something useful with your life. The Crash Pad is something you should be really proud of.'

'Excuse me?' Surprise nearly had her sliding off the seat. 'You've changed your opinion.'

'Not really. I always thought it was a great venture. I just...' he trailed off.

'Just what?'

He rubbed the back of his neck. 'I assumed your parents had bankrolled you, and it was a pet project you'd drop the moment things got tough.' He gave her a sheepish smile. 'Sorry.'

'Ah, so that's why you've been such a shit to me? It makes sense now.'

He cringed. 'But I know better now. And I get why you're so invested. You don't want your parents to be proved right.'

'That's not why I'm doing this,' she snapped, infuriated by the implication.

Jamie raised an eyebrow. 'No?'

'Well, not entirely.' She folded her arms defensively, not wanting to admit he might be right.

He laughed. 'Look, it's fine. We all need motivation. And maybe having that extra drive to make the shelter a success is what'll help you succeed.'

'Maybe.' She glanced out the window, realising where they were. 'Turn right into Royal Crescent and then left into St. James's Gardens.'

He followed her instructions, whistling when he saw the size of the properties ahead. 'Jesus. What number?'

'No number. Just head for the gates at the end.'

'The ones with the security hut outside?'

'Yup. Home sweet home.'

Jamie slowed the car. The security guards came out to meet them, no doubt suspicious of the less-than-impressive budget car approaching. Even the hired help were snobs.

'Are they going to shoot me?'

'I hope not. I need a ride home later.' She wound down the window and stuck her head out. 'It's me, guys.'

On seeing who it was, the guards scurried to open the gates. It wouldn't do to piss off the boss by denying her daughter access. They ushered them through the ornate gates.

Jamie peered through the windscreen. 'Where do I park?'

'You don't. Just pull up by the front door and give your keys to one of the parking attendants.'

'How stupid of me. Everyone has parking attendants, right?' He shook his head. 'And that is not a front door. Well, not like any door I've ever seen.'

'You're right. It's the gateway to hell, but unless you want to climb over the railings it's the only way into the house.'

He switched off the engine. 'That entrance is bigger than my whole flat.'

'Mine too,' she said, getting out of the car. 'We can feel inadequate together.'

He joined her on the gravel driveway. 'Need my jacket?'

'I'm fine.' She rubbed her arms. 'We'll be inside soon.'

'Sure about that?' He looked up at the three flights of marble steps ahead. 'That's quite a climb.'

When she laughed, he offered her his arm, which she accepted. No point being stubborn, especially as she needed all the support she could get. Plus, he was warm. And he smelt nice.

They walked up to the opulent white building with its black iron porch and glass ceiling. The raised flowerbeds either side were filled with exotic plants and ornamental grasses. A far cry from her rooftop garden in Streatham. The marble steps were lined with potted topiary bushes decorated in twinkling white fairy lights.

She shivered, more from nerves than the cold. She didn't enjoy attending events like these. She always felt like she was on show – another ornament to be admired. The expectation for her to 'behave' weighed heavily and she clutched Jamie's arm a little tighter.

He turned to her. 'Relax. What's the worst that can happen?'

'Oh, you have no idea. The last party I attended I tipped a bowl of fruit punch down Sadiq Khan's suit.'

Jamie stilled. 'The Mayor of London?'

'Not on purpose. But my mother was glaring at me, willing me to make a good impression and offer him a drink. I was so nervous my hands turned to jelly and the next thing I knew he was covered in punch.' She shivered at the memory. 'Believe me, I don't even have to try to make a bad impression. Nature did it for me.'

Jamie shook his head and chuckled. 'I can't believe the Mayor of London was at your house. Will he be here tonight?'

'Probably. Unless he knows I'm coming.'

Jamie dipped his head. 'If you're going to make a scene, can you let me know in advance?'

'Why? So you can hide?'

'No, so I can film it.' He dazzled her with that smile of his again, and she felt a little dizzy. 'Do you have any idea how much money I could make from a clip like that?'

She smiled back; she couldn't help it. She much preferred this Jamie to the prickly version she'd first encountered. 'I'll be sure and let you know.'

'Good.' He leant closer and she was hit by a wave of manly scent. 'And if at any point you want to leave, just let me know and we're out of here, okay?'

'Okay.' She nodded, touched by his kindness. 'Assuming you're not hooking up with my mother by then.'

'Funny.'

The grand black ornate doors ahead were decorated with two giant holly wreaths. They slowly opened as they approached and two footmen greeted them and showed them into the lobby.

Jamie's face was a picture when he saw the vast white space decorated with crystal chandeliers, vases of white flowers, and select ornaments and paintings, each one carefully chosen to enhance the space and evoke awe.

Centre-stage was a twenty-foot Christmas tree, shipped in from Norway no doubt, and trimmed with glass figurines and twinkling white lights. The star on top could rival anything the Milky Way had to offer. It glowed brightly, lighting up the whole lobby, like it had its own solar system.

Double doors ahead led them through to the drawing room, where the majority of guests mingled and chatted, clinking glasses and laughing.

An array of sparkling evening gowns glistened under the chandelier lighting, balanced by the sombre tuxedoes on display.

Sam recognised a few faces. Mainly other rich families they'd socialised with over the years. Lord and Lady Sabell were here with their daughter, Isabelle. Most likely Hylton Sabell would also be present, her brother's oldest and booziest friend, but she couldn't see him.

At the far end of the room, a six-piece jazz band were playing a swing version of 'Silent Night'. Waiters dressed in pristine uniforms circled with trays of champagne cocktails.

At the other end of the room a platform had been erected, no doubt for the auction later. Or maybe there would be an entertainer. She wouldn't be surprised if Frank Sinatra himself was on the bill. Her mother had connections in high places. Even Heaven.

'Talking of her mother. A flash of silver appeared in her periphery.

'Incoming missile,' she whispered to Jamie. 'The mothership is about to land.'

'Samantha, darling!' Her mother's voice penetrated the collective chatter in the room and the jazz band. Quite a feat. She arrived, all smiles and kisses, enveloping her daughter in a hug that didn't actually involve any touching – a talent of the rich. 'I almost didn't recognise you.' Her sharp eyes scanned Sam's appearance. 'Why aren't you wearing the dress I sent you?'

'It didn't fit,' she lied, avoiding eye-contact.

'I suppose you have lost weight,' her mother said, with a suspicious look. 'Is that dress couture?'

'Of course.' Although made for someone else – and several years ago. But she wasn't about to mention that.

'Well, that's something.'

'She looks stunning, doesn't she?' Jamie's voice attracted her mother's attention. 'As do you, Christina.'

It was true, her mother was a vision in a floor-length silver gown, complete with chiffon train and bespoke Sabell & Sutton necklace – worn no doubt to impress the owners, who'd joined her father over by the cocktail bar. 'Why, thank you.' She held out her hand, which Jamie dutifully took.

'Thank you again for inviting me, Christina.'

God, he could lay on the charm.

'My pleasure.' She gave him the once over, clearly impressed by what she saw. 'Remind me to introduce you to my bridge ladies later. They'll enjoy meeting you.'

'*Devouring* you more like.' Sam's hushed comment induced a nudge from Jamie, who whispered, 'Behave.'

Her mother's astute gaze flitted between them. 'Remind me again what you do, Jamie?'

He looked startled. 'What I do?'

'Yes, what line of business are you in?'

Sam recognised the look in her mother's eye. Jamie was being assessed as suitable beau material.

God, she really hoped he said something like 'bin collector' or 'shop cashier'. Not that she had anything against those professions. Far from it. But she knew it would freak out her mother. Come to think of it, what did Jamie do? He'd never really said.

He was prevented from answering by her brother and a woman approaching.

'Hey, Sammy! Look at you, all dressed up.' Max crushed her in a hug, evoking a tut from their mother.

'And look at you,' she said, pulling away and nodding to his blue velvet blazer. 'Where's your comets, Bill Hayley?'

'Hey, this is Armani. It cost over two grand.'

'So did my car, but I wouldn't wear it to a party.'

He poked his tongue out at her.

Her mother tutted again and checked to make sure no one had seen her son's inappropriate behaviour. 'Really, Maxim. Show a little more decorum, please.'

'I think he looks hot,' the blond woman with him said, straightening his matching blue velvet bowtie. 'A real stud.'

Stud? Sam supressed a laugh. 'I'm just glad he didn't opt for the matching shoes,' she said, winking at her brother.

Her brother poked his tongue out again.

'Children, please,' her mother said through gritted teeth, still managing to smile at her guests.

Max nodded to the woman draped over him. 'This is Xanthe. She's a model.'

'And *girlfriend*,' Xanthe said loudly, making her brother and her mother simultaneously flinch. 'Pleased to meet you.'

'Pleased to meet you too.' Sam smiled. Mostly because of the horrified look on her mother's face.

Xanthe was definitely not suitable girlfriend material, her appearance was far too risqué and provocative. Her white dress was slashed to the crotch revealing long tanned legs, and the top section of her dress had so many cut-outs Sam was surprised it stayed in place. The woman had enormous boobs and the material was barely covering them. One ill-timed sneeze and they'd overspill for sure.

Her mother was glowering. She was far from charmed.

Max on the other hand looked smitten.

Sam turned to Jamie, wondering what he made of Xanthe. She expected him to be as fixated on the stunning blonde as her brother was, but she discovered he was looking directly at her. 'Drink?' he said, nodding to a nearby waiter.

'God, yes,' she said, leaning into him. 'A large one.'

He grinned. 'Coming right up.'

Thank God for Jamie.

...Now there was a sentence she'd never imagined herself saying.

Chapter Thirteen

Jamie couldn't believe what he was witnessing. He'd spent the last two hours wandering from room to room with his mouth hanging open. Part in awe, part horrified by the extravagance on show. A hot cocoa bar. Chocolate fountains with guests coating pink marshmallows under the cascade of melted Swiss confectionary. A photographer taking portraits against the backdrop of picturesque falling snow – indoors. And a cocktail bar offering all manner of tipples – including wines and champagnes that usually cost several hundred quid a bottle. All for free. And all at his disposal.

But the ultimate display of wealth had come during the auction. A signed Anthony Joshua boxing glove sold for eight hundred quid. A George Michael print by Daniel Mernagh fetched over six hundred pounds. And a luxury seven-night stay in an exclusive villa on Bali had gone for thousands. It was crazy. And fascinating. And very confusing.

Not least, because the information he'd been able to glean about Max Tipping was puzzling. Jamie had surreptitiously watched the guy interact with those around him all evening. His behaviour was loud and laddish with men of his own age, flirtatious and suave with women of any age, and focused and congenial with dignitaries, business moguls and members of parliament, regardless of age. Sadiq Khan might not be here, but several other MPs were. Along with TV celebrities and sports stars. Max Tipping charmed them all.

When Jamie had tried to explore the house under the guise of needing the loo, he'd been redirected to a suite of lavatories set up outside in a marquee for the guests to use. Nothing like the disgusting affairs he'd experienced at Glastonbury, but fancy units with sensor-flushing loos, warm-air hand dryers and a selection of festive-scented handwashes on offer.

So here he was, at gone eleven p.m, still no closer to discovering whether Max Tipping was a misunderstood philanthropist, or a money-laundering crook.

He sipped his zero-alcohol lager and looked around the packed room. The band had resumed playing and several guests were dancing to 'Rockin' Around the Christmas Tree'. Others were standing in groups chatting, or had spilled onto the patio to escape the heat of the room.

Christina and Richard Tipping were entertaining a group of business types over by the baby grand, and Max Tipping was talking to a Southampton footballer, whose name Jamie couldn't remember. Max's date for the evening was hanging on his arm, although her seductive pout was aimed squarely at the footballer.

Jamie searched for Sam. He found her trapped in a circle of men, looking pained. She was nodding and smiling, but he could tell she wasn't enjoying it. She glanced over and caught his eye. Her expression said, 'help me.'

He made his way through the crowd, avoiding elbows and wayward drinks.

For someone who usually adopted the casual look, she certainly could pull off glamour. He'd nearly fainted when she'd opened the door to him earlier. He wasn't sure which had floored him most, the sight of her exposed shoulders revealing the curve of her long neck or the way her dark red lipstick had emphasised her full lips. Throw in her smoky dark eyes and the fit of her dress enhancing her slender figure, and it'd taken him a good few seconds to formulate a coherent sentence.

Yet strangely, Jamie still preferred her casually dressed. She didn't look right dressed up. There was no doubt she was a beautiful woman, but she didn't look relaxed. Her smile was forced and her posture was stiff and rigid. When she was at the shelter she was animated and energised. Slightly clumsy, and never restrained. But tonight, she was liked a caged tigress, miserable from being imprisoned, and eager to escape her shackles.

When he reached her, he heard the man next to her say, '…so you see, Samantha darling. These homeless types do tend to bring it on themselves.'

Sensing she needed rescuing, he edged his way into the circle. 'Apologies for interrupting. You promised me a tour of the house, Sam.'

Her smile radiated relief. 'You're right, I did. Excuse me, gentleman. Thank you for your time this evening. Enjoy the party.'

He took her hand and led her away. 'Networking not going well?'

She shook her head, making her dangly earrings sway. 'It's a disaster. I don't know why I thought these people would care. They're only interested in charitable ventures that look good on their Forbes Rich List profiles. One woman actually suggested I redirect my efforts towards a more worthwhile cause. Do you know what she came up with? A care home for retired opera singers.'

He laughed, but caught her when she stumbled. 'How much have you had to drink?'

'Not nearly enough,' she said, straightening. 'And it's too crowded in here.'

She redirected him into the grand lobby and up the sweeping staircase, lined with swathes of thick mistletoe and lit with fancy candles that smelt of vanilla and nutmeg.

His eyes scanned the walls, looking for family photos or clues about Max Tipping's life. But his gaze kept reverting to the curve of Sam's neck and the expanse of pale flesh running from her hairline down to the bodice of her dress. It was hard not to stare.

'This is my old bedroom,' she said, opening a door off the hallway. 'Cosy, isn't it?'

She kicked off her shoes and jumped onto the huge white bed, bouncing on top of it and flopping back, spreading her arms out.

He leant against the doorframe. 'Are you being sarcastic?'

'You think?'

The space was divided into two, each area bigger than the entire footprint of his flat. Two steps led from the bedroom down to the lounge area, complete with huge flat-screen TV and built-in log-burner. It was an impressive space, stylish and classy. And very white. The walls were painted white. The accessories were white. The cushions and throws were variations of white. The wooden flooring was a pale grey-white. Talk about cold.

The only colour came from Sam's dress, a wash of teal against the white covers beneath.

'Was it like this when you lived here?'

'God, no.' She wriggled up the bed, leaning against the pillows behind and messing up their strategic placement. 'You can come in, you know.'

He glanced behind him into the hallway. 'Supposing your parents come up. Won't they worry about finding a strange man in your bedroom?'

'Like they'd care, or notice. They're too busy schmoozing downstairs.'

He came into the room and closed the door. 'So what did this room look like before?' He glanced around, trying to imagine a younger version of Sam. 'I'm guessing lots of pink. Dolls on the bed. And a stack of medals and rosettes from winning horse-riding competitions.'

She laughed. 'Is that how you see me?'

He tried to envisage her as a teenager. 'Justin Timberlake, Gareth Gates and Westlife posters on the walls.' He pointed at the skylight above. 'Fairy-lights and glow-in-the-dark stars and moon stickers on the ceiling.' He came over to the bed. 'A locked diary in your bedside cabinet covered in hearts, and a Girls Aloud duvet cover.'

She shook her head. 'You couldn't be more wrong.'

'Enlighten me.' He leant against the fitted wardrobes running the length of the room.

'I did have posters,' she said, shuffling to a cross-legged position. 'But they weren't of popstars. They were mostly anti-war posters. Or ones promoting peace and veganism. The Gay Pride ones never lasted long. Every time I returned from boarding school they'd been removed.'

'You went to boarding school?'

She grabbed a cushion and hugged it to her chest. 'Up until the age of sixteen, when to my parents' horror I refused to attend finishing school in Switzerland and enrolled in the local sixth-form college.'

He tilted his head. Sam Tipping was full of surprises. 'I bet that went down well.'

'Only surpassed by my opting to study social work at a non-red brick university. In Wales, no less.' She faked a gasp, her hand coming up to her neck. 'Oh, the shame of it.' Climbing off the bed, she discarded the cushion. 'For the first year, they insisted I holiday with them in the Alps and attend the usual calendar events like the polo and Royal Ascot, as I'd done many years before. But they soon gave up when I kept disappearing off to music festivals and arranging camping trips with my hippy uni friends.'

'A bit of a rebel, huh?'

She stopped, as if considering the thought. 'I didn't mean to be. I think it was just due to the age gap.' She wandered over to him, lifting her dress when she trod on the hem. 'I was a 'welcome surprise', born ten years after my brother and twelve years after my sister. It was like growing up an only child. I was the odd one out. They wanted to attend lavish functions and holiday in exotic destinations, whereas I wanted to go on sponsored walks and attend rallies protesting animal testing. It wasn't exactly an ideal fit.'

He guessed it wouldn't be. 'It was brave of you to follow your own path, though.'

'Or stupid.' She sighed. 'Life would've been a lot easier if I'd succumbed to their demands.' She slumped against the wardrobes, her expression sad.

He had a sudden urge to reach out and touch her. She looked so vulnerable.

He didn't, of course.

'The real insult came when I sold the Dulwich flat they'd bought for me for my twenty-first birthday and used the money to set up The Crash Pad.' She inspected her red nails. 'I wasn't very popular.'

'I imagine you weren't.'

She pushed away from the wardrobes. 'Like I said, I'm either very stupid or very brave. Come on, I need some fresh air. The champagne is making me talk nonsense.' Her hand slipped into his and she led him over to the door. 'I need food.'

So much for being an investigative journalist. He was putty in this woman's hands.

But instead of heading back to the party where buffet food was being restocked throughout the evening, she led him down the less-grand back stairs.

'Where are we going?' he asked, realising they were entering the servants' quarters. He felt like he was in a modern-day episode of Downton Abbey.

'Kitchen. Halloumi Bites and Beetroot Blinis won't suffice. I need real food.' She still had hold of his hand. He didn't mind – which was strange, as he didn't usually like hand-holding. Or, at least, he never had before. But her hand was warm and soft and he was in no hurry to let go.

The kitchen looked like something from a fancy hotel. It was huge, with a mass of steel worktops and chefs running about in white tunics.

A tiny dark-haired woman appeared wearing a black uniform. 'Miss Samantha!'

'Altamira!' Sam hugged the woman.

The woman cupped Sam's face in her hands. '*Minha querida. Tão bonito.*'

'It's so good to see you.' She hugged the woman again, almost crushing her. 'This is our housekeeper,' she said, turning to Jamie. 'I love her more than anyone else in my family.'

The woman wiped away a tear. '*Eu também a amo.*' And then she addressed Jamie. 'She a good girl.'

Sam smiled. 'This is my friend, Jamie.'

The woman gave Sam a sly look. 'Handsome, no?'

Sam's cheeks coloured. 'He's just a friend. A work colleague.'

'He make nice boyfriend.' The woman winked at Jamie. 'Miss Samantha beautiful, no?'

Jamie caught Sam's eye, and for a moment the noise in the kitchen faded away.

Her blue eyes held his and her cheeks glowed from the champagne, and once again he was knocked sideways by just how stunning she was. 'Very beautiful.'

The woman nudged Sam. 'See? He like you.'

'Honestly, what with you and my mother.' She gave him an apologetic smile. 'Sorry.'

Another lingering look followed that sent a wave of heat rushing to his face. He loosened his shirt collar, unsure quite what was happening. But then she seemed to shake away whatever thought she was having and the moment was gone. 'Altamira, are you serving chilli wraps?'

'At midnight. Not before. Madam Christina's instructions.'

Sam slipped her arm around the tiny housekeeper. 'It's very nearly midnight. Only twenty minutes to go. Can we please sneak ours now?'

The woman smiled. 'You don't tell Madam Christina.'

Sam crossed her heart. 'My lips are sealed.'

And such nice lips, he thought, before checking himself. Where had that come from?

'You vegan too?' the woman asked him.

'Err... no.'

She looked pleased. 'See? Perfect boyfriend. Meat on his bones.' She squeezed his bicep and then giggled naughtily.

It was an eye-opening insight into Sam Tipping's world. Not the perfectly presented façade upstairs with its designer décor and who's-who guest list of acquaintances, but a glimpse of the real Sam. The woman he saw at the shelter, looking after homeless teenagers and caring for her volunteers. She was more at home and intimate with the housekeeper than she was with the rest of her family.

Jamie was starting to realise just how much he'd misjudged her.

Armed with an ice-bucket of chilled champagne and their chilli wraps – his filled with beef and hers a spicy bean-mix – they snuck out the backdoor and into the gardens.

'This way,' she said, leading him across the lawn to the swimming pool.

They descended the steps down to the poolside. It was cut in a large kidney shape, surrounded by plants and palm trees. On one side a canopy provided shelter, under which an outhouse contained several individual changing rooms. The other side was open-plan, leading seamlessly into the grounds, like an infinity pool, but with lawn rather than sea.

'Here,' she said, sitting by the edge of the smaller section of pool. 'It's heated, I promise.' She tucked her skirt between her legs and dangled her legs in the water, her face radiating pure bliss. 'Lovely!' She wiggled her toes. 'Take off your shoes and socks.'

He hesitated for a second and then thought, what the hell, and did as she suggested.

Rolling up his trouser legs, he sat beside her. She was right. The water was bath-warm. It was glorious.

She paddled her legs in the water. 'How's your chilli wrap?'

He took another bite, savouring the kick of spicy beef. 'Delicious.'

'Fab, aren't they? Altamira's an amazing cook. Although I think she cursed me as a teenager. She'd never encountered a vegan before. I don't think they have them in Brazil.'

'What age did you become vegan?'

Sam chewed on her wrap. 'About fourteen, I think. We were on holiday in Mexico and a farmer was loading sheep into a rickety wooden truck. The truck was full, but he kept on herding more in. The sheep had to climb on top of each other because there was no room.'

He stopped eating his wrap.

'I screamed at my dad to do something, but he told me to stop making a scene. I ran over to the farmer and pleaded with him to stop, but he didn't understand me. The only person who tried to help was Max, but the farmer shooed him away. My dad told my brother off for interfering.'

Another insight into the Tipping family dynamic.

Lifting the champagne bottle from the ice bucket, she eased off the metal clasp. The cork released with a bang and shot into the air. 'Bubbles?'

'Better not, I'm driving.'

'Mind if I do?'

'Course not.'

She poured a flute and took a long sip. 'I needed that.'

He placed his chilli wrap on the ground next to him. 'Are you close to Max?'

With a small sigh, she looked up at the clear sky. 'In a way. Certainly closer than I am with either my parents or my sister. Tara lives in LA, so we rarely see her. She's a high-flying plastic surgeon. You'd be shocked if I told you some of the A-listers she's had under the knife.' Jamie could well believe it. 'Max is equally driven. He loves his job and makes shed-loads of money.'

But does he do it legitimately, Jamie wondered?

'But he has a softer side too. I've lost count of the number of mates he's bailed out when a business venture has gone belly-up.'

Finally, something useful. 'Does he invest in the companies? Or buy them out?'

She took another sip of champagne. 'Neither. He just gives them the money they need to clear their debts. Or quit and start a new project. He's not in it for the money.'

'But you said he likes making money?'

'Oh, he does, but he also likes giving it away.' She turned to him and smiled. 'So you see, not all bad.'

'Has he invested in The Crash Pad?'

She shook her head. 'He would if I asked him to, but it's bad enough my parents are against the project. There's no need for Max to fall out with them as well.' She took another swig of champagne. 'And besides, if he invested he'd only want to take over, or start telling me how to run the place. As he has no clue about life as a homeless person, I'm not about to invite his opinion.'

A beat passed, before she suddenly laughed.

'What's so funny?'

'I was expecting a snarky comment about me not having a clue about being homeless either.'

'I've already apologised for that,' he said, feeling guilty for ever having made her feel that way. 'And I promised not to make any snide remarks tonight. I've kept my promise, haven't I?'

Knocking back the rest of her champagne, she got to her feet, wobbling a bit in the process. 'You have.'

'What are you doing?'

'Swimming.' She unzipped her dress. 'Coming?'

'Are you crazy? No way.' His brain told him to look away. His eyes refused to budge. The teal dress loosened and then slid down her body, landing in a heap by her feet.

Holy crap.

She stood there wearing only a black strapless bra and lace knickers.

His brain nearly exploded.

She stepped out of the dress and lowered herself into the pool.

Her skin shone under the moonlight and her smile cut through the darkness like a laser beam. She looked serene and angelic. Like a mermaid. Perfectly at home in the water.

Jamie, on the other hand, was struggling to breathe.

'Sure you won't come in?' She crooked her finger at him. 'It's lovely.'

He shook his head, his eyes locked on hers.

She extended her arms and circled, gliding through the water with seemingly no effort. And then she swam over to him, the water barely moving.

When she reached him, she rested her arms on his thighs and looked up at him. 'Are you having a nice evening?'

Unable to speak, he simply nodded.

When she smiled, something shifted in his chest. What was happening? And then she pushed herself up and brushed her lips softly against his.

Holy crap.

'You taste of chilli,' she said, kissing him again, this time letting her lips linger a little longer. 'And heat.' Another kiss, this one longer, her lips parting, moist and incredibly tantalising.

He opened his mouth to speak. To point out that she was tipsy. That this wasn't a good idea. That she'd be mortified in the morning when she remembered what she'd done. But no words would come. Only a response to her questioning kiss, asking him, teasing him, inviting him to kiss her back — so he did. He was powerless to refuse, unable to pull away.

Her arms slid around his neck, pulling him closer. He could feel the wet seeping through his shirt. She was pressed against him, kissing him, drawing him in.

It was like being drugged. He was paralysed. Not by fear, by lust.

He wasn't aware of moving, until his hands registered the sensation of her skin. He was touching her. His fingers splayed across her back, her ribcage, moving of their own accord, exploring the curves of her body.

He began to shake. Whether it was cold, or panic, or pure desire, he had no idea. But his whole body pulsed with electricity, his resistance seeping away with every stroke of her tongue, her hands, laced into his hair, pulling him closer.

And then an explosion.

A loud bang above, followed by a whizzing sound.

Far from breaking the moment, the noise spurred them on. The intensity of the kiss increased, gathering speed and energy, dragging him past the point of sanity.

Another explosion. A whizz. A bang.

He was unravelling.

His arms tightened around her. His mouth pushed against hers. His body reaching for her... desiring her... wanting her... and then he fell into the pool.

Shock was the first thing to hit followed by panic.

The water dragged him under, his suit weighing him down.

He heard muffled cries. Another explosion. Voices above.

And then hands on his collar, dragging him to the surface.

He gasped for air.

Another explosion. A glitter of red and gold filled the sky.

The sound of collective 'ooos' and 'ahhhs' from the gathering crowd.

Another bang. This one blue and silver.

Fireworks.

And then the sound of Christina Tipping's voice. 'Samantha! Are you... *naked!?*'

Chapter Fourteen

Thursday, 29th November

When Santa's sleigh flew across the room and smacked Emily on the head, she wondered if this was what hell would be like. It was certainly her own personal idea of hell.

Crammed inside a room packed with hundreds of people wasn't enjoyable. Especially when those people were stomping on the wooden flooring and singing along to 'All I Want For Christmas Is You'. Add in tacky red tinsel hanging from the ceiling, inflatable reindeer flying about and wilted mistletoe dangling from the doorways, and it was her worst nightmare.

But her fellow students didn't seem freaked out by watching the angel Gabriel flossing on the dance floor, or the sight of a giant penguin stuck in the doorway, its black bottom poking out from beneath its wobbly white body. Everybody else was having fun. It was only Emily who was counting down the minutes until she could escape.

Needing to keep herself busy, she bagged up the last of the disposable plates and carried the rubbish through to the college kitchens, holding her fluffy tail aloft so it didn't get trampled on.

She gazed down at her avocado-green furry onesie, complete with red-striped scarf and furry green mittens.

Thankfully, the Grinch outfit had come with a hood and a substantial set of facial whiskers, so her identity, like her anxiety, was well hidden.

Returning to the main hall, she discovered the penguin had made it through the doorway. The sight beyond revealed a gaggle of bodies dressed in the most bizarre and elaborate costumes imaginable. There were regular Christmas favourites such as snowmen, elves and shepherds, but far from wrapping themselves in a sheet and sticking a tea-towel over their heads, these people had taken dressing-up to a whole new level. Giant turkeys, a rotund Christmas pudding, and even a Christmas cracker – complete with 'Pull Me If You Want A Bang!' slogan attached to the front.

The low point was an apparition of Charles Dickens's decomposing ghost Marley appearing from nowhere and rattling in front of her, closely followed by the Ghost of Christmas Past. Despite logic dictating these were not undead beings, but real live bodies donned in cobwebs and fake blood, Emily recoiled as the warped skulls loomed at her through the pulsating lighting.

Recreating A Christmas Carol seemed to be of huge amusement to these particular students of London's South East College. But that's because they hadn't encountered the real underworld. They might not be so willing to party with the dead if they'd ever woken up next to a corpse. A memory that still haunted her to this day.

It was time to go home. Her nerves could only stand so much.

She made her way across the room, dodging wayward elbows and plastic cups of beer. She had brief encounters with a Victorian caroller and a scantily-clad Mrs Claus before finally making it outside. Freedom, at last.

It was gone 11:30 p.m. She'd lasted longer than anticipated. Thankfully, the buses were still running and she could catch a ride home. It was a dry night, no wind, so she was warm enough in her fur outfit as she headed to the bus stop. A few cars honked their horns as they drove past, her costume causing some amusement.

The bus arrived a few minutes later. It was virtually empty, something she was extremely grateful for. She headed upstairs and curled into a seat by the window, watching the distant streetlights flickering.

When a group of lads staggered onto the bus and started making drunken comments about her 'pussy', she decided it would be safer to get off and walk the rest of the way home.

As she ambled past Crystal Palace Park, she tried to see through the fencing, hoping for a glimpse of the dinosaurs hidden in the bushes. As a child, she'd always been fascinated by dinosaurs. When she'd first arrived in London, she'd frequently visited the park. They had a petting zoo, a maze and a boating lake, and she'd been happy to spend hours wandering around, climbing over the triceratops and forgetting the realities of her life. For a while, at least.

Turning onto Anerley Road, she made her way towards Gipsy Hill.

As the Tesco express came into view, a flash of green caught her eye. Several bodies were huddled in the doorway, bedded down for the night. It was too dark to recognise anyone, but there was something about the sight of a green beanie that made her slow.

Alfie owned a similar hat. Was it him?

She hesitated when she reached the corner and glanced back. The doorway was out of sight. Her brain told her to resume walking, go home, drink hot chocolate and sleep.

Her conscience told her to go back and check.

But what if it was him? What then? Would they engage in polite conversation, before she said goodnight and headed off home to her warm flat where a comfy bed awaited? Or would he be embarrassed for her to see him sleeping rough, vulnerable and dirty?

It was no good, she needed to find out. She'd never sleep otherwise.

Retracing her steps, she saw it was definitely Alfie. He'd moved from the doorway and was leaning against the wall, wearing a thick padded coat that looked too big for him and hung to his knees. 'You came back?' he said, smiling.

She stopped walking. 'You saw me?'

'You're not exactly easy to miss.'

She frowned. 'But my face is hidden under a hood. And I'm wearing whiskers.'

His smile didn't let up. 'And very cute you look too.'

She felt herself blush.

He pointed to her Doc Marten boots. 'I recognised the rainbow laces.'

'Oh.'

He gave her a questioning look. 'Just out of interest, why are you dressed as the Grinch?'

'Christmas party at college.'

'Ah, right. Fun?'

'Not really. I don't like parties.' She felt self-conscious, exposed as she stood around chatting dressed as a green, pot-bellied children's book character.

'Why did you go then?'

'I was part of the catering team. Fancy dress was a mandatory requirement.' She moved out of the way when a couple tried to pass with their dog, which pricked up his ears — until he realised she wasn't a real feline and ambled off unimpressed.

She turned back to Alfie. 'No luck at the shelter tonight?'

'The beds had all gone by the time I got there. But I made good tips delivering pizzas, despite being given the wonky scooter, so not all bad.'

She looked at the solitary blanket by his feet. 'Is that all you have?'

'It's enough. It keeps me dry.' A commotion by the Tesco express doorway made him look over. Another homeless person was trying to make room to lie down. 'I'd better go. Looks like I've got competition for my space.' He picked up his rucksack. 'Will you be at the shelter tomorrow?'

She nodded, feeling like she should do something, but wasn't sure what. 'I don't have morning classes on a Friday, so I'll be on the lunchtime shift.'

He smiled. 'Good. See you there. Night, Emily.'

'Night.' But as he walked off, something made her say, 'You could stay at my place tonight.'

He stopped, but didn't turn back.

'It's not fancy, or anything. And you'd have to sleep on the sofa, but it's better than a doorway.'

A beat passed before he turned. 'Are you sure? Will your landlord be okay about it?'

She hadn't thought about that. But it was too late now, she couldn't retract her offer, it would be cruel. 'Of course,' she lied, knowing damn well her tenancy agreement didn't allow for co-inhabitants. But it was only for one night. And no one would know. And she couldn't walk away and leave him to sleep rough. She just couldn't. 'So do you want to come back with me?'

'Christ, yes.' He slung his rucksack over his shoulder. 'This is really kind of you, Emily. Thank you.'

'No problem.'

Except it was.

She was inviting a man back to her flat. Something she'd never done before. Something she shouldn't be doing. It wasn't sensible. Or safe. Had she learnt nothing from living on the streets? Never let your guard down. The moment you did, trouble happened.

But this was Alfie. Kind, sweet, ever-smiling, Alfie. Who complimented her cooking, encouraged her dreams, and wanted to make something of his life.

She glanced over.

But could she trust him? She knew nothing about him. Chatting at the shelter wasn't the same as inviting someone into your home. Maybe she should have kept walking and not gone back.

She fiddled with her hands, glad her mittens prevented her from biting her nails.

'So why don't you like parties?' he asked, as they walked past Norwood library.

'Too noisy. Too crowded.'

'Didn't you go to parties as a kid?'

She cast her mind back. 'Not really. I was an only child. And Mum wasn't well a lot of the time, so I stayed home to look after her.'

'That must've been hard.'

'I never minded.' Which was true, certainly in the early days. Caring for her mum had been like playing with a giant doll. She'd tuck her up in bed, spoon-feed her soup and sing nursery songs until she fell asleep. It was only when her mother's behaviour became violent that it stopped being fun. 'Did you go to parties?'

He nodded. 'When I was younger, yes. But then—' He pulled her out of the way when a lad on a pushbike mounted the pavement. 'Hey! Watch where you're going, mate.'

'Sorry!' The lad rode off.

Alfie tutted. 'Idiot. You okay?'

'Fine.' She wanted to tell him she could look after herself. That she'd survived on the streets a lot longer than he had. But she didn't. He was just looking out for her. And she'd never really had that. Someone who gave a damn. It was an alien feeling.

They resumed walking.

'You were about to tell me about when you were young?'

'Oh, right, yeah. Well, my dad left when I was five. Up until then things were fine. Even when he left and it was just me and Mum, we were happy. But then she married my step-dad and the dynamics changed.'

'Didn't you get on?'

'It wasn't that.' He paused, as if in thought. 'I guess it's hard trying to parent someone else's kid. I didn't like him telling me what to do and he didn't want to be seen backing down. We argued a lot.'

They walked by the Thai restaurant. The door opened and a waft of fragrant spices filled the air. 'What did your mum do?'

'Not a lot,' he said, as a man emerged with a takeaway bag. Alfie eyed the food enviously. 'I don't think she wanted the hassle.'

Emily pointed ahead. 'This is me, on the left.'

He turned to look at the block of redbrick flats. They weren't anything special to look at, just rows of soulless identical boxes, but it was her home, and it was a lot better than living on the streets.

'The stairwell is straight ahead,' she said. 'There's a lift, but I don't like using it.' It stank of wee and made an awful grating noise, like it would plummet to the bottom at any moment. 'But it's only two flights.'

'No problem.' He followed her up, glancing at the graffiti on the walls and the discarded rubbish on the steps.

'So what changed at home?' she asked, when they reached the first floor.

He followed her down the corridor. 'My stepdad left. Don't really know why. I suspect Mum was already seeing the bloke she's with now, Mick. He's a nasty piece of work.'

'You don't like him?'

'Christ, no. He drinks too much and shouts even more. But Mum won't hear a word against him. She's obsessed. When she asked him to move in, I told her it was a bad idea, but she said she needed him.'

Emily unlocked her door. 'So he moved in?'

'Yep, and immediately started nicking money from my mum's purse.'

She stepped inside her flat. 'That doesn't sound good.'

'It wasn't. But Mum wouldn't kick him out, even when I told her what he was up to. In the end, she got sick of the arguing. She said she couldn't take it anymore.'

Emily beckoned him inside. 'But instead of kicking him out, she asked you to leave?'

'I thought she was joking at first. Turns out she wasn't.' He followed her into her flat and then stopped. 'Oh, wow!'

She liked his reaction.

The living area and kitchen were open-plan. It wasn't big, but it was her home and she was incredibly proud of it.

He moved around the room, admiring her Ikea shelves filled with second-hand books. 'Did it come like this?'

She kicked off her Doc Martens and removed her mittens. 'No, it was a white shell when I moved in. A local charity kitted me out with the basics, a fridge, oven, sofa and that coffee table.' She pointed to the glass-topped table. 'They got me a bed too. Norah gave me the rest. All the nice stuff, like the cushions, the throw and the rug. She said she was having a clear out and it saved her a trip to the charity shop, but I don't believe her.'

'You think she bought the stuff new?'

Emily shrugged. 'Not sure, but look at it? It's lovely.'

'It's amazing.' He looked in awe.

'I even have a TV.' She padded over to the unit in her socked-feet. 'It's second-hand, but it works. Not that I watch it much.' She'd yet to get into television. It wasn't something she was used to.

Alfie looked impressed. 'You could subscribe to Netflix.'

'Maybe.' She wasn't sure what to do now she was home and he was here. In her home. Amongst her stuff. It seemed surreal. 'Would you like something to eat?'

His expression indicated yes, but he shook his head. 'I don't want to put you out.'

'It's no problem. I have leftover curry in the fridge. It won't take me a minute to heat it up.' Plus, it would give her something to do. She needed to occupy her hands.

'If you're sure?'

'Of course. Make yourself at home. I won't be long.' She went into the tiny kitchenette and emptied the leftover curry into a saucepan, all the while watching the man in her living area.

He removed his trainers and coat and stuffed them inside his rucksack. He then checked he was dirt-free before sitting down. The sofa wasn't new and was covered in a patterned throw, but it was a nice gesture all the same.

Smiling, she stirred the curry.

But when he started laughing, she glanced over, suddenly self-conscious. 'What?'

'It's funny to see the Grinch cooking. Not something you see every day.'

Embarrassed, she lowered the zip on the furry onesie and pushed the hood away from her head. 'Better?'

'Much. I can see your face now.' She felt her cheeks flush. 'Although you could do with a shave.'

Her hand shot up to her face. 'Excuse me?'

'Whiskers,' he said, pointing to her chin.

It was a moment before she laughed. Even then it was shaky. She wasn't sure how she felt about being teased. 'You had me worried there.'

He grimaced. 'My idea of humour.' He relaxed against the sofa. 'So what about you? What's your backstory?'

Her backstory?

She busied herself unearthing a bowl from the cupboard. 'I told you my story.'

'Not in any detail.' He waited, watching her set cutlery on a tray. When it became obvious she wasn't going to answer him, he said, 'I won't judge. Or tell anyone anything. I promise.'

She focused on the curry. 'Why do you want to know?'

'I'm curious, I guess. I'd like to get to know you better.' When she glanced over, he shrugged. 'You seem... cool.' It was his turn to look embarrassed. 'You know, a nice person. And you can never have too many nice people in your life, right?'

She realised he was as nervous as she was. 'I guess not.'

'So how did you end up sleeping rough?'

She dished up the curry and carried the tray over to him. 'I hope it's hot enough.'

'It smells incredible.' He took the tray. 'Thanks. Aren't you having any?'

'I had mine earlier.' She sat at the opposite end of the sofa and curled her feet under her. 'Good?' she asked, when he took a mouthful.

'Christ, yes.' He tucked into the food, his expression a mixture of relief and pleasure.

It warmed her heart to see.

He didn't say anything, but his eyes kept drifting to hers in a curious manner.

Eventually, she sighed and gave in. He'd shared his story, so it was only fair that she told him hers. 'I grew up on a housing estate in Birmingham. I never knew my dad. I have no idea who he is. Mum would never talk about him. She fell out with her parents before I was born, so I've never met my grandparents either.'

He spooned in another mouthful of curry. 'Bummer.'

She reached for a throw and hugged it to her chest. 'My mum suffered from depression and anxiety. She was on medication since I was born. Social Services were forever visiting. They tried to take me away a few times, but the courts would always give her another chance when she told them how much she loved me.'

'Did she love you?'

It was a valid question. 'I'm sure she did, yes.' She cuddled the throw closer. 'When she had a good spell, things were great. We'd go to the park or museum and she'd buy me a toy dinosaur. We'd have ice cream and it would be like nothing was wrong. But then her health would deteriorate, she'd stop eating, she wouldn't get dressed for days... and then the self-harming would begin.'

It felt strange to say the words aloud, like she was relaying the story of someone else's life, not her own.

Alfie lowered his spoon. 'Did she hurt you?' His voice was soft and low and the sound of his concern caused a twinge in her chest.

She looked down at the throw, focusing on the geometric patterning. 'Not in the beginning.' Which was true. It was only as things escalated that the target of her violence switched focus. 'One night, a few days after my fourteenth birthday, she burnt the dinner. She started throwing food and pans around the kitchen, screaming and crying. I tried to calm her down, but she was in such a rage she couldn't even hear me. She started hitting the wall. Like really punching it, making her knuckles bleed. I grabbed her and pulled her away, but...' she trailed off, recalling what happened next.

'She hit you instead?' The sound of his voice brought her back to the present.

'I blocked the first few blows, pleading with her to stop, but she was too far gone.' She fiddled with the throw, turning it over and over, trying to keep herself from shaking. 'When I was released from hospital I was placed with a foster family in Watford. I wanted to go home. To be with my mum, to take care of her. But the authorities wouldn't let me. I wasn't even allowed to speak to her. It was like I was being punished too.'

'So you ran away?'

She dropped her head against the sofa. 'I came to London. I don't know why, or what I expected would happen. I just had to get away.'

'And that's how you ended up sleeping rough?'

'Yes.' She gave him a look. 'Keep eating.'

'Sorry.'

'It was okay to begin with. I liked the freedom and not having to do or be anything. And it was easier to be around people who didn't ask questions or want anything from me, than try to fit in with regular family life. I sofa-surfed with a few girls I met and used the shelters, but when the police showed up, I had to move on. I was a minor. I didn't want them taking me into care.'

He finished the last mouthful of curry. 'Christ, that was good. Thank you.' He wiped his mouth using the kitchen towel she'd given him. 'Mind if I wash my hands?'

'Course not. There's hand soap by the sink.'

He got up and went into the kitchenette. 'How did you end up here?'

She angled her head so she could watch him. 'I grew tired of feeling afraid all the time. And lonely. And I guess, pointless.'

'I know that feeling,' he said, rinsing his hands.

'When I turned eighteen and knew I wouldn't be taken into care, I registered as homeless with the local council. I was put up in bed and breakfast to start with and then a room in a shared place. Then I got a call to say they had a flat for me. And here I am.'

He dried his hands. 'It's a great place.'

'I like it.'

'I'd love a place like this.' He ran his hand over the worktop. 'With nice furniture, and food in the cupboards.'

He opened a kitchen cupboard. 'Look at that? Three types of cereal?'

She smiled. 'Decadent, I know.'

'Downright indulgent.' He returned to the sofa, pausing to look at her. 'Was that the right word?'

She laughed. 'It was, yes.'

He sat down, no longer at the opposite end of the sofa, but right next to her. 'It's just you're so smart. I don't want to make an idiot of myself.'

She averted her eyes, but her pulse rate quickened. 'I'm hardly smart. I left school at fourteen. I didn't even take my exams.'

'School doesn't make someone intelligent. It's what's inside here.' He tapped the side of his head. 'I went to school every day and barely passed my exams. But you know stuff. You've lived and experienced life. You're more intelligent than I'll ever be. School or no school. And besides, you're at college now, aren't you? I bet you're top of your class.'

Was he teasing her again? Emily felt her cheeks burn.

'You are, aren't you? I knew it.' His expression softened. 'Good for you.'

She clutched the throw, glad of the barrier. It wasn't that she was afraid of him, it was more that he unsettled her in a way she couldn't describe. 'It's not always easy, and I have to work twice as hard as everyone else, but it'll be worth it if I pass the course.'

'Damn right, it will.' He looked around the room. 'And does this feel like home?'

'Kind of. It's taken me a while to adjust.' For weeks, she hadn't even bought bedding, too afraid the council would change their mind and evict her. But she was slowly getting accustomed to regular living. 'Some nights I wake up on the floor. I don't remember moving, but it's like my brain can't accept I have a bed. And that it's mine. And no one can take it away from me. Bonkers, huh?'

'Not bonkers.' He reached out for her hand. 'Understandable.'

The warmth of his touch was like a bolt of electricity. She pulled away, shocked by her reaction. Panic and instinct and... something she couldn't fathom.

Whatever it was, she was flooded with regret when she saw the hurt look on his face. She hadn't meant to offend him. 'Would you like some hot chocolate?' she asked, trying to make amends.

He gave her a half-smile. 'Only if it's no trouble?'

'It's fine. I was making myself some anyway. It helps me sleep.' She went into the kitchenette, her mind a whirl. Why had she pulled away? He was only being kind. Showing compassion and empathy. She was an idiot.

While she waited for the milk to heat, she fetched a pillow and blanket and placed them on the sofa. 'I hope you'll be warm enough. The flat isn't double-glazed.'

'Neither is Tesco's doorway.'

'Good point.' She swallowed awkwardly. 'There are towels in the bathroom if you want a shower. And there's a spare toothbrush in the cabinet. Help yourself.'

'Thanks, Emily. You have no idea what this means.'

Shrugging away the compliment, she finished making the hot chocolate and handed him a mug. 'Goodnight, then. Hope you sleep okay.'

'I'm sure I will. And thanks for this.' He took a sip. 'Delicious.'

She headed for the bedroom, thinking how unnerving it was to have a guest in the flat. And one who made her feel so nervous and self-aware and... excited.

Excited?

'Emily?'

She turned abruptly. 'Yes?'

He was sitting on the sofa, looking up at her through his pale blue eyes, his expression tender and hopeful. 'Thanks for telling me your story. For what it's worth, I think you're amazing. And kind and brave. And I really hope this is the start of something wonderful for you. You deserve to be happy.'

It was a while before she found her voice. 'Th... thanks... You do too, Alfie.'

He raised his mug to her. 'Cheers to that.'

His tender smile was her undoing. She turned and darted into the bedroom, closing the door behind her and leaning against it. Why was her heart beating so fast? Why did she feel so... heightened? So alive?

She ran over to the bed and jumped under the covers, pulling them over her head. She needed a barrier. Protection. To hide. From what, she wasn't sure.

Herself, probably.

Chapter Fifteen

Saturday, 1ˢᵗ December

The day of the donation drive had arrived. It was chilly, but the sun was shining and the rain had held off. Social media advertising for the event had gone well, promising a good turnout, and the local paper had published a full-page spread supporting the event. All was good.

But as much as Sam tried to focus on the positives of her situation and not allow her mind to venture into more humiliating territory, the only word that sprang to mind as she took in the sight ahead of her was chaos. Utter chaos.

It had started yesterday when the twenty-foot blue shipping container had been delivered to the shelter. The delivery truck had barely been able to squeeze into the car park and unload the thirty-ton monstrosity onto the forecourt, taking out huge clumps of overhanging branches as they eased it into position behind the main building, where it now took up half the outside space.

This had been followed by another delivery early this morning. Stacks of boxes containing one hundred wash kits, one hundred sleeping bags, and one hundred waterproof one-man tents that had been unloaded onto the forecourt.

Before she'd had the chance to move the boxes into the shipping container, people had begun turning up with donations – despite the event not officially starting for another hour. Thankfully, her trusty volunteers had arrived early and were helping her to move the boxes and try to regain some sense of order.

Well, except for Jamie. He'd yet to arrive. Something she was incredibly grateful for.

She picked up another box and carried it over to Norah, who in turn carried it over to Emily, who concluded their human chain by handing it to Fraser for loading into the shipping container. It was a lot better than her original plan of lugging each box into the container herself.

As long as she kept busy, she didn't care. It was when she stopped being active that her mind tumbled back to the events of last Saturday.

The memories threatened to surface again and she forced them away. She was stressed enough as it was.

Somehow she'd managed to avoid seeing Jamie since the night of her mother's soiree. A miracle in itself. He hadn't been at the shelter for the two days following the party, and the rest of the week their paths hadn't crossed. Mostly down to her efforts to avoid him. When he'd been working from home dealing with preparations for today's donation drive and the social media advertising, she'd been covering shifts at the shelter. Likewise, when he'd come into the shelter to volunteer in the evenings, she'd disappeared under the guise of needing to deal with 'urgent tasks'.

Not that she'd been skiving off. Far from it. She'd got a lot done this week. Humiliation proved to be a good motivator.

On Tuesday, she'd visited the local GP surgery and managed to persuade a few of the doctors to run monthly health checks at the shelter. Some of the kids hadn't seen a doctor for years, so it was a vital service. She'd tried a couple of local dentists in the hope they'd come on board too, but they were less willing to commit. No profit in it. Still, she wasn't giving up. She'd try a different practice next week.

On Wednesday, she'd sold her car. Extra funds were desperately needed, so it was time to ditch the Merc. She'd used the money to buy a second-hand white Fiat Scudo van and purchased the giant shipping container, which would hopefully resolve their storage issues – especially if today's donation drive proved a success.

The rest of the money she'd deposited in the bank. It wouldn't do to blow it all in one go. After all, this was the last of her assets. She had nothing left to sell.

She carried another box over to Norah.

If avoiding Jamie this week had been challenging, avoiding her mother had proved impossible. When Sam hadn't answered any of her calls on Sunday, her mother had sent a text threatening to turn up at the shelter unless she spoke to her. Unwilling to have another public humiliation, she'd called her mother back.

What followed was a painful forty-minute rant by her mother about the inappropriateness of Sam's behaviour at the soiree. The level of embarrassment she'd caused her family. And how it was fortunate the press hadn't witnessed the incident in the pool otherwise the family's disgrace would have been plastered over the tabloids for weeks to come.

Sam had tried to reason with her mother that it wasn't that bad, but she knew she was only trying to convince herself.

A point hammered home when her mother informed her she'd spent hours on the phone trying to persuade the soiree guests not to upload any incriminating photos of her daughter in the pool onto social media. Talk about embarrassing.

But it wasn't the thought of a few excruciating photos that worried Sam. Or the damage to her reputation by getting tipsy and skinny-dipping in the family pool. It was the horror of having 'frolicked' – as her mother had referred to it – with Jamie Lawson that upset her most. Not just upset her. Mortified her. And made her so ashamed she wanted to crawl into the shipping container and never emerge.

'Everything okay, Sam?' Norah's out-stretched arms indicated she was ready for another box.

Sam blinked. 'Sorry, Norah. I was miles away.'

'Anywhere nice?'

God, no.

Norah glanced over Sam's shoulder. 'Oh, good. Another pair of hands. Jamie's here.'

Oh, hell.

Sam's heart dropped to her stomach. 'I think we should switch places,' she said to Norah. 'Jamie can stay out here and I'll take over from Fraser.' She raced off before Norah could question her rationale.

She wasn't up to facing Jamie. Not today. Not ever.

She ran into the shipping container. 'I'll take over in here now, Fraser.'

Fraser straightened and wiped his brow. 'You sure? I'm happy to carry on.' He stretched out his back.

'You look like you could do with a break.' Which was true. The poor man looked shattered. 'Why don't you grab a drink?'

'Now you come to mention it, I am thirsty.' He picked up his army coat from the floor. 'Want anything?'

'I'm fine, thanks. You go.' She almost pushed him out the container. 'Enjoy your drink.'

A puzzled–looking Fraser left.

Sam looked around the container. Fraser had done well. He'd stacked the boxes at the far end, leaving plenty of space for the bedding that would hopefully be dropped off by the public later.

And then she heard her name being called, 'Sam? You in here?'

Blast! It was Jamie. She needed to hide.

She ran over to the boxes. Without pausing for thought, she climbed up the stack and laid on top, praying she was out of sight. The boxes wobbled beneath her, but she kept still, hoping they'd settle and not give away her position.

A moment later, she heard his voice again. 'Sam?'

He'd entered the container. Footsteps echoed on the bouncy plywood flooring. They grew nearer. And then stopped.

She strained to hear, wondering if he'd left. And then the box beneath her creaked. It held for a few seconds, but then sagged in the middle. She clung on, but her fingers struggled to gain purchase on the bendy cardboard.

He must have heard the movement, because he said, 'Sam? Where are you?'

Damn it! The box made another creaking sound. Why wouldn't he just go away?

And then a rumbling sound filled the container. Like an earthquake about to erupt. Only it wasn't the ground splitting apart – it was the pile of boxes.

She felt a jolt. Then a drop. The box beneath her collapsing. More moving. Shifting. Knocking her off balance. There was nothing to hold onto. The boxes tilted and moved apart.

She fell in instalments, like a cartoon character tumbling down a waste disposal unit. Bumping her lower, sending boxes toppling as she slid downwards, ending up wedged under a pile at the bottom.

For a moment, there was silence.

Had she got away with it? Maybe he'd left before she'd fallen?

But then the sound of footsteps approached. Boxes being moved. A concerned voice. 'Sam? Is that you? Where are you?'

It was too much to hope he wouldn't find her.

The box above her lifted and his concerned face appeared. 'My God, are you okay?'

'I'm fine.'

'Are you hurt?'

'Nope.'

His intuitive eyes scanned her prone position. 'Are you sure?'

'I'm sure.' She went to move, but she was wedged in.

'Need a hand?'

'Nope, I can manage.' She pushed against the boxes. One tumbled off the pile above and whacked her on the head. Helpful.

'Certain about that?' There was a note of amusement in his voice.

Oh, he thought this was funny, did he? She pushed harder at the boxes, determined to escape. It was bad enough she was trapped, but did he have to enjoy it so much?

And why did he have to smell so good? His musky fragrance mingled with the smell of cardboard, making her feel unsteady. Lightheaded, even. Yet another reminder of last Saturday night – a reminder she could do without.

He began moving boxes, clearing a path to her. When the last box was removed, he held out his hand. 'Here, let me help you.'

'No, thanks.' She didn't need or want his help. She rolled onto her stomach, got to her knees and then hauled herself upright, using the boxes to aid her. When she turned to face him, she found him smiling. 'What's so funny?'

'You.'

'Glad I amuse you.' She tried to move past him, but he blocked her way.

Why did he have to look so good? Who wore a smart shirt and dark jeans to a donation drive? Well, she wasn't falling for it. She was stone cold sober today and not about to let his seductive charms hoodwink her into misbehaving.

Not that she'd been blameless. But he wasn't totally innocent either, he'd definitely joined in.

'You've been avoiding me,' he said, refusing to budge.

'I've been busy. Can you move please?' Her hands went to her hips. She tried to look intimidating – which was impossible to pull off when you were wearing bleach-splattered dungarees and a lopsided ponytail.

'Not until you talk to me.'

'We've got nothing to talk about.'

He raised an eyebrow. 'Really?'

'One hundred percent.' But then she realised there was no point avoiding it.

She'd hoped, rather foolishly, he'd pretend it never happened. That he'd carry on as though they hadn't shared an intimate moment in her parents' pool and not mention it, enabling them to behave normally around each other. But he obviously wasn't going to let her off the hook.

She avoided eye contact. 'I'm guessing you're referring to last Saturday?'

'Last Saturday?' He feigned forgetfulness. 'We went to your parents' party, right?' He mulled it over and then shook his head. 'Nope, it's gone. You'll have to remind me.'

The sod was enjoying this.

'I may have got a little… tipsy.'

'I do recall you knocking back the champagne cocktails.'

'And as such, my behaviour may have been somewhat out of character.' Was it ever? She'd been positively uninhibited.

'Are you referring to the midnight swim? Kissing me? Or pulling me into the pool?'

She winced. 'All three.'

It was hard to know what had triggered her unravelling. Whether it was her parents' disapproval, or her inability to charm any of the dignitaries into supporting The Crash Pad, she didn't know. Maybe it was simply being back in her old room and evoking memories of being an unhappy teenager and wanting to escape.

What else could have driven her to remove her clothes and kiss Jamie Lawson?

The thought made her groan. Yes, she'd been tipsy, but she hadn't been so far gone she hadn't known what she was doing… which was a lot worse than being able to blame it entirely on the alcohol. One minute she was in the water, the next she'd swum up to him and launched herself at him.

Maybe if she'd stopped at that moment, they'd both have forgotten about it and laughed it off as a drunken mistake. But she'd kissed him again… and again. Intoxicated by the way he'd tasted, his mouth urging her on, heating her blood until she'd lost all semblance of control.

'You know my suit is ruined?'

She jerked at the sound of his voice. 'I'll buy you another one.' Why did her face feel so hot? Come to think of it, why were her hands so clammy? Was she ill?

He grinned. 'Don't worry, it was hired. I lost my deposit, that's all.'

'I'll give you the money.'

'Don't be daft.' His smile became ponderous. 'But you did take me by surprise. I mean, one minute you act like you hate me, the next you're—'

'Stop!' She lifted her hand. It was bad enough she'd thrown herself at him, she didn't need him reminding her.

His eyes softened. 'Don't get me wrong, I had no objections. I mean, it wasn't like I didn't enjoy it.' He didn't? 'But it was kind of confusing.'

Swallowing had suddenly become difficult. 'How so?'

'Well, you've been avoiding me. Which tells me you're either embarrassed by what happened, or you're worried I've got the wrong idea and think something's going on between us.' He expression turned questioning. 'Am I right?'

Talk about blunt.

Did she really have to spell it out? It was a drunken mistake, a moment of madness. It wasn't like she had feelings for him, she'd just got carried away and the moonlight and music had seduced her. The champagne had softened her inhibitions. The build-up of stress and anxiety had tipped her over the edge, making her crazy and reckless, and desperately needing an escape. But how could she explain that without offending him?

Somehow she needed to try. After all, it wasn't his fault she was a drunken-lush. 'The thing is… well… you see, it's not that you're not attractive, but—'

'It's okay.' He nudged her arm. 'I'm teasing you.'

She blinked in surprise. 'You are?'

'Sure. I thought it would be fun to make you squirm.' He shrugged. 'It's no big deal.'

'It's not?' She felt herself frown. Why wasn't it?

'It was just a kiss. You'd had too much to drink. And I was up for a good time. Add in the music, moonlight and fireworks, and it was bound to spill over. It happens at parties. People get carried away. Don't stress it, I'm not.'

A weight settled in her stomach. 'You're not?'

'Course not. I'm not saying it wasn't hot.' A grin creased his cheeks. 'But it didn't mean anything. For either of us.'

'Right.'

What he said made sense. It was a mistake. It wasn't a disaster, no one had died. It was just a drunken fumble at a party. She was making too much of it.

'So you don't need to avoid me, or worry I'm hurt, or I've fallen for you. I haven't, okay?' He opened his arms. 'See? No harm done.'

'Well… good. I'm glad.' Why didn't she sound it?

'So can we dispense with the awkwardness and just be mates.'

'Mates?'

'Yeah. I enjoyed Saturday, it was fun. And I like volunteering here. I'd like it if we could forget what happened and be like we were before. We were getting on okay, weren't we?' He sounded relaxed, and genuine, and completely unaffected by their encounter.

Which was good, right?

'Err… yes, I suppose we were.'

'Right. So… mates?' He held out his hand.

She shook his hand. 'Mates.'

'Need a hand with these boxes?' He turned away and began tidying up, as though they'd just been discussing the weather.

'Err… thanks.' She picked up a box, wondering what was wrong with her. It wasn't like she was interested in Jamie Lawson. The kiss had been a mistake. She didn't fancy him. He didn't fancy her, he'd just said as much.

It was a drunken fumble. A tipsy 'hook up'. It had meant nothing. He wasn't looking for a romance. He was happy to forget it had ever happened and be… mates.

Mates. Right.

That was good… wasn't it?

Chapter Sixteen

Jamie turned away so Sam wouldn't see the disappointment on his face. For a brief moment, he'd allowed himself to believe she might be interested in him. Ever since last Saturday night, he'd been replaying the events in his mind, desperate to hold onto the way it had felt to kiss her, to touch her, and to get lost in the heady moment of ecstasy – until he'd fallen in the pool, obviously. That part he was happy to forget. But right up until that moment, he'd felt himself unravelling, letting go of the tight rein he had on his emotions and allowing himself to just… feel.

He shoved the box on top of the others, moving them into position and repairing the damage done by her attempts to hide from him, which hadn't been great for his ego.

She'd been so desperate to avoid him she'd almost killed herself. That was not the action of a woman who was smitten. It was the action of a woman who was riddled with regret and mortification. And that hurt more than he wanted to admit.

He needed some space to regroup. He couldn't be around her right now. 'I could do with a drink,' he said, shoving the last box into position. 'Want anything?'

'I'm good, thanks.' She stepped down from the pile of boxes, her ponytail swaying with the movement. 'You have one, though. Take a break. As long as you like. No rush to hurry back.'

Wow, she really wanted him gone. Something he should be grateful for, but wasn't.

'I won't be long,' he said, exiting the shipping container and heading for the main building.

Despite ending up in the swimming pool and seeing the horrified look on her parents' faces when they'd discovered their daughter skinny-dipping with him last Saturday night, he'd woken on Sunday morning overcome by an unexplained sense of hope.

He'd foolishly allowed himself to imagine what might happen if they got together. Like a proper couple. It wasn't an unpleasant thought... which was confusing, as before last Saturday he'd have laughed at the idea of them even being friends, let alone anything more intimate.

But learning more about Sam's upbringing and getting to understand how she'd come to be the person she was had softened his aversion to her.

He'd spent all of Sunday wishing his phone would ring, hoping she'd call with an offer to pick up where they'd left off Saturday night.

By the end of Monday, he'd given in to temptation and phoned her on the pretence of needing to talk about the donation drive. She'd ignored his call. She'd responded with a text saying whatever he had planned was fine. It was short, to the point, and didn't invite a response.

He'd hoped her clipped response was due to embarrassment about what had happened, and that she just needed some space before seeing him again. So he'd stayed away, hoping when they did meet again she'd be open to them exploring their connection. Because whatever else had happened last Saturday night, they'd definitely clicked in the chemistry department.

But no. She hadn't been pleased to see him. Quite the opposite. She'd bolted and taken the drastic action of climbing onto a pile of boxes.

He'd done the only thing he could and pretended the kiss hadn't meant anything. That he wasn't interested in her and that it was laughable to imagine them getting together.

What else could he do? If he told her how he really felt, she'd terminate his position at the shelter and ruin his chances of ever getting a story on her brother. So he'd swallowed his pride, faked disinterest, and pretended to be... mates. Had he really said that?

He pushed open the door to the shelter and headed for the main area.

What an idiot he was.

He must have audibly groaned, because when he reached the cafe, Alfie turned to him. 'You okay?'

'I'm fine,' he lied. 'Are you working here today?' The kid was wearing one of the red Crash Pad aprons.

'I'm covering until Emily takes over. She wanted to do her stint outside first. I tried to persuade her to let me do the heavy stuff, but she insisted on doing it herself.'

Jamie smiled. 'She's tougher than she looks.'

Alfie looked disgruntled. 'She's not as tough as she makes out.'

Jamie could imagine. Most abandoned kids became street-wise and developed a thick skin, but it was a fragile barrier, a mask for the bruises lying beneath. He was the same. Alfie too.

He noticed the wistful look in the kid's eye. He guessed it matched his own mournful expression. What a pair, eh?

'So you're running the cafe?'

'Just serving drinks until it opens properly. Emily'll take over then and I'll help outside.' He gestured to the coffee machine. 'Drink?'

'Just tap water, thanks.' He watched Alfie fetch a jug from the fridge and pour him a glass of water. 'Nice of you to volunteer.'

'We all need to give something back, right? Society won't work otherwise.' He added a slice of lemon to the glass and handed Jamie his water.

The kid never failed to impress him. 'Any luck finding a place to live?'

'Nothing permanent.' Alfie averted his eyes. 'Although a mate has been letting me crash on their sofa for a few nights.'

It wasn't hard to guess who the 'mate' was.

'Kind of them.'

'I know.' His cheeks flushed and Jamie's suspicions were confirmed.

'What about the job hunting? Still no joy?'

Alfie wiped the countertop with a cloth. 'I've applied for loads of positions, but mostly I don't hear back. If I do, it's a no thanks. I did get an interview yesterday, which was cool. As an auxiliary in a care home.'

Jamie took a sip of his water. 'Is that a field of work you're interested in?'

'Kind of.' He stopped wiping. 'I mean, I like old people and I used to look after my granddad when he was alive. It sounded like a cool job. You know, helping people.' He resumed cleaning.

'So what happened? Didn't the interview go well?'

'It went fine. The lady was nice and she said I'd be a good fit for the team. She felt I had the right attitude and skills to be a carer. She was keen to have me.'

'But?'

Alfie shook out the cloth over the bin. 'Same old problem. No fixed abode. No references. No proper job history and no way for them to do a background check. The elderly residents are vulnerable, so the care home has a duty of care to protect them. I'm considered a risk.'

'I'm sorry, mate. That sucks.'

Alfie returned to the counter. 'She said I could contact them again if I get settled somewhere. She'd see if the owners would agree to a trial period. I guess that's something.'

'You must have impressed her.'

'Maybe.' He leant on the counter. 'I got a call-back for an office cleaning job, so it's not all bad.'

Jamie took another swig of water. 'I admire your optimism.'

'No point feeling sorry for yourself. One day things'll turn around. I know they will.'

Jamie really hoped so. And then he was struck by an idea. 'How would you feel about letting me make a documentary about you?'

Alfie tilted his head. 'What, like a video?'

'Yeah, a video diary. What it's like to be a young homeless person on the streets and the challenges you face.'

Alfie looked intrigued. 'Is that what you do for a job?'

'No, but it's what I want to do eventually. Be a documentary film-maker.'

'Sounds cool. What would I have to do?'

'Nothing too onerous. I could follow you as you apply for jobs and when you talk to the council about getting housed. You know, to show how hard it is. Maybe I could ask you questions about your life and how you came to be homeless.'

Alfie straightened. 'I don't want to bad mouth anyone. Especially my mum.'

'Of course not. It's entirely up to you what you say. I won't push, or include any footage without your permission. You get final say in the edit. …Will you do it?'

Alfie ran his hand through his hair. 'You think it'll help others?'

'I'd hope so. I have this mate who works for the *South London Herald*.' He didn't need to mention he also worked there. 'I'm sure he'd be willing to run the story on their website. Other newspapers might be interested too.'

Now the idea was formulating in his mind, he realised he was excited to make it happen. It was the perfect subject matter. A great way to kick-start his transition into filmmaking.

'And it would be good advertising for The Crash Pad,' he added, warming to the idea further. 'We could show what a difference this place makes. Hopefully it'll turn around public opinion about why it's needed.'

This seemed to sway Alfie. 'You have yourself a deal,' he said, extending his hand.

Jamie shook his hand.

And then his phone rang.

'Excuse me. I should take this.' He moved out of earshot, wondering why his boss was calling him on a Saturday. 'Hi Gareth. Anything wrong?'

'What's happening with the Max Tipping case?'

'I'm working on it.'

'You've been telling me that for nearly a month. What have you found out?'

Good question. He thought about it. 'Well… the guy likes boozy lunches, playing golf and is dating a model called Xanthe.'

'All of which I could've found out in this month's *GQ*. What about his business dealings?'

'I know he's helped out a few friends when their companies got into trouble.'

'Helped out how? Buying and selling shares? Pumping the stock market with false information? What?'

'By paying off their debts.'

'Is that it?'

Jamie looked around, hoping for divine intervention. It didn't come. Even the sight of the beach mural on the wall failed to inspire him. 'Maybe that's all there is to find out.'

'Or maybe you're not digging deep enough. What's happening with the sister?'

Jamie flinched.

But then he remembered his boss had no idea what had happened last Saturday night. He wasn't about to enlighten him. 'She's not that close to her family. I've tried asking her questions, but she doesn't divulge much.'

'Then there's no point wasting any more time on her. Quit with the volunteering. We need to find another way in.'

Jamie nearly choked on his water. Stop volunteering? He didn't want to stop. He was enjoying the work. He was making a difference, contributing to society. He wasn't ready to walk away. From the shelter. …Or from Sam. Especially Sam.

He realised Gareth was still talking, '… rumours are mounting in the financial world. It won't be long before this story breaks. The name Hylton Sabell keeps coming up, why? What's his connection to this? Find out. I don't want another paper beating us to this story. You hear me? Not when I was given advance information. You need to expose this story first.'

'I hear you.'

'You'd better. Your job is on the line.'

Oh, crap. But what did he expect? He was failing in his first assignment.

And then something bizarre happened. Call it fate, or pure luck. But like a mirage emerging from the hot barren desert, Max Tipping walked into the shelter.

Jamie couldn't believe it. 'Err… boss? Max Tipping has just turned up at The Crash Pad.'

'Are you shitting me?'

'I'm serious, boss. He's literally standing a few metres away.'

'Then what are you doing still on the line. Get me that story!'

The line went dead.

Okay. It was time to prove himself a decent journalist.

He headed over. 'Hi, Max. Looking for Sam?'

Max Tipping turned at the sound of his voice. He seemed distracted. His attire was the familiar city-boy suit, complete with waistcoat and silk handkerchief tucked into his top pocket, but he didn't look his normal pristine self today. His hair wasn't quite so neat, he had dark circles under his eyes and his suit looked a little creased – like he'd slept in it. Maybe he'd had a wild night celebrating a big win on the stock market? Or perhaps drowning his sorrows in booze following a huge loss. Who knew?

Whatever the reason, it was a moment before he spoke. Even then, all he said was, 'What?'

'I said, are you looking for Sam? I'm Jamie… remember?' He was given a blank look. 'We met at your parents' party last Saturday?' He held out his hand, but Max ignored it.

'The bloke in the pool, right?'

Jamie inwardly cringed. 'That's me.' He tried to make light of the situation. 'Has your mother recovered?'

'No idea. Where's my sister?'

Okay, the man wasn't in the mood for chit-chat. 'Outside.'

'I didn't see her.'

'Did you check inside the shipping container?'

'Excuse me?'

'We're having a donation drive today. People are dropping off bedding for us to give to the homeless. We needed more storage room, so Sam bought a shipping container. It's parked around the back of the building.'

Max's eyes grew wide. 'The crazy things my sister comes up with.' He turned and walked off.

Not crazy, Jamie thought. Eccentric, definitely. But also unselfish, compassionate and caring. He decided not to voice this. Max Tipping didn't seem like the kind of guy who'd appreciate being corrected.

He followed Max outside.

For the first time since starting his investigation, he was alone with Max Tipping. The man was within reach. It was the break he'd been waiting for and he needed to capitalise on the situation. But how? Think, he told himself.

'So… did you enjoy the party on Saturday?' he said, jogging to keep up. 'It was quite the shindig.'

Things must be desperate if he was using words like 'shindig'. Be more casual, he told himself. Like two blokes chatting down the pub.

'Your mate looked like he was having a good time. Hylton, isn't it? He can sure knock back the booze. Is he a friend from school?'

But Max Tipping clearly wasn't interested in engaging in small talk and kept walking.

Jamie needed another way in. Something contentious. Something that would provoke a reaction. ...And then it came to him. He could use his recent research into insider trading.

'Shocking news about Stephen Richards, isn't it?' he said, struggling to keep pace with the man, and hoping he was up-to-date with the goings-on at Forsythe Banking Group. There'd been extensive coverage on all the news channels, so the man would have to be a hermit not to be aware of the latest scandal to hit the banking sector.

But Max kept walking, pushing his way through the front door to the car park area.

Jamie tried again. 'I imagine everyone in the trading sector was quite shocked?' It wasn't the subtlest line of questioning, but time was of the essence.

Still no response.

Max upped his stride.

Jamie did the same. 'It's not every day the global head of sales of a multi-national company gets arrested.' The shipping container was in sight. He was running out of time. 'But in a way, you have to admire the man. I mean, it takes some balls to backdate contracts to inflate quarterly earnings and temporarily prop up the company's stock price. Right?'

Max stopped dead.

Jamie almost ran into the back of him.

The man turned and pinned Jamie with what could only be described as a death stare. 'Is there a point to this?'

'No, I just—'

'Are you police?'

Police? 'God, no.'

'A journalist?'

Oh, hell. Jamie swallowed. 'Why would you think that?'

'Then what's with all the questions?' Max's expression was hard, the tight muscles in his jaw like granite.

'I'm interested in the stock market and Sam mentioned you worked in that field. I was trying to make polite conversation.'

Max eyed him suspiciously.

What he would have said next, Jamie had no idea because at that moment Sam emerged from the shipping container, spotted her brother and came running over. 'Max? What are you doing here?' She hugged him. 'Have you come to help with the donation drive?' Her huge smile lit up her face.

Max raised an eyebrow. 'Why would I do that?'

Her smile faded. 'Oh, well… shame. We could've done with the help.' She looked disappointed, but then rallied her spirits. 'So why are you here? Did Mother send you? Am I still in the doghouse?'

Max rubbed his forehead. 'Are you surprised? What were you thinking?'

Sam glanced at Jamie. 'It was a momentary blip. Anyway, you're hardly Mr Squeaky Clean. You and Hylton were knocking back the booze too.'

'But we didn't end up in the swimming pool cavorting with the hired help, did we?'

Jamie felt his hackles rise. Hired help? Wow, so that's how he was viewed, was it? Charming.

Sam punched her brother's arm. 'Jamie's standing right there. And he's not the hired help, he's a volunteer. Who, unlike you, is here to help today. So quit with the mean remarks.' She offered Jamie a smile. 'I apologise for my brother, he's not normally such a snob.'

Max gave Jamie an apologetic glance. 'Sorry. Bad mood. Hangover.'

Jamie nodded. He figured it was as good as he was going to get. 'No worries, been there myself. Heavy night?'

'Something like that.' Max's expression turned rueful.

'Splashing the cash on Xanthe, no doubt.' Sam gave her brother a loaded look. 'That woman looks expensive. And high maintenance. You get no sympathy from me.'

Max opened his mouth as if to say something, but shook his head and backed away. 'I shouldn't have come. My mistake.'

'Hey, where are you going?' Sam caught his arm. 'You just got here.'

'You're busy.' He gestured to the multitude of people dropping off bags on the driveway. 'I'll come back another time.'

'Or you could stay and help?' Sam asked tentatively. 'You look like you need to talk.'

Max hesitated. 'Don't worry about it. It's nothing. Carry on with your... thingy.'

'Donation drive.'

'Right. I'll call you later.'

'Okay.' Sam looked deflated. 'Make sure you do.'

Max kissed her on the cheek. 'Take care, Sis... I love you.'

Sam startled, like she'd never heard those words before. 'Crikey. Right... well, I love you too, you big softie.' But it was to his retreating back. 'Are you ill? Should I call a doctor?'

Max glanced back and waved. 'I'm fine. Go and save the world,' he said, trying for a smile that failed to be convincing. 'You raging vegan.'

'Right-Wing Tory!' she called after him.

'Hipster!' he shouted back.

She watched her brother leave, her expression concerned. 'What on earth was that all about?'

Jamie didn't know the man well enough to make a judgement, but his behaviour was obviously out of character. 'Isn't he normally like that?'

'God, no. I mean, the name calling, sure. He's loud and competitive and crass, but he's never... morose.' She fiddled with her ponytail. 'Maybe Xanthe dumped him? Surely he wouldn't be upset about that. I mean, you met the woman. She didn't strike me as his soulmate.'

'Maybe he has work problems?' He felt bad for asking. Sam was obviously worried about her brother and he was using the situation to dig for dirt. But that's what investigative journalists did, right? He was just doing his job.

Sam shook her head. 'He often has work problems, but he doesn't let them get to him.' Picking up a bag of bedding, she slung it over her shoulder.

Jamie picked up a bag of his own. 'What kind of work problems?'

'Oh, I don't know. Demanding clients. Pressure to make a stack of money. Poor economy, stuff like that. The recession affects everyone, even loaded stock brokers.' She headed into the shipping container and threw the bag on top of the pile.

He followed her. So Max did talk to her about his work then? 'Sometimes during difficult times people are persuaded to make decisions they wouldn't normally make.'

Sam turned to look at him. 'How do you mean?'

He pretended to think about it. 'I don't know much about it myself. But I have a friend who dabbles on the stock market and he tells me sometimes traders feel pressurised into leaking or buying information to ensure a killing.'

She looked shocked. 'Max would never do that. He's a combative arsehole at times, but he's not a cheat.'

'I'm not saying he is,' Jamie quickly backtracked. 'But from what I've heard, they don't see it as cheating. More like... levelling out the playing field.'

She dismissed the idea with a wave of her hand. 'It's not Max's style. He's had knockbacks before. Lost shed-loads of money, but he's always bounced back. He's never resorted to illegalities. He doesn't have to – he's loaded. And besides, he knows what a scandal would do to our parents. He'd never risk that. He's too scared of our mother, for a start.' She headed out of the container. 'Whatever's wrong, it's not work related.'

Jamie followed her. 'Do you want to go after him? I can hold the fort here, if you like.'

'No, I'm sure whatever it is, it can wait.' And then she stopped and turned to him. 'Thanks, though. I appreciate the offer.'

'No problem. That's what mates do, isn't it? Help each other out.'

A flash of what looked like disappointment crossed her face. 'Mates, right. I forgot.' With that, she turned and walked off.

He was left to contemplate his next move and ignore the sinking feeling in his gut. Not only was he doing a rubbish job of pretending he hadn't fallen for her, he was also no nearer to finding out what Max Tipping was up to.

Was Sam right when she said her brother would never get involved in anything dodgy? Or was the man up to his eyeballs in scandal and his sister clueless to his shady dealings?

Until he knew for certain, he'd better stick around. Because no matter what his boss said, if things went pear-shaped then Sam would need a mate. And he'd promised to be that. A mate. Nothing more.

Yeah, right.

Chapter Seventeen

Monday, 3rd December

The temperature outside was eight degrees but it felt colder. The wind had picked up, stripping the trees of their leaves and making everything look more wintery. It was gone eight p.m. and The Crash Pad had closed its doors for the night. All fifteen beds had been taken and the guests had been fed and were either currently watching TV, lazing about in the recreation area, or tucked up in their beach huts exhausted. Norah and Fraser were on the night shift, so Sam was free to go home and try to catch up on some much-needed sleep.

Except she couldn't do that. Not yet.

Opening the rear doors of her recently acquired white van, she began loading the garments into the back, still amazed by how much more space she had.

The donation drive had been a massive success. Most of the bedding donated had been of decent quality and was clean and in good condition. They'd been able to prepare over two hundred takeaway parcels, which would keep them going for several months.

They'd begun the trial last night and had given away seven sets of bedding, complete with a tent, a wash kit and a hot meal. Despite being told there was 'no room at the inn', the teens and young adults being turned away had seemed delighted with their parcels, reacting as though Santa had arrived bearing gifts… which was satisfying and heart-breaking in equal measures.

But it wasn't enough. She needed to do more. Not just for those approaching The Crash Pad for assistance, but for those who weren't – which was the driving force behind her new project.

The shelter door opened and Jamie appeared, having finished his volunteer shift for the evening. Thankfully, the awkwardness following their swimming pool encounter had faded as the week had progressed and they'd been able to move past feeling embarrassed and become… well, maybe not 'mates', but they were certainly on friendlier terms.

He stopped by the van. 'What's all this?' he said, inspecting the pile of clothing draped over the railings. 'I thought you were heading home?'

'I will be soon. This is my latest initiative,' she said, lifting one of the padded jackets. 'As well as bedding, several people donated coats, gloves, and scarves on Saturday.'

He rubbed his arms, his thin grey sweater no match for the biting wind. 'I'm guessing you have a plan to use them?'

She nodded. 'I want to distribute them to people sleeping rough. I need to do some more research into where homeless people hang out in Streatham, but in the meantime, I'm going to let people come to the coats, rather than the other way around.' She threw another pile of clothing into the boot. 'It might mean some coats get nicked, but if it keeps a few people warmer, then it's worth the risk.'

He leant back against the railings. 'So, what's the plan?'

'I'm going to attach the coats to trees and lampposts, and anywhere else that's visible with a note pinned to the front.' She showed him one of the printed signs. *Please only take me if you're homeless.* 'Tucked inside the pockets of each coat is a scarf, a pair of gloves, a pair of thermal socks and a chocolate bar.'

He looked puzzled. 'People donated socks?'

'Well, no, I had to buy the socks… and the chocolate bars, but everything else was donated. I didn't want to see it go to waste. What do you think? Is it a good plan?'

He pushed away from the railings. 'It's a great plan, but you're not doing it alone.'

She waved away his concern. 'I'll be fine. I won't venture anywhere unsafe. I'll leave the coats in public places.'

His wavy hair lifted in the wind. 'I still think someone should come with you.'

'There isn't anyone available.' She loaded more coats into the van.

'There's me.'

'You've done your shift for this evening.'

He picked up the last pile of coats. 'So have you.'

'Yes, but you were on the night shift last night. You must be exhausted.'

'I'm fine.'

'Seriously, Jamie. I'll be okay. Go home and get some sleep.'

'I will once we're done. And two people means it'll get done quicker. Then you can get home to bed too.' He dumped the coats in the van and shut the doors.

She could tell he wasn't going to be dissuaded. 'In that case, thank you. I appreciate your help.'

'Good. Because I wasn't taking no for an answer.' He opened the passenger door. Or tried to. It was stuck and needed a good yank. 'A little different to the Merc, huh?'

Her hands went to her hips. 'Are you going to criticise my van now?'

'I wouldn't dare. I'm just saying, it's quite a change.'

'Yeah, well, as you pointed out, driving around in a Merc wasn't exactly appropriate.' She climbed into her new van, still getting used to the smell of plastic rather than luxury leather... which, as a vegan, was a definite positive.

He climbed in beside her. 'I hope that's not why you changed it? You shouldn't take any notice of anything I say. I told you, I was being a judgemental prick.'

'I know.'

He laughed.

She gave him a half-smile. 'Don't flatter yourself. I changed my car because it was the right thing to do,' she said, starting the engine. 'I needed something more practical.'

'Well, this is certainly practical.' He took in the basic dashboard and rock-hard seats. 'Not a luxury gadget in sight.'

'And it's cheaper to run and does more miles to the gallon. Plus, the boot is huge, which means I don't need to visit the wholesalers so often. If I'm going to distribute coats on a regular basis, I'll need the appropriate transportation.'

'You want to make this a regular thing?'

'I figured if we held donation drives throughout the year, we'd collect enough stuff to run the project every winter.'

'Nice idea.'

'I think so.' She pulled away, having to floor the accelerator to get the economic one-litre engine to respond. It certainly didn't have the power of the Merc.

'Is it helping having a commercial washing machine?'

'Crikey, yes. It saves so much time, not to mention money.' She glanced at him as they pulled onto the main road. 'I never really thanked you for getting me that, did I?'

'Sure, you did. I'm just glad it helps.'

'Can I repay you for it? I have money left over from the sale of my car.'

He gave her an exasperated look. 'I told you, it was a gift. Keep the money. You're bound to need it for something else. Repairs for this probably,' he added, when the glove compartment door flopped open.

She reached over and shut it. 'Well, I'm very grateful. Thank you.'

'You're welcome.' He smiled and once again she was struck by how handsome he was, even in the dark.

Not that it mattered. But whereas she used to think he was all looks and no substance, she had to admit her opinion of him had changed. He was a decent bloke. Which didn't help dampen her attraction towards him. Maybe if he'd remained a judgemental grump, it would be easier to ignore him.

She sighed and turned onto Ambleside Avenue, wondering which house belonged to Harold. The elderly man still came into the shelter every day for his lunch, wearing his new slippers. He seemed happy enough, and the kids liked him, so she didn't see any harm in allowing him to use the facilities.

She glanced at the houses lining the road. Some of the properties were grand, others had been converted into flats. She spotted a cute bungalow with a neat front hedge and coloured Christmas lights flashing in the windows. She hoped that was Harold's home, he deserved to live somewhere nice.

The traffic lights were in her favour and she swung onto Tooting Bec Road. 'How was the night shift? Fraser said it ran smoothly.'

'It did.' Jamie turned to look at her. 'He's an interesting character, isn't he?'

'Fraser?' She indicated right and pulled into the lido car park. 'I suppose he is. I've got a lot of time for Fraser. He's one of the good guys.'

'He's had a hard time though, hasn't he?'

She parked under the overhanging trees. 'Did he tell you about himself?'

'He did, yeah. About how he joined the army at sixteen, but had to be medically discharged a few years back with PTSD. I didn't realise he'd had problems with alcohol. But he said he's working hard to remain sober so he can regain access to his kids. He's only allowed supervised visits at the moment.' He unbuckled his seatbelt and then stilled. '*Shit*. Please tell me you know all this and I haven't just dropped him in it?'

She opened the van door. 'Don't worry, Fraser wanted me to know everything before I took him on.' She climbed out and went around to the boot. 'But he doesn't tell many people, so keep it to yourself, okay?'

'Of course.' He looked around. 'Where are we?'

'Outdoor swimming pool. It's one of London's hidden treasures, it's been here for over a hundred years. Haven't you ever been?'

He shook his head. 'Not much of a swimmer.'

'Really? Didn't you learn as a kid?' She slipped on her hoodie and zipped it up.

'Not really, no.' He broke eye contact.

Had she touched a nerve? She hadn't meant to.

She handed him a couple of coats. 'You know, Fraser must like you. It's not usual for him to open up like that. Apart from Norah and Emily, I don't think many people know about his background.' She picked up a few more coats and shut the doors.

'It was a quiet night, so we played pool. I guess we ended up… sharing.'

She headed for the trees. 'A budding bromance, eh?'

He followed her. 'He started off telling me about Afghanistan and how he lost his leg. One thing led to another and we ended up talking about our lives.'

Unzipping the first coat, she draped it around a tree. 'And what information did you share with him? Or aren't I allowed to know?'

'Nothing very exciting.'

'Fair enough. It's your business, I won't pry.' She zipped up the coat and fixed the sign to the front. But having said she wouldn't pry, she couldn't resist pointing out the imbalance in their relationship. 'It occurred to me the other day I don't really know much about you. Anything, in fact. And you know all my dirty little secrets.'

He looked at her. 'I do?'

'Well, some of them.' She moved to the next tree. 'It would be nice to know something about you. You know, seeing as how we're *mates* now.'

He didn't immediately respond.

Instead, he attached a jacket to one of the lampposts. 'There's not much to say really. I support West Ham. I hate early mornings, moaners and Marmite. I watch a lot of crap TV, and eat a lot crap takeaways. I have a few close mates, but I don't socialise much. I tend to overthink things. I'm quick to judge and slow to trust.'

His honesty shocked her. 'Wow, that's quite an insight.'

He shrugged. 'You wanted to know.' He turned and walked back to the van, not inviting any follow up questions.

But he'd piqued her curiosity.

She attached another coat to a tree and joined him by the van. He was leaning against the passenger door, looking across Tooting Bec Common.

She leant next to him. 'Why are you slow to trust?'

It was a while before he answered. His face was a picture of concentration, like he was trying to work it out himself. 'People have let me down in the past.'

'So you figure it's easier to keep people at arm's length, than risk getting hurt again?'

'Something like that.'

'That's sad. But understandable, I guess.' When nothing more was forthcoming, she pushed away from the van. 'We'd better get going, or we'll be out all night.'

He followed her lead and they returned to the van.

They headed out of the car park and re-joined the A214. Tooting Bec Common was busy, filled with visitors enjoying the Christmas market. A group of kids were messing about and laughing, drinking from beer cans and eating roasted chestnuts from one of the stalls, a world away from the kids at the shelter.

They drove past the drinking fountain and cricket pitch and common cafe. She kept her eyes peeled, looking for suitable places to stop. She wondered if Jamie had ever been homeless. Is that what had driven him to volunteer? Was that why he found it hard to trust people?

'What about your family?' she asked, as they circled the common and headed back towards the town centre. 'Are you close?'

He noticeably stiffened at her question. For a moment, she feared he was about to tell her to mind her own business. Instead, he rubbed his forehead, as if contemplating his answer. 'Only with my foster mum.' His voice was quiet and she could tell he'd risked a lot by voicing those words aloud. She imagined he didn't divulge that information to many people.

'You were brought up in care?'

'From the age of seven.' His hands squeezed his thighs, his unease tangible. 'I went to Peggy's when I was fourteen. I stayed with her until after I left uni.'

They turned into the high street and drove past Nandos. Above the road, a set of huge star-garlands hung down, zigzagging across the road, creating a magical twinkling tunnel. It was a pretty sight.

She wanted to ask him about his childhood but decided he might clam up if she was too intrusive. Instead, she asked, 'What did you read at uni?'

The question seemed to relax him. 'Media studies. I have this insane dream to become a documentary film-maker.'

'Why is it insane?' She spotted a parking space outside the Odeon cinema. She bumped the van onto the kerb before coming to a halt. The Skoda certainly didn't have the same ease of parking as the Merc. Then she remembered something. 'Is that why I saw you filming Alfie today?'

Jamie exited the van and waited for her on the pavement. 'He's agreed to let me follow his story. He's a fascinating kid.'

Opening the rear doors, she unearthed the next batch of coats. 'I don't know much about him, just snippets from what Emily's told me.'

Jamie took a few coats from her. 'He's had a rough time of it, but he has this endless positivity. It's like he genuinely believes everything will work out if he keeps trying.'

'And you don't?'

'I'm not sure anymore.' He hooked a coat around a parking pillar. 'I switch between thinking the kid is delusional, to desperately wanting a happy ending for him.' Buttoning up the coat, Jamie made sure the sign was visible. 'People have let him down badly and yet he's not bitter. He's been hurt, but he's still a hopeless romantic. He's continuously rejected for jobs and housing and yet he keeps trying. I admire him.'

She attached a coat to the pedestrian crossing. 'Maybe he reminds you of you?'

He paused, as if thinking about it. 'Nah, I'm way more cynical.'

She fixed another coat to the railings. 'But you've obviously had to work hard to turn your life around. Statistically, children who enter the care system struggle at school and find it harder to integrate into society. But look at you. You're smart, you have a degree. You have career aspirations and you're contributing to society. I'd say that was a pretty successful outcome for a someone who was taken into care aged seven.'

His expression was undecipherable.

'What I mean is,' she continued, 'that's a particularly difficult age for a child to be separated from his birth family.'

'You're not going to start analysing me about my attachment issues, are you?'

She narrowed her eyes at him. 'Do you have attachment issues?'

'No.' He looked grumpy. 'Yes.' And then he walked
back to the van and climbed inside. He clearly didn't want
to have this conversation in public, or maybe at all.

Sam returned to the van and waited until there was
a gap in the traffic so she could pull out. There were a
zillion questions she was burning to ask, but she knew it
was better to let him take the lead. This was a sensitive
topic.

Just when she thought it was conversation over, he said
quietly, 'Like I said before, I'm quick to judge and slow to
trust.'

He was giving her the green light to resume their
discussion. She wondered if he had many people to talk
to about this. It would be a shame if he'd never had
professional counselling. 'Is there anyone you trust?'

He squeezed his thighs again. 'I trust my foster mum,
Peggy.'

'No one else?'

'What is this, a therapy session?' He didn't sound
snappy, more... embarrassed.

'I didn't mean to pry. It's just...' she trailed off,
wondering whether it was appropriate for her to voice
her thoughts.

'Just, what?'

She turned into the layby next to the cemetery. 'You're
starting to make sense to me, that's all. I guessed something
had happened to you, but I didn't know what. Now I do.
Some of it, anyway.' Climbing out of her seat, she gave
the area a quick scan. 'This looks like a hot-spot. What
do you think?'

He looked to where a few bodies were curled into the porch-way of the church. 'There's more over there,' he said, nodding to a man and his dog sheltering beneath the ornate stone archways.

She went to the van and collected the remaining coats. 'Probably best if we stick together, it's dark inside the cemetery.' She was glad Jamie was with her. In fact, she wouldn't be venturing inside otherwise.

It didn't seem respectful to attach the coats to the gravestones. Fortunately there were a series of signposts positioned along the walkway.

'My dad was a drug addict,' he said, surprising her. 'He was also a dealer. He left before I was born. Last anyone heard he was in prison.'

She tied a coat to a thin post. 'What about your mum?'

'She was a drug addict too. That's why I was taken into care.'

And she thought her parents were challenging. 'You never went back home?'

He shook his head. 'I never heard from her again until a couple of years ago. She wrote to me via social services. That's how I discovered she'd gone on to have three more kids.'

'Were they taken into care too?'

'Not that I know of.' He sighed. 'Apparently, she's sober now. She writes to me at my foster mum's, but I don't read her letters. I know what she wants, though. She wants to see me.'

'And you don't want to see her?'

'No.' He walked off, turned, and then walked back. 'Yes.' He rubbed his forehead. 'Oh, shit, I don't know.'

'So you keep thinking about it and torturing yourself about what you should do?'

He slumped onto a stone bench. 'About a thousand times a day.'

She attached another coat to a signpost. 'Do you find yourself getting angry? Replaying the same argument in your head, demanding to know how she could let you go?'

Jamie dropped his head into his hands. 'Yes.'

'Then maybe you need to see her. Not for her sake, but for your own.'

'Please don't tell me I need to forgive her. I'm sick of people telling me that.'

Sam could understand that. After carrying the last remaining coat over to the bench, she sat next to him. 'I don't think it's about forgiveness. I think it's about acceptance.'

His head lifted to look at her. 'How do you mean?'

'We're all a product of our upbringing. We're shaped and influenced by those around us. But at some point, we have to take all of that information and make informed choices about who we are and what kind of life we want to lead.'

She draped the last coat around his shoulders. He was shivering but she didn't think he'd noticed.

'Take me, for example. I grew up feeling like I never fitted in and I was a constant disappointment to my family. It made me unhappy at the time, but it doesn't anymore.' She paused. 'Well, not as much as it used to. The reason being, I've accepted who I am. And more to the point, I've accepted who they are.'

Pulling the scarf from the coat pocket, she wrapped it around his neck. 'We have different values and morals. Different ambitions and goals. But you know what, that's okay. We don't have to be the same. I'll love them anyway and they'll always love me, however much they grumble about my choices.'

'So what are you saying?'

'I'm saying, you can't make the same decision, because you don't have all the facts.' She unearthed the chocolate bar from the coat and unwrapped it. 'You're trying to reach a decision based on events that happened over twenty years ago. But you've changed. Your mum has too, by the sounds of it. The only way to gain peace is to visit her and see whether she's someone you want to have in your life, or whether she's someone you don't want anything to do with.'

She broke off a piece of chocolate and handed it to him. 'It's no longer anybody else's decision about what happens to you. The power is with you. It's your life. Your choice.'

Seemingly on autopilot, he took the chocolate. 'You think I should see her?'

'Only you can decide that. But if you really didn't want to see her, then you wouldn't be feeling this conflicted.'

With a thoughtful expression on his face, he chewed his piece of chocolate. 'Won't seeing her reopen old wounds?'

'Probably. But sometimes the only way a wound can heal is by reinjuring it. You have questions. She has the answers. Worst-case scenario? It's a terrible visit, you hate every minute of it, and you leave vowing never to return.'

'Is that supposed to persuade me?'

'But the pain will fade. And in the long-term you'll be glad you went because it gave you closure.' He didn't look convinced. 'Best-case scenario? Your mum's turned her life around, she begs for your forgiveness, and she becomes the mother figure you always wanted.'

He made a scoffing sound. 'Highly unlikely.'

'The more likely scenario is that it'll be an awkward visit, mixed with both good and bad moments, and you leave feeling emotionally exhausted and sad about all the what-might-have-beens. Either way, it'll help you accept what has happened to you and enable you to make a choice about your own future and the kind of man you want to be.'

He turned to face her. 'Will you come with me?'

Sam blinked in surprise. 'Pardon?'

'To visit my mother. Will you come with me?' His eyes were earnest and pleading… and heartbreakingly sad. 'I've spoken to therapists and social workers and so-called experts about this over the years and none of them have made as much sense as you did just now. Please come with me.'

Crikey, she hadn't expected that. But how could she refuse? After all, he'd suffered one of her mother's painful soirees. 'If you think it'll help. But isn't there someone else you'd rather take?'

'No. I want you there.' His hand covered hers. 'Please?'

She stared into his intense eyes and felt the ground shift beneath her. 'If you're sure.' Maybe delving into such personal territory wasn't such a smart idea, after all.

And then her phone rang, slicing through the bubble of intimacy that seemed to have surrounded them.

She glanced at the screen. Talking of difficult mothers.

'Excuse me a moment. I need to take this.' She stood and moved away from the bench. It seemed insensitive to be chatting with her mother when Jamie had just been telling her how awful his own was. But far from the usual preambles, her mother's opening question was, 'Is Max with you?'

'Max? Of course, not. Why?'

'He's gone missing.'

'Missing?' She turned to Jamie. 'What do you mean, he's gone missing?'

Chapter Eighteen

The M25 was busy. Thankfully, they'd left early, so despite the heavy congestion they were due to arrive in Canvey Island on time. Jamie wasn't sure whether that was a good thing or not. Sitting in traffic had given him time to think. Too much time. His already nervous state had been enhanced, causing his driving to become erratic.

Sam had refrained from comment. Instead, she'd sat in silence in the passenger seat, ignoring his fingers drumming against the steering wheel and letting him stew in his own thoughts. Just as she was stewing in hers. They both had their problems.

He glanced at Sam. 'Still thinking about Max?'

'It's hard not to,' she said, pushing her dark hair away from her face. She was wearing it loose today and he liked it. Not that his opinion mattered, but she looked more relaxed with her hair down. 'We know he's safe, so that's something. I just wish I knew where he was.'

'Have you had any further communication from him?'

She shook her head. 'Just the one text saying he's okay and not to worry.'

'Easier said than done.'

'Tell me about it.' She rolled her eyes. 'My brother's forty years old and he's never needed time to "think things through" before. Max is a doer, not a thinker. And I mean that in the nicest possible way.'

Jamie's stomach dipped when he saw signs for Canvey Island. 'Midlife crisis?'

'That's what my mother thinks. In which case, why doesn't he just buy a bloody Harley Davidson and be done with it? But disappearing off the face of the planet? Not even contacting work? It's so unlike him.'

'I know you don't think it's work-related, but it seems strange he'd risk his career by going AWOL.'

'That's what worries me. I tried speaking to his colleagues, but they're as baffled as we are. If they know anything, they're keeping quiet.'

'Have you spoken to Xanthe?'

Sam groaned. 'I tried to, but she launched into a tirade about how my brother was letting her down by not attending some fancy function with her this weekend. She's not worried about his safety or the state of his mind, only how it impacts her. Talk about self-centred.'

'You know, you didn't have to come today. I'd have understood if you'd wanted to stay home and search for your brother.'

She ran her hands through her hair and twisted it above her head. 'Honestly, I'm glad of the distraction. And anyway, my parents are looking for Max. They're talking about hiring a private investigator.' She gripped the seat when he got too close to the car in front.

He slowed down. Agitation was making him twitchy with the accelerator.

'Personally, I think we should give Max some space,' she said, her nails digging into the seat. 'That's what he's asked for and we should respect that. But they don't want to sit back and do nothing. Besides, I promised to come with you today, and I wasn't going to back out.'

He was grateful. Although in truth, he was still questioning why he'd asked her to come in the first place. It had been a spur of the moment reaction to them talking about his childhood. Why he'd divulged so much, he had no idea. He'd never told any of his previous girlfriends about his past, yet for some reason he'd blurted everything out to Sam. And she wasn't even a girlfriend. Just a *mate*.

Whatever the reason, he'd woken the next morning feeling an acute sense of mortification and wishing he'd never opened his big mouth. But the idea of facing his mother alone had filled him with dread. So much so, he knew he wouldn't be going if Sam wasn't with him.

'Enough about my problems,' she said, reaching for the water bottle. 'How are you feeling about seeing your mum?'

'Sick to my stomach.'

'I think that might be down to your driving.' She gave him a wry smile. 'Water?'

'No thanks.' He took the exit for Canvey Island. 'I never knew it was possible to feel this nervous. Or conflicted.' He hadn't slept last night or eaten anything this morning. His stomach was in knots.

'Whatever happens today, you'll be glad you came.'

'I wish I shared your confidence.'

'Are you worried your mum won't like you?'

He jolted. 'Why would you say that?' His loss of concentration caused him to swerve across the road. 'She's the one who fucked up, not me. I don't care what she thinks about me. Why would I?'

'Sorry, sorry.' She grabbed the dashboard, waiting until he'd steadied the car. 'Forget I said anything. My mistake.'

Damn right. He wasn't the one on trial, his mother was. He had no interest in impressing her. This was about her proving to him she was worthy of being a part of his life. He didn't need his mother's approval, he'd done fine without her. Great, in fact. He'd beaten the odds, gained a degree, got a good job. He had dreams and goals and aspirations, all without any input from his mother.

So why did he feel so frickin' nervous?

He glanced at Sam. 'Sorry for snapping.'

'You've nothing to apologise for. I was out of line. I forgot I wasn't a social worker anymore.'

Taking the exit for Thorney Bay, he tried to dissect her words. 'You must've asked the question for a reason?'

'It doesn't matter. I was talking nonsense.'

He rubbed the back of his neck. He felt sweaty and uncomfortable in his own skin, probably because she'd struck a nerve. 'It's illogical for me to want her to like me,' he admitted, his clammy hands gripping the steering wheel. 'But are you implying it wouldn't be unusual?'

As if considering her response, she hesitated before replying. 'You wouldn't be the first person to feel that way. Kids don't think like adults do. Their brains haven't fully developed. They lack logic, so they have no idea their home life isn't regular, or safe, and they don't understand why they're being taken away. They assume it's something they've done, that's it's their fault and they're being punished for misbehaving.' She paused. 'Did you feel like that?'

He nodded. 'I promised the policewoman I'd behave better if she let me go home.'

'Oh, Jamie.' She reached over and squeezed his hand. 'Most kids react the same way. And even though as adults we're able to reason why these things happen, it doesn't always eradicate the feeling that there was something we could've done to prevent it. But you know it wasn't about you, right?'

'Logically, yeah.'

'And it's still not about you.'

He frowned. 'How do you mean?'

'If your mum doesn't react the way you're hoping for today and be the kind, caring, stable woman you want her to be, it's not a reflection on you. Okay?'

'Okay.' He knew she was right.

'But for the record, if she isn't impressed and doesn't think you're an amazing human being, then she's batshit crazy.'

With an abrupt laugh, he felt something easing in his shoulders. She thought he was amazing?

'If at any point it gets too overwhelming today, just let me know and we're out of there, okay? Tug on your left ear as a sign and I'll invent an emergency so we can escape.'

He rubbed his chest, trying to control his breathing. 'Thanks.'

She patted his hand. 'I'm on your side, remember?'

The sign for the mobile home park came into view. It was a big park with numerous dwellings spread around the area. He followed the numbers and parked across from where his mother lived. He almost couldn't look.

Sam strained to see out of the window. 'Are we here?'

He nodded. They were here.

The sight ahead was a far cry from the rundown area of his childhood. The property was a bungalow, painted cream with white shutters and bay windows. A pinecone wreath hung from the front door next to an inflatable Father Christmas. It looked nice. Happy. Safe.

He climbed out of the car, needing some fresh air. It was a blustery day, but the sun occasionally appeared from behind the wispy clouds, casting the sandstone paving in a wintery sheen.

Sam joined him on the walkway. 'Ready to do this?'

'God, no.' He turned to her. 'How do I look?'

'Handsome.' And then she blinked, as if she'd said something out of turn. 'I mean… smart. Well-groomed. Appropriately dressed for making a good impression.' She averted her gaze.

He was glad she approved. 'Thanks.'

They crossed the pedestrian walkway. 'You look nice too, by the way.'

'Thanks. I didn't think paint-splattered dungarees would be suitable.' She smoothed down the front of her red jumper as they stepped up to the front door.

He took a deep breath, not quite ready to ring the bell.

As if sensing his anxiety, Sam's warm hand closed around his. He was more grateful than he could express. 'You got this,' she whispered.

And then the door shot open. A woman with long blonde highlighted hair wearing a sports polo shirt and fitted jeans stood in the doorway.

They must have the wrong house. No way was this his mother. But then she said, 'Jamie?' and he instantly recognised her voice.

Shit, it *was* his mother.

Shock rendered him speechless. His recollection of his mum was of a skinny woman with sallow skin and rotten teeth. Not a woman with rosy cheeks, manicured nails and a perfect veneer smile.

'Come in, come in,' she said, seemingly caught between wanting to reach for him and being scared to touch him. Thankfully, a dog appeared in the hallway and barked, saving him from being hugged. He wasn't ready for physical intimacy.

His mother caught the dog's collar. 'It's all right, Cooper, they're friends.'

He still hadn't spoken. He was too shocked.

Sam came to his rescue. 'I'm Sam, a friend of Jamie's,' she said, stroking the dog's mane. 'What a lovely home you have, and such a gorgeous dog.' She crouched down and ruffled the Labrador's ears.

'Thank you. Yes, he's a sweetie. I'd be lost without him.'

Jamie flinched. She hadn't been lost without her son though, had she?

'I'm Kirsty,' she said to Sam. 'Come through to the lounge. I've made lunch; I thought you might be hungry after your journey. Was the traffic bad?'

Sam glanced at Jamie, waiting for him to answer. When he didn't, she said, 'Not too bad. The M25 was slow.'

'Isn't it always.' His mother gestured to the brown leather sofa pushed against the wall. 'Take a seat. I'll put the kettle on.'

His mother disappeared into what looked like the kitchen. He glanced around the room. It was light and airy. A family-sized dining table and chairs were positioned in front of French windows which led to a garden. He could see a football goal set up at the end of the lawn. A reminder he had brothers. Three of them.

Sam squeezed his hand. 'Sit down,' she whispered. 'Remember to breathe.'

He hadn't realised he'd been holding his breath. He sat on the sofa next to her. It was worn and faded in places and he could imagine a family lying on it watching the huge TV attached to the wall. A small Christmas tree sat in the corner, the decorations mismatched and seemingly homemade. There were numerous pictures hanging from a picture rail. Photos of football teams. Sports certificates. A school photo of three boys.

A lump constricted his throat.

Next to the TV was a display unit with more photos and ornaments. This time he recognised the subject. There were a range of photos from when he was born to the age of seven. Pictures of him smiling, cuddling a teddy, playing with a train set. But nothing after that. It was creepy. Like he'd died.

His mother returned carrying a tea tray. The china mugs and milk jug matched. She placed the tray on the coffee table where triangular-shaped sandwiches sat on a china plate, along with a selection of cakes and a bowl of crisps. It was nothing like he remembered. Meals had been irregular, leftovers thrown together from tins of food in the bare cupboards. He'd lived off cereal, mostly, feeding himself whenever he'd been hungry.

'How do you take your tea?' His mother looked directly at him.

Despite the assurance in her smile, he could see a slight shake in her hands. It was the first action he recognised, although he suspected this wasn't down to drug use. At least, he hoped not.

He opened his mouth with the intention of saying, 'Milk, no sugar,' but what came out was, 'Are you clean?'

If she was surprised by his direct line of questioning, she didn't show it. She simply nodded and said, 'Yes, eighteen years now.' She waited for another question. When it didn't come, she poured the tea. 'Help yourself to milk and sugar.'

Sam edged forwards and added milk to one of the mugs. 'Thank you, Kirsty. You've gone to so much effort.' She handed Jamie a mug of tea, urging him to drink it.

Sam's watchful eyes darted between estranged mother and son. As if sensing the pair needed a kick-start, she said, 'Maybe you could tell Jamie about your recovery? I imagine it wasn't easy.' She turned to Jamie, her hand resting on his knee. 'Is that okay with you?'

He nodded, grateful for her taking the lead, he seemed to have lost the ability to speak. And he was supposed to be an investigative journalist.

Kirsty remained kneeling by the coffee table. 'If that's what you want?' She looked at him with an anxious expression.

He nodded again. It helped to think of her as 'Kirsty', rather than wrestling with the fact that she was his mother.

She sipped her tea. 'I guess... I hit rock bottom after social services took you away,' she said, her voice steady and even, a contrast to the shake in her hands. 'I was angry and distressed, and I couldn't see it was my fault. I blamed the so-called do-gooders who'd stolen my son from me.'

If she was looking for sympathy, she was going to be disappointed. But her eyes remained cast downwards, as if overwhelmed by a sense of shame. 'I spiralled into a shocking state. I don't remember much about that time.'

He had no idea he was shaking, until Sam's hand slid up his back and gently rubbed, trying to get him to relax. 'That must've been difficult for you, Kirsty,' she said.

Kirsty began to rock, slow movements back and forth, which only stopped when the dog nudged her arm. She did a double-take and then patted the dog's head, and whispered, 'Good boy.'

A few moments later, she continued, 'It was a difficult time, yes. But I accepted the offer of a treatment programme and went into rehab. A few months after leaving, I met Mike. He supported me through my recovery and gave me something to live for.' Stroking the dog's ears, her smile was sad. 'Following rehab, I went through a period of deep self-loathing. I didn't feel like I deserved happiness. But Mike persuaded me otherwise. It took a long time, several years, in fact. Eventually we got married and it felt like I'd been given a second chance. We went on to have three boys. Liam, who's seventeen and in sixth form. Logan, who's fourteen, and Levi, who's just turned eleven. They're at school today.'

'Is Mike at work today?' Sam's hand still discreetly rubbed his back.

'Mike passed away a couple of years ago. Brain aneurism. It's just me and the boys now.'

Sam's hand stilled on Jamie's back. 'I'm very sorry for your loss, Kirsty. What an awful thing to happen.'

'But I didn't relapse,' she added quickly, her eyes darting to her son's. 'I didn't want to fall back into old habits, or risk losing the boys.'

He must have looked pained, because Sam resumed rubbing – harder this time – like an over-zealous Swedish masseuse.

Kirsty began fiddling with a leather strap tied to her wrist. 'Rehab taught me it isn't enough to just stop using drugs, you have to create a new life where it's easier not to use in the first place. There were too many triggers in my previous life. Reminders that would make me angry, or sad, or lonely, which would make the temptation to escape unbearable.'

Was he one of those triggers?

She took a deep breath. 'I knew if I was serious about reforming my life, then I had to make drastic changes. So, that's what I did, with Mike's help. We moved area, had the kids and made a home together. After he died, I had to change again and learn to be a single parent. So, I trained as a football coach.' She pointed to a team photo on the wall. 'I coach my youngest son's team.'

'That's amazing,' Sam said, turning to him. 'Isn't it, Jamie?'

He wanted to follow Sam's lead and join in the conversation, drink tea and eat the food on offer, but his mind and stomach were too knotted.

Kirsty offered him cake. 'Are you sure you wouldn't like something? More tea, perhaps?'

But he was feeling too claustrophobic. Too agitated.

He stood up. 'I need some air.'

She looked disappointed at the idea of him leaving.

Sam got to her feet. 'Good idea. Why don't we take the dog for a walk?'

On hearing the word 'walk' the dog went into a frenzy of excited barking and running around the room. Kirsty got up and grabbed the dog's collar. 'The beach is only down the road. We can take him there. He loves the sea. I'll get his lead.'

When she'd dragged the dog from the room, Sam turned to him. 'You okay?'

He shook his head. 'No. It's not what I expected. She's so... together and positive. With her perfect home and her perfect kids. Like she's got it all worked out.' He let out a shaky breath. 'My brain can't process it. I was expecting to find a flake... not a flipping... zen football coach.'

She touched his arm. 'It's a lot of information to absorb, I know. But don't panic, okay? You're doing really well.'

He raised an eyebrow. 'I've barely said a word.'

She smiled encouragingly. 'But you're still here, aren't you? You haven't run screaming from the room, threatening never to return or burst into hysterical tears.'

'I'm close,' he admitted.

She took his hand. 'Then it's a good thing we're going outside. You'll feel less tense in the open air. Trust me.' She tugged on his hand and they exited by the front door.

Kirsty joined them a few moments later, striding off down the pathway, the dog hot on her heels. 'This way.'

Jamie watched her, thinking how strong she looked. Her head was held high, her shoulders pulled back, and when she gave the dog a command he instantly obeyed.

It was totally irrational, but he couldn't help feeling disappointed she wasn't still a pathetic nervous wreck. It would have been easier to deal with. He'd have felt reassured she wasn't a woman capable of taking care of a kid, and he could have left feeling vindicated in his decision not to have her in his life.

They walked under the 'Welcome to Canvey Seafront' sign and passed the carousel and arcade of shopping booths, boarded up for the end of season. Kirsty removed the dog's lead and he immediately ran off, heading for the sea.

'He loves water,' she said, shielding her eyes from the sun. A beat passed before her gaze switched to Jamie and she gestured to the expanse of beach. 'Walk with me?'

Jamie searched for Sam, but she was running down to the water's edge, throwing sticks into the sea for the dog to fetch.

'Sam's rather lovely,' Kirsty said, mirroring his thoughts. 'Good friends are important to have.'

When he didn't offer a response, she walked off down the beach, albeit slowly.

He debated whether to follow. It would be easier to stay put, but that would be cowardly. He needed to see this through.

The sand was damp and hard to walk on, but the ache in his legs detracted from the ache in his chest.

When he caught up with Kirsty they walked together, not exactly companionably, but in step, listening to the crash of waves and sound of seagulls diving into the water.

He had no idea how to engage in conversation with this woman.

Thankfully, she spoke first. 'I have so many questions for you,' she said, her face angled towards the sea. 'But today isn't about me. It's about you. I can't even imagine the rage you must feel. You probably hate me. Quite rightly. But I'm hoping we can move past that and reconnect, I want that more than anything. Ask me anything you want. Don't hold back.'

But the words refused to come. He focused instead on the way his trainers left imprints in the sand.

'Cooper is a therapy dog, you know? I get quite depressed when I think about my past and what happened to you.' Her step slowed. 'Or rather, what I did to you. It's not like it was an accident, or something that was unpreventable. It was a direct result of my drug addiction. My selfishness resulted in you being taken into care.' She stopped and looked at him. 'I'll never forgive myself for that. Never.'

What was he supposed to say to that? I'll never forgive you either?

Then he remembered what Sam had said. It wasn't about forgiveness; it was about acceptance. And in order to achieve that, he needed some answers.

'You said you got sober eighteen years ago?'

He could sense her looking at him. 'That's right.'

'I would've been twelve. So why didn't you apply for custody?'

'That's a fair question.' She took a step closer. 'I did consider it, but when I spoke to social services they advised against it, said it would be too distressing for you. For me too. My recovery was in its fledgling stage, so any stress might've triggered a relapse. It was too risky.'

'Jesus.' Taking him back was considered too risky? He turned to her, suddenly angry. 'Do you have any idea how unhappy I was? I spent seven years being passed from one placement to another, feeling utterly alone and unloved. And you didn't think it was worth the *risk* to take me back?'

Her cheeks paled. 'I wanted to, believe me I did... but... I didn't trust myself not to let you down again.' She reached for him, but he pulled away. 'I'm trying to be honest with you, Jamie. By the time I felt strong enough to fight for you, it was too late.'

He frowned at her. 'How do you mean?'

'You were with Peggy. I wasn't allowed direct contact, but I knew you'd gone to a good home. Peggy kept me informed of your progress via my social worker. I knew you were doing well at school, you were playing football, and flourishing in your new environment.'

She made it sound like it had been easy. Well, it bloody hadn't been. It had taken him years to settle and trust Peggy.

'Peggy told me she loved you like you were her own son and I honestly felt you were better off with her than returning to me. I mean, look at you. No wonder she's so proud of you.'

'Don't,' he said, moving away. He couldn't cope with the cacophony of emotions swirling inside him. Thinking about Peggy would only send him over the edge.

She waited a while before approaching him again. 'You have no idea how sorry I am. For everything. I wish I could go back and relive that part of my life again. You deserved so much more. But I can't change the past, what's done is done. But I can change the future. I want to be a part of your life, Jamie. I want you to be a part of your brothers' lives. And they want that too.'

He felt tears threatening. He ran his hands into his hair, staring up at the vast expanse of sky, watching the birds hovering in the wind, wishing he could join them and fly away.

'It's completely up to you. Whatever you decide, I'll accept your decision.'

He backed away. 'I need time.'

'Take all the time you need. We're not going anywhere.' After a long pause, she turned and searched the beach. 'Now, where's that dog gone?' She wandered off, calling Cooper, putting on a brave face although he knew she was crying. He'd seen the tears before she'd turned away.

He slumped forwards, resting his hands on his knees. The tightness in his chest hurt. He didn't want to cry, not in public.

A hand touched his back, rubbing the muscles, soothing his pain. 'How's it going?'

He opened his eyes.

He could see Sam's wet feet standing next to him covered in sand.

'She's sorry. She wants to be in my life. And she wants me to meet my brothers. Like it's that easy?'

'It won't be easy. But that doesn't mean it won't be worth it in the long run.'

'I just feel so… angry. Like I don't want to let her off the hook. I want to punish her, to make her suffer like she made me suffer. Which makes me an arsehole, right?'

'No, it makes you human. But staying angry at her not only punishes her, it punishes you too. And you deserve so much more. Do you really want to spend your life bitter and twisted? Letting go of your anger might be the only way you can accept what's happened and move on with your life.'

He straightened.

She placed her hands on his shoulders, her face close to his, her hair tousled from the wind. 'Your mum has had years to sort her life out and come to terms with her mistakes. You haven't. This is all new and raw, and you need time to process and adjust. No one's saying you have to make a decision right now. Today is an important step. But it's only the first step in a very long journey. The good news is, it's done. The worst is over.'

His head dropped, weighed down by the decision ahead of him.

She lifted his chin. 'Go home, sleep on it, and see how you feel tomorrow. Or after the weekend, or next week. There's no rush. And if you do decide you want to try and build a relationship, then start small. Maybe a weekly phone call? Get to know her. Allow her to get to know you. Build up to meeting your brothers once you've adjusted to having your mum back in your life.'

She cupped his cheek. 'But you don't have to make any decisions today, okay?'

'Okay.' He rested his forehead against hers. The tickle of her loose hair soothed him, as did the feel of her hand touching his cheek. It was the first time he'd felt calm all day. 'Can we go home now?'

'Yes, but not while you're this knotted up. Your driving was bad enough on the way here. You'll kill us both if you drive home this tense.'

'I'll be fine.'

'No, you won't.' She pulled away, shocking him by dropping to her knees.

What the hell? 'What are you doing?'

She gave him a sarcastic glare. 'Don't get any daft ideas. You need to let off some steam.'

Aghast, he watched her roll up his trouser legs. 'Do you remember what happened last time we ended up in the water?'

'I'm sober this time,' she said, untying his trainers. 'Now take off your shoes.'

He did as he was told. Why, he wasn't sure. 'It's too cold. We'll freeze to death.'

'Then we'll stick to the sand. Come on, it'll be fun,' she said, grabbing his hand. With a tug, she dragged him down to the sea, laughing at his disgruntled expression.

Her laughter increased when a splash of freezing water touched his legs and he yelped and tried to run off. But she wasn't letting go. She dragged him further down the beach, encouraging him to let go and enjoy himself.

As crazy as it was, it proved to be the perfect stress-reliever. Her infectious laughter seemed to fill a void inside of him and before long he was splashing her back, picking her up and threatening to dunk her under the water. She clung to him, her arms around him soothing and tight.

Outwardly, it was playful and fun. Inwardly, he clung to her like she was a lifebelt, the only thing keeping him afloat.

Chapter Nineteen

Monday, 10th December

Emily left the college campus still buzzing from doing well in her practical exam. Her course tutor was delighted with her progress and said she was one of the most mature students she'd ever taught. She was sure Emily would be able to secure a good job placement once she'd completed her course, going so far as to offer to line up a few interviews within the industry if she wanted to gain some work experience ahead of graduating. It had been a huge compliment, especially as Emily was barely halfway through the first term of her two-year course.

Distracted from being in such a heady daydream, she almost missed her bus. Thankfully, the driver spotted her and pulled over, allowing her to board. Heading for a seat at the back, she settled in for the short journey.

Tempting as it was to get carried away by all the praise and get a job in a fancy restaurant, she was happy to stay volunteering at the shelter. A proper job would be hard work and long hours. Not that she was afraid of hard work, but it would add an extra pressure to her studies.

She enjoyed her work at the shelter, it fitted with her college hours and allowed her the freedom to experiment with her cooking. Sam was more than happy for her to try out new recipes, and she got a boost from helping kids like herself. So it was important for her to stay at The Crash Pad, at least for the duration of her course. Even after that, hopefully. If she could combine working full-time with volunteering, she'd have the perfect life.

She gazed out of the window, beyond grateful she no longer had to sleep rough on nights like this. It was dark and raining, the pavements wet from cars splashing through the puddles. How lucky she was to be going home to a warm flat and a comfy bed.

It was crazy to think how much her life had changed in recent months. She'd gone from being homeless, with no money, or real friends and family, to living independently and enrolling in college. She could still hardly believe it.

It made her smile to think how nervous she'd been on her first day at college, unsure of whether she'd even last the distance. But her determination to better her life had pulled her through those first few days. Well, that and having the support of her friends.

Norah's cookery lessons had given her confidence in the practical classes, and Sam's belief in her abilities to manage shifts at the shelter had helped her self-belief. Along with Fraser always having her back, she felt like she wasn't battling alone. She had support. Friends. A family, even.

And then there was Alfie.

Sweet, kind, funny Alfie, who encouraged her to dream big and be more positive about the future.

Just thinking about him made her smile.

The bus pulled up at her stop and she got off, pulling up the hood of her jacket to keep dry as she walked up towards Central Hill Estate.

As she neared the block of flats, she glanced up at the second floor and counted the windows from left to right until she reached her flat. The lights were on, which meant Alfie was home. Her heart gave a little flutter. She was getting used to him being there.

She crossed the road and entered the stairwell. He'd been staying with her for nearly two weeks now. For the first week, he'd packed his bag every morning intending to leave. He'd reach the front door, before she invited him to stay another night.

He'd never assumed it was okay for him to stay, and she appreciated that. In truth, she still wasn't entirely comfortable about sharing her space with someone else and she'd felt on edge the whole time. But after a week of sharing meals, watching TV and chatting about their respective days, she'd started to relax. She'd begun to sleep better. It felt good to have someone to talk to.

So, last Friday she'd told him he didn't need to pack his bag each day. He was welcome to stay until he found somewhere permanent to live. He'd looked relieved, and happy. But also unwilling to outstay his welcome. She'd assured him she was okay with him staying. And strangely, she was.

Reaching her front door, she inserted her key. She could hear the TV on in the background.

No sooner had she opened the door, when Alfie appeared in the corridor. 'I was looking out the window for you,' he said, smiling in that open way of his. 'I saw you coming. Dinner's ready. I hope you're hungry?'

She shrugged off her jacket. 'You made dinner?'

'Well, sort of. Beans on toast.' He gave her a sheepish grin. 'But I added grated cheese. That's posh, right?'

She laughed. 'Very posh. You didn't have to do that.'

'Sure, I did. You're helping me out by letting me crash here. And you cook for me all the time, I need to pull my weight.' He shoved his hands in his jeans pockets and bunched his shoulders. He looked cute in his X-Men T-shirt.

She followed him into the lounge. It was spotless, like it was every night. The cushions were plumped up, the throw straightened, the sides dusted and the crumbs hoovered up. 'You don't have to clean every day, you know.'

He ruffled his dark hair. 'It's my way of saying thank you.'

And then she noticed the tiny Christmas tree perched on the coffee table, the little angel on top twinkled brightly, making her smile. 'Cute tree.'

'I know, right?' He looked sheepish. 'I got it down the market. Do you like it?'

'I love it.' She kicked off her boots and dumped her college bag on the floor. 'My very first Christmas tree. Dinner smells good.'

'Take a seat. I'll bring it through.' He pressed mute on the TV and padded off in his socked-feet. 'Orange juice?'

'Yes, please.'

Having fruit juice in the flat was a real treat. It had been hard enough finding water on the streets, let alone anything fresh. Buying cartons of juice was her way of celebrating how far she'd come.

'How was college?' he said from the kitchen. 'Did you pass your practical?'

'Yes.' She didn't like to mention she'd come top of her class, it seemed like bragging.

Alfie appeared with her orange juice. 'Top of the class?'

Her cheeks grew warm. 'Maybe.'

'You were, weren't you?' He grinned and handed her the juice. 'Good for you. What about the written exam?'

'I passed that too.'

'Brilliant.' And then he clocked her expression. 'But?'

'My grammar and spelling need a bit of work.' She'd been embarrassed by the number of red circles on her paper.

'Surely it's whether you can cook that counts?'

'Not if I want to run my own restaurant. I'll need to be able to write emails and stuff.'

He sat down beside her on the sofa, close enough that their shoulders bumped. 'Don't be despondent. You're just out of practice, that's all. You probably haven't had to write anything down for years.'

'The other kids use computers or tablets,' she admitted. 'I'm the only one who hand-writes anything.'

The girls in her class had openly laughed when they'd seen her scribbled essay. It had taken the edge off her success in the practical exam. Not that she cared what the other kids thought, but it had stung just the same.

'You're showing skills those other kids don't have,' he said, nudging her. 'I bet they use spellcheck. If they had to hand-write their work I bet it wouldn't be any better than yours.'

She shrugged. 'Maybe. I might enrol in an adult learning class. They have them at the college. And it's only one night a week. I'm sure Sam won't mind if ask to reduce my shifts.'

'I'm sure she won't. Sounds like a plan.' He nudged her again. 'You still passed the exam, though. So don't beat yourself up too much. Okay?'

He was right. She just didn't like feeling dumb. 'How was your day?'

'Good. I met with Jamie and we did some filming.' The toaster popped in the kitchen and he jumped up. 'Back in a minute.' He ran into the kitchen and began buttering the toast. 'He came with me to work and asked questions while I delivered pizzas. It was funny to see the look on people's faces. One bloke asked if I was famous.'

She relaxed back in the sofa. 'What did you say?'

'I told him I was. I said I was filming for the TV show Secret Millionaire.' He grinned. 'Trouble was, he never tipped me. Said if I was loaded I didn't need the cash.'

She giggled. 'That's a shame.'

He dished up the beans. 'It was cool, though, being filmed. No idea whether it'll make a difference. But you've got to try, right?' He sprinkled grated cheese over the top. 'Does your oven have a grill?'

'Middle button on the right.'

He lit the grill and slid a plate underneath. 'Always better if the cheese is melted.'

'Agreed.'

'By the way, you have post.' He nodded to the letters on the coffee table.

She picked them up. Most of them were for the previous tenant. She'd have to drop them off at the post office. There was a letter from the water company about her meter reading and an official-looking brown envelope from the council with the words *This Is Not A Circular* written in bold.

Strange. She was up to date with her council tax. What could it be?

'Start without me,' he said, carrying in her dinner on a lap-tray. 'Mine isn't ready yet.' He placed it on the coffee table. 'I nearly forgot, Fraser gave me this today.' He picked up a DVD case. 'Season one of *How To Get Away With Murder*. We could watch it later, if you want?'

But she was too preoccupied reading the letter from the council.

'Emily? Everything okay?'

She could hardly believe what she was reading. 'Someone's reported me.'

'Reported you?' He came over. 'What for?'

'To the council. For illegally sub-letting.'

He stilled. 'Oh, crap.'

Her eyes scanned over the words. 'According to my tenancy agreement, sofa-surfing isn't permitted.'

'Can I see?'

She handed him the letter, feeling slightly sick.

He read it wordlessly, and then swore when he realised his dinner was burning under the grill. He ran into the kitchen and grabbed the plate, which was hot, and he promptly burnt his hand, dropping the plate. 'Shit!' He fell to his knees.

Emily ran into the kitchen. 'No! It's still hot. You'll burn yourself.' She ran the cold tap. 'Come here.'

'But the mess—'

'The mess can wait. Come over here, put your hand under the tap.' She caught his T-shirt when he reluctantly got to his feet and dragged him towards the sink, shoving his hand under the water. 'Hold still.'

He did as she asked, but she could feel him shaking. Or was she the one shaking? She didn't know. Her hand was holding his under the cold water. Her other arm was around his waist. It was the closest they'd ever been. Their bodies touching, their heads next to each other. So close that if she turned they'd bump noses.

'I'm sorry,' he whispered.

'You've nothing to be sorry for.'

'I've put you at risk. The letter says you'll be evicted unless you comply with the terms of your tenancy. I'll leave tonight.' He tried to pull away, but she held onto him.

'The letter also says I have seven days, so we don't need to do anything tonight. Tomorrow we'll try and find you somewhere else to go. I'll talk to Sam, see if she can secure you a bed at the shelter.'

'You don't have to do that. It's my problem, not yours.'

'But I don't want you to go,' she said, tears blurring her vision.

He looked into her eyes, his expression kind and filled with tenderness, and desperately sad. 'I don't want to go, either. I've loved staying here. With you.'

'We can sort this,' she said, her voice faltering.

'I won't risk you losing this place. You've worked too hard, come through so much. I have to leave.'

'But not tonight. Please?'

'It's better not to risk it. I'll be okay, you know I will.' He bent his head and dropped a kiss on the end of her nose. For once, she didn't flinch from the contact.

In fact, she didn't mind him kissing her. Touching her. She didn't want to let him go.

'You have no idea how grateful I am for you letting me stay, Emily. I'll never forget your kindness.' He pulled away.

She felt like he was taking her heart with him.

It felt so unfair, so cruel. Why had someone been so mean as to report them? They hadn't been doing anyone any harm.

He dropped to the floor, but she ushered him away. 'I'll do this.' She fetched the dustpan and brush. 'How's your hand?'

'It's fine,' he said, but she could see the red marks on his fingers. 'I'll pack my things.'

While he collected his stuff together, she swept the broken plate and spilled dinner into a rubbish bag, all the while fighting back tears. She felt like her heart was breaking.

'That's everything,' he said, a few minutes later, standing by the coffee table wearing his big coat and green beanie, his rucksack by his side.

'It's too late for a bed at the shelter tonight,' she said, desperate for him to stay. 'Why don't you stay here tonight? One more night won't make a difference.'

'It might,' he said with a shrug. 'I can't risk it. Take care, Emily.'

'Wait!' She rummaged through a kitchen drawer and ran over to him. 'At least take this.'

He looked down at the burn cream and smiled. 'Thanks.'

'What else can I give you? Money? Food? You haven't eaten. At least stay for some dinner. Have mine. Look it's there ready to be eaten.' She pointed to the tray of beans-on-toast. 'You don't have to leave right now.'

'I do,' he said, quietly. 'Every moment I stay is torture.' A tear spilled from his eye, and with that, he turned and walked away from her. 'Thanks for everything, Emily. You take care now, you hear?'

She ran after him. 'When will I see you again?'

'Soon,' he said, reaching the front door. 'I'll be at the shelter. It'll be just like it was before.' But his voice

sounded strange, like he was fighting to hold it together...
and she knew things would never be the same again.

When the door shut behind him, she burst into tears.

On the other side of the door, Alfie did exactly the same thing.

Chapter Twenty

Sam wasn't having the best of weeks. None of the dentists she'd approached about running a clinic at the shelter had responded, Norah had been off sick for a couple of days with a nasty virus, and Emily was distraught over the council threatening to evict her for letting Alfie sofa-surf at her flat.

As if that wasn't enough, Max was still missing, her mother's stress levels were through the roof, and now the lights had blown in the cafe – five minutes before they were due to open for the night shift. Things were not going well.

She fetched her torch and the stepladders from the maintenance cupboard. It was tempting to call for Fraser, but he was manning the front desk with Emily and Norah, ready to deal with the queue of young people needing a bed for the night. She had to deal with this latest emergency herself.

Lifting the cumbersome stepladders, she gingerly made her way into the darkened kitchen to locate the fuse board. A chicken stew bubbled away on the stove, along with a tomato pasta sauce. She needed to tread carefully. Knocking over the saucepans wouldn't help to improve her week, or ease Emily's anguish if her food was ruined.

Plus, it would leave a lot of guests very hungry and that wasn't something she was prepared to risk.

As she carried the stepladders over to the wall, her phone pinged with a message.

It was Jamie, apologising for running late. On any other night, it wouldn't be a problem, but with an electrical issue to contend with she could have done with him here. Not that it was his fault. Maybe he'd gone to see his mum today and that's why he was delayed? She hoped so. Kirsty was a rare phenomenon, a drug addict who'd managed to turn her life around in the face of deep tragedy and loss. She deserved a second chance. As did Jamie.

Sam positioned the stepladders by the wall and secured the latch. She was about to climb up when her phone rang. It was her mother. Maybe she had news of Max?

Pressing the speaker icon, Sam placed her phone on the counter and climbed the ladder. 'Hi mum. Any news on Max?'

'It's not good,' her mother said, sounding distraught.

Oh, God. 'What's happened? Is he hurt? Worse? ... Tell me?'

'We still haven't tracked him down.'

She stilled. 'Then what?'

Her mother sniffed. 'They think Max has been involved in insider trading.'

'Absolute nonsense. Max would never do that. And who are *they*?'

'The police.'

'The police?' Sam nearly fell off the ladder. She steadied herself. 'When did you speak to the police?'

'Today. They turned up at the house looking for Max with a man from the Financial Conduct Authority. They want to interview him.'

'What about?'

'They wouldn't tell me. Your father became quite forceful and threatened to involve our lawyers, but they refused to divulge any information.'

Sam frowned. 'Then how do you know Max is accused of insider trading?'

'Because that's what the press are saying. They're camped outside the house.'

Oh, God. That wasn't good. Her poor parents.

'Can they do that?'

'Apparently so. According to the police anyway. They can't move them on unless they're creating a disturbance or obstructing traffic. They don't have the resources.'

Sam aimed her torchlight at the wall, her annoyance levels rising. 'But they have the resources to investigate Max over a bunch of ridiculous rumours? Talk about hypocritical.'

'Now darling, that's why I called. Your father and I don't want you getting all riled up and making matters worse.'

'How would I make things worse?' She lifted the lid on the fuse box.

'By getting all… you know, political and outraged. The last thing we need is another photo of you holding a banner with a grammatically incorrect slogan splashed across the front of the *Guardian*.'

Sam sighed. Not this again. 'That was fifteen years ago, Mum. I was a teenager. And it wasn't political. It was moral. Protesting against fox hunting is an animal welfare issue.'

'It was still the talk of many a dinner a party for months afterwards.'

And that was what really bothered her mother.

Sam shone the torch on the row of fuses, looking for the one that had tripped. 'Only because most of your friends partake in fox hunting.'

'That's beside the point. We cannot afford to deal with any more unflattering stories appearing in the papers. Need I remind you we only narrowly avoided a scandal a few weeks ago when you ended up in the swimming pool *naked*?'

'I wasn't naked.' How many times did she have to say it? 'I was wearing underwear. And I've apologised on numerous occasions.'

'Nonetheless, we need to tread very carefully with this latest incident. We spoke with our lawyer a few moments ago and he agreed it would be in the best interests of the family if you closed your charity project.'

'What?' Sam wobbled on the ladder. 'No way!'

'Just until this scandal blows over.'

'No.'

'Once Max returns we can resolve this. It's for the best.'

'No, Mother. I won't close The Crash Pad.'

'Be reasonable, darling.'

'Reasonable? I have a queue of kids outside waiting for a bed for the night. Plus scores of others who'll be offered a meal and bedding. There's no way I'm turning them away. I have a responsibility to help them.'

'And what about your family? Don't you have a responsibility to support them too?'

'This isn't my mess, it's Max's.'

'But it impacts all of us. You must close the shelter. If you don't, it'll only continue to add fuel to the story.'

Sam lifted her hands to the ceiling in exasperation. 'How will it?'

'Do I need to spell it out?'

'Yes.'

'If Max's reputation is in question, then we need to avoid any further bad press.'

'And how is running a homeless shelter for young people inviting bad press, Mother?'

'We've been over this. It's about perception. You might believe these youngsters are worthy of charitable support, but most hardworking tax payers don't. I know this project means a lot to you, but it's time to see reason and return to the real world.'

The real world? Sam gripped the top of the stepladders – partly so she wouldn't fall off, but mostly so she wouldn't punch the wall. 'This *is* the real world, Mother. Not everyone has money and privilege and a loving home. We might live in a consumer-driven society, where social media constantly tells us that body image and material wealth is the be-all-and-end-all, but it's a load of bollocks. We still have poverty in this country. We have inequality and discrimination and a homelessness problem. I'm not going to abandon my principles to avoid one measly press report over something that isn't even true.'

She flicked the fuse switch. The lights came back on. Hallelujah. She descended the ladder. 'Now, I have to go, Mother. The shelter is about to open.'

'But, Sam—'

'Goodnight, Mother. Call me if you hear any news of Max.'

She hung up on her mother before she said something she'd regret. There would be hell to pay for cutting her off, but she was too mad to continue arguing. Close The Crash Pad? No flipping way.

But her troubles were far from over.

Fraser appeared in the kitchen doorway. 'We have a problem.'

Oh, great. 'What kind of problem?'

'The press are outside. They're asking for you. Do you know what they want?'

She closed her eyes. 'Unfortunately, yes.' This was not a good development. 'I'll deal with it, Fraser. You concentrate on processing the guests.'

'Will do.' He came over and retrieved the stepladders. 'I'll put these back for you. Let me know if I can help.'

'Thanks, Fraser.' She patted his shoulder and headed for reception.

She'd hoped her mother had been overreacting about the extent of press interest in the story, and far from finding broadsheet paparazzi gathered outside the shelter, it would just be one local reporter chancing his or her luck. But it didn't look that way.

She found Emily and Norah in reception.

Emily looked worried. 'They keep knocking,' she said, pointing to the glass doors where a sea of faces stared back. 'They wanted us to let them in, but we refused.'

'You did the right thing.' She touched the girl's arm, noticing the dark circles beneath her eyes. 'Are you okay?'

Emily nodded. 'I'm fine.' She didn't look it.

'I've a good mind to go outside myself and give them a piece of my mind,' Norah said, looking disgruntled. 'Bunch of low-lives. What do they want, anyhow?'

'Info about my brother,' Sam said, steeling herself for a confrontation with the press. 'And thanks for the offer, but I don't want you getting involved. This is my problem, not yours. Stay inside out of harm's way. I'll go outside and try to move them away from the entrance.' She walked over to the door. 'Lock it behind me, okay? Don't open it until

Fraser's back and then process the queue as normal. We're not going to let these bastards win.'

'Be careful,' Emily called, as Sam unlocked the door.

'And don't take any crap,' Norah added, closing the door behind her as she exited.

'I won't.' But her words were all bravado. Despite her mother's warning, she was shocked to discover a horde of journalists bustling for position and an array of long-lens cameras being thrust into her face.

Talk about aggressive. And why were there so many of them? 'Move away from the door,' she yelled, trying to clear the entrance.

But they weren't budging.

'Where's your brother?' one of them called.

'Is Max here?'

'When did you last speak to your brother?' another shouted.

They jostled and pushed, showing no regard for the people queuing at the door. Several of the teens looked frightened, torn between wanting to flee, but not wanting to give up their place in the queue.

Sam's blood boiled. 'Didn't you hear me? I said, move away from the door!'

'Tell us where Max is,' came a shout.

'Did you know your brother was selling information?'

Sam tried to push her way through the crowd, shoving them away from the queue. 'My brother hasn't done anything of the sort.'

'Then why's he in hiding?'

'He's not in hiding.' A camera flashed in her face, making her blink.

'Then where is he?'

'None of your business.' She pushed the camera away.

'Has he spoken to the police?'

Sam figured trying to reason with them wasn't the answer. She needed another approach. She opted for their family lawyer's favourite response, 'No comment' ...which might have sufficed had it not been for the man's next question.

'How do you feel about Hylton Sabell's involvement? The betrayal must sting?'

Why on earth were they asking about Hylton? What did this have to do with her brother's oldest friend? He wasn't even a trader; he ran his family's longstanding jewellery business. 'I have no idea what you're talking about. Now, for the last time, will you please move away from the door before someone's injured.'

'Were they in it together?' another reported shouted.

'How much did Max get paid?' another yelled.

'Talk to us, Samantha. Tell us your side of the story.'

She honestly had no idea what they were on about. 'If you don't leave immediately, I'm calling the police.'

Not that they'd do anything. Although, if this didn't count as a disturbance of the peace, she didn't know what did.

'We're not doing anything wrong,' another shouted. 'The public has a right to know the truth.'

The truth? Right, that did it. They weren't going to take the moral high ground with her, the cheeky buggers. 'And these vulnerable teens have a right to a home,' she said, knowing she shouldn't retaliate, but unable to stop herself. 'Why don't you report on that instead? A real story. Something worthwhile. Something that might actually make a difference.'

'Begging doesn't sell newspapers,' a reporter shouted. 'Insider trading does.'

Sam's hackles rose. 'Maybe they wouldn't have to beg if society took care of their own.'

'Come off it, they're scroungers the lot of them.' The man's shouts were accompanied by him thrusting his camera forwards and clipping her forehead. The flash fired right in her eyes, blinding her vision.

'Leave her alone,' a voice shouted. Only it wasn't a reporter, it was a young male voice. A voice she vaguely recognised.

A scuffle followed, as the lad pushed through the crowd of reporters.

Sam blinked, her vision clearing. Alfie was coming towards her.

'I said, leave her alone.' He shoved the reporter who'd hit her with his camera, sending him reeling backwards.

Another reporter stepped forwards. 'That's assault,' he said, taking a photo of Alfie. 'I'm reporting you to the police.'

'Do what you like,' Alfie said, squaring up to the man. 'I ain't scared of you.'

'You're probably too pissed to be scared. Use all your benefit money on getting stoned, did you?' The reporter took another photo.

'I'm not on benefits,' Alfie said. 'I work. I don't need handouts.'

'Why are you here then, scrounging for a bed?'

Sam had had enough. 'Because he's homeless, you sanctimonious prick,' she said, so enraged she forgot her mother's request for her not to retaliate and make matters worse. 'Now get away from him, before I shove that camera down your throat.' She lunged forwards, aware of cameras flashing away in the dark. She didn't care.

Except she stumbled, crashing into the reporter and causing them both to fall heavily to the ground.

What happened next was a blur of camera flashes, shouting and pushing.

Someone trod on her leg. She tried to get to her feet but lost her balance. A few of the girls queuing were crying. She could hear swearing and threats of violence. This was not good.

And then the faint sound of sirens cut through the night air.

Thank God.

A hand touched her shoulder. 'Sam? Sam, take my hand.'

It was Jamie. He was standing over her, shielding her from the angry mob, his expression one of perplexed concern.

She took his hand and he yanked her to her feet.

'Head down,' he said, putting his arm around her. 'This way.' He led her through the mass of bodies, shoving people out of the way, getting her to safety.

She could see Fraser pulling reporters away from the kids. Norah was wagging her finger at a few more. Alfie was moving the girls in the queue to safety.

Sam felt she should be doing more. 'The kids. I have to look after the kids.'

'Fraser will look after the kids,' he said, signalling for Emily to open the door. 'I need to get you out of the way.' But before he could ease her inside, blue flashing lights appeared.

The police had arrived.

Chapter Twenty-One

Jamie's head was spinning. He didn't know what to tackle first. Emily struggling to hold off a reporter who was trying to push through the main doors – Alfie grabbing hold of the said reporter and almost rugby-tackling him to the ground – Fraser physically picking up another reporter and moving him away from the kids – or Norah screaming abuse at the police for automatically assuming it was the kids who were causing trouble and not the overly-enthusiastic press.

He opted for getting Sam to safety.

'Where are we going?' she said, resisting his efforts to remove her from the fracas and lead her around the back of the building.

'You being here is inflaming the situation,' he said, manoeuvring her towards his car. 'I need to take you home.'

'I can't leave!' She wrestled free from his clasp.

'You have to, Sam. These reporters are not going to give up.'

'But the police are here. That will calm things down. And once we get the kids inside, we can close the doors and ignore the reporters. They'll soon get bored and go home.'

He gave her an incredulous look. 'No, they won't. They've smelt blood and they're not going anywhere without something to print.'

'There's nothing *to* print. I haven't told them anything. I don't know anything,' she said, raising her hands in exasperation.

'They don't know that.' Plus, she probably knew more than she realised. But he wasn't about to enlighten her on Hylton Sabell's involvement. Not right at that moment. Her safety was more pressing. The kids too.

'Think about it,' he said, resting his hands on her shoulders. 'What happens tomorrow morning when you open the doors and let the kids out? The reporters will swarm, the kids won't react well to be photographed, and the whole thing will kick off again. The only way those reporters are going away is if you're not here.'

She looked like she wanted to argue, but knew he was right. 'I'm supposed to be on the night shift. It's not fair on the others.'

'The others can manage and it'll be easier for them if they don't have to contend with that mob outside.' He looked into her eyes, currently flashing with a mixture of concern and anger. 'Think of the bad publicity for the shelter.'

'You sound like my mother,' she said sulkily, folding her arms.

'But unlike your mother, my concern is for the shelter's reputation, not your family's. If you stay, I guarantee there'll be stories in all the papers tomorrow. They'll accuse you of protecting your brother. They have photos of you pushing that reporter and threatening to shove his camera down his throat.'

She groaned. 'Oh, God.'

'Worse. They'll print photos showing Fraser and Alfie fighting with reporters. And trust me, it won't be an impartial account of what happened here tonight. They'll spin it so Fraser looks like an ex-army thug with anger management issues, and Alfie's a loser kid typical of a rough-sleeper. I know how these things work. If they can't get the story they want, they'll use a different angle.'

She gave him a quizzical stare. 'You sound very know-ledgeable.'

'I studied media, remember?' He avoided eye contact, trying to disguise his subterfuge. 'We were told stories about how the press skewer the facts to create a more interesting story.'

'Well, it's disgusting,' she said, shaking her head. 'And immoral. It shouldn't be allowed.'

'Maybe, but that's how it is.' He opened the passenger door. 'So are you going to do the sensible thing and let me take you home?'

Hesitating, she turned back to look at The Crash Pad. A beat passed, before her shoulders sagged in resignation and she climbed into his car. 'I'm not happy about this. It feels like giving into bullies.'

'It's just for tonight. Hopefully things will calm down tomorrow, or another story will break and divert their attention elsewhere.' He ducked to speak to her through the open door. 'I'll go and check the police have everything under control before we leave. Okay?'

She nodded. 'I'll be happier once I know everyone's alright.'

'Back soon.' He closed the door and jogged around to the front of the building.

He wasn't lying when he said he wanted to ensure everything was okay. But he also had an ulterior motive for removing Sam from the fracas. He wanted to quiz her before the other reporters got in first. It wasn't the most honourable thing he'd ever done, but his career was on the line.

Ignoring the guilty feeling weighing in his stomach, he approached the shelter entrance. There were no signs of any scuffles or arrests. He'd been worried the police might take Fraser and Alfie into custody if any of the reporters had claimed they'd been assaulted. But thankfully the police didn't look eager to escalate matters.

A couple of coppers were moving reporters away from the entrance. A couple more were escorting the kids inside the shelter.

Sadly, by the time Alfie had finished being quizzed by the police, he'd lost his place in the queue. As the shelter closed its doors for the night, he was left on the outside… much to the horror of Emily, who was pressed against the glass, tears running down her cheeks as she watched him walk away, his shoulders sagged, his head dropped.

It was a tragic sight. And so unfair that having gone out of his way to protect the shelter staff, the kid's reward was a night sleeping rough.

Life sucked at times.

But Jamie had Sam to deal with. And a story to submit before six a.m. tomorrow.

He ran back to the car and updated Sam, assuring her everything was under control and the team didn't need her and were aware of his plan. 'But let them know you're okay, or they'll worry,' he said, securing his seatbelt.

'Of course,' she said, unearthing her phone. 'I'll text Norah and Fraser.'

'Keep your head down until we're away from the shelter,' he said, as they pulled away.

She ducked low, waiting until they were clear of the reporters before resuming typing.

Jamie concentrated on driving, trying to get his head around what had happened tonight.

He'd been late for his shift because his boss had called him into the office for a bollocking. What had followed was a twenty-minute lecture on how Jamie was failing in his first assignment and showing ineptitude and incompetence when it came to undercover reporting. Gareth had shouted various obscenities, waved his hands about in an aggressive manner, and berated him for not being ahead of the story, despite being given advance intel.

Jamie had apologised, agreed, and accepted his boss's assessment of the situation. He'd even offered his resignation, but to his surprise – and slight disappointment – Gareth had rejected his offer to leave. Why was he disappointed? Because if he was honest, he didn't want to run the story. He was conflicted, torn between wanting to progress his career and not wanting to hurt the woman he'd grown to like and admire. He couldn't do both.

But Gareth had given him 'one last chance' to use his connection with Samantha Tipping to get the story. He should be feeling grateful. Instead, he felt sick to his stomach.

So here he was. Pretending to be a mate and acting as though he was protecting Sam from the immoral hard-nosed press, when in fact he was using the situation to get the story himself.

However he viewed it, he was being a shit. He was letting his boss down by being a crap reporter. And he was letting Sam down by lying to her and betraying her trust.

It wasn't a good feeling.

He turned into Melrose Avenue and immediately spotted the press camped outside.

Sam saw them too. 'Oh, my, God. They know where I live?' Her voice cracked.

He drove past the house without slowing. 'Keep your head down so they don't clock it's you and follow us.'

'What do I do now?'

He couldn't take her to his place, there might be stuff lying around that would give him up as a journalist. He could drop her off at her parents… but that would scupper any opportunity to dig for dirt. No, he had to take her somewhere the press would never find her.

'Where are we going?' she asked, as they headed for the Blackwall Tunnel.

'Peggy's.'

She angled her body to look at him. 'Your foster mum?'

He nodded. 'You'll be safe there.'

She fiddled with her ear. 'Meeting your birth mother and your foster mother in the same week? No pressure.'

'It's the safest place.' He ignored the nerves pressing against his skin at the idea of introducing Sam to Peggy. 'So how come the press were at the shelter tonight?' He tried to sound innocent. 'Have they found Max?'

She shook her head and rubbed her temples, looking exhausted. 'My mother phoned me this evening to warn me the press had got wind of his disappearance and they were camped outside their place. But I had no idea they'd show up at The Crash Pad.'

'Is Max's disappearance really that big a deal? I mean, I know it is for your family, but why are the press so interested?' His efforts to sound clueless felt clunky and obvious, but she didn't seem to notice.

Instead, she frowned. 'They think Max is involved in insider trading. And please don't say, I told you so. I'm not in the mood, okay?'

'I wasn't going to.'

'I still don't think it's true,' she said, vehemently. 'There's been a mix-up, that's all. A misunderstanding. Once Max returns and explains it'll all be straightened out.'

'I'm sure you're right.' He kept his eyes fixed ahead, afraid she'd become suspicious if he kept questioning her.

He'd never felt so inept. But this was what happened when you allowed yourself to become emotionally involved with a potential information source. You could no longer be impartial. Ruthless.

Neither spoke for a while. She was lost in thought. He concentrated on driving.

He was just thinking he'd blown any chance of getting any more information, when she said, 'One of the reporters said the oddest thing tonight. He asked me how I felt about being betrayed by Hylton Sabell.'

Jamie faked a frown. 'Who's Hylton Sabell?' he asked, knowing full well who he was. On paper, at least. He needed to find out the unofficial version.

'He's my brother's oldest friend. They went to school together.'

'Is he a city trader?'

'Crikey, no.' She fidgeted in her seat. 'And that's what's puzzling me. Hylton heads-up his family business, Sabell & Sutton.'

'Is that a finance company, or something?'

'It's a jewellers. Haven't you heard of them? They're one of the most famous brands in the world.'

He shook his head. It was only a partial lie. He'd genuinely never heard of them until recently when his boss had instructed him to expand his research into Max Tipping's friends as well as his business associates.

'They've been around for a couple of hundred years. They specialise in high-end bespoke pieces. Their customers include royalty, celebrities and millionaires. A Sabell & Sutton piece is a very collectable item. People buy them as an investment.'

'Do you own any pieces?'

'If I did, I'd have sold them by now,' she said, raising an eyebrow. 'My mother has several pieces, unsurprisingly.'

'I wonder why this reporter asked you about him?'

'That's what I can't fathom.' She looked genuinely perplexed. 'I could understand it if they thought Hylton was hiding Max somewhere, the man has properties all over the world, but it was the insinuation he'd betrayed my brother that's puzzling me.'

'Betrayed him, how?'

'I've no idea. The reporter didn't elaborate, and I wasn't about to indulge him by asking.' Her head dropped back against the headrest.

So she really didn't know what was going on? In a way, he was relieved. 'Are you close to the Sabell family?'

She shrugged. 'I guess. Our families holidayed together when we were young, and Hylton and Max still socialise in the same circles. They meet Mother's stringent criteria for what constitutes *worthy* company,' she said, rolling her eyes. 'Any function attended by a Sabell is automatically an A-list party.'

Jamie turned into Crownfield Road. 'So you have no idea how Hylton's involved with your brother's insider trading?'

'*Alleged* insider trading,' she said, shooting him a glare. 'And no, I have absolutely no idea.'

He'd nearly slipped up there. 'Sorry. You could always call him?'

'Who, Hylton?'

'He might know where Max is.' He pulled up outside Peggy's.

'I doubt it. And Mother would've already contacted him. Besides, I don't want to get involved. I'd rather hear the truth from Max himself.' She glanced out of the window. 'Are we here?'

'Yep. This is Peggy's.' He secured the handbrake and opened the driver's door.

Sam joined him on the driveway. 'Won't Peggy mind us just turning up like this? Shouldn't we have called first and checked it was okay?'

'Peggy won't mind.' He walked up to the door and rang the doorbell. A few moments passed before a light went on in the hallway.

The door opened and Peggy appeared wearing a bright orange and yellow kaftan, her hair wrapped in a turban. Her face registered disbelief, followed by pure delight. 'Jamie? What a lovely surprise!' Then her smile wavered. 'Is everything okay? Are you hurt? Is something wrong?' Her eyes switched between him and Sam.

'Everything's fine. Can we come in?'

'Of course! Come in, come in.' She ushered them both inside, giving him a tight bear hug. Taking his face in her hands, she administered a huge kiss… followed by the evil eye, indicating he needed to make introductions.

'Peggy, this is my friend Sam. She runs the night shelter where I volunteer.'

'Oh?' Her curiosity switched to suspicion – she was astute enough to remember he was only volunteering at the shelter to get inside information on a story. 'Is that right?'

Sam extended her hand. 'It's lovely to meet you. Jamie's told me so much about you.'

'Has he now?' Peggy took Sam's hand, but far from shaking it, she pulled her into a tight hug. 'Any friend of Jamie's is welcome here.' She glared at him over Sam's shoulder, indicating she'd be expecting an explanation later. 'Now, what can I get you? Tea? Coffee? Something stronger? Have you eaten?'

'I'm fine, thanks. Is it okay if we stay here tonight, Peggy?'

Peggy's eyebrows raised. 'Is there a problem?'

'Not really. But it's not safe for Sam to stay at her place tonight.'

'Not safe?' Peggy looked alarmed.

'It's a temporary situation,' he said, wondering how to placate Peggy's curiosity. 'I can't go into detail. It's a sensitive subject involving Sam's family.'

Peggy folded her arms. 'I see.'

Sam looked uncomfortable. 'I don't want to intrude. I can get a hotel room for the night.'

'Nonsense.' Peggy touched her arm. 'You're more than welcome to stay. You can sleep in Jamie's old room. He can sleep on the couch,' she said, slipping her arm through Sam's and leading her upstairs. 'Make yourself useful and put the kettle on, Jamie. Sam looks like she could do with a strong brew.'

He knew better than to disobey. He made a pot of tea and carried two mugs upstairs.

'I left yours downstairs, Peggy,' he said to his foster mum, a not-so-subtle hint that he wanted some privacy.

Peggy's hands went to her hips. 'No cake? I brought you up better than that, boy.'

He rolled his eyes and handed Sam her tea. 'I'm sorry. Would you like some cake?'

'No, thank you. But thanks for the offer.' She turned to Peggy. 'Are you sure it's okay for me to stay? I don't want to cause any friction.'

Peggy laughed. 'Don't worry about that. Sixteen years I've been waiting for this one to bring home a nice girl. You stay as long as you want.'

Not embarrassing at all.

Jamie should have known Peggy would never leave voluntarily. She was too intrigued, too invested in his happiness to pass up an opportunity to delve into his personal life.

Her inquisitive eyes inspected Sam's baggy hoodie and faded jeans. She nodded in approval at what she saw.

And why not? Sam was a beautiful woman – inside and out. She was also way out of his league. Something that was becoming more apparent with each passing day.

But Peggy surprised him by heading for the door. 'I'll leave you to settle in. Help yourself to anything you need. Don't be shy.' She touched his hand on the way out. 'We'll talk later.' She gave him the evil eye again.

Not if he could help it. He knew what would be coming – a lecture about ethics and honesty and invest-igating a person while pretending to be their 'mate'. His actions were not cool.

So why *was* he doing this? It was a question that kept nudging its way into his brain.

Sam looked around the medium-sized room, with its cobalt-blue walls and wrought-iron bedstead. 'So this was your childhood bedroom? Cosy.'

'It wasn't like this when I lived here.' He shut the door.

'What was it like?' Then she held up her hand. 'No, wait… let me guess.' She looked around the room, tapping her lip in contemplation.

'This is payback, isn't it?' He shrugged off his jacket and hung it over the bedframe. 'Revenge for the assumptions I made about your bedroom as a teenager.'

'I think it's only fair,' she said, smiling.

'Need I remind you how that game ended?'

Her cheeks turned pink. 'Does Peggy have a swimming pool?'

'In Leytonstone?' He kicked off his trainers.

'Then I think we're safe.' She unlaced her boots and carried them over to the door, placing them on the floor. 'A teenage Jamie. Now there's a conundrum. I'm guessing… a bit of a geek?'

He shrugged. 'Depends on your definition of geek.'

'Moody… filled with angst… spending all your free time playing computer games with the lights out and curtains closed. Grunting responses to anyone who interrupted.'

He shook his head. 'Not guilty. Well, except for the grunting. I was a typical teenager in that respect. Not for long, though. Peggy soon straightened me out.'

Sam climbed onto the bed and crossed her legs. She looked like a teenager herself with her polka dot socks poking out from beneath her jeans. 'And how did she do that?'

He cast his mind back. 'Peggy wouldn't tolerate solitude. Rules of the house were that we ate meals together as a family, we attended church every Sunday, and we had to talk about our problems and not bottle them up.'

'Sound advice. Did you adhere to the rules?'

'Not straight away.' He went over to the window and closed the white voile curtains – another new addition since his time in the house. 'When I first arrived, I was an angry fourteen-year-old who thought he knew it all and didn't need anyone. My previous placements had been short-term affairs, so I assumed this one would be too. Why bother trying to bond, I thought, when I'd be moved on in a few months.'

Sam looked sad. 'So you acted out?'

'Christ, yeah.'

'How?'

He shrugged. 'Played truant mostly. It'd always worked before when I wanted to cause trouble. My previous foster placements hadn't really cared enough to make me stop doing it. But with Peggy, I had the shock of my life. I'd only been here a week when I skipped school and headed to the park, intending to spend the day dossing about with a football. But the bloody woman tracked me down. She'd gone on the hunt the moment the school had phoned her.' He ran his hand through his hair. 'She gave me such a bollocking. She dragged me back to school and sat outside the classroom guarding the exit so I couldn't run off again. Talk about humiliating.'

Sam's eyes grew wide. 'Seriously?'

He thought back to those years and the battles between them. 'She'd give me chores to do when I answered back. She grounded me if I was late home. She even withheld my pocket money if she caught me cursing.' He shook his head, smiling despite the difficulties. 'But the one thing she never did was stop me playing football.'

'You played football?'

He went over to the chest of drawers and pulled open the top drawer. His medals were still there, along with his certificates and the ticket stubs from the games she'd taken him to. His twice-yearly treat, a trip to see West Ham at Upton Park.

'I was pretty decent when I was younger, I played for the county and the London Football Academy. I had training three nights a week, plus games on Saturdays. She took me to every single session. She said I needed a physical outlet for my anger and a reward for my good behaviour.'

'So her methods worked?'

'Only after she forced me to attend boxing classes.'

Sam laughed. 'I can't imagine you boxing.'

'I was terrible at it. I hated being hit, and I never wanted to punch my opponent. Two fundamental flaws. I promised Peggy I'd behave better if she let me quit.'

'And did she?'

He nodded. 'I realised I was never going to beat Peggy. She wasn't like anyone I'd ever met before.' He sat on the edge of the bed. 'It's also when I realised she was never going to give up on me either, no matter what I did.'

Sam's expression softened. 'The definition of unconditional love.'

He rubbed his chest. 'It was the turning point. I stopped fighting her and started letting her... I don't know... love me, I guess.'

Sam blinked away a tear. 'What an amazing woman.'

'Of course, it took me years to realise how lucky I was. Or that I'd become as attached to her as she was to me.'

Sam looked quizzical. 'Is that why you're so resistant to get close to your birth mother? It feels like a betrayal to Peggy?'

He was about to deny it when it struck him that that was exactly how he felt.

Sam edged closer to him on the bed, taking his hand. 'It would be entirely understandable, it's taken you years to get over being taken into care and learning how to be part of a family again. Why would you want to repeat that process again? It was hard enough the first time around.'

His throat tightened. It always did when he thought about his birth mother. Sam was right, even the idea of getting to know Kirsty again was exhausting. All that angst and miscommunications, having to talk about his feelings and be emotionally vulnerable. The idea turned him cold. But the thought of spending the rest of his life tied up in knots didn't thrill him either. He was damned either way.

Sam was looking at him. Her pupils had dilated in the dim lamplight and her eyes looked huge. 'You know, for someone who's been through so much, you're incredibly insightful and well-adjusted.'

'Are you kidding me? I'm a mess.'

'No, you're not.' She touched his cheek. 'You're bruised and confused, but not a mess.'

He expected her to drop her hand, but she didn't.

She held his gaze, her expression endearing and serious. Her palm grew warm, creating a buzz in his blood. 'Look how you helped me tonight. I couldn't think clearly, but you took control and got me out of a dire situation.'

Guilt heated his face. She wouldn't be saying that if she knew his motivation.

'You're a good man, Jamie Lawson.' No, he wasn't.
'I was an idiot not to see it sooner.' Leaning closer, she brushed her lips against his.

Oh, hell. He should pull away. It wasn't right. He was duping her.

By then she kissed him again and his body refused to move. He was drugged by her touch... her smell... her honesty.

But he wasn't being honest with *her*, was he?

He should definitely pull away. Her judgement was clouded by adrenaline and the drama of earlier. She wasn't thinking straight.

She kissed him again, her touch soft and teasing.

And now *he* wasn't thinking straight.

Logic told him to put a stop to things before they escalated.

It was one thing to pretend to be a friend while secretly digging for information on her brother. It was another thing entirely for that 'friendship' to become intimate. That would be unforgivable. It would be a betrayal of her trust and kindness, after all she'd done for him.

A good man wouldn't take advantage of a loaded situation like this.

He pulled away. 'Sorry, but we can't.'

The sudden movement caused her to fall into his chest. She looked crestfallen.

'Not in Peggy's home,' he added, trying to soften the rejection. 'It doesn't feel right.' It was a feeble excuse, but it was all he could come up with.

She scrambled back up the bed. 'Of course. What was I thinking?' She looked embarrassed.

'Not that I don't want to,' he said, because he did. 'But not like this. Not until we can do this properly.'

And by properly, he meant… not until she knew the truth about why he was a part of her life. Not until the story about Max was out in the world and he could confess to being an undercover journalist. And not until he could explain that falling for her was not part of the deception, and that his feelings for her were very, very real.

He got off the bed, defying every nerve ending in his body that desperately wanted him to stay. 'Hope you sleep okay. See you in the morning.'

Her hand touched her neck, self-consciously. 'Thanks again for everything.'

'No need to thank me.' Because he'd done nothing heroic. Far from it. 'I did it because I care about you.' At least that part was true.

He closed the bedroom door before his resolve cracked.

Chapter Twenty-Two

Sam woke with a jolt, confused and unsure about where she was. Her surroundings were strange and unfamiliar. A grey light seeped through the white voile curtains casting the room in shadows, reminding her she was in Jamie's old childhood bedroom.

Relieved, she sat up and rubbed her eyes, her face hot from the recollection of a dream in which she'd been frolicking in her parents' swimming pool with Jamie. Only it wasn't just a dream, was it?

Flopping against the pillows, she tried to rid her mind of the images imprinted on her brain. She wasn't accustomed to having erotic dreams. But then, it'd been a long time since she'd been interested in anyone. Her dormant senses had been reignited.

Pushing back the duvet, she swivelled to a seated position, letting her toes enjoy the sensation of the deep-pile rug beneath.

She hadn't meant to kiss Jamie. But then, she hadn't meant to the time before either. One minute she was in control of her actions, thinking coherently and behaving rationally, and the next she was throwing herself at him.

But it wasn't like he hadn't reciprocated. A man didn't moan, pull you closer, and tug on your hair to deepen the kiss if he wasn't a willing participant… right?

As mortified as she'd felt when he'd abruptly ended their kiss, he was right to put the brakes on. It wouldn't have been appropriate for them to spent the night together. Not at Peggy's: it would have been disrespectful.

Fanning her face, she pushed herself up from the bed. She needed a cold shower.

A pile of towels were neatly folded on the chest of drawers where she spotted a prom photo poking out from the drawer. Even aged eighteen Jamie had looked good in a tux. His build was slimmer, his face clean-shaven and his red-brown hair accentuated the glint in his eyes. She imagined he hadn't been short of female attention.

But his companion in the photo wasn't a teenage cutie in a glitzy prom dress. It was Peggy. She was beaming into the camera looking pristine in a long gold dress, a white corsage attached to her wrist. Jamie had taken Peggy to his prom?

Fighting the lump in her throat, she carefully replaced the photo and shut the drawer.

Picking up the towels, she headed for the bathroom. A lanky teenage boy had just exited. He nodded a greeting and then scuttled into his bedroom, embarrassed at having been caught in his underwear.

She could hear music playing behind another door. She wondered how many kids Peggy had staying with her at the moment.

Once showered and dressed, she headed downstairs.

A series of framed photos lined the staircase, each one draped in shiny gold tinsel and flashing with Christmas lights. So many kids. Mainly teenagers, all looking happy and well cared for. Peggy had obviously been fostering for most of her life. The world needed more Peggys.

As she descended the staircase she could hear voices coming from the kitchen. Faint at first, but then clearer as the discussion became more agitated. Were Jamie and Peggy arguing?

Sam hesitated, torn between heading back upstairs or entering the kitchen and dispelling the disagreement. But then she heard her name. Was she the cause of the argument? Perhaps Peggy had been unhappy about being ambushed last night?

Then she realised her staying the night wasn't the issue.

'When are you going to tell her?' Peggy's tone was angry. 'She deserves to know the truth. I did not raise you to be deceitful, boy.'

'Soon,' Jamie replied, sounding flustered. 'When the time's right.'

'And when will that be?' Peggy demanded.

Sam couldn't have moved if she wanted to. Trepidation began to crawl up her arms, making her skin itch. Jamie had been deceitful?

'Once this is all over,' he said. 'I'll tell her everything.'

Sam had no idea what they were talking about, but it didn't sound good.

'So the poor girl gets to find out by reading it in the newspaper?' Peggy's voice rose another notch. 'Have you lost your mind?'

'I'll tell her before then. Today. As soon as I've submitted the story.'

Story? Sam pushed opened the kitchen door. 'What story?'

Two sets of eyes turned to look at her. Peggy and Jamie were standing either side of the kitchen table, their hands resting on top as they glared at each other.

On seeing her, they immediately straightened. The colour drained from Jamie's face. 'Morning.' His eyes didn't meet hers. 'What can I get you for breakfast?'

Did he think she'd be that easily deterred?

'What story?' she repeated, feeling slightly sick. Her hands had started to shake.

A teenage lad appeared in the kitchen.

Peggy went over and ushered him out of the room. 'Not now, Ash. Jamie and Sam need a moment.'

'But I'm hungry,' the kid complained as he was dragged out.

Sam waited until the door shut behind them. 'What story, Jamie?'

'I can explain,' he said, looking anywhere but at her. He was dressed in the same clothes as yesterday, his hair mussed from sleep.

She stood her ground. 'I'm waiting.'

He mumbled an expletive and rubbed his forehead. 'I work for the *South London Herald*.'

Her throat suddenly felt dry. 'You're a journalist?' He nodded. He'd kept that piece of information quiet and she had a feeling she was about to find out why. When nothing more was forthcoming, she prompted, 'And?'

'I was assigned to do a story about your brother.'

Oh, God. Her face grew hot. 'When?'

The question seemed to throw him. 'Pardon?'

'When were you given the assignment? It's a simple enough question.'

He hesitated. 'Six weeks ago.'

'Right.' Her heart rate doubled. 'What was the story?'

He moved away from the table, his movements jerky and awkward. He shoved his hands inside his jeans pockets and then instantly removed them, like he had no idea what to do with them. 'I was tasked with investigating rumours of insider trading at Quinton International.'

Her heart rate accelerated even more. 'So you've known for over a month that my brother was under suspicion?' Before even she'd known. Before her family had known.

He nodded again.

'How?'

'My boss was sent a photo of Max receiving a large envelope. We think it contained money.'

That didn't sound good. 'Who from?'

'A man.'

'A man?' Her voice rose. 'What man?'

'We believe it was Hylton Sabell.'

Oh, God. This was just getting worse.

She rubbed her chest, trying to stem the pounding sensation that was rattling her ribcage. Her mind flitted from one question to another, trying to make sense of the puzzle. And then another thought occurred.

'Is that why you volunteered at The Crash Pad?'

This time his nod was barely visible.

The impact was crushing. Her pulse suddenly seemed to slow and she felt light-headed, as if the overwhelming disappointment had severed an artery. 'You volunteered at a shelter for homeless youths so you could get information for a story?'

Jamie's shoulders were bunched by his ears, his head lowered. He looked vulnerable and wounded... and guilty as hell.

A slow rage began to burn inside her. 'Let me get this straight. You pretended to be a decent, kind, and caring bloke who wanted to help those less fortunate... so you could get the dirt on Max?'

He closed his eyes.

She took his silence as confirmation. 'You… complete arsehole.' She moved towards him. 'You criticised me. Made judgements about my family and my motivations for starting up the project, and the whole time you were working as an undercover journalist?' She pointed a finger at him. 'You accused me of being fickle and superficial. You shamed me and mocked my efforts. You acted like some kind of superior being, and yet the whole time you were using me?'

'It wasn't like that.'

She opened her arms. 'What was it like then? What have I missed?'

He opened his mouth as if to speak, but changed his mind. He looked tortured and conflicted, moving about the kitchen as if desperate to escape. But she wasn't letting him off the hook that easily, he deserved to squirm.

She folded her arms. 'Well? I'm waiting.'

It was a while before he found his voice. 'When I first volunteered it was because of my job… but then I grew to appreciate what you were trying to do at the shelter.'

'Oh, big of you. Good to know I have your approval.' Her tone dripped with sarcasm. 'So why didn't you confess why you were really there?'

'Because you didn't trust me at that point, and I thought you'd get rid of me if I admitted I was a journalist.'

'You're right. I didn't trust you, and with good reason, it seems.'

He took a step closer. 'But the more time I spent at the shelter, the more invested I became.'

Her hands went to her hips. 'In which case, you should've gone to your boss and requested someone else be assigned to the story due to a conflict of interest.'

'My boss wouldn't have agreed to that. It was my first undercover assignment.'

'Oh, poor you. Yet another money-driven individual prepared to put work ahead of what's morally right. And I thought you were different? More fool me. You're pathetic, you know that?'

He looked deflated. 'Yes.'

'And selfish. You wanted it all. To get the dirt on my family, write your crappy story, and not be made to feel bad about duping people who genuinely cared about you. Am I wrong?'

A small shake of his head.

'And I thought I'd misjudged you? Turns out my first assumption was bang on. You're a spineless... selfish... arrogant arsehole.' She banged the kitchen table. 'You point the finger at others, questioning their intentions and morality, but you're the one whose character is flawed.'

He flinched. 'I didn't mean for this to happen.'

'I'm sure you didn't.' She was in his face now, expecting him to back off, surprised when he didn't. 'You were hoping to submit your story, receive your promotion or whatever, and walk away completely unaffected at having hurt innocent people.'

She could see him blinking furiously, as if trying to hold it together. She didn't care. 'You know what? Maybe it's not your fault. By your own admission you have attachment issues. You're a lone wolf, unwilling to forgive anyone who's made a mistake. Well, congratulations. Because the upshot of not caring about anyone makes it a hell of a lot easier to walk all over them.'

'I care—'

'Bullshit.' She batted his hand away when he reached for her. 'If you truly cared, you wouldn't be submitting the story. Because unless I've missed something, you are submitting the story… right?'

He stayed silent.

'Just as I thought.' She needed to leave. Her resolve wouldn't hold out much longer and she wasn't prepared to let him see her cry. She would retain her dignity, even if it killed her. 'Thank you for your help over the last few weeks – even if your actions were part of an agenda,' she added, pointedly. 'I genuinely wish you good luck with your birth mother. I hope you can find it within you to forgive her and accept that none of us are perfect. Not even you.'

He caught her arm when she turned to leave. 'I'm sorry.'

'Me too. I'm more sorry than I can express.' She fixed him with a glare. 'I'm sorry that I trusted you, that I believed in you… and that I let my guard down around you and allowed myself to think just for one moment I might've found a man I could…' she trailed off, stopping herself short from saying it. There was no point. He didn't know the meaning of love. And sadly, most of that wasn't his fault.

His hand tightened around her arm. 'I don't want it to end like this.'

'That's not your decision.' She shook free from his hold. 'Stay away from The Crash Pad. You're no longer welcome. My volunteers deserve better. As do the kids.'

She headed for the door, barely able to see from the tears pooling in her eyes. Somehow she made it down the hallway and out through the front door.

Once outside, she stumbled onto the pavement, suddenly remembering she didn't have any transportation.

She rummaged in her pockets, hoping to find enough money for a bus. But her pockets were empty.

And then a taxi pulled up.

A tall black man exited and opened the passenger door. 'Morning, Miss.'

'I'm sorry, but I don't have any money,' she admitted, her face wet from crying.

'No problem,' he said, in a slow Caribbean drawl. 'Miss Peggy instructed me to take you anywhere you need to go.'

Sam glanced back at the house. Peggy was peering out from behind a curtain, looking forlorn. She gave a short wave and blew a kiss.

Sam mouthed 'thank you' and climbed in the taxi, more grateful than she could express. All she wanted to do was go home. Not that she would get any peace there if the press were still camped outside, but she needed some privacy. She wanted to cry, scream, and yell at the unfairness of it all, and she couldn't do that with an audience.

Her phone pinged with a message.

Meet me at the lido cafe. xxx

It was from Max. Thank God, he was okay.

The taxi driver turned up the reggae music on the radio. 'Where to, Miss?'

'The lido cafe in Tooting Bec Common, please.'

'No problem.'

Shutting her eyes, she leant against the headrest, her mind playing tug-of-war between worrying about her brother and thinking about Jamie. Only now the dynamics had changed.

Max was home safely. He was alive and asking to meet with her. His troubles weren't over, but at least he was back from wherever he'd been hiding. She could talk to him, hear his side of things and try to make sense of this crazy situation. Something that was impossible to do when thinking about Jamie.

Only an hour ago, she'd been imagining them together. Wondering if they could make a go of things. Now, she never wanted to see him again. He'd betrayed her in the worst possible way. He'd used her, pretended to be something he wasn't so he could sell a few bloody newspapers.

What an idiot she was. How had she been so blind-sided? When she'd first met him, she couldn't deny her attraction, but she'd also sensed he was hiding something. Turns out, she was right. She should have trusted her instincts and not allowed herself to be sucked in by his good looks and sad backstory.

No wonder he'd been so cagey about his line of work. He'd obviously surmised it wasn't really lying if he omitted the truth. Well, not in her book. Concealing the fact that he was a journalist was downright deceitful. And only volunteering at the shelter to investigate Max? Well, that was completely unforgivable.

She hiccupped when a sob escaped and quickly covered it with a cough. Not that she could be heard above 'No Woman, No Cry'.

For the rest of the journey, she focused on Max. She would not dwell on Jamie. What was done was done. She just hoped her brother would forgive her when he discovered she'd been duped by an undercover journalist. Not that she'd divulged much, but that had never stopped a journalist embellishing the truth before.

What angle would Jamie's story take, she wondered? She could almost imagine the headline: *Tippings Insider Trading Shock – An insight into the lives of the spoilt and rich.*

She shook her head. So much for not dwelling.

And then a horrible thought occurred – had Jamie tipped off the rest of the press? Is that how they knew where she lived?

Oh, God, the pain was unbearable. Talk about betrayal.

The car slowed, and she was surprised to discover they'd arrived at their destination. Stressing over Jamie had warped time.

'You need me to wait?' the driver asked, parking up.

'No, I can walk home from here. Thanks for the ride.'

'No problem, Miss. You take care, now.'

'I will.' She climbed out and stretched. She'd gone from feeling relaxed to feeling like a tightly wound coil about to burst its springs.

The taxi pulled away, leaving her alone.

Patting her jeans pocket, she checked she still had her phone and headed across the empty car park.

In the height of summer the lido would be packed to the brim. But few people were hardy enough to endure an outdoor swim in an unheated pool in mid-December. The cafe remained open all year-round though, catering to dog walkers and fitness fanatics who used the rural space to exercise.

Tooting Bec common glistened in the morning sunlight. The grass was damp underfoot and the bare tree branches contrasted with the pale sky above, creating a maze of intricate patterns.

Reaching the lido, she was unsurprised to find it deserted. The row of changing cubicles ran the length of the pool, their multi-coloured doors all closed. The water in the pool was a pale grey, a reflection of the sky above.

Sam had loved coming here as a kid. Her parents had never taken them swimming, but their housekeeper, Altamira, used to bring them here in the summer with a picnic and an inflatable ring. Being so much younger than her siblings, she'd enjoyed being tossed around the pool and yelling and screaming to her heart's content. In fact, she'd much preferred it to the exotic holidays abroad, where she was always expected to be on her best behaviour.

She spotted a lone figure sitting at one of the wooden tables, his shoulders hunched, a baseball cap covering his head. As she approached, she could see creased grey suit trousers beneath a thick padded jacket, the collar turned up. If her brother was aiming for incognito, he'd failed.

He glanced up when she reached the table. 'You came.'

'Of course, I came.' She noticed her messy reflection in his sunglasses. Her ponytail had drooped to one side, but now wasn't the time to worry about appearances.

'I wasn't sure you would.' He sounded tired, shaky and very unlike Max.

'Why on earth would you think that?'

He gave a half-hearted shrug. 'I thought the family might've disowned me.'

'Don't be daft. We'd never do that, no matter what you've done.' She gave him a playful shove. 'Aren't you going to give your sister a hug?'

He looked momentarily unsure, but rose to his feet and opened his arms.

Wrapping her arms around him, she held him tight. A few moments passed before she felt his body relax and he hugged her back. He smelt musty and faintly of beer. No doubt he'd been drowning his sorrows.

She rubbed his back and kissed his cheek before pulling away.

'I need tea,' she said, her throat dry from spending the morning yelling at Jamie. 'Do you have any cash on you?'

He pulled out his wallet and gave her a twenty-pound note. 'Get me another coffee, will you.' His hands were trembling. 'Three sugars.'

'Coming right up.'

The cafe wasn't busy, just a couple of dog-walkers queueing for a drink. It hadn't changed inside. It was still basic, but clean, and she had a sudden flashback of enjoying a hot chocolate after swimming. How much simpler life was back then.

She made her purchase and returned to Max with their drinks and two Danish pastries. 'I couldn't resist,' she said, sitting opposite him and handing him his change.

'I'm not hungry.'

'More for me, then.' She wrapped her hands around the large carton of tea. It wasn't freezing outside, but spent-adrenaline and no jacket was making her shiver. 'Have you spoken to Mum and Dad?'

'Not yet. I went by the house, but the press are camped outside.' His voice sounded flat. 'How long have they been there?'

She instantly felt guilty. Not that it was her fault – other than having been stupid enough to let an undercover journalist infiltrate her trusted circle of friends. But it still stung. 'Since yesterday.' It felt like a lot longer. 'Rumours are circulating.'

He looked dejected. 'I knew it was only a matter of time.'

She took a sip of tea, glad of the warmth. She waited for her brother to elaborate, but nothing was forthcoming. She needed to take the lead. 'I gather Hylton Sabell's involved?'

He glanced up, surprised. 'How did you know?'

'One of the journalists asked me about him.' She raised her hand when his eyes widened. 'Don't worry, I didn't tell them anything. Mainly because I don't know anything.' Which was entirely true. 'You need to tell me what's going on, Max. I don't want to read a pack of lies in the newspaper tomorrow.' Lies written by flippin' Jamie Lawson. The thought made her feel sick. 'What's going on?'

He stared at the table, not moving.

'Is it true you're being investigated for insider trading?'

He nodded. 'But it's not what you think.'

'I don't think anything, Max. But I know you. I don't believe you'd knowingly sell information – which means there's something else going on.' She reached across and took his hand. 'Talk to me.'

He took a swig of coffee before answering. 'I guess it started years ago. I've always talked about my work to Hylton, nothing overly confidential, but we'd chat over dinner or on the golf course about the stock markets. He didn't seem that interested, and he wasn't in the same line of work, so it never felt like a big issue.'

She broke off a piece of pastry. It was buttery and delicious and her stomach growled in appreciation. She hadn't realised how hungry she was. But then, she hadn't eaten since yesterday lunchtime. 'Go on.'

'I guess we'd kind of... show off. You know, brag about how much money we were making. Him from jewellery, me from the stock market. It was just boozy banter. Men competing to see who had the biggest—'

'I get the picture.' She held up her hand.

'—ego.'

'Oh, right. So what happened?'

'He used the information to play the stock market. It was small at first, so it went under the radar. But then he started taking bigger risks. His last deal made forty grand.'

'Crikey.'

'The transaction was made a few seconds before the stock price dropped, so it attracted attention. The deal triggered an investigation and that's when the Financial Conduct Authority got involved.'

'But surely Hylton would know you'd get into trouble? Why would he take such a risk? The man's loaded, for Christ's sake. He's never struck me as greedy.'

'He's not. But Sabell & Sutton aren't as secure as everyone thinks. In fact, they're having serious financial difficulties. The London flagship store isn't doing well and he didn't want anyone getting wind of it. Especially not his family. He thought if he could inject some cash into the business he could prop it up without anyone knowing.'

'Not the greatest plan.'

He shrugged. 'Desperate people do desperate things.'

'How do you know all this? Have you spoken to Hylton?'

'Not recently, but I already knew he was having financial problems. He told me a few months back.' He removed his baseball cap and ran his hands through his dark hair. 'He asked me for a loan and I agreed. I've been giving him money ever since to cover the staff wages. But I only knew he'd been making deals on the stock market after the FCA visited me at work.'

She sipped her tea. 'How did they know the information had come from you?'

'Hylton told them when he was questioned.'

'He squealed on you?'

'He was offered a plea-deal if he co-operated. I guess he felt he had no choice.' Max looked so utterly morose her heart broke for him.

'But surely he told them he hadn't paid for the information? And you weren't knowingly selling him insider information?'

Max removed his sunglasses. His eyes were bloodshot. 'The FCA have photos of me exchanging envelopes of cash with Hylton.'

'But you were giving *him* the money, it wasn't the other way around.'

'The photos don't make that clear.'

Oh, God. Did Jamie have a copy of those photos? 'Surely you can explain to the FCA that the money was a loan, and it wasn't payment for information?'

He shrugged. 'Like the FCA are going to believe that.'

'But didn't Hylton tell them?'

Another shrug. 'I've no idea what he told them. He's blocked my number.'

Sam was furious. 'Bastard.'

Max took a long swig of coffee. 'His lawyer probably told him to do it.'

'That's no excuse. Loyalty and friendship should come first. I can't believe he threw you under the bus like that.' She'd wring Hylton Sabell's bloody neck if she ever got hold of him. Talk about a traitor.

'It's my own fault. I was stupid enough to give him the information.'

'You had no idea he was going to use it for financial gain.'

Max scratched his unshaven chin. 'But if he hadn't had the information, he wouldn't have been tempted to use it, would he? Like I said, desperate people do desperate things.'

'Like disappear for ten days and not tell their loved ones where they are?'

He didn't offer a response.

She softened her voice. 'Where were you, Max? We were worried sick.'

'It doesn't matter. I'm back now. I'm ready to face the music.'

For the first time in her life, Sam felt like the older sibling. It was usually her that messed up. This time, she needed to step up to the plate. Max had contacted her, which meant he wanted her help and advice.

'Right... well, the first thing we need to do is let Mum and Dad know you're okay.' That was the easy part. 'Then you need to speak to a lawyer. You need expert advice, someone who'll help you build a defence.' She took his hand. 'Because you're not going to take the fall for this, okay?'

'But I'm guilty.'

'Only of naivety. Not of insider trading.' She dug out her phone. 'I'm calling Mother to let her know you're okay. And then we'll get a taxi back to the house and you can contact a lawyer. Do you know someone who could represent you?'

He nodded.

'Good. Then call them and get them over to the house pronto.'

But before she could make the call, her phone pinged with a message.

It was from Norah.

> Sorry to bother you, Sam. Hope you're okay. Thought you should know Harold has died.

Sam stared at the screen. Oh, no. Not Harold. Not lovely, kind, lonely Harold.

Tears raced to the surface and she clutched her chest, unable to prevent a sob escaping. And she'd foolishly thought her day couldn't get any worse.

Chapter Twenty-Three

Saturday, 15th December

Emily stifled a yawn. It had been a long night. Not that she normally slept well when covering a night shift at the shelter, but last night she hadn't slept at all. Just as she hadn't the previous night. Why? Because Alfie hadn't turned up again.

Finishing up her stint at The Crash Pad, she stacked the dirty cutlery on to the empty plates and tidied the chairs, exhausted from a busy breakfast shift.

That was two nights now Alfie hadn't queued for a bed and two days that he hadn't shown up for lunch. In fact, she hadn't seen him since Wednesday night when he'd got into an altercation with the journalists camped outside – who thankfully had now departed. Had she upset him? Was he hurt? Had he found somewhere to live?

Maybe he'd got another job? But then surely he would have told her? Not that he could have contacted her. Her blessed phone had packed up so she hadn't been able to call him either.

She piled up the empty plates. The bright décor and beach mural painted on the wall usually cheered her, but not this morning. She felt tired and sluggish, her limbs weighed down by worry.

As she lifted the plates, her foot caught on the chair leg and she lost her grip. There was a huge crash as the plates hit the floor, the chatter around her lulling as the kids finishing their breakfast looked over.

Emily looked down at the mess, tears threatening to surface.

She wasn't normally clumsy, but her mind wasn't focused on her job today, which was unforgivable. And now she'd cost the shelter money. She felt awful.

Before she could tidy the mess, new volunteer Lucie raced over with a dustpan and brush. 'Don't worry,' she said, dropping to the floor. 'I've got this.'

Until recently, seventeen-year-old Lucie had been a frequent user of The Crash Pad, queuing for a bed each night and grateful for the facilities on offer. But she'd now been housed in bed and breakfast and was awaiting a permanent room. Keen to support the charity that had helped her so much, she'd applied to be a volunteer.

Emily pulled herself together. 'You don't have to do that, Lucie. It's my mess, I should clear it up.'

'It was an accident.' Lucie smiled up at her. 'No one's fault.'

She appreciated the girl's kindness, but it was entirely her fault, she hadn't been focusing on her work.

Lucie swept up the broken crockery. 'I'm happy to help.'

Emily believed her, because despite what some of those horrible reporters had claimed, most of the kids here weren't lazy or scroungers, they just wanted what everyone else wanted – a home, security, and someone who gave a damn about them. Was that so much to ask?

'I'll fetch a cloth,' Emily said, heading into the kitchen.

It wasn't only worrying about Alfie that was upsetting her. It was also hearing the news that Harold had died. He'd been such a sweet man. She was really going to miss him. She'd looked forward to seeing him every day. He was like the granddad she'd never had, asking her about college, complimenting her cooking and telling her stories about London in decades gone by.

And now he was gone.

Emily wiped her eyes. She hated crying.

She was also worried about Sam. When her boss had arrived for the night shift yesterday, she could tell something was wrong. Her eyes were downcast and there was a permanent tremble in her hands. She'd batted away questions and assured everyone she was fine, but no one believed her. Mainly because when Fraser had asked where Jamie was, she'd snapped, 'Don't know. Don't care. He won't be volunteering here anymore.'

With no further explanation, she'd busied herself making beds and sweeping the floors like a demon possessed, as if determined to keep herself occupied.

Emily had no idea what had happened. But it would be a shame if Jamie stopped volunteering. He was a nice guy. She'd come to trust him, which wasn't something she found easy to do. There weren't many people she genuinely cared about. And right now, they all seemed to be leaving her.

Consequently, on seeing Norah walking into the kitchen ready for the start of her shift, she ran over and hugged her. 'I'm so glad you're here.'

Norah chuckled. 'That's a nice welcome.' Then she frowned. 'Has something happened?'

'Alfie never showed up again.'

'Ah, sweetheart, I'm sorry.' She stroked Emily's hair. 'Have you asked around? Maybe one of the other kids knows where he is?'

'I tried, but they don't know anything.'

'That's a shame.'

She rested her head on Norah's shoulder. 'And I'm sad about Harold.'

'Me too, love.' Norah patted her back. 'How's Sam taking the news?'

'Not great. Plus, I think her and Jamie had a falling out. She said he won't be volunteering here anymore.'

Norah raised an eyebrow. 'Lover's tiff, eh?'

Emily was shocked. 'Are they...?'

'I wouldn't be surprised. There was certainly chemistry there.' She winked at Emily. 'But I'm disappointed he's stopped volunteering. I thought he fitted in well here.'

'Me too.'

Norah tucked her fair hair behind her ears. 'How's Lucie getting along?'

'Great. She processed the queue last night and helped me serve breakfast this morning. She's a quick learner.'

'At least that's something positive.' Norah dumped her handbag on the table, her concerned gaze settling on Emily. 'You look exhausted, love. Get off home to bed, your shift is finished.'

Emily shook her head. 'I need to help Lucie clean up first. I dropped a pile of plates.'

'I'll do that. You go home.' She took the cloth from Emily. 'No arguments.'

'You don't have to—'

'Go! I insist.'

'Okay.' She squeezed her friend's hand. 'Good luck with Lucie.'

Emily left the kitchen and headed for reception, glad she wasn't leaving Norah to manage the cafe alone. Her friend was right: she was exhausted. With any luck bone-deep tiredness would override her anxiety and she could grab a couple of hours sleep this afternoon.

But her plan to escape was interrupted when she heard Fraser calling her.

She turned to see him limping towards her. 'I've just heard about an assault,' he said, reaching her. 'It happened a couple of nights ago, down by the Tesco Express near Gipsy Hill.'

That was one of Alfie's regular spots. 'An assault? What... what kind of assault? Was someone hurt?' She had a horrible feeling she already knew the answer.

Fraser looked tired, he hadn't had the best night either. 'I'm not certain.'

'But you think it's... Alfie?'

'I think so, yeah.' He scratched at his dark stubble. 'Judging by the description. It sounds like him. I'm sorry, Ems.'

'Is he badly hurt?'

'I don't know any details.'

'Where is he?'

'St. George's hospital.' He gestured outside. 'You want me to drive you?'

She shook her head. 'You're needed here. I'll catch the bus.'

'It'll take forever.' He unearthed his phone. 'Get a taxi. My shout.'

'You don't have to do that.'

'Course I do.' He was already dialling. 'You're family. Alfie too.' He rested his free hand on her shoulder. 'We stick together.'

Tightness constricted her throat. He was right. They were family. 'Thanks, Fraser. I'll wait outside.'

The next thirty minutes went by in a blur. It wasn't far to the hospital, only a couple of miles, but it was long enough to exacerbate her stress levels, her mind whirling from the news that Alfie had been assaulted.

Almost before the taxi had pulled up, she was jumping from the vehicle and racing towards the main reception.

The queue at reception seemed to take forever to move. All the while her stress levels continued to increase. How badly was he hurt? Was he conscious? Was he alone?

Oh, God, he shouldn't be alone. No one should be. She needed to be with him.

Finally, she reached the front of the queue. 'My friend has been assaulted,' she said in a rush. 'He's been admitted here. Please can you tell me where he is?'

The receptionist barely looked up. 'Name?'

'Emily Martin.'

The receptionist sighed. 'The patient's name.'

'Oh, right, sorry. Alfie Evans.'

The receptionist tapped away on the keyboard. It seemed to take forever. 'He's in the acute medical ward.'

'Acute?' That didn't sound good. 'Where's that?'

'Fifth floor. St James wing. Cavell ward.'

'Right. Thanks.' She ran off.

'Other way!' The receptionist pointed to a corridor. 'The stairs and lifts are at the end.'

Emily skidded to a halt and switched direction. 'Thank you!'

The word 'acute' tugged at her brain as she ran towards the lift and jabbed at the button, willing the elevator to arrive. But whatever fear she felt, she had to overcome it. Alfie needed her. He didn't have anyone else.

The first thing that struck her when she stepped out of the lift on the fifth floor was the smell. A mixture of cleaning products, antiseptic, and patients suffering from poor health.

Life on the streets had desensitised her to rancid odours, so the fact that she noticed the smell meant she'd readjusted to clean living. Her flat was always spotless, and she showered every day – a luxury that had yet to wear off.

Her hands were shaking as she scuttled down the corridor, passing cubicles, searching for Alfie. She must have looked lost because a friendly nurse caught her eye. 'Who're you looking for?'

'Alfie Evans.' Her voice shook as she said his name.

'Bed nine.' The nurse pointed to the left. 'Are you a relative?'

'Friend.'

'We haven't been able to trace a next of kin. Do you have any contact details?'

She shook her head. 'He's estranged from his family.'

'Oh, that's sad.' The nurse glanced across to his bed. 'He seems like a nice boy.'

'He is. Really nice. Can... can I see him?'

'Of course.' The nurse patted her arm. 'It'll be good for him to have a visitor.'

Emily thanked her and headed for bed nine.

The cubicle curtain was partially closed. She paused and took a breath before nervously poking her head through the gap, scared of what lay behind it. The sight beyond sickened her. A young man was lying on the bed wearing a blue gown. He was hooked up to a drip and attached to a monitoring machine that beeped every few seconds. If she hadn't known it was Alfie, she might not have recognised him.

His eyes were closed. The right one was badly swollen and so black it looked like he was wearing eye-shadow. His left eye had a deep purple bruise below that covered most of his cheek.

Tears threatened again. But she couldn't collapse now, she had to hold it together. Taking a deep breath, she moved closer to the bed.

As if sensing her presence, his eyes flickered open – well, the left one did. The right stayed shut, the swelling preventing it from opening.

It took a moment, but his mouth broke into a smile. 'Emily?'

'Hey, there.' She moved to the side of the bed. 'I hear you had a bit of trouble.'

'You should see the other guy,' he said, reaching for her. His fingers closed around hers and he squeezed tightly. 'I'm so glad you're here.'

She swallowed past the lump in her throat and perched on the side of the bed. 'I would've come sooner, but I only found out what happened this morning. Are you okay?'

'I'll live.' He winced. 'Two broken ribs and a fractured cheek bone.'

She noticed a tube attached to the side of his chest.

'Oh, and a collapsed lung.'

'A collapsed lung?' That sounded alarming.

'Don't worry, it's reflated now. How's that for a posh word?' He smiled, but his voice was weak and it sounded like it pained him to talk.

She spotted his phone lying on the cabinet next to him. The screen was smashed. 'What happened?'

'Two guys on a moped tried to mug me.'

She flinched. Why would anyone target a homeless person? 'What were they after?' Rough sleepers were an easy target, but not exactly known for having much to steal.

His eyes flickered to the broken phone. 'It doesn't matter.'

'Of course, it matters.' She followed his line of sight. 'Were they after your phone?' Not that it was a particularly new or high-spec version. It didn't make sense.

He hesitated. 'It wasn't that one they were after.'

'You have another phone?'

He didn't answer.

'Alfie, what's going on?'

He rolled his head to look at her. 'I bought you a new phone, okay?'

'Me? Why?'

'It was supposed to be a surprise.'

'But... why would you do that?'

'Because your old phone is rubbish.' He looked right at her. 'I know the girls at college take the piss. So I thought I'd get you a smart phone. I thought you could use it to get internet at your flat and, you know, catch up with technology. You said you felt left behind.'

Emily couldn't believe what she was hearing. It was true she felt overwhelmed by technology, but that was her problem, not his. 'It doesn't mean you had to buy me a phone. How did you even afford it?'

'I've been saving up my tips from the pizza place.'

'Oh, Alfie. You need that money for yourself. You could've paid for a bed and breakfast... or bought new shoes, or a winter coat, or—'

'I wanted to buy you a phone.' He tugged on her hand. 'It was my way of saying thank you for letting me stay. And sorry for the trouble I caused.'

'You didn't cause me any trouble.'

'You were threatened with eviction.'

She looked at his bruised and swollen face. 'You still didn't need to buy me a phone.'

His right hand rested on his chest. A gadget was attached to his finger. 'Is your old phone broken?' he asked, quietly.

She dragged her eyes away from the monitor screen. 'Why do you ask?'

'I tried calling you.'

'Oh. When?'

'The night I was brought in here. I could've done with seeing a friendly face.' His grip on her hand tightened and she felt tears welling again. He must have been so frightened.

'I'm sorry. My phone packed up, but I only realised when I tried calling you last night.' His tender expression made her feel suddenly shy. 'I was worried when you didn't show up at the shelter again.'

'That was nice of you.' He held her gaze for a long moment and then nodded to the cabinet. 'It's in there.'

'What is?'

'Your new phone.'

She blinked in surprise. 'The muggers didn't nick it?'

'Are you kidding me? No way was I letting them have it. Take a look.'

He'd fought the muggers off?

Letting go of his hand, she opened the cabinet, removing the phone. It was still in its box. She lifted the lid.

'It's not top of the range, but it's better than the one you have.' He touched her arm. 'Do you like it?'

'Yes, but—'

'The police reckon the shop I bought it from is dodgy. They think the owner's in league with the muggers and he tells them about new sales. They follow customers when they leave the shop and wait for an opportunity to strike.'

'That's awful. And this happened Wednesday?'

He nodded. 'I was going to give it to you that night, but it all kicked off with those journalists.' He trailed his fingers across her forearm. 'Is Sam okay?'

'She's fine. Physically, anyway.' The hairs on her arm responded to his touch.

He adjusted his position, wincing as he did so.

She waited until he'd settled and looked more comfortable. 'She's had a falling out with Jamie. He won't be volunteering at the shelter anymore.'

'Poor bloke. He'll be gutted. ... You know he's into her, right?'

'So it seems.'

'It's sad if you like someone and they don't like you back.' His voice was tender and soft, and she noticed he'd averted his gaze.

'What makes you think she doesn't like him?'

'She told him she just wants to be friends.'

'Oh.' She stared down at his hand, which had stilled. His fingers were long and narrow and she wanted so much for him to continue touching her. 'Does Jamie know about the attack?'

He shook his head. 'I doubt it.'

'I think he'd want to know. Can I tell him?'

He pointed to the new phone. 'Call him. You have a new phone.'

She sighed. 'Alfie, I can't accept it. Especially as your phone is broken. You need to have it.' She unwrapped the charger and plugged it into the wall behind. 'But I promise to let Jamie know you're here. I'm sure he'll want to visit.'

He looked dejected. 'I wish you'd take it.'

'Why don't we talk about it when you're out of hospital?' She didn't want to upset him by refusing, but it was such a generous gift. How could she accept? 'You keep it for now.' She attached the phone to the charger. 'How's the pain?'

He briefly closed his eyes. 'It's been worse. I'm due for pain meds soon.'

She flattened down the bedsheet, not quite sure what to do. 'Do you know how long you'll be in here?'

'A few days. A week, maybe. Depends on when they take the drain out.'

'It looks uncomfortable.'

'I can't really feel it.'

Typical Alfie, always putting on a brave face. 'Liar.'

He smiled, but it quickly faded. 'It hurt a lot more not seeing you for the last couple of days. I missed you.'

She swallowed awkwardly. 'I missed you too.'

'You did?'

'Of course.' Was he kidding? She hated not seeing him every day.

'Because I'm your... friend?'

It was odd to see Alfie looking uncertain. He was normally so confident, so self-assured. And up until a few days ago, she'd have said they *were* just friends. But now...? Something had changed. She wasn't sure what.

'You're more than my friend, Alfie.'

The beeping on the monitor sped up. 'I am?'

'Yes, you're family.'

'Right.' The beeping slowed and he turned his face away. 'You mean, like a brother?'

'No, more like…' She fiddled with her hands, resisting the urge to bite her nails. 'It's hard to explain. I don't know how to describe it.'

He rolled his head to look at her. 'Is it like a nice feeling?'

She nodded. 'Yes… and no.'

'No?' He frowned.

'It's nice when I'm with you… and horrible when I'm not.'

A faint smile touched his lips. 'Is that right?'

'Yes, I mean…' She sat back down on the side of his bed, careful not to disturb the equipment. 'When you turn up at the shelter, I feel happy. But when you had to leave the flat, I felt sad. And when Fraser told me you'd been attacked?' She covered her face with her hands. 'It was awful.'

'Emily?'

'I think about you all the time – which is sometimes nice and sometimes very confusing. But mostly it's scary, because I've never felt like this before… and it makes me feel vulnerable… and nervous and—'

'Emily?'

She lowered her hands. 'Yes?'

'I love you.'

Her breath hitched. 'You… do?'

He nodded. 'And I think you might love me too.' He sounded nervous. The monitor screen confirmed this.

Did she? …Love him?

Emily's experience of love was skewered. Shaped by disappointment and loss. She'd only ever associated love with feeling sad. But Alfie made her feel happy. And cared for. And wanted. She didn't feel sad when he was around. 'I don't know for certain… but I think I might.'

He laughed. 'That'll do.' He lifted his right arm. 'Come here. Lie with me.'

She glanced around. 'Are we allowed?'

'No idea.' His expression softened. 'But I need a cuddle.'

How could she refuse? She walked around the bed and climbed onto the mattress next to him. 'Are you sure I won't hurt you?'

'You could never hurt me. And I would never hurt you.'

She believed him. Reaching up, she brushed the hair away from his forehead and asked, 'What happens now?'

'Under normal circumstances, I'd kiss you.'

She stilled. 'You would?'

'But I'm a little incapacitated.'

'Oh.' She was so close she could see the flecks of grey in his blue eyes.

'You might have to kiss me, instead.' His voice was barely a whisper.

Was she really going to do this? Kiss a boy? And in hospital too. It was hardly the most romantic of settings. But Emily didn't care. It was Alfie, and she'd wanted to kiss him for a very, very long time.

Balancing on her elbow, she looked down at his bruised and swollen face. His left eye was locked on her, encouraging her, coaxing her closer. The monitor had gone into a frenzy of beeping. She was just about to kiss him, when he lifted his hand and said, 'Wait.'

Had she done something wrong? Had he changed his mind?

He removed the gadget from his finger. 'Otherwise the nurses'll think I've had a heart attack.'

Gently, she lowered her lips to meet his. The kiss was soft and warm and sent a wave of excitement racing through her. Was it a fluke? She tried again, just to be certain. She closed her eyes and kissed him, letting her lips linger a little longer. Yep, it was there again. That giddy feeling. She could get used to this.

She kissed him again, feeling the sensation right down to her toes.

Yep, she definitely liked kissing.

He was smiling. 'When I get out of here, I'm going to take you on a proper date. Where would you like to go? A fancy restaurant in London?'

She rested her head on his shoulder. 'You know where I'd really like to go? Crystal Palace Park to see the dinosaurs. It's my special place.' She felt slightly embarrassed admitting it. Would he think it silly? That she was too young and clueless?

But he smiled and said, 'Sounds perfect.'

She trailed her fingers through his hair. The colour had returned to his cheeks and he seemed less pained. 'You look… happy.'

'I am.' A tear dropped from the corner of his eye onto the pillow. 'I told you, I just needed to find the right girl.'

A nurse drew back the cubicle curtain. It was the friendly nurse from earlier. Her concerned face broke into a smile as her gaze switched from Alfie to the monitor screen. 'You haven't died then?'

He grinned. 'The opposite.'

The nurse's hands went to her hips. 'I shouldn't really allow this.'

'Think of the medicinal benefits,' he said. 'I'm feeling better already.'

'I'll bet you are.' She came over to the bed and replaced the gadget on his finger. 'I'm going to pretend I never saw anything. But keep this on, okay?'

He nodded. 'I'll be a good boy.'

'Glad to hear it.' She left grinning, closing the cubicle curtain behind her.

Alfie turned to Emily. 'Are you going to kiss me again?'

She smiled. Boy, was she ever.

Chapter Twenty-Four

Monday, 17th December

As Jamie entered the offices of the *South London Herald*, he knew his life was about to take a dramatic turn. He strode across the office, holding the article he'd written in his hand, ready to give it to Gareth. He was proud of the story, it was the best thing he'd written. He'd stayed up all last night perfecting the wording, editing it so that it had the right balance of drama, intrigue and human interest.

The only problem was – it wasn't the article Gareth was expecting.

Gurdip looked up from his workstation as Jamie walked by. 'You're still employed then?'

'For the moment.' Although probably not for much longer.

'The boss isn't happy,' Gurdip called after him.

'Nothing new there then,' he replied, and carried on walking.

He reached the far end of the room where Gareth's large tinted-glass office was situated. Frances was exiting the office. She looked annoyed, but her face brightened on seeing him. 'Hey, stranger. Long-time, no-see.'

'Hi, Frances.' He tipped his head towards the door. 'Is he in there?'

'Unfortunately, yes. I've just been torn off a strip for failing to buy him the correct coffee. He's switched to skinny lattes, apparently.' She rolled her eyes. 'Like I'm a mind-reader.' She turned to walk away, and then paused. 'Just so you know, I've been assigned Pet of the Week.'

'Good for you.'

She tilted her head. 'You're not mad?'

Was she for real?

'I'm delighted.' He'd had his fill of dysfunctional pets. He was ready to tackle meatier stories. But whether that was for the *South London Herald*, or an alternative news-paper, remained to be seen. 'Good luck with it.'

She nodded to the door. 'Break a leg. He's not in the best mood.'

Great. He took a moment to compose himself and knocked assertively on the door.

'I'm busy!' barked Gareth, glaring at him through the glass.

Tough. He knocked again. 'We need to talk. Can I come in?'

A beat passed before Gareth marched over and yanked open the door. He stood there looking daggers. 'The prodigal arsehole returns.'

Jamie winced. It wasn't the first time he'd been called an arsehole that week.

'Get in here.' Gareth walked back to his desk. 'Close the door.'

Jamie did as he was instructed.

The TVs mounted on the wall were switched on as usual, depicting various news stories from around the world, but the sound was muted. Jamie went to sit in the plastic 'interrogation' chair, but Gareth yelled, 'Did I say you could sit?'

326

Jamie remained standing.

'The *Daily Mirror.*' Gareth picked up a newspaper from his desk and threw it at Jamie. 'The *Sun.*' Another newspaper was tossed across the room at him. 'The *Telegraph.*' This one was thrown against the wall. 'The *Express,*' he said, slamming it on the desk. 'You know what they all have in common?'

Jamie could guess.

'They all feature stories about Max Tipping.' Gareth picked up today's copy of the *South London Herald.* 'Is there a story in our paper? No, there fucking isn't!' He threw the newspaper at Jamie, forcing him to duck.

Jamie had seen Gareth angry before, but this was a whole new level of rage. He needed to tread carefully.

But when he opened his mouth to speak, he realised Gareth wasn't done. 'Did you even go to the press conference Max Tipping held on Friday?'

Jamie nodded. 'I did.'

'Then why don't I have an article?' Gareth banged his hand on the desk. His armpits were sweaty and he had large dark patches on his blue shirt. There was a manic look about him. Jamie feared the man might have an aneurism if he continued ranting – a situation that would be exacerbated when Jamie admitted he hadn't written the article.

Why? Because when he'd sat down to write it the words wouldn't come.

He'd tried to focus on the facts and not include any details about the Tipping family, but without that insight there was no story. It was a boring repeat of the facts. Yet he couldn't bring himself to write anything personal about Sam, or Max, for that matter.

Besides, since Max Tipping's press conference last Friday everyone now knew the story. There was nothing more to tell. He'd admitted to unintentionally committing insider trading. He'd confessed his guilt and handed himself over to the authorities for questioning. The story was done.

But would his boss agree?

Gareth marched over. 'You had a head start on the story. I gave you that photo of Max Tipping weeks ago. You assured me you wouldn't let me down and you'd get the story done.'

'I know.'

'You've had over a month to gather evidence and dig the dirt on the Tippings.' He opened his arms. 'And what have you given me? Nothing.' He jabbed a finger at Jamie. 'You convinced me to let you continue volunteering at the sister's charity, because you assured me you were close to a breakthrough.' He was so close Jamie could smell his coffee-breath. 'You even had direct contact with Max Tipping on the day he fucking disappeared! And yet still, nothing. What happened?'

It was a valid question. Admitting he'd been sidetracked wouldn't help Jamie's cause, though. His interest had been piqued elsewhere – and not by the dodgy dealings of Max Tipping, but by the good work carried out by his sister. It was hard to care about insider trading when teenagers were queuing outside a homeless shelter in need of a bed.

Then there was the issue of Sam herself, and how he'd lied to her and betrayed her trust. But he couldn't allow himself to think about that right now. One problem at a time.

Jamie braced himself. 'I came up with a better story.'

Gareth looked incredulous. 'A better story?'

'Yes.'

'A better story than exposing Max Tipping for insider trading before anyone else knew about it?' He threw his arms in the air. 'This I've got to hear.'

Jamie wanted to step away, but he knew he had to stand his ground. He could almost imagine the looks on his colleagues faces in the main office. Gareth's office wasn't soundproof and his rantings could often be overheard. Would Gurdip and Frances be sympathetic to his plight, or enjoying the floorshow? Both probably.

'When I first volunteered at the shelter, I felt the same way you did,' Jamie said, maintaining eye contact with his boss – which was hard when he was being eyeballed like his head would look good on a stick. 'I assumed the Tippings were a privileged spoilt family, and the sister's charity was most likely a front for her brother's dirty money laundering. But it quickly became apparent that wasn't the case. Not in relation to Sam, anyway.' The rest of the family he wasn't so sure about, they certainly liked their wealthy trappings.

'*Sam?*' Gareth almost spat the name. 'How very *cosy*... Don't tell me you fell for the woman? Is that what this is about? You've been dicking around?'

'That's not—'

'Don't get me wrong, she's hot. And if getting inside her knickers gets you insider information, then I'm all for it. But please don't tell me the reason you haven't submitted the story is because you have *feelings* for the bloody woman?'

'It's not like that.' At least, that wasn't the only reason. He'd be lying if he said he hadn't fallen for her.

Gareth looked disbelieving. 'I think that's exactly what happened.' He started pacing the office. 'First rule of journalism. Never fall for the piece of skirt you're invest-igating.'

His boss really was a tosser. But challenging him about his non-PC stereotypical assumptions wouldn't cool the situation. 'What I meant was, my opinion changed when I saw the work of the charity. It's not a hobby, or a sham. It's an amazing project, which achieves extraordinary outcomes for the kids who use it. It's an essential part of our community.'

Gareth laughed. 'Which all sounds very *worthwhile*,' he said, air-miming quote marks to accentuate his sarcasm. 'But it has nothing to do with Max Tipping. I want a hard-hitting corruption exposé to print. Not a story about how *nice* the man's sodding sister is.'

Jamie wiped away a shower of spittle that landed on his shirt. 'That's what I'm trying to say. We don't focus on Max Tipping at all. There's no story there. The man made a mistake, which he's now admitted to. It holds no interest.'

Gareth look unconvinced.

'But there's another story waiting to be told.' He gestured to the folder he was holding. 'It's a story I think will create real interest for our readers. The plight of homeless teenagers in South London.'

Gareth baulked. 'Are you for real? Why would people want to read about homeless kids? It's fucking depressing.'

'But that's just it. It's not. It's incredibly uplifting.' Jamie was determined to say his piece, whatever the outcome. 'Yes, there's sadness and desperation, but there's also inspiration and hope. The shelter doesn't just provide the kids with a bed for the night. There's a non-profit cafe, which is open to all the community, and a rooftop garden, which provides home-grown produce and promotes sustainability. Kids missing out on a bed are given a sleeping bag and hot food. Winter coats are distributed across South London. The shelter has set up health checks for the kids with local GPs, and when we organised a donation drive for bedding and winter clothing, the response was incredible. The local community responded in droves. There was so much stuff donated we had to store it in a shipping container.'

'We?' Gareth looked appalled. 'Who is this *we*? Next you'll be telling me you want to continue volunteering there.' He did. Unfortunately, Sam didn't want him there and he couldn't really blame her. Gareth rubbed his forehead. 'You really have got it bad, haven't you? She was that hot in the sheets, eh?'

Jamie ignored him, hard as it was. 'I've also made a video. A diary that follows one of the kids as he struggles to get off the streets.'

Gareth slumped into his sumptuous leather chair. 'And you're telling me that isn't depressing?'

'It's also incredibly inspiring. And it highlights the vicious circle these kids find themselves in.'

'Who cares—'

'Please hear me out.' He moved closer to the desk, ignoring Gareth's shocked expression. His boss wasn't used to being interrupted. 'This kid, Alfie, is classed as an adult because he's eighteen, so the council won't house him. He can't get a decent job, because he doesn't have a fixed abode, and he can't rent anywhere, because he doesn't have enough income. He works evenings delivering pizzas, which means he misses out on a bed at the shelter, and he refuses to claim welfare benefits because he's convinced he can make it on his own. The kid wants to be self-sufficient, but the system obstructs him at every turn.' Jamie placed his hands on Gareth's desk. 'You're telling me that isn't a hard-hitting story?'

Gareth leant forwards, matching Jamie's pose. 'Where's the drama?'

'You want drama? The kid was mugged the other night. He's currently in hospital with multiple fractures and a collapsed lung. Two thugs on a moped tried to nick his mobile phone. A phone he'd been saving up to buy for his girlfriend.'

Gareth didn't immediately reply. He sat back in his chair and swivelled slowly from left to right, eyeing Jamie suspiciously. 'And this story's ready to run?'

Jamie lifted the folder. 'It's all here. I can email it through.'

'And the video?'

'Edited and ready to stream. I visited the kid in hospital yesterday and we filmed the final section. It's powerful stuff. Heartfelt. Dramatic. And yes, it's sad and frustrating and bleak at times, but the kid's a natural in front of the camera. He's charming, good-looking and funny. People are going to love him, root for him. He's not a drunken bum lying in a gutter begging for money. This is a kid who believes in hard work, making the best of a bad situation and who's a helpless romantic.'

Gareth chewed on his thumbnail. 'I wanted the Max Tipping story.'

'I know. But this is better. No one else has it. It's an exclusive. We run the story front page and the video online. It has the potential to go viral.'

Gareth remained unconvinced. 'I don't know.'

Jamie needed to think fast. 'Okay, how about this. We still briefly mention the Max Tipping case, but instead of focusing on the insider-trading angle, we show the other side of the family. We flip the story on its head and come at it from a completely different perspective. We *defend* the Tippings.'

Gareth stilled. 'Go on.'

Jamie was on a roll. 'We lead with the photo of the Tipping family opening the shelter. The one that was in the paper a few weeks ago. Max Tipping's in that photo, so anyone following the story will be intrigued. But we offer an alternative view. We show how being privileged can also lead to extreme altruism and compassion.' He leant on the desk. 'You wanted a coup? An original story? Something no other newspaper has? Well, this is it.'

Gareth raised a bushy eyebrow. 'And if I say no?'

Jamie shrugged. 'Then I quit and take the story someplace else.'

Gareth jumped up from the chair, sending it spinning backwards. 'You little shit!' He marched around the desk. 'You think you can threaten me? Back me into a corner? I was writing articles for daily newspapers while you were still in nappies, you cheeky fucker.' He grabbed Jamie by the shirt collar, drawing him close.

Just when Jamie thought he was about to be fired or punched, Gareth said, 'But we might just make a journalist of you yet.'

Jamie let out a relieved sigh.

'Now get out, and email me that fucking story, before I fire your scrawny arse!'

Jamie ran for the door. 'I'm on it.'

'And Jamie?'

He turned back. 'Yes?'

'Defy me again and I *will* fire you. Understand?'

Jamie nodded. 'Yes, boss.'

He left Gareth's office and walked across the office, trying to appear composed, which wasn't an easy task when his heart was thumping madly and his mind was an excited whirl. He'd won. He'd convinced his boss to print his article. He could hardly believe it.

He became aware of Frances and Gurdip watching him. He almost laughed at their surprised expressions when instead of packing up his things and leaving the building, he switched on his computer and sat down.

'You still have a job?' Gurdip's head appeared over the partition.

Jamie grinned. 'I do, yeah.'

Gurdip and Frances exchanged a puzzled glance. As much as he wanted to share his good news, he had one last task to do before filing his story. He didn't know why he hadn't thought of it before.

He picked up his phone and dialled his foster mum's number.

She answered immediately. 'It's about time, boy.'

'Peggy? I have a favour to ask.'

Chapter Twenty-Five

Tuesday, 18ᵗʰ December

Sam stirred from her afternoon nap and rolled over... hitting the floor with a thud. She'd forgotten she wasn't lying in a comfy bed, instead curled up on a pile of duvets in the laundry room at The Crash Pad. She hadn't meant to sleep, but the warmth of the room, coupled with the low whir of the washing machine had lulled her into a deep slumber.

Rubbing her elbow, she sat up and shook herself free from the duvets. That's what happened when you hadn't slept properly for several nights. It caught up with you at the most inconvenient of moments.

It wasn't even as if her brief nap had improved her spirits. She still felt flat, her limbs weak and wobbly and her stomach knotted so tightly it ached. The correlation of stress and worry that had built over recent weeks had culminated in a heavy heart. If she wasn't worrying about Max, she was sad about Harold. If she wasn't concerned about Alfie, she was replaying the argument with Jamie in her head. It was exhausting.

There were no windows in the room, so she had no idea what time it was. Blinking away the sleep, she checked her phone. Almost five p.m. So much for grabbing a quick ten minutes. She'd been asleep for nearly an hour.

She also had two missed calls and a text message waiting for her. She didn't recognise the caller. It was an unknown number. But the text was from Norah.

> Have you seen Jamie's article in the South London Herald? x

No, she hadn't, and she had no intentions of reading it. Seeing the articles in the other newspapers had been bad enough – and those journalists hadn't had inside access to the family. She could only imagine what personal information Jamie would reveal. The pain of which still threatened the onset of tears.

She wouldn't succumb, however; she was tougher than that. She got to her feet and straightened out her crumpled dungarees. It was ridiculous to cry over a man. She'd never been this feeble before.

But then, no one had affected her this way before. And it hadn't even been real. Jamie had duped her, pretended to be interested when all the time he was making notes for a story about her brother. She was such an idiot.

Come to think of it, *he* was the idiot. Her only crime was trusting him.

Either way, she felt crap.

Despite her anger, it still hurt that Jamie had betrayed her. When no story had appeared in yesterday's paper along with all the other newspapers, she'd foolishly wondered if he'd changed his mind and had decided not to expose them. Clearly that was just wishful thinking. It looked like the story had gone to print as planned

– confirmation that Jamie was a callous, gossip-driven journalist, and not the caring, thoughtful man he'd pretended to be.

Well, she wasn't going to give him the satisfaction of hurting her further. Whatever was written in that article, she didn't want to know.

The door to the laundry room opened and Norah flicked on the overhead light. 'Here you are,' she said, coming into the room, carrying a newspaper. 'We've been looking for you everywhere.'

Fraser was with her. 'Are you okay, Sam? We were worried about you.'

Sam squinted, her eyes adjusting to the light. 'I'm fine. I was just doing some laundry.'

Norah looked sceptical. 'In the dark?'

Sam removed the dried bedding from the washing machine. 'Yeah, well, I may have fallen asleep.'

'I'm guessing that's why you didn't reply to my message.' Norah glanced at Fraser.

He was leaning against the door, his brow furrowed.

'Have you seen this?' Norah held out the newspaper.

'No.' Sam folded the duvet. 'And I have no desire to. I've had my fill of stories about Max. I don't need to read any more lies.'

Norah and Fraser exchanged a glance.

'Well, that's the thing, love.' Norah sounded tentative. 'The story Jamie's written isn't about Max. It's about you.'

Sam turned sharply. 'Me?'

Norah nodded. 'And The Crash Pad.'

Oh, God. What had Jamie done? Why had he written about her? About her project?

Norah offered her the newspaper again. 'You need to read it. It's not what you think.'

With a shaking hand, Sam took the newspaper.

'Front page,' Fraser said, with a wry smile.

Front page? Heavens. It was worse than she thought.

She lifted the paper. The first thing she saw was the photo that had been taken on the opening day of The Crash Pad. The headline above was written in large bold lettering.

Where the Heart Is

by Jamie Lawson

Her eyes scanned over the first few lines...

> Nestled in the backstreets of Streatham lies a hidden gem. A home like no other. Where the food is home-cooked and served with love, and the rooms are colourful and comfy. Once a week is film night, shown on the big TV. Help is on hand 24/7 and the kindness never lets up. You might think it's a typical home. Where a family lives. Safe and warm and protected. But this is no ordinary family. The parenting is supplied by volunteers: an ex-army serviceman, a retired paediatric nurse, and a teenage runaway. And the kids? Homeless. And all under the age of 21, who are loved and cared for unconditionally by one remarkable woman. Samantha Tipping.

Sam glanced up from the paper. 'It's... not about Max?'

Norah shook her head. 'He gets a mention, but as a supporter of the project. Your parents too.'

338

Sam couldn't believe it. She wanted to read every word, absorb the enormity of what she was reading, but it was hard to focus with tears in her eyes.

The article spanned two further inside pages. It covered everything from the donation drive to the new monthly health checks. He'd written about the takeaway project, the distribution of winter coats and the challenges of limited funding, local objections to the project, and inaccurate assumptions about life as a homeless teen. He'd even written about Alfie, and how the system often let down young people who didn't have the support of a loving family.

At the bottom of the article was a plea for extra volunteers and funding for the shelter. It concluded with a paragraph about Jamie's own experience of volunteering.

> As a former foster kid, I thought I knew what 'suffering' meant. That without the support of family, we struggle as human beings to thrive and achieve and be happy – because if our families can't commit to us and show us love and attachment, who else will? But I now realise that family doesn't necessarily mean blood-relations. Sometimes the people who love us the most and have our best interests at heart, are those who choose to be a part of our lives, rather than those we're related too. Why? Because our 'adopted' families don't stay out of duty or obligation. They stay because they've chosen to. And that's the true definition of love. The finest example of this can be found at The Crash Pad, where no kid is made to feel unwanted, or unloved, or left to go hungry.

Sam felt unsteady. It was remarkable. Confusing... and very unexpected. She slumped against the washing machine. 'I... I don't know what to think?'

Fraser pushed away from the door. 'We thought you should see it before—'

'Before you started getting calls about people wanting to volunteer,' Norah cut in, glaring at Fraser as though he'd nearly slipped up.

He cringed. 'Right. Yes. What she said.' He gave an apologetic shrug. 'Talking of which...' He cleared his throat, his eyes darting from Norah to Sam. 'There's a man here who wants to volunteer. He's in the cafe.'

Great, but the last thing Sam needed right now.

'Can you deal with it, Fraser? I'm not in the right headspace.' She was still too thrown by the article and needed time to process it.

Fraser looked conflicted. He glanced at Norah, as if unsure what to do.

'He specifically asked for you,' Norah said, looking uncharacteristically shifty. 'I think it might be better if you dealt with him and we need to get ready for tonight's shift.' She pushed Fraser towards the door. 'Isn't that right, Fraser?'

'What? Err... right. Yes. Definitely.' He was out the door before Sam could object.

'I'd better help him,' Norah said before rushing for the door.

Sam rubbed her cheeks, trying to re-energise her flagging spirits. How she was supposed to concentrate and appear composed and professional when her head was all over the place, she had no idea.

Folding the newspaper under her arm, she headed out of the laundry room.

The man in question was sitting at a table in the cafe. He had his back to her. He was wearing a smart reddish-brown leather jacket, the colour a match for his...

Oh, no way!

She turned, intending to run away, but he must have heard her, because he jumped up and called after her. 'Hi. My name's Jamie Lawson. I'd like to volunteer.'

She skidded to a halt and turned to face him. 'Excuse me?'

He looked just as he had on the first day he'd come here. Smart. Handsome. Sincere. Well, she wasn't falling for his charm a second time. She was more savvy now.

Before she could enlighten him as to exactly what she thought of his offer, he said, 'I've heard good reports about the charity and the amazing work you do here.' He walked towards her. 'I'd like to volunteer, if you'll have me.'

She wasn't sure whether she was hallucinating, or still asleep and dreaming. 'Is this some kind of joke?'

'Not at all.' He shook his head. 'I'm being completely genuine.'

She gave an unladylike snort. 'Well, that'd be a first.'

He ignored the slight. 'Recent events have made me re-evaluate what's important in my life, and what kind of man I want to be. It's time for me to be the change I want to see in the world.'

Was he quoting Gandhi? Did he think she was an idiot?

She folded her arms. 'Oh, really?'

He rubbed the back of his neck looking nervous. 'A wise person once told me every kid deserves somewhere they feel looked after and safe,' he said, carefully. 'And that's what you provide here. A haven for those who don't have the love and support of their families. It's a great project and I'd like to be part of it.'

So, he was pretending like they'd never met, was he? Did he think it would be that easy? That she'd forget all he'd done and offer him a fresh start? He could think again.

'All our volunteers require a background check,' she said, going along with the pretence. 'What will I discover if I look into you, Mr Lawson? Are you an upstanding member of the community? Do you have references that hold up to scrutiny, or were they penned by a mate down at the pub?'

He flinched. 'I haven't always been an upstanding member of the community,' he said, quietly. 'But that's why I'm here. To make amends for those mistakes. I've lied. I've hurt people I care about and I've betrayed their trust.'

Finally, something they agreed on.

'Is that so?' She wanted so badly to hold onto her anger, but it was hard when he was looking at her through those huge caramel eyes. Eyes that appeared genuine and endearing and did strange things to her insides.

'Why here?' she managed, although her voice had lost some of its sting. 'I'm sure there're loads of places better suited to your particular skillset.'

He struggled for a response. 'Maybe… but I think this project is perfect for me.'

'Why?'

He took a deep breath. 'Because I can relate to these kids. I was taken into foster care aged seven. I know what it's like to grow up feeling unwanted and scared.'

However mad she was with him, she knew voicing those words aloud would have been incredibly painful for him.

'It's taken me years to come to terms with being abandoned,' he continued, his voice unsteady. 'And I've only been able to do that because of the support and love of people who took the time to give a damn. I'd like to… no, I *need* to return the favour.' He pulled an envelope from his pocket. 'And I do have references. Genuine ones. The first is from my boss at the *South London Herald* where I work as a journalist. The second is from my former foster carer, Peggy Miller. I hope you'll find them satisfactory.'

His hand was outstretched. Despite the visible shake in it, she couldn't bring herself to accept the envelope. Partly because she was clutching herself so tightly, she didn't trust herself not to collapse if she let go.

'I'm sorry to disappoint you, Mr Lawson. But we're unable to accept your application at this time. Thank you for showing an interest in The Crash Pad. I wish you luck in finding a more suitable position elsewhere.' Her words came out evenly and devoid of any emotion. She had no idea how. It was like she was on autopilot, her calm exterior was a mask for the torment raging inside her.

He lowered his hand. 'Well… thanks for your time. I appreciate you seeing me.' He walked off.

She realised she hadn't mentioned the story. 'Jamie?'

He turned back, his expression hopeful.

'Thank you for the article.' She gestured to the newspaper. 'I appreciate you not writing about Max.'

He held her gaze. 'You're welcome. And I meant every word. This truly is an amazing place and you're an extraordinary woman. I'm sorry I let you down.' And with that he was gone.

A wave of emotion threatened to wipe out her legs. She slid onto a chair and dropped her head onto the table.

She felt sick. She'd been so mean to him, so cruel. And she was never cruel to anyone. It wasn't a good feeling. No matter what he'd done, she shouldn't have been so… bitchy.

It would have taken a lot for him to come here, admit his mistakes and reveal his background. She should have shown more compassion, even if she had rejected him.

Had she done the right thing in rejecting him? Her head said, yes. Her heart wasn't so sure.

But she couldn't have someone volunteering at the shelter she didn't trust, and he was still a journalist. This time the story had been positive and supportive. What about next time? How could she be certain he wouldn't run with a story if something scandalous happened at the shelter, or Max messed up again? She couldn't take the risk.

Her phone rang, making her startle. She checked the screen. Unknown caller.

She pressed accept. 'Hello?'

'Am I speaking to Miss Samantha Tipping?' the male voice asked.

'Yes. I'm Sam Tipping,' she answered warily, worrying a reporter had got hold of her number. 'Who is this?'

'My name is Stanley Lawrence. I'm the probate solicitor dealing with the estate of Mr Harold Arthur Jones.'

She was hit by another wave of sadness. It still hurt that Harold had died. Maybe he was calling with details of the funeral?

'How can I help you?'

'Were you aware that your charity is the sole beneficiary of Mr Jones's estate?'

Sam blinked. 'Err… no, I wasn't. You mean, Harold left us something?' She knew money hadn't been in abundance, so it couldn't amount to much. She was touched nonetheless.

'In the form of property, yes. He was, as the saying goes, asset rich, cash poor.'

If Sam was surprised before, she was in total shock now. 'Are you saying Harold left us… property?' Surely he didn't mean actual property? He probably meant a trinket, or a piece of furniture, or something.

'His property in Streatham, to be precise. Valued as of today at 1.2 million pounds.'

Sam nearly dropped her phone. She clutched it tighter to her ear. 'But… why? Surely he had relatives he could've left the house to. Why leave it to us?'

'Mr Jones had no children or surviving family members. However, his neighbour enlightened me as to why your particular charity was chosen as a beneficiary. Mr Jones's late wife, Dorothy, was a resident of the care home that was situated on the site where The Crash Pad now resides. Mr Jones was very appreciative of you allowing him to visit the charity every day, where he felt he could be close to his late wife.'

Sam was speechless, choked up with a chaotic mix of emotions. She wished she'd known that's why Harold like coming to The Crash Pad.

'It will take some time to complete probate and deal with any capital gains tax arising from the sale of the property,' he continued, 'but I anticipate being able to settle the estate early next year. Do you have any questions for me at this time?'

About a zillion, but none she could manage to articulate right now. Instead she settled for, 'No, I don't think so.' She needed to get her head around this latest bombshell.

'I'll be writing to you in due course, but if you have any questions in the meantime, please don't hesitate to get in touch.'

'I will. Thank you.' And then a thought struck. 'What about the funeral? Can you send me details, please? There're several people who I'm sure would like to attend.'

'I'll get my assistant onto it right away.'

She ended the call, her mind spinning. The charity would be inheriting over a million pounds? That would keep them running for years. She could expand, build an extension so they could have more beds. The possibilities were endless.

She looked upwards and placed her hand over her heart. 'Thank you, Harold. I hope you rest in peace with Dorothy. You have no idea how much this means to me… to us.'

But maybe he did. Harold was an astute man. Maybe he knew exactly what an influx of cash would do to a charity like theirs. Bless him.

Aware that her eyes were wet for the second time that day, Sam headed into the bathroom to wash her face. Honestly, she couldn't remember the last time she'd cried so much. She needed to get a grip.

When she arrived back in the cafe a few minutes later, she saw Emily arriving for the night shift. She was helping a fragile-looking Alfie to sit at one of the tables. The poor lad looked a sight. His face was a rainbow of purples, blues and yellows, and he was clutching his side, wincing.

She went over. 'Hey there, Alfie.' She bent down and kissed his cheek. 'I'm sorry to hear about what happened. How are you?'

'Not too bad,' he said, smiling. 'Happy to be out of hospital. I missed Emily's food.' He glanced up at Emily, who blushed.

At least the experience hadn't dented their blossoming romance.

'I hope you didn't mind me bringing Alfie in with me?' Emily looked concerned. 'But I didn't want to leave him outside in the cold.'

'Of course, not. You're more than welcome here, Alfie.' Sam rested a hand on his shoulder. 'I hope it goes without saying you're guaranteed a bed here tonight. And every night until you're fully recovered.'

It was totally against the shelter's protocols, but no way was she allowing this kid to sleep rough in his condition. She couldn't do that to him. Or Emily. The poor girl had been in bits since the council had made Alfie leave her flat.

'Cheers, Sam. But no need.' His eyes were still fixed on Emily.

'It's the least I can do,' she continued. 'Especially after the way you stuck up for me last Wednesday with those dreadful journalists. I owe you.'

He turned to her. 'I meant, it's not necessary, because I have somewhere to live now.'

'You do?' She looked between Alfie and Emily, who was grinning. 'Oh, Alfie. That's fantastic news. Have the council found you somewhere?'

'Christ, no.' He shook his head. 'It's all down to Jamie.'

Sam tilted her head. 'Jamie?'

'Yeah, he got me housed with his former foster carer, Peggy. She has a room spare and has agreed to rent it out to me. How cool is that?'

Sam was dumbfounded. Her mind struggled to process the information. 'Peggy?'

'Yeah, she's super nice. Jamie took me there today. Can you believe it?' His grin widened. 'I keep pinching myself. It's like a proper family home, with nice stuff, and other lads my age.'

Sam leant against the table for support. 'I'm absolutely thrilled for you, Alfie. I've met Peggy, she's a wonderful woman. I think you'll be really happy there.'

'I think so too.' He gazed adoringly at Emily, who continued to blush.

Sam couldn't believe it. Jamie had intervened and helped Alfie?

Emily interrupted her thoughts. 'Have you seen the video Jamie made?'

'Video?' Sam asked with a frown.

'It went live today and already has over three hundred likes.' Emily handed her phone to Sam, the video onscreen and ready to play. 'Jamie's done such a great job.'

The video started with a night-time shot of a kid sleeping in a doorway. *This is Alfie*, the caption below read. *He's 18 and homeless.*

It then showed Jamie asking Alfie questions about life on the streets. The video cut to a shot of Alfie delivering pizzas on a rickety old scooter, followed by an interview at the housing department and queuing outside the shelter. Throughout it all, Alfie smiled, joked and came over as the most positive, adorable kid on the planet. It ended with him in hospital, beaten and bruised, but still hopeful of a happy ending.

It was powerful stuff and left Sam yet again blinking away tears.

She passed the phone back to Emily. 'Thank you for showing it to me.'

Emily shook her head. 'Wait, there's more.'

There was further footage of Jamie outside The Crash Pad talking directly into the camera. He spoke about the project and the amazing volunteers who worked tirelessly to support and help homeless teens. His voice was assured and professional, and he spoke eloquently and passion-ately, urging people to support the shelter by donating money, or bedding, or a few hours a week of their time.

By the time the credits rolled, Sam was deeply regret-ting her actions of earlier.

She shouldn't have been so hard on Jamie. He'd apolo-gised and more than made amends for his behaviour. But instead of forgiving him, she'd rejected his offer to volunteer.

And now it was too late. He was gone.

'Excuse me a moment,' she said, standing up.

Emily looked worried. 'Are you okay?'

'I'm fine. It's a great video. Thank you for taking part, Alfie. It means a lot.' She touched his shoulder.

'It was all Jamie's idea.' He rested his hand over hers. 'I hope it helps?'

'I'm sure it will.' She swallowed past the lump in her throat. 'Now, if you'll excuse me. I just need a moment before the guests start arriving.'

She needed someplace quiet. Someplace she wouldn't be disturbed, where she could kick and scream and yell. Because despite hoping her tears were done, she had a feeling more were about to fall.

And it was her own stupid fault.

Her phone beeped with a message. It was from Fraser.

> Problem in the rooftop garden. Need help.
> Please come. ☹

She stopped walking. What the…?

She rubbed her forehead. What on earth was Fraser doing in the rooftop garden? He was supposed to be on the door tonight. The shelter would be opening soon.

Puzzled, she headed for the loft ladder, noticing it was extended.

What was the emergency? Had he had an accident? Sprayed the produce with weed-killer? Stabbed his foot with a garden fork? It was hard to fathom.

She climbed the ladder, heading into darkness.

And then she saw lights.

Hundreds of tiny twinkling lights.

Chapter Twenty-Six

It took Sam's eyes a moment to adjust to the subdued lighting. The night sky was filled with patchy clouds, pushed along by the gentle breeze. Despite the onset of winter, it was never cold up here. The surrounding walls and dense foliage created a cocoon that rendered the space a few degrees above the ambient temperature.

She looked around. The entire rooftop garden had been decorated with twinkling Christmas lights. It looked magical. Ethereal. And incredibly romantic... which was rather worrying, since it was Fraser who'd summoned her up here. She didn't think for a moment he had designs on her, but it was puzzling nonetheless.

Closing the hatch behind her to avoid any accidents, she moved between the raised flowerbeds. 'Fraser...? Are you up here?'

A man stepped out of the shadows. It wasn't Fraser.

'Hi,' he said, pausing by the winter jasmine, their pale blooms enhanced by the soft lighting.

She blinked in surprise. 'Jamie...? What are you doing up here?'

'Plan A didn't work. So I thought I'd try Plan B.' He gave a self-deprecating shrug.

Her brain had ground to a halt and she couldn't fathom what was happening. 'I'm sorry?'

'Plan A was me turning up earlier wanting to volunteer and hoping you'd pretend I hadn't been an arsehole and give me a second chance.'

Guilt nudged her in the ribs. 'And Plan B?'

He gestured to the abundance fairy lights. 'Making a fool of myself by trying to be romantic. It always works in the films,' he said, with a half-hearted shrug.

He was trying to be romantic?

'How did you get all this up here?' she said, puzzled as to how this had happened right under her nose. 'And when? I've been here all day.'

'Fraser helped me. We did it while you were asleep in the laundry room.'

She'd be having words with Fraser. 'But that was before you spoke to me about volunteering?'

'I know. I felt I needed to have a back-up plan in place before I attempted Plan A. I had a feeling Plan A might not work. And I'm still not sure Plan B will, but I had to give it a try.'

It was a struggle not to smile at his ramblings. He was nervous. Flustered. And far from looking his normal assured self, he looked vulnerable and exposed.

Any remaining resistance melted away. It was impossible to stay mad at someone so endearing. Not that she was about to tell him that; not yet. She was curious as to what he was about to say.

'So here's the thing,' he said, walking towards her. 'When I first met you I behaved like a complete dick. I had this preconceived idea of what you'd be like and I had no qualms about pretending to be someone I wasn't.' His forehead creased into a frown. 'I don't have a defence, other than I was here to get a story. It was work. A job. It never occurred to me I'd end up feeling conflicted.' He rubbed the back of his neck. 'Then something strange happened. I started to feel invested in the shelter. It challenged my perceptions about family and community, and before long I'd almost forgotten why I was here. In fact, if my boss hadn't kept reminding me my job was at stake, I wouldn't have wanted to write the flipping story. I'd lost my appetite for it.'

She'd certainly sensed his confliction; she just hadn't known the cause of it.

He looked upwards, as if talking to the expanse of sky above. 'Before I came here, I kept people at arm's length. It felt safer that way. If you didn't care about anyone, they couldn't hurt you.' His gaze lowered to hers. 'But you made it impossible for me not to care.'

A sense of hope began to build inside her.

'I resisted it at first, but you wore me down with your endless compassion, enthusiasm and determination to help the kids who turned up here every night.' He moved closer to her. 'I'm not sure when it happened, but at some point, I realised I wasn't pretending anymore. I genuinely cared about what happened to these kids and to the volunteers who supported them. I wasn't here because I had to be, but because I wanted to be.'

He was now in front of her. Tantalisingly close. Sam could see the creases on his forehead, a sign of his anxiety. She wanted to reassure him, to end his suffering, but she sensed he needed to externalise his feelings. Something she knew he didn't do very often.

'The next thing I knew, I'd fallen for you.' Her heart crashed against her ribs, and she blinked away a rogue tear. His voice had lowered, almost as if he was afraid of being overheard. 'And I didn't know what to do. I knew I couldn't keep lying to you, but I knew admitting the truth would ruin things between us. I guess I wanted to delay that happening. It was selfish, I know.'

But understandable. She realised that now.

He ran his hand through his hair. 'For years, Peggy's been trying to get me to understand that family isn't just about who we're related to, but who we choose to have in our lives.' He dropped his hand. 'I get that now. I didn't before because I'd never met anyone who I was afraid of losing... until you.' He took a step closer. 'And the thought of not having you in my life scares me shitless.'

She felt the same way.

He reached for her hand. 'I've done everything I can think of to show you how sorry I am. And I'm not beyond begging, if that's what it takes. But I need you to believe me when I say I'll never lie to you again.' His voice cracked. 'So can you please put me out of my misery and forgive me, because I... you know... love you.' This last part was mumbled.

She almost laughed. Not because it was funny, but because he muttered those words as if it was the first time he'd ever said them. Maybe it was?

As endeared as she was by his declaration, she wasn't beyond teasing him a little first. 'I'm sorry, I didn't quite catch that. What did you say?'

He cleared his throat. 'I said... I love you.' He pulled her closer, so she bumped into his chest. 'I love you,' he said, louder. 'I love you!' he shouted to the sky above.

A dog started barking in the distance, making her laugh.

His eyes searched hers, bright with joy and trepidation. 'Am I forgiven?'

'Of course you are, you daft thing.'

'You mean, Plan B worked?'

It was time to confess. 'Actually, Plan A worked. I was just too stubborn to admit it.'

'I don't understand.'

She sighed. 'It was only after you'd left… or I'd thought you'd left… that I regretted being such a cow to you. Then I saw the video you'd made about Alfie and realised what a huge mistake I'd made.'

He gave her a sheepish look. 'Did you like it?'

'I loved it,' she admitted. 'And it was so kind of you to get him a room at Peggy's.'

'I know it doesn't solve the bigger problem and there are loads more Alfies needing a home, but it seemed like a good fit. Peggy's thrilled. It was love at first sight. The kid's going to be spoilt rotten.'

She smiled. 'It's no more than he deserves.'

'I want to help other kids like him… kids like me, who've lost their way and need a hand.'

She placed her hand on his chest. 'We could do with another volunteer at The Crash Pad, if you're interested?'

His laugh was shaky. 'I'd like that.' And then his expression turned mushy. 'What about us?'

She wasn't done teasing. 'What about us?'

He swallowed awkwardly. 'Is there a chance we could try again?'

She pretended to think about it. 'Well, my mother's holding another soiree next month. She's keen to repair the damage done to her social standing by my wayward brother. I could always blag an invite. Maybe ask her to heat the swimming pool?'

He laughed. 'Christ, could you imagine?' He lowered his face to hers. 'I have very fond memories of that swimming pool, but next month? I was hoping for something a little sooner. Like perhaps… tonight?' His eyes dipped to her mouth.

'You were?' She pretended to glance around. 'Well, we don't have a swimming pool, but we do have a water-butt… though I saw a frog in it earlier. It might be a bit of a squeeze.' She sighed. 'I guess we'll have to settle for frolicking in the vegetable patch.'

His laugh was playful. 'You're a complete nutter, you know that?'

She shrugged. 'Why else would I have fallen in love with you?'

He stilled. 'You love me?'

She rolled her eyes for effect. 'Crazy, huh?'

His face broke into a smile and he drew her closer. 'Absolutely bonkers.'

Taking her face in his hands, he kissed her. A slow tender kiss that was sensual and perfect. She succumbed, happy in the knowledge that her heart was safe. He was a good man. Not perfect, but who wanted perfect? She certainly wasn't without fault. And he didn't seem fazed by her many failings, so that was a bonus.

They could be imperfect together.

Epilogue

Two years later…

Sam used the money she'd inherited from Harold's estate to build an extension at The Crash Pad. They now have an extra fifteen beds, a cinema room, a medical unit and a classroom so they can run workshops to help improve young people's chances of getting off the streets. She named the annex Harold's Hideaway.

Following on from Jamie's article, the shelter was inundated with requests to donate and volunteer. They now have a fully-staffed rota running The Crash Pad, which allows Sam the time off she needs to campaign for votes.

Having taken on-board Jamie's advice (stolen from Gandhi) – *Be the change you want to see in the world* – she decided to become a Lambeth councillor so she could influence change from inside the Local Authority and fight for more homeless provision in South London. This seemed preferable than continuing to embarrass her mother by protesting with a placard outside parliament.

Her mother is delighted by the prospect of having a daughter 'in government' – and has already designed posters for when Sam becomes Mayor.

Jamie continues working at the *South London Herald* and Gareth has promoted him to head investigative journalist. He allows Jamie to focus on stories that expose inequality and injustice, as well as support the work of local charities – much to the chagrin of his colleagues, who are still stuck covering Pet of the Week.

Jamie also has a weekly podcast, which he uses to air documentaries and highlight local issues. He was named one of this year's top social media influencers and has over 100,000 followers. Channel 4 have approached him about making a documentary about homelessness in the UK. He's agreed.

Jamie still volunteers twice a week at The Crash Pad, although never on a Sunday. Sundays are reserved for daytrips to Canvey Island to see his birth family. They frequently end up playing football on the beach. His half-brothers are skilled players, Sam not so much: she usually ends up in the sea with Cooper, his mum's dog. Kirsty and Sam have become friends. Jamie's glad. He's closer to his birth mother than he'd ever imagined he could be… but his heart still belongs to Peggy.

Norah still runs the The Crash Pad cafe and has opened a weekend cookery school, hoping a few of the kids might find their true calling and develop a flourishing career in catering. She's yet to find another protégé like Emily, but she lives in hope.

Fraser is now the manager of The Crash Pad. Thanks to an influx of donations and grants, he receives an annual salary for the role. He has plans to introduce self-defence classes and install a gym at the shelter. Last week, he attended court and was awarded shared-custody of his two children. He hasn't had a drink in over three years.

Emily graduated from catering college with top marks and now works at the prestigious Café Jardin in central London. Her aim is to be running her own restaurant by the age of thirty. She still volunteers at The Crash Pad on her day off and still lives in her flat on the Central Hill Estate – but she no longer sleeps on the floor. In fact, three nights a week, she sleeps over at Peggy's.

Alfie is now in full-time employment and works at a local care home. The residents adore him. So does Peggy. He's saving up to buy his own place – with Emily.

Max Tipping served nine months of a two-year prison sentence for insider trading. He was released just in time to attend his sister's wedding – something his mother was delighted about.

Christina Tipping had imagined a large society wedding for her youngest daughter, with a prestigious guest list and coverage in all the top magazines – recompense for the damage done to the Tipping reputation by her errant son. So imagine her horror when Sam and Jamie announced they were getting married in the rooftop garden at The Crash Pad.

She has yet to recover.

Acknowledgements

Thank you so much for reading *A Winter's Wish*! I sincerely hope you enjoyed following the stories of Sam & Jamie and Emily & Alfie as much as I enjoyed writing them.

The book is dedicated to all the staff and volunteers who work for Citizens Advice, and whom I've had the privilege to call my friends over the last twenty years. It never ceases to amaze me how tirelessly these people work, providing free, confidential, and impartial advice to those who need it most. Whether it's a problem with homelessness, debt, a relationship breakdown, or dealing with a dodgy builder, the team always go that extra mile to ensure the person is supported and helped as much as possible to resolve their situation. And all done with compassion, kindness, and with no judgement. Citizens Advice is truly a place where everyone is treated equally, and no one is discriminated against or treated unfairly, and that makes it a very special and heartwarming place to work.

As always, a huge thank you to my agent, Tina Betts, who has stuck by me through the ups and downs and always encourages me to keep writing. It's hugely appreciated. And a big thank you to my lovely editor, Emily Bedford, who has given me such constructive and helpful feedback on my second book for Canelo, enabling me to make it the best it can be. Thank you!

Finally, thank you to all the fabulous readers, bloggers and fellow authors for supporting my journey, sharing posts, posting reviews and generally being wonderful people. In particular, the fabulous Rosanna Ley, who read an early draft of *A Winter's Wish* and gave me some invaluable feedback. It's very humbling to have the support of such a talented and prolific author. I feel very lucky. Thank you!

If you'd like to follow me on social media or make contact then I'd love to hear from you:

Twitter @tracyacorbett

Facebook @tracyacorbettauthor

Instagram tracyacorbett

Website tracycorbettauthor.co.uk